Shine *Like the* Dawn

Books by Carrie Turansky

Novels

A Refuge at Highland Hall

The Daughter of Highland Hall

The Governess of Highland Hall

Snowflake Sweethearts

A Man to Trust

Seeking His Love

Along Came Love

Surrendered Hearts

Novellas

Moonlight Over Manhattan

Mountain Christmas Brides

Where Two Hearts Meet

Christmas Mail-Order Brides

Kiss the Bride

A Blue and Gray Christmas

A Big Apple Christmas

Wedded Bliss?

Praise for
Shine Like the Dawn

"*Shine Like the Dawn* is a shining gem of a story. Turansky creates characters that are vibrant along with a sweet romance that elicits a satisfying sigh. Intrigue, secrets, and dangerous conflicts make the plot riveting until the very end."

—Jody Hedlund, author of *Luther and Katharina,*
ECPA Book of the Year

"Reading a Carrie Turansky novel is the next best thing to taking a trip to England, with the added luxury of stepping back in time. *Shine Like the Dawn* is an Edwardian gem, layering rich spiritual truths with love, loss, secrets, and forgiveness, always showcasing God's abundant restoration. This hope-infused story is as lovely as the cover!"

—Laura Frantz, author of *A Moonbow Night*

"From the first compelling page to the last heart-lifting moment, *Shine Like the Dawn* drew me in, made me smile then cry—all while keeping me on the edge of my seat. Turansky's latest English historical romance, rich in mystery and intrigue, brings to life warm and memorable characters nestled between a charming Edwardian village and its local grand estate. Uplifting and highly recommended."

—Cathy Gohlke, Christy–award winning author
of *Secrets She Kept* and *Saving Amelie*

"With her trademark heart and attention to historical detail, Carrie Turansky paints a picture of loss, inner torment, and—ultimately—healing. Set against a backdrop of Edwardian England, *Shine Like the Dawn* is aptly named because it shows the illumination that floods the soul when forgiveness replaces bitterness and a hurting heart finds its way back to the Maker of Light. A moving, life-impacting, engrossing story."

—Kim Vogel Sawyer, best-selling author of *Guide Me Home*

"Enter a world of innovations, mysterious manor houses, sweet romances, and whispers of suspense, all wrapped within a novel that gives off Elizabeth Gaskell's *North and South* vibes. In typical sweeping style, Carrie Turansky takes us on a journey to another time and place with added intrigue to keep us wondering to the very end—a story worth adding to your reading list."

—Pepper D. Basham, award-winning author
of the Penned in Time series and *A Twist of Faith*

"In this charming novel—filled with mystery, surprise, romance, and courage—Carrie Turansky skillfully transports us to Edwardian England. Readers will root for our heroine as she faces the shocking loss which dominates her life and reaches toward a future filled with faith, hope, and perhaps . . . love. Captivating."

—Sandra Byrd, author of *A Lady in Disguise*

"With a vivid setting in beautiful but tumultuous Edwardian England, Carrie Turansky masterfully tells a tale of family, love, trust, and betrayal. A charming story for every lover of historical romance!"

—Roseanna M. White, best-selling author
of the Ladies of the Manor series

"Lovers of English drama set during any era will certainly enjoy Carrie Turansky's latest novel! With a mix of themes from both *Downton Abbey* and *North and South, Shine Like the Dawn* will intrigue and enthrall readers until the very last page!"

—Dawn Crandall, award-winning author
of *The Hesitant Heiress* and *The Cautious Maiden*

Shine Like the Dawn

a novel

CARRIE TURANSKY

MULTNOMAH

Shine Like the Dawn

Scripture quotations and paraphrases are taken from the King James Version and the Holy Bible, New International Version®, NIV®. Copyright © 1973, 1978, 1984, 2011 by Biblica Inc.® Used by permission. All rights reserved worldwide.

The characters and events in this book are fictional, and any resemblance to actual persons or events is coincidental.

Trade Paperback ISBN 978-1-60142-940-7
eBook ISBN 978-1-60142-941-4

Cover design and photography by Mike Heath, Magnus Creative

Published in the United States by Multnomah, an imprint of the Crown Publishing Group, a division of Penguin Random House LLC, New York.

Library of Congress Cataloging-in-Publication Data
Names: Turansky, Carrie, author.
Title: Shine like the dawn / by Carrie Turansky.
Description: First Edition. | Colorado Springs, Colorado : Multnomah, 2017.
Identifiers: LCCN 2016050786 (print) | LCCN 2016058940 (ebook) | ISBN 9781601429407 (paperback) | ISBN 9781601429414 (ebook) | ISBN 9781601429414 (electronic)
Subjects: | BISAC: FICTION / Christian / Historical. | FICTION / Christian / Romance. | FICTION / Romance / Historical. | GSAFD: Christian fiction. | Love stories.
Classification: LCC PS3620.U7457 S55 2017 (print) | LCC PS3620.U7457 (ebook) | DDC 813/.6—dc23
LC record available at https://lccn.loc.gov/2016050786

Printed in the United States of America
2017—First Edition

10 9 8 7 6 5 4 3 2 1

This book is dedicated to my heart-sister, Judy Conroy,
for her faithful friendship, powerful prayers,
and endless encouragement.

Commit your way to the LORD;

trust in him and he will do this:

He will make your righteous reward shine like the dawn,

your vindication like the noonday sun.

PSALM 37:5–6

PROLOGUE

August 22, 1899

Sunlight blinked off the rippling surface of Tumbledon Lake and into Margaret Lounsbury's eyes. She squinted and adjusted the brim of her straw hat to shade her view, then took hold of the oar on her side of the sixteen-foot rowboat.

"Are you ready?" Her father, Daniel Lounsbury, dipped his oar into the water and looked across at Maggie. Pleasant lines fanned out from the corners of his dark-brown eyes. A reddish-brown beard covered the lower half of his tanned face, but it couldn't hide his smile.

"Yes!" She returned his smile and lowered her oar for the first stroke.

"The sun's bright today, especially out on the water." Her father looked across the lake to the rocky shore and lush woodlands beyond. Five years earlier, he and his team had dammed a section of the Debdon Burn, filling the small valley with water and creating this beautiful lake in the northernmost section of the estate. It was just one of his many accomplishments as lead landscape architect for Sir William Harcourt of Morningside Manor.

"Do you have a special spot in mind for our picnic?" Maggie's mother, Abigail Lounsbury, sat in the rear of the boat with Maggie's younger sister, Violet, on her lap.

"I found a lovely little glen surrounded by birch trees." Father turned and grinned at Maggie's older sister, Olivia, seated up front. "It will be the perfect place to celebrate your birthday. It looks like a fairy forest."

Olivia's eyes sparkled. "I can't wait to see it."

Maggie's heart lifted, and she pulled her oar through the water, matching her father's strong strokes. With the warm sunshine on her shoulders and her family around her, she couldn't imagine a happier day.

The breeze picked up and blew a strand of Maggie's hair across her cheek.

"It looks like rain is coming our way." Her mother nodded to the west, a slight crease in her brow. She adjusted her hold on Violet.

Heavy, gray clouds rose above the trees beyond the shoreline, though the rest of the sky remained mostly clear.

Father lifted his gaze and studied the clouds for a few seconds. "I'm sure we've no cause for concern." His confident tone eased Maggie's mind. There was no one who knew more about plants, animals, and the weather than her father. If he didn't believe a storm would threaten their afternoon picnic, there was no need to worry.

A graceful white egret rose out of the grass on the far side of the lake and flew across the water toward them. Violet squirmed on her mother's lap with a gleeful shriek. She looked as though she would climb over the side of the boat any moment if Mother didn't keep a tight hold on her.

Father chuckled. "It seems Violet would like to go swimming."

Olivia turned toward them. "There's not much Violet doesn't like, except perhaps cooked carrots and going down for a nap."

Maggie smiled. Olivia was right about that. Violet had started resisting her naps a few months after she celebrated her first birthday, and she'd never been fond of carrots.

"No swimming today," her mother replied in a serious tone, but Maggie could see the glow of good humor in her eyes.

"Keep up, Maggie," Father called, stroking his oar through the deep water.

She focused on rowing again and picked up her pace to match Father's. As they reached the center of the lake, Maggie heard an odd sloshing sound and looked down. Water slapped against the side of her shoe. She pulled in a sharp breath and lifted her foot. "Father, look!"

He followed her gaze, and his eyes flashed wide. He jerked his oar from the water and scanned the hull of the boat.

Mother straightened. "What is it, Daniel?"

"We seem to have sprung a leak." His voice remained calm, but the muscles in his jaw grew taut.

"What?" Olivia shot a startled glance at Maggie.

Mother wrapped her arms more tightly around Violet. "How large a leak?"

"I don't know." Father frowned as he continued to search the floor of the boat, then he grabbed his dripping oar again. "Come on, Maggie, we've got to get back to shore."

Maggie's hand trembled as she reached for her oar.

Olivia rose, rocking the boat side to side. "Aren't we closer to the other shore?"

"Olivia, sit down!" Father's sharp tone startled them all. Olivia sank onto the bench, and Father plunged his oar into the water.

Maggie's heartbeat pounded in her ears as she strained to keep up with Father's rapid pace. But even if she could match his deep, steady strokes, would they make it back to the dock before water filled their boat?

What if they couldn't?

She was a strong swimmer. Father had taught her that skill when she was only seven. She could make it. But Mother and Olivia had never wanted to learn how to swim, and Violet was too young.

Maggie clenched her jaw and pulled the oar through the water, her arms burning from the strain, but their swift pace across the lake only seemed to bring more water into the boat. It splashed around Maggie's ankles and the hem of her dark blue skirt.

"Daniel, it's too far! We'll never make it!" Mother's frantic voice sent tremors racing down Maggie's legs.

"Pull, Maggie!" Father grunted and heaved his oar around again.

Maggie gripped her oar and darted a glance toward the shore. Panic climbed up her throat, stealing her breath. They were only halfway there. Mother was right. Water sloshed up Maggie's leg and soaked her skirt. Soon lake water would pour over the side and the boat would go down.

"Father!" Olivia scooted forward as far as she could, but there was no escaping the rising water lapping at her legs.

Violet grabbed her mother's neck and broke into pitiful cries.

Father's gaze darted from one family member to the next. "We'll have to swim. Maggie, you take Violet. I'll help your mother and Olivia."

Fear froze Maggie. She blinked and tried to focus on the distant shore. It was at least half a mile, maybe more. If Violet would calm down, she might be able to swim with her sister, but how could Father help Mother and Olivia?

Father pulled Violet from Mother's arms.

"No, Daniel!" Mother reached for her youngest daughter. Her face had gone pale, and her eyes shimmered with tears.

"Be calm, Abigail. Maggie will take care of Violet." He passed Violet to Maggie.

Her hands shook as she grabbed her squirming sister, but she held on tight.

"We're counting on you, Maggie." Love and fierce determination radiated from his eyes. "Safeguard your sister. Don't turn back for any reason."

Maggie swallowed hard. "Yes, Father." She blinked her burning eyes, wanting to say she loved him and she would do her best, but there was no time.

"Go on now." He helped her over the side of the boat and into the cold water.

Kicking to stay afloat, she rolled over onto her back and pulled Violet onto her chest. Slipping her arms under Violet's, she pushed off from the side of the boat.

The shock of the cold water and the weight of her skirt and blouse pulled her down, but she thrust herself through the water, holding tight to Violet and kicking as hard as she could.

Oh God, have mercy on us! Save my family!

Tears and lake water flooded her eyes, blocking her view of her family and the boat. Water rushed past her ears, but it couldn't block out her mother's fearful cries, her father's shouts, or her sister's heartrending calls for help. But she pushed on, her promise to her father giving her strength.

Violet whimpered and tossed her head from side to side, then she lay back on Maggie's chest, stunned by the cold water and frightening events.

Maggie swam on, listening for her father's confident call or his strokes in the water behind her. But all she heard was her own heavy breathing and the splashing water as she kicked her way closer to shore.

Finally, her feet touched the muddy bottom, and she dragged herself and Violet out of the water. Her legs trembled and water poured from her clothes, pulling her down. But she forced herself to stay standing. Turning, she wiped her face and scanned the water.

Nothing broke the rippling surface of the lake. No boat. Not one member of her beloved family. Numb with dread, she blinked and stared across the quiet lake.

Where were they? How could they all just disappear?

Violet cried and clung to Maggie's leg through her soggy skirt. A gust of wind sent a cold shiver through Maggie, and her teeth chattered hard.

Clouds scuttled across the sky, blocking the sun and casting a gray shadow over the scene. Heavy raindrops splattered on the ground, and then the heavens opened and rain poured down on her head and shoulders. Still, Maggie stood, staring across the lake.

Her father had been wrong. A storm had come. A more terrible storm than she could've ever imagined.

Maggie searched the lake once more, straining to hear the voices of those she loved, but the only sound was the cry of the egret as it rose from the water's edge and flew across the lake toward the eastern shore.

She sank down on the muddy shore and pulled Violet into her arms while rainwater and tears ran down their faces.

Four Years Later
April 1903

Maggie turned the hat block and examined the broad-brimmed, yellow straw hat. Red silk roses circled the crown, with little blue cornflowers sprinkled in between. It looked perfect. She could imagine wearing it to a garden party or afternoon tea in London.

She released a soft sigh and sat back on her stool. Not that she would be going to London to attend events like those any time soon or wearing this lovely hat.

"I like the color combination and the choice of flowers, but you'll need to add several ostrich feathers if you want to please Mrs. Huntington." Grandmother Hayes looked across at Maggie from behind the long glass display case on the opposite side of the millinery shop. Her silver-rimmed spectacles rested halfway down her nose, and her rosy cheeks creased as she sent Maggie a knowing smile.

Maggie clicked her tongue and looked back at the hat. "I suppose you're right." She didn't like flamboyant designs with piles of feathers and gobs of ribbons, but that seemed to be what most women wanted, especially those on their way to London for the season.

Maggie took two yellow ostrich feathers from the box on the shelf, then reached for her needle and thread. Grandmother had owned this shop for almost twenty-five years, ever since she'd become a widow and needed to provide for herself. She knew everything there was to know about pleasing her customers, and she'd taught Maggie how to fashion the most stylish hats in Northumberland.

But arthritis had stiffened Grandmother's hands in the last few years, and now Maggie did most of the intricate work. Grandmother still made a few hats, oversaw the shop, and guided Maggie with design suggestions.

Maggie smiled, tenderness for her grandmother warming her heart. What would she and Violet have done without Grandmother Hayes? She had taken them in when no other relative could be bothered.

"Can we have buns with our tea today?" Maggie's six-year-old sister rested her chin in her hand and sent Maggie an imploring puppy-dog look. She sat on a stool behind the opposite counter, next to Grandmother.

Maggie pressed her lips together and looked down at the hat in her hands. Violet was a dear, but she had a sweet tooth that never seemed to be satisfied.

Her little sister clasped her hands below her chin. "Please, Maggie. I love buns, and we haven't had any in such a long time." Just last week they'd bought buns from Mrs. Fenwick's Teashop. But to a six-year-old she supposed a week qualified as a long time. "You said you would think about it." Violet smiled and batted her long, dark eyelashes at Maggie.

Maggie stifled a groan. She hated to say no to her sister, but if they spent those shillings on tea treats, it would mean cutting back somewhere else.

When Maggie didn't answer, Violet's face brightened. "You wouldn't have to stop working. I could get them. I'm old enough."

The teashop was directly across the street. Violet loved to be trusted with the coins and allowed to make the purchase and bring back the buns in a paper sack.

"Please, Maggie." Violet's plaintive voice pulled at Maggie's heart.

There were so many times she had to say no. Perhaps she could find some way to stretch the budget just a bit more. "All right. I suppose we can buy some buns today. Bring me the canister."

Violet hopped off her stool, grinning like she'd won the grand prize in a footrace, and hurried past the curtain that separated the front room of the shop from their tiny private sitting room and kitchen in the back. The only other rooms in the building were a small bedroom upstairs that Maggie shared with Violet and another small bedroom behind the kitchen for Grandmother.

The bell over the front door jingled. Maggie looked up as Mrs. Eugenia Huntington and her eighteen-year-old daughter, Elyse, walked in. Both women were dressed in stylish walking suits and wore large, elaborate hats.

Grandmother stood. "Good afternoon, Mrs. Huntington, Miss Elyse."

Mrs. Huntington returned the greeting, and Elyse nodded to Grandmother and Maggie. Elyse was preparing for her first season in London. Maggie had heard through one of her friends that Mrs. Huntington had ordered enough evening gowns and day dresses for Elyse to fill several trunks. And then, of course, there were all the hats, gloves, parasols, and shoes to go with them.

A pang shot through Maggie's heart. She would have traveled south, more than three hundred miles, to London and taken part in the season if her parents were still living. She might even have received a marriage proposal by now. Her late father had been a well-respected landscape architect and acquainted with many fine families in London and all around the country.

But the deaths of her parents and sister had changed everything.

The only future she could imagine now was one tied to the millinery shop, where she would spend her days designing hats she would never wear to help provide for her grandmother and sister.

Grandmother came around the end of the counter. "Maggie is just finishing one of the hats for Miss Elyse, but I believe the others you ordered are ready."

"Yes, these two are finished." Maggie reached up and took a wide-brimmed lavender hat from the shelf and placed it on the glass countertop. Then she reached for a cream-colored hat with pink roses circling the crown and set it next to the other.

"Oh, they're lovely." Elyse beamed as she crossed the shop toward Maggie.

Mrs. Huntington followed, but her brow creased as she regarded the hats. "I'm afraid they're both too plain." She nodded toward the lavender hat. "This one needs more flowers and ribbons, perhaps even some netting and lace."

Elyse turned to Mrs. Huntington. "But Mother, I think—"

The older woman lifted her finger and silenced her daughter. "Your hats must be unique and draw attention so you will stand out from the crowd."

Maggie clamped her lips together, struggling to hold back her reply. Adding more adornments would draw attention, but it would make the hat look overdone and gaudy. Perhaps she could convince Mrs. Huntington to change her mind once she saw how lovely the hat looked on Elyse. "Why don't we try it on to test the fit?"

Mrs. Huntington's frown remained in place, but she gave a slight nod. Her daughter unpinned her hat and stepped forward. Maggie placed the lavender hat on the young woman's head. They all turned toward the mirror on the countertop and examined Elyse's reflection.

Grandmother adjusted the angle of the hat, tipping it a bit more to the side. "The color certainly highlights her blue eyes and flatters her skin tone."

Mrs. Huntington studied the hat. "It definitely needs more flowers and ribbons. And perhaps a trailing vine off the side. We want it to look impressive from every angle."

Maggie rolled her eyes behind Mrs. Huntington's back. There was hardly room to add any more flowers, and a trailing vine would look ridiculous. She was just about to say so when Grandmother sent her a warning look.

Maggie stifled a sigh. How many times had her grandmother told her she must listen to the customer's wishes and find a way to please her?

She reached under the counter for her basket of silk roses. "Perhaps we could add a few more flowers on the side." She chose three smaller roses and tucked them in with the rest of the bouquet covering the crown of the hat.

Mrs. Huntington surveyed the design with lifted eyebrows. "That's better, and now the ribbons."

Maggie reached for a spool of green velvet ribbon. "This color would be a good contrast to the flowers." She looped a few pieces around the roses and stood back.

"That's a good choice." Grandmother reached up and tucked the ribbon in at the back.

Mrs. Huntington sighed. "There's no time to start over. We leave for London tomorrow morning. I suppose it will have to do."

Heat flushed Maggie's cheeks. There was nothing wrong with the hat! It was just as fine as any she would find at the shops in London. Maggie and her grandmother subscribed to several catalogs to make sure their designs kept pace with the latest fashions.

Grandmother stepped forward, blocking Mrs. Huntington's view of Maggie. "Let's try on the other." She placed the cream-colored hat on Elyse, while Maggie stood back with her arms crossed.

Elyse turned her head from left to right, examining herself in the mirror. "I like the way the brim is lifted on the side, with the flowers placed underneath."

Mrs. Huntington stepped to the left, inspecting the view from that angle. "Perhaps some more netting and feathers would make it look fuller."

Grandmother lifted her silver eyebrows and glanced at Maggie.

Maggie set her jaw and reached for the basket of netting from the shelf behind the counter. She might not agree with Mrs. Huntington, but she couldn't ignore her suggestions.

Grandmother took some cream netting from the basket and wove a piece in with the flowers. "We can gather this over the crown and add a few more feathers to give it a bit more height."

Mrs. Huntington nodded. "Yes. That's what it needs."

Violet had been waiting patiently during the whole exchange, but now she tugged on Maggie's sleeve and held up the canister.

"Excuse me a moment." Maggie turned away from the women, popped the lid off the canister, and took out two coins. Bending down, she whispered in Violet's ear. "Be careful when you cross the street, and wait your turn nicely in the shop."

Violet returned an eager nod. "I will." Then she hurried out the door, setting the bell to jingling.

Maggie watched Violet through the window. Her sister stopped and looked both ways, then dashed across the street and into Fenwick's Teashop. Maggie turned back to their customers.

"Maggie is just about finished with the third hat." Grandmother held out the yellow straw hat with the red roses and little blue cornflowers.

"Oh, that's very pretty." The young woman's eyes sparkled as she gazed at the hat.

Maggie rose up on her toes with a pleased smile. At least Elyse Huntington had good taste and knew a lovely hat when she saw one.

Mrs. Huntington wrinkled her nose. "No, Elyse can't wear that. It's much too informal for the London season."

Maggie pulled in a sharp breath. She might not have been to London recently, but she'd seen photographs and advertisements for hats very similar to this one in magazines published there.

Grandmother pushed her spectacles up her nose and looked back and forth between Mrs. Huntington and her daughter. "Surely Miss Elyse will be attending garden parties or boating events, and this hat would certainly be appropriate for—"

The older woman shook her head and pushed the hat away. "It looks like a hat worn by a shopgirl or the village schoolmarm."

Fire flashed through Maggie. "There is nothing wrong with—"

A motorcar horn blasted outside on the street.

A child's scream pierced the air.

Maggie's heart lurched, and she spun toward the door.

Nathaniel Harcourt peered out the soot-dusted window as the train slowed and approached the village station.

The conductor walked down the aisle. "Heatherton. This stop is Heatherton."

The brakes screeched, steam hissed into the air, and the train jerked to a stop. Nate rose from his seat, took his hat and small leather bag from the overhead rack, and started down the aisle. The four-hour trip from London had given him plenty of time to consider the next stage of his journey, but it had done little to ease his apprehension about returning to Morningside.

He stepped down from the train and scanned the platform. Men, women, and children dressed in traveling clothes disembarked behind him, while several others waited to board the train and travel north to Scotland. For a moment he considered climbing back aboard and continuing the journey, but his stepmother's letter had made it clear. His father was seriously ill, and he should not delay.

The train hissed again, and a steamy cloud puffed out around him. He gripped the handle of his bag and stared across the platform.

A porter approached. "Do you need help with your luggage, sir?"

"Yes, thank you." They made their way to the baggage car, where Nate claimed his trunk and the porter hauled it onto a waiting cart.

"Would you keep my trunk here at the station until I send someone to retrieve it?"

"Yes, sir." The porter quickly tied a ticket to the leather handle, then tore the ticket in half and gave the bottom piece to Nate.

He thanked the porter, passed him a few coins, and then started down the street, intent on finding a horse so he could make the final four-mile journey home to Morningside.

Home . . . His chest tightened, and he focused on those walking past, trying to push aside his conflicting thoughts.

It had been four years since he'd left Morningside, crossed the huge iron bridge spanning the deep ravine with the gardens and stream below, then boarded the train in Heatherton to travel south and accept his naval commission.

He'd been determined to distance himself from his family and his painful past, and that was what he'd done. But today he would travel that same road in the opposite direction to keep his promise to the Almighty and try to make amends.

Was there still time . . . or was it too late?

Could he restore his relationship with his father, or would his father's unexpected illness steal away that opportunity? And what about his stepmother and half sister, Clara? Could he bridge the gap that had always kept them so far apart?

There was only one way to find out. He must finish this last leg of his journey and face his family.

He scanned the village street, and his tension eased a bit. Heatherton looked much the same as it had the day he'd left. Small shops lined both sides of the street, and at the end he saw the sign for the Red Lion Inn. Mr. Hastings kept a stable behind the inn, and with any luck Nate would find a horse he could hire there.

He walked past the small village hospital and glanced at the arched doorway into the side garden. Was Dr. Albert Hadley still taking care of the medical needs of those in the village and surrounding area? He'd always appreciated the doctor's calm, caring manner and practical wisdom. Nate walked on past Saint Peter's Church, with its tall spire, quiet churchyard, and neatly trimmed cemetery.

The roar of an engine sounded behind him. He grabbed his hat and jumped out of the way as a speeding motorcar raced past.

The driver looked over his shoulder with a broad grin and waved to Nate.

The fool! He ought to slow down and look where he's going before he kills himself or someone else. Nate darted a glance down the street, and his breath hitched in his chest.

A little girl, who looked no more than five or six, stepped into the street, carrying a small parcel.

A surge of energy shot through Nate. "Look out!"

The girl's eyes widened, but rather than turning back, she dashed ahead, directly into the path of the speeding motorcar. The driver blasted his horn, jammed on his brakes, and swerved to the left.

Nate took off running toward the girl, but the car rammed into her, and a heartrending scream tore from her throat. She flew up into the air and landed a few feet away in the middle of the street.

Nate dropped down beside her before the driver had even climbed out of his motorcar. She writhed on the ground, crying. He shot off an urgent prayer as he looked her over. She had not lost consciousness, and he saw no blood. Those were good signs. He laid his hand on her shoulder. "Everything is going to be all right. Try to stay calm."

The little girl squeezed her eyes shut, sobbing and rocking back and forth as she held her leg.

Villagers ran from the shops and gathered around.

"What happened?"

"Isn't that Mrs. Hayes's granddaughter?"

"Someone run for the doctor."

"Let me through!" A young woman pushed past the others. "Violet!" She knelt beside the girl and leaned in close, her back to him.

"My leg!" Tears flowed from the little girl's eyes.

"What happened?" The young woman looked up at the crowd.

The driver of the motorcar stepped forward, tweed cap in his hand. "I'm sorry, miss. I tried to stop. But I didn't see her until it was too late."

"How could you be so careless?" She turned and shifted her fiery gaze to Nate. "We have to move my sister . . ." She blinked and stared at him.

For the first time Nate looked the young woman full in the face, and a shockwave rolled through him. "Maggie?"

Hurt filled her eyes, and she turned away. "We need to move her out of the street." She looked around at the other villagers, ignoring him.

"I'll help you." Nate reached for the little girl.

Maggie's hand shot out to stop him.

But no one else stepped forward, so he gently scooped Violet off the ground. She cried out as he lifted her.

"What is it, darling?" Maggie leaned in close again, her face lined with agony that matched her sister's.

"My leg hurts." A fresh round of tears cascaded down the little girl's flushed face.

Nate gritted his teeth and looked away. During his naval career, he'd seen many men wounded in battle and transported hundreds of prisoners during the South African Boer War, but seeing his childhood friend and her young sister in this painful situation struck him in a completely different way.

"Step aside." Dr. Hadley moved through the crowd toward them. "What happened here?"

"Violet was hit by that man in his motorcar." Maggie pointed to the guilty driver, and the man lowered his head.

"Let's take her to the hospital." The doctor looked up at Nate, and his eyebrows rose. "Nathaniel Harcourt?"

"Yes, sir."

"I didn't realize you had returned."

"I've just arrived on the train from London. I haven't even been to Morningside yet."

The doctor gave a firm nod. "It's good you've come. Your father will be glad to see you. But let's take this young lady to the hospital." He set off, clearing a path through the crowd. "Make way, please."

Nate followed the doctor, carrying Violet. Maggie walked beside him, her eyes fixed on the doctor's back, her posture rigid. It made sense that she would be upset about Violet's injuries, but why was she angry with him? He wasn't responsible for the accident. He glanced her way. "I didn't know you'd returned to Heatherton."

She arched one eyebrow. "We've lived here for the last four years."

Surprise rippled through him. How could that be? He'd searched for her after the boating accident, but he'd not been able to find her. "They told me you'd gone to Scotland to live with relatives."

"Your parents sent us to my great-aunt Beatrice in Edinburgh, but she had no desire to care for us. A few weeks later, she sent us back to Heatherton to stay with Grandmother Hayes. We've been here ever since."

So Maggie had been in Scotland, but his stepmother had told him she was in Glasgow, not Edinburgh. The address she'd given him had turned out to be a butcher shop, and the proprietor said he'd never heard of Margaret Lounsbury.

After that ill-fated trip to Scotland, Nate returned to Morningside and confronted his father and stepmother, demanding to know what had happened to Maggie and Violet. But they both claimed they knew nothing more about where the girls had gone.

He looked back at Maggie. "So you live here now with your grandmother?" That thought lifted his spirits, but the feeling quickly deflated as he observed her cool, impassive expression. Why did she seem so distant? It was almost as if she thought he was somehow responsible for today's pain and problems.

The doctor pushed open the side door to the hospital and ushered them inside. It took a moment for Nate's eyes to adjust from the bright sunlit street to the dim doctor's office.

"Bring her in here." The doctor walked into the next room and motioned toward the examination table.

Nate gently placed Violet on the table and stepped back. Maggie moved closer and took her sister's hand. The little girl's tears had slowed, and she looked around the room with a curious expression. Her eyes were blue but much lighter than Maggie's smoky blue-gray eyes. Still, he could see the family resemblance in the shape of Violet's nose and mouth.

The doctor turned to him. "Thank you, Nathaniel. I appreciate your help."

Nate shot a questioning look at Maggie.

For a brief moment he saw the uncertainty in her eyes, or was it hope that he would stay? She quickly masked her emotions and looked away.

"I'll wait in the office," he said. "I'd like to hear how Violet is doing before I go."

"Very well." The doctor turned back to his patient.

Maggie's gaze softened, but she shifted her focus to her sister.

Nate walked into the adjoining office and crossed to the window. Leaning on the windowsill, he looked out at the street. Three children ran past, and a cart pulled by a strong bay drove on toward the center of the village.

How long would it take the doctor to do his examination and discover the extent of Violet's injuries? He glanced at his watch. It was just after four. There were still a few hours of daylight, plenty of time for him to find a horse and make his way to Morningside.

But even if it took longer than expected, he wasn't leaving until he knew Violet was going to be all right. Waiting for word from the doctor would ease his mind and give him a chance to show Maggie that, though they'd been separated for more than four years, she could still count on his help and friendship.

Maggie gently brushed a tendril of light-brown hair off Violet's forehead. For the last thirty minutes she'd stood by to comfort her sister as Dr. Hadley set Violet's leg and then applied the plaster cast. "Rest easy, Violet. I'll be back in just a few minutes."

Her little sister's eyes widened. "Where are you going?"

"I have to go to the shop. I'm sure Grandmother is anxious to hear how you're doing." Her grandmother's arthritis made it difficult for her to walk a long distance, but she might try to come to the hospital if Maggie didn't hurry home with some news soon. "I'll collect a few things and then come back to stay with you."

Dr. Hadley wiped his hands on a towel. "We'll watch over Violet. Take whatever time you need."

"Thank you, Doctor. I should be no more than fifteen minutes."

Maggie glanced at Violet's knee-to-foot plaster cast, and her throat tightened. She'd come very close to losing her little sister today, and that thought was almost more than she could bear. She swallowed hard and tried to push away her frightening line of thinking. For Violet's sake she must not break down.

She pulled in a calming breath. Violet would be all right. She had fractured her left leg and had a few cuts and bruises, but her injuries were not life-threatening. Still, the doctor wanted to keep her overnight at the hospital to allow the cast to dry and be sure there were no other complications. Maggie would stay with her.

"Don't worry, Maggie." The doctor patted her arm. "Everything is going to be fine. We'll keep a good eye on Violet until you return."

Maggie thanked him again, then crossed the room and pushed open the door. It swung wide, and she ran directly into Nate's solid chest. She gasped and pulled back.

"Sorry." He reached out to steady her, and his touch sent a jolt up her arm. "How is Violet?"

Maggie stepped back, shaken by the collision and her conflicting emotions. Nate had been her friend from the time she was twelve years old until she turned seventeen, but when she'd needed him most, he had failed her. She steeled her heart and turned away. "She'll be fine."

"Maggie, wait." He stepped into her path and looked down at her. His deep-brown eyes scrolled over her face, reflecting what looked like sincere concern, but she didn't trust him or that look. "I'm sorry about Violet. I saw the motorcar race past. I shouted and tried to warn her, but it was too late."

Her stomach clenched. "Yes, too little, too late." And she wasn't the least bit sorry for the touch of bitterness in her voice.

His dark brows dipped. "What is it? Why are you angry with me?"

His questions stunned her for a moment. "Did you think I would forget the way you and your family treated Violet and me after our parents and sister died?"

He frowned. "I don't know what you mean."

"Really? You expect me to believe that?" She paced a few steps away, trying to control her churning emotions, then turned and faced him again. "My father treated you like a son. We welcomed you into our home and our hearts. How could you act as though we meant nothing to you?"

He blinked and gave his head a slight shake. "I'm sorry, Maggie, but honestly, I have no idea why you're upset with me."

The pain in her chest turned to fire, stirring her hot reply. "Where were you, Nate? Why did you disappear when we needed you most?" She opened her mouth to say more, but her throat swelled, making it impossible. She rushed past him and pushed open the door, blinking away hot tears.

She had tried to let go of the hurt and disappointment, but it still tore at her heart. She'd trusted Nate, depended on him, believed he would stand up to his father and stepmother and take up their cause.

But he hadn't.

"Maggie!"

Ignoring his call, she strode down the street, determined not to look back. She couldn't. Her heart was too sore.

How could he say he didn't know why she was upset? That couldn't be true. He had been home at Morningside that summer. He must have been privy to his parents' decisions after the boating accident.

The painful memories came flooding back, and with them all the reasons she'd assigned for his failure to care for them in their time of need. He'd always longed for his father's approval, and when it came time to choose between Maggie and his family, he'd closed his heart to her, bowed to his parents' wishes, and stayed away from the funeral. Then he'd ignored her letters and pleas for help while she and Violet had been sent off to their great-aunt in Scotland who wanted nothing to do with them.

She pulled in a calming breath, and a troubling thought pricked her heart. Nate appeared genuinely baffled by her accusations, and she'd never known him to be dishonest. Had she misjudged him? Could it be true that he'd not known how his family had treated them? Frowning, she turned and searched the street, but Nate was gone.

Even if there was some explanation and he was unaware of his parents' actions, why hadn't he answered her letters—or at least tried to discover where they were and if they were all right? If he truly had been a caring friend, he would've done that much.

But he hadn't. Instead, he'd left her alone to face the darkest days of her life.

Nate rode across the iron bridge leading to Morningside Manor as the sun sank behind the house and forested ridge beyond.

His gaze dipped to the deep ravine and rugged hillsides below the bridge. The plants and trees had filled out and grown much taller since he'd left. No one would imagine that the land had once been a rocky, deserted moor. But with good planning and hard work, Maggie's father and his team of assistants had transformed the estate into beautiful gardens and glens, with two large lakes, several carriage drives, and myriad stone paths winding throughout.

Lush ferns, creeping heather, and pink and purple rhododendrons covered the craggy hillsides now. Birds called from the tall evergreens, and the sound of rushing water rose from the rocky streambed below.

Warmth spread through his chest as he took it all in. He'd had a hand in the creation of this beauty. For several years, he'd spent most of his summer holidays working alongside Daniel Lounsbury as he oversaw the landscaping projects. As time passed, Nate's admiration for Daniel grew, and their friendship deepened. The older man often invited Nate to join his family on their rambles, fishing outings, and picnics. Nate loved those times, and he grew very fond of them all . . . especially Maggie.

Their earlier meeting in the village flashed through his mind, and his happy memories dissolved like mist vanishing off the lake. Apparently four years was not long enough to ease the ache in her heart brought about by the accident and loss of her parents and sister.

He clenched his jaw, questions throbbing through his mind.

Why hadn't his father and stepmother called him home from his cousin's estate as soon as they'd learned about the boating accident? Instead, they'd waited almost a week before they told him about the terrible tragedy. He'd missed the funeral and his opportunity to console Maggie. That must be the reason she was still upset with him. She had no idea why he'd been absent.

His parents' callous response to the accident had dealt a terrible blow to his relationship with them. He'd left Morningside the next day and gone to Scotland, searching for Maggie. But he ran into a dead end there and returned home determined he would stay at Morningside only long enough to inform his father he was accepting a commission in the Navy. Then he would collect a few belongings and leave as soon as possible.

Looking back, he wished he'd allowed his temper to cool and found a way to leave on better terms, but he couldn't change the past. The only option was to make the most of the present.

He urged his horse up the path and lifted his gaze to his family's imposing manor house. Three stories high and built of sand-colored stone, it looked as though it clung to the cliffs. The house's design was a bit of a jumble with all the wings and rooms that had been added over the years. The tall tower on the left and several of the upper sections across the front displayed dark timber in a crisscross design against a white background in the Tudor style.

He passed the main arched entrance and rode on to the stable, leaving his horse there with a young groomsman. Then he made his way back toward the house. Stepping into the cool, dim entrance hall, he was surprised to see Jackson, the aging butler, shuffle toward him. He couldn't believe the old man hadn't retired by now.

Jackson blinked. "Master Harcourt . . . is that you?"

"Yes, Jackson, it's good to see you."

"I'm sorry, sir. Should I address you as Lieutenant Harcourt?"

"No, please, just call me Nathaniel."

"Oh no, sir, I couldn't address you by your Christian name."

"You may call me Mr. Harcourt, then."

"Very well, sir."

Nate glanced toward the upper gallery. "Is my father upstairs?"

"Yes, sir, in his bedroom. Mrs. Harcourt is with him, as well as Miss Clara."

"Thank you." Nate strode past Jackson and mounted the carpeted steps.

The house seemed unchanged, but what of his family? He'd had very little communication with them in the last four years, only a few letters from his father. His stepmother had never written—at least not until penning the letter he'd found waiting for him when he returned to London yesterday. In it she urged him to come home as soon as possible.

Nate knocked at his father's bedroom door, and a female voice invited him to enter. He opened the door and stepped in. The curtains were drawn, and the scent of beeswax and camphor hung in the air. A lamp on the bedside table and another on the fireplace mantel gave the only light in the dim room.

His father lay in the center of his bed, his eyes closed, his pale, wrinkled face a dreadful shade of gray. A few strands of wispy white hair fanned out above his forehead.

Nate's steps stalled, and he swallowed. His father looked much worse than he'd expected. He shifted his gaze to his stepmother, Helen Harcourt. She sat on a straight-backed chair across the room, dressed in a high-necked black dress, as though she were already in mourning. His half sister, Clara, sat beside her, holding a book in her lap. They both looked up and met his gaze as he approached.

His stepmother's sharply drawn eyebrows arched. "Nathaniel, I hardly recognized you."

He nodded to them. "Hello, Helen. Clara." He moved to his father's bedside and searched his face. "How is he?"

Helen rose and crossed to the other side of the bed. "Dr. Hadley was here this morning."

He looked up, and she gave her head a slight shake, obviously reluctant to say more, but the resignation in her gray-green eyes told the rest of the story.

Nate nodded, trying to absorb the news. He bent over his father's still form and took his hand. "Father, can you hear me?"

The old man's eyes slowly opened, and he looked up at Nate. "Is that you, son?" His voice was no more than a hoarse whisper.

"Yes, sir." Nate tightened his hold on his father's hand.

"I'm glad you've come." His father squeezed back.

"I would've been here sooner, but I only received Helen's letter yesterday when I arrived in London."

Father's watery gaze shifted to Helen. "I want to speak to Nathaniel—alone."

Her posture stiffened, and she sent Nate a cool glance. "Very well. Come along, Clara."

His half sister closed her book and slowly rose from her chair. She met Nate's gaze as she passed, her eyes shadowed with sorrow. He watched them disappear out the door, then he turned back to his father.

"Are you well, my boy?"

"Yes, Father. I'm well."

"I wish I could say the same." He started to chuckle, but it turned into a dry, wracking cough.

Nate laid his hand on his father's shoulder and waited for his cough to subside. "I'm sure with time and good care you'll be feeling better."

"No, Dr. Hadley is a fine physician, but he doesn't offer much hope for my recovery."

"Surely there is some treatment that would help your condition."

"We've tried, but I've only grown weaker, and now . . ."

Nate started to protest, but his father lifted his hand. "I have some things I want to say, and I'll rest easier knowing I've said them. Sit down, Nate." He nodded to the chair beside the bed.

Nate pulled the chair closer and took a seat. "I'll be glad to listen to whatever you have to say, but I hope you'll allow me to speak first."

"As you wish."

"My time in South Africa and my experiences in the war . . . made a deep impression on me."

Memories of the prisoner-of-war camps that held the wives and children of Boers, the Dutch farmers who had fought the British, rose in his mind. He'd never seen such devastation and terrible suffering. It had made him ashamed and desperate to do something to change the situation. But before he could, his own painful illness had struck him down and taken him to death's door.

How could he recount the lifesaving care he'd received from missionary doctor Alfred Thurston and the promises he'd made during his recovery?

Life was too short, and family relationships were too important, to let the past destroy the possibility of healing and renewal. His wartime experiences had prompted his return, even before he'd received Helen's letter.

He focused on his father again. "I'm sorry for the way I left and for the distance it put between us. I was young and impulsive."

The deep lines around his father's mouth softened. "It's all right. I was young once, ready to take on the world and right every wrong. But look at me now." His watery gaze drifted to the fireplace for a moment, then he looked back at Nate. "I owe you an apology, son. My actions toward you and many others have not always been . . . honorable."

Nate shook his head. "There's no need to—"

"Yes, there is a need. A man gains perspective at the end of his life. And looking back, I can see I invested too much time in my experiments and inventions and not enough with the family, and you in particular."

Nate's throat tightened, and he took his father's hand again.

"There are many things I wish I had done differently," Father said softly.

"We all have regrets, but it's never too late to set things right."

"It's too late for me, but not for you."

Nate studied his father's face, uncertain of what he meant.

"Soon all of this will be yours." His gaze traveled around the room, but Nate knew he was speaking of more than the house. "That will be a blessing, but also a great responsibility. I'm sorry I haven't done more to prepare you for what's to come."

"Don't worry about me. Just focus on resting and recovering your strength."

Father tightened his grip on Nate's hand, his gaze intense. "Listen to me, Nathaniel. I know my time is short, but I'm not afraid. I've made my peace with God."

Nate's heartbeat quickened, and he studied his father's face. Had his father experienced a spiritual awakening similar to what Nate had experienced in South Africa? Nothing would give Nate as much peace as knowing he and his father would be together again in heaven one day.

"I need you to take care of some important matters for me," his father continued.

"Of course. Whatever you need."

His father nodded and took a shallow breath. "After I'm gone, you must promise to take care of your stepmother. I know she can be difficult, and you've not been close, but I want to be sure she and Clara will have everything they need."

"Yes, of course. I'll look after them."

"Good." He paused for a moment, as though gathering strength. "There is a woman in New York, Natalie Fredrick, who receives a sum of money each quarter. My solicitor, Miles Randolph, handles those payments. You must make certain they continue until she confirms they're no longer needed."

Nate frowned. "Who is Natalie Fredrick?"

His father looked away. "She is someone I promised to help, and that promise must be kept."

His father's explanation stirred more questions in Nate's mind, but he didn't want to press him. "Of course. I'll make sure the funds are sent."

"And finally, you must promise to make things right with Daniel Lounsbury's daughters."

Nate's pulse jumped. "What do you mean?"

"I'm ashamed to say it, but I owed their father a great deal of money at the time of his death."

"How much money?"

He named the amount and sent Nate a guilty glance.

Nate stared at his father, stunned by his confession.

"I know. It was wrong, but funds were tight at the time. We were constructing three new warehouses at Clifton, and Daniel Lounsbury had agreed to wait for his wages. He said his needs were met. Then the accident happened, and—"

"You withheld the money?"

"I meant to pay it back, but I put it off until it was an uncomfortable memory."

"And now?"

"I want the matter settled. Give the money to his daughters." He met Nate's gaze. "You'll see they're paid what's owed?"

"Yes. I'll take care of it right away."

Father lay back and closed his eyes. "Thank you. I can rest now."

The weary lines around his father's eyes and mouth softened, and his breathing seemed easier. If accepting these responsibilities would give his father a measure of peace, then he was glad to take them on.

But what would Maggie say when he told her about the money? She was barely speaking to him now. But perhaps this good news would bridge the gap and help restore their friendship.

Determination coursed through him. He would see that the debt was paid and his father's wishes were fulfilled. It was the least he could do for his father . . . and for Maggie.

3

"Bring her in this way." Maggie pushed open the front door of the millinery shop, causing the bell to jingle.

Joseph Neatherton, their neighbor and friend, carried Violet inside. Though he was a year older than Maggie, she often thought of him as she would a younger brother. Today he looked the part, with a lock of shaggy blond hair falling over his forehead and into his pale-blue eyes. He was definitely in need of a good haircut and a new pair of trousers.

Joseph looked back at Maggie. "Where shall I put her down?"

"In our sitting room." She motioned toward the back of the shop.

Grandmother pulled back the curtain and hobbled out. "Oh, there she is! Thank you, Joseph. We're so grateful for your help."

"I'm glad to do whatever I can for you." He glanced at Maggie rather than Grandmother as he spoke, then carried Violet across the shop and ducked when he passed through the low doorway. Maggie doubted he would've actually hit his head on the doorframe, but he would've come very close.

Joseph placed her little sister in the chair by the fireplace. "There you go, Miss Violet."

Grandmother pushed a small footstool toward Violet, then Maggie helped Violet raise her leg. "How is that?"

"My leg hurts a little, but it's all right." Violet released a soft sigh and sank back into the chair.

Joseph grinned. "It looks like you're glad to be home."

Violet nodded. "The doctor is nice, but I didn't like staying at the hospital."

"It was good he let Maggie stay with you." Joseph's steady gaze settled on Maggie again.

She glanced away, pretending not to notice. Joseph was thoughtful and eager to please, but she didn't want to encourage him, especially when she thought of him only as a friend.

"Well, I should be going." Joseph straightened his shoulders. "My father is going to Newcastle upon Tyne, and I'll be overseeing the shop today."

Grandmother patted him on the arm. "You're a fine young man, Joseph. Your father is proud of you, as he should be. One day you're going to make a very fine husband for some fortunate young lady." She lifted her silver eyebrows and sent Maggie the slightest nod.

Heat flooded Maggie's face. Could her grandmother make her hopes any more obvious?

Joseph gave a self-conscious chuckle and rubbed his jaw. "You're kind, Mrs. Hayes."

Maggie snatched a pillow and placed it under Violet's leg, keeping her focus off Joseph, hoping to give the impression she hadn't caught her grandmother's meaning.

Joseph brushed his hands down his wrinkled trousers. "Well, I should be going. There's always plenty to do at the shop. This is a busy week for us."

Maggie leaned toward Violet. "Isn't there something you want to say to Joseph before he goes?"

Violet searched Maggie's face, then she looked up and sent him a sweet smile. "Thank you, Joseph."

"You're welcome, Miss Violet." He knelt on the other side of the chair. "Just do me a favor and stay out of the way of motorcars, all right?"

"I will. I promise."

"I'm glad to hear it." He looked across at Maggie with a hopeful, expectant expression.

She glanced away. Why couldn't Joseph be content as her friend rather than hinting he wanted to be her suitor?

The bell out front jingled, and relief flashed through Maggie. "I should see who that is. Excuse me." She hurried across the room, pushed the curtain aside, and froze in the doorway.

Nate Harcourt stood by the front door, his hat in his hand, his broad shoulders filling out his coat. "Good morning, Maggie."

She swallowed and nodded. "Good morning . . ." She couldn't finish the greeting. Calling him Nate seemed too informal, but addressing him as Mr. Harcourt didn't seem right either.

Oh, why wouldn't her traitorous heart stop racing?

"I came to ask about Violet. How is she today?"

The kindness in his eyes was unmistakable, and the warmth of it threatened to melt away another layer of Maggie's resentment. She looked away, then let the curtain drop behind her and took a few steps forward. "She's home and is as well as can be expected."

He nodded. "I'm glad to hear she doesn't have to stay at the hospital another day. I'm sure one night was hard enough for someone so young."

Joseph stepped out of the sitting room and crossed to stand beside Maggie. He frowned slightly and exchanged a glance with her.

"This is Mr. Nathaniel Harcourt of Morningside Manor." She motioned toward Joseph. "And this is our neighbor, Joseph Neatherton. He helped us bring Violet home from the hospital."

The men nodded to each other, but both maintained serious, assessing looks. Maggie could feel the tension in the air as though some sort of silent challenge passed between them.

Nate held out his hand. "I'm pleased to meet you."

Joseph hesitated a split second, then shook Nate's hand. "And I, you."

Nate shifted his hat to his other hand. "So you're Maggie's neighbor?"

"Yes. My family owns Neatherton's Shoes and Boots." He nodded to the right, toward his shop.

"Ah, I see." Nate's gaze flicked back and forth between Maggie and Joseph.

Joseph lifted his chin. "Many people say we make the finest footwear in Northumberland."

"Then I must pay you a visit soon. I'm in need of a new pair of boots."

Joseph's gaze dropped to Nate's feet and then rose to his face again. "You've been away for some time, haven't you?"

"Yes, I've spent the last few years in South Africa with the Navy."

Maggie's stomach tensed as she thought of Nate's involvement in the war. Joseph's sister, Lilly, worked at Morningside Manor as a housemaid and was

Maggie's closest friend. Lilly said Nate didn't write home often, but when he did, his father passed some news to his valet, who then shared it with the rest of the staff.

"So you've been fighting the Boers?" Joseph asked.

"Yes, though I spent most of my time patrolling the coast and transporting troops and prisoners of war."

Joseph's wary expression eased, replaced by a look of grudging admiration. He rocked back on his heels, then turned to Maggie. "I should be going, but I'll stop back later and see if there's anything else you need."

"Thank you, Joseph, but you don't have to do that."

"It's no trouble at all." He smiled at Maggie, then nodded to Nate and walked out the door.

She shifted her gaze to Nate. Would he excuse himself and leave as well? Part of her wished he would, but the traitorous part wondered if she should invite him to stay.

"I'd like to talk for a few minutes, if you have time." He glanced toward the door.

Would he explain himself and try to make amends? Hope fluttered in her stomach, but she pushed it down. "If you wish."

"I'd prefer it be in private."

Her heart rate picked up speed, and she glanced over her shoulder. She could hear Grandmother's soft voice beyond the curtain, though Maggie could not make out her words.

Nate took a step closer, his expression easing into a gentle smile. "Come on a walk with me, Maggie."

His invitation stirred fond memories, and for a moment she felt seventeen again. Oh, how she longed to say yes, but she shook her head. "Violet has just come home. I don't think I should leave."

"Please. It's important." His earnest tone sparked her curiosity.

Surely she could spend a few minutes with him. There was no danger to her heart in that. "All right. Wait here a moment."

She crossed the room and pushed the curtain aside. "I'm going out, but I won't be long."

Grandmother sat across from Violet, a cup of tea in her hand. "Where are you going?"

Maggie took her shawl from the hook on the wall. "Just for a short walk . . . with Nathaniel Harcourt."

Grandmother's silver eyebrows rose. "Nathaniel is here?" She rose, set her cup aside, and walked past Maggie into the shop. "Nathaniel, it's been too long. How are you?" She reached out her hand.

"Hello, Mrs. Hayes. It's good to see you again." His eyes glowed as he took her hand and sent her a broad smile.

"It's wonderful to see you as well." Her eyes crinkled at the corners. "You've made quite a name for yourself in the Navy. We read all about it in the newspaper."

He gave his head a quick shake. "I've done my duty. There are many others who have done much more."

"Well, we're all proud of you and very glad you've come home safely."

His brow creased slightly. "Thank you, ma'am."

Why did he seem reluctant to accept her grandmother's praise? Wanting to ease his discomfort, Maggie motioned toward the door. "Shall we go?"

Nate stepped forward and held the door open for her. She passed outside, into the cool spring morning, and Nate followed.

They set off down the street, and Maggie's uneasiness grew as they walked on in silence for several seconds.

"So, Violet seems to be improving?" He tipped his head and looked her way.

"Yes. She's still in pain, but the doctor says if she stays off her feet for eight weeks, her leg should heal."

"She'll need crutches, then."

"Yes, Dr. Hadley is having a pair sent over later today."

"How do you think she'll do with those?"

"I'm sure it won't take long for her to learn to use them. She's strong and determined. We'll probably be chasing her in no time at all."

He grinned and broke into a soft chuckle.

"You find that funny?"

"She sounds very much like you."

Maggie couldn't hold back her smile. "We are alike in some ways, but she has her own gifts and talents."

"Such as?"

"She's very musical and has a lovely voice, unlike me, but very much like my mother and sister."

His smile faded and his eyes softened. "It's good to hear you speak of them."

Her throat tightened, and she had to push out her words. "I don't want to forget them."

"Of course not." He was quiet for a few more steps. "There's something I must tell you." His expression grew serious. "My father is not well. His recovery is doubtful."

She shivered and clutched her shawl tight around her. "I heard he was ill, but I didn't realize it was that serious."

"I'm afraid so. Dr. Hadley told him to prepare himself and put his affairs in order."

She didn't know Mr. Harcourt well, but the news was still unsettling. Mr. Harcourt was a skilled engineer and industrialist and a leading partner in Clifton Engineering Works, the largest employer in the area. But he'd never impressed her as a man who was truly happy. His changeable opinion about the landscaping plans for Morningside had been a continual frustration for her father.

"What caused his illness?" she asked softly.

"His heart has grown quite weak in the last few years. That's affecting his lungs, and his breathing is very labored." He shook his head, lines creasing his forehead. "His appearance is so changed I hardly recognize him."

She started to reach for his arm, wanting to comfort him as she would've done years ago, but that didn't seem appropriate now. She clasped her hands instead and walked on. "I'm sorry. This must be very difficult for you and your family."

"Seeing him so weak is hard, but his illness has caused him to reflect on his life and prompted him to take care of some matters that have been weighing on his conscience." He glanced her way.

She wanted to ask what matters he was referring to, but she supposed that was private information his father might not want shared with anyone.

Nate walked a few more steps before he continued. "He asked me to speak to you and express his regret for withholding funds he owed your father at the time of his death."

Her steps stalled. "He owed money to my father?"

Nate nodded. "Apparently he owed him almost a year's wages."

She stifled a gasp. "A year's wages?"

He smiled. "Yes, and now that money will be yours, and you can do whatever you'd like with it. Just think, you could add on to your shop or save for the future or even take a holiday."

Maggie stared at him, still stunned by the news. "But . . . why didn't he pay it right away?"

Nate sobered. "He should have, but he said his finances were strained because of building projects at Clifton, and your father had agreed to wait for the money, saying his needs were met."

She stiffened. "That doesn't give him the right to withhold the money for four years."

"No, it doesn't, and he regrets that now. I'll be meeting with Mr. Hornshaw, the estate manager, later today to find out the exact amount owed to you, then I'll see that it's paid."

Maggie clutched her shawl and battled her surging emotions. How could one of the wealthiest men in the north of England conveniently forget to pay a huge sum of money owed to her and her sister while they often struggled to afford their basic needs?

It wasn't right!

But if she took the money, would Mr. Harcourt believe his guilt was absolved? Shouldn't he have to take responsibility for withholding those funds for so long? Perhaps she should require him to pay interest or write a letter of apology. Even that wouldn't make up for what he had done.

She turned to Nate. "I can't accept your father's money."

His dark eyebrows dipped. "Why not? Your father earned it, and it would've been passed on to you."

"Yes, but if your father thinks he can just sign a bank draft and gain a clear conscience—that I would forgive his hardness of heart and dishonesty—then he is greatly mistaken."

Nate's mouth firmed into a straight line. "Withholding the money was wrong. My father realizes that, and he wants to make it right."

She bristled. "It's very convenient for him to pay it now, when he's ill and has no more need of it."

Nate stared at her, his gaze reflecting disappointment. "He is dying, Maggie. He wants to settle his debts and go in peace. Please, accept the money. If not for his sake, then for mine."

The load of hurt she had nursed for so long filled her chest with a painful ache. How could Nate say that? Didn't he realize how unfair this was? If she took the money, even for his sake, it would be like saying it didn't matter that she and her sister had been discarded like yesterday's trash and then cheated out of funds owed to her father.

"I can't." She spun away and strode back toward the shop.

Maybe now he would finally realize how much his disappearance had wounded her, how much she'd grieved, not only her parents' and sister's deaths, but also for the way he had left her to face it all alone.

She walked on, straining to hear his voice calling her back and his firm steps on the street behind her. But all she heard were her own footfalls crunching on the gravel road.

Her heart sank, and doubts rose in her mind. Was she being unfair by refusing the money and holding Nate responsible for his father's decisions?

She slowed and glanced over her shoulder, searching the street. But Nate was gone. He had probably stepped into the Red Lion or taken a side street out of town. Anywhere to get away from her and her hard-hearted refusal to be reconciled to him and his father.

And she couldn't blame him for that.

Lilly Neatherton took a stack of clean sheets from the linen closet and set off down the hall toward Mrs. Harcourt's bedroom. She'd have to hurry if she was going to change the bedding before the mistress returned to her room, and Mrs. Burnell, the housekeeper, would give Lilly a royal scolding if she didn't make quick work of it.

"Psst, Lilly!" The whispered voice came from the far end of the hall.

Lilly glanced over her shoulder.

Sophie, one of the other housemaids, stood at the open doorway to the servants' stairs. She lifted her index finger to her lips and motioned Lilly to come closer.

Lilly set the sheets on a chair in the alcove and hurried to meet Sophie. "What is it?"

"Rob Carter is downstairs at the courtyard door, asking for you."

Lilly's breath hitched in her chest. What was Rob doing here? He knew Lilly was not allowed to receive male callers at Morningside.

Sophie tipped her head. "Well, are you going to see him or not?"

Lilly bit her lower lip and glanced down the hall. It must be important or he wouldn't dare come. She turned back to Sophie. "Would you change the sheets in Mrs. Harcourt's bedroom for me?"

Sophie smiled. "Of course, but you'd better hurry. If Mrs. Burnell finds out about Rob . . ." She clicked her tongue. "I wouldn't want to be in your shoes."

"Pray she doesn't." Lilly took the stairs as quickly as she could, then slipped down the lower hallway and out the back entrance. She quietly closed the door and glanced around the stone courtyard.

Rob stood in the shadow of the house a few feet away. His eyes lit up when he saw her.

She hurried toward him. "Rob, what are you doing here?"

"I had to see you." Lines creased his forehead. "It's my dad. There was an accident at Clifton."

Lilly gasped. "What happened?"

"He caught his hand in one of the machines." Rob looked down and clenched his fists. "I was working on the other side of the building. One of the men ran over and got me. We had to take him to the hospital."

She laid her hand on his arm. "Oh, Rob, I'm so sorry."

He pressed his lips together. "He's in a lot of pain. They're keeping him at the hospital for now. I went home and told Mother. She was beside herself, and the girls were in tears."

"That's terrible."

"Mother ran over to the hospital, and she's with him now. She told me to go back to work, but I couldn't." He took off his cap and rubbed his hand down his face. "It's bad, Lilly. I'm not sure if they can save his hand. And if they can't, I don't know what we're going to do. My wages are barely enough to cover the rent. How are we going to pay for everything else?"

Lilly squeezed his arm. "Don't worry. I'll help you, and I'm sure our friends will as well."

Rob shook his head. "I couldn't take your money, Lilly."

"Of course you can. It's not my money; it's ours." Rob had proposed to her last October, and they'd both promised to save as much as they could so they'd be able to set a date and be married. But sometimes Rob's father spent his wages at the pub, and Rob had to buy food for his family or pay the rent for their small cottage in the village.

"What did the doctor say about his hand?"

"We'll have to wait and see how it heals. But the way it looked . . ." He closed his eyes for a moment, and his Adam's apple bobbed. "I don't know if he'll ever go back to work at Clifton or anywhere else."

Lilly's shoulders sagged and her eyes burned. How would they ever save enough to get married if Rob had to support his family? All these months of saving and waiting, only to find they must put off their hopes and dreams again. She bit her lip and silently scolded herself. She ought to be thinking about Rob's father and mother and how to help Rob through this hard time.

"And that's not all." Rob lifted his sorrowful gaze to meet hers. "My dad's accident has stirred up all kinds of trouble at Clifton."

Lilly's stomach tightened. "What do you mean?"

"All the time we were waiting for the wagon to come and take Dad to the hospital, the men gathered around, muttering and complaining."

"What did they say?"

"They blame the company for making us work such long days, and others say the equipment is old and not safe to use."

"People say all kinds of things when they're upset."

"Yes, but this time they're more than upset."

Lilly frowned and studied his face.

"They're tired of asking the management for changes and seeing nothing happen. It's been years since they raised anyone's salary. And this is not the first serious accident." He leaned toward her, his gaze intense. "Here's what it comes down to—if the board at Clifton won't listen, the men are going to call for a strike."

"A strike?" A dizzy wave swept over Lilly, and her legs went weak.

Rob nodded, his jaw firm and his blue eyes serious.

"But that could mean weeks without wages." Her mind spun with thoughts of the suffering a strike would cause. Not everyone had savings to see them through. Families would go hungry, and some might be turned out of their homes if they couldn't pay their rent. "Surely you don't want to strike."

"No, but I don't want to be the next one crippled by an accident either." He narrowed his eyes. "If we want things to change, we have to band together, speak up for our cause, and press the management to do what's right."

"Oh, Rob, be careful. You don't want to get in trouble and lose your job."

He placed both hands on her shoulders. "Don't worry about me, Lilly. I'll be all right."

She leaned toward him, and he pulled her into a tight embrace. She wrapped her arms around his waist and rested her head against his chest. The rough wool of his jacket brushed against her cheek. She closed her eyes, soaking in his strength and praying they'd find a way through these troubles.

Nate shifted on the hard chair opposite the desk of Mr. Robert Hornshaw, Morningside's estate manager, and watched the older man pull a leather-bound account book from his desk drawer. Hornshaw adjusted his spectacles, flipped through several pages, then looked up at Nate. "Daniel Lounsbury was paid quarterly, if I remember correctly." He ran his finger down the page. "Here's an entry for a payment made to him in September of 1898, the year before the accident." Hornshaw turned the book so Nate could see and pointed to the figure.

Nate leaned forward and scanned the entry. "Were any payments recorded later that year, or in 1899?"

Mr. Hornshaw cocked one eyebrow, and his mustache twitched. "I don't believe so." He made the statement without even checking the book. That piqued Nate's interest.

"How much did my father owe Mr. Lounsbury at the time of his death?"

"He died in August, didn't he?"

"Yes, on the twenty-second."

Hornshaw rubbed his chin. "I never could quite reconcile that in my mind."

"What do you mean?"

"That boat was almost new. I'm not sure how it could've sprung a leak."

Nate frowned. "Are you sure about that?"

"Yes, sir. We acquired it in May of that year. I took it out twice myself to do some fishing on the lake. It seemed sound to me at the time."

Nate pondered those comments while Hornshaw wrote a few numbers on a small piece of paper and did the calculations.

Hornshaw passed the paper across the desk to Nate. "I believe this is what was owed to Mr. Lounsbury."

Nate's eyebrows rose. The amount was more than his father had suggested, quite a bit more. He rubbed his chin. Had his father simply miscalculated, or had he intended to pay Maggie less than was due?

Maggie's accusations rose in his mind, stirring doubts about his father's sincerity. He glanced at the figure on the paper again, then sat back in his chair. "Do you know why my father neglected to pay Mr. Lounsbury's wages to his family after his death?"

Hornshaw rubbed his hand down his mustache. "I really couldn't say."

"Wouldn't he discuss a matter like that with you?"

"Usually, but I don't recall him saying anything about it, at least not after Mr. Lounsbury died."

"Before his death, then? What was the arrangement?"

Hornshaw pushed the pencil and paper aside, then looked across at Nate. "Your father said Mr. Lounsbury understood the situation at Clifton was putting a financial strain on him, and he agreed to wait for his wages."

Nate nodded. At least Hornshaw's story matched what his father had told him. But it wouldn't help to know those details or the amount owed if he couldn't convince Maggie to accept the money. Still, he intended to press on and find a way to see it through.

"My father would like me to make arrangements to pay off that debt."

Mr. Hornshaw nodded. "I'll prepare the bank draft and take it to your father for his signature."

"He'd like it done today. I'll wait for the draft and take it to him myself."

"Very well." Mr. Hornshaw set to work, wrote out the draft, and passed it to Nate. "There you are, sir."

"Thank you. I appreciate your help." Nate stood and shook hands with the estate manager, then left his office.

As he walked back across the estate to the house, his conversation with Maggie ran through his mind again. She had always been spirited and determined, but hearing her refuse the money and accuse his father of selfish motives had been hard to bear. He had hoped she would be glad to receive the money, even grateful. Instead, she seemed to consider it another reason to hold on to her anger against him and his family.

His father lay on his deathbed and was trying to make amends. Where was her compassion? Probably buried beneath her stubborn pride and the unforgiving spirit that seemed to have taken hold of her heart and turned her hurt into bitterness and resentment.

He must remember that Maggie had suffered a terrible loss, and grief had a way of distorting events and impacting the way people responded. Still, a lack of forgiveness, even when it seemed justified, only ended up hurting the one who refused to forgive. He had learned that painful lesson in the last few years, and he was beginning to see the benefits of extending forgiveness, even to those who might not deserve it.

Forgiving his father had freed him and given him a greater measure of peace.

And for that reason, he must find a way to convince Maggie to accept the funds she so obviously needed.

But how to do it . . . that was the question.

"Mr. Harcourt!"

Nate looked up.

Andrew, one of Morningside's footmen, hurried up the drive toward Nate. "A message for you, sir, from Mrs. Harcourt." He passed the folded note to Nate.

Nate opened it and scanned the words.

Come at once. Your father has taken a bad turn. The end is near.
Helen

A blanket of dread fell over Nate's shoulders like a heavy weight. He looked up. "Has someone gone for the doctor?"

"Yes, sir. Phillip left about ten minutes ago."

Nate nodded, stuffed the note in his pocket, and jogged toward the house. He would not disappoint his father—he couldn't. Somehow, he would find a way to carry out his father's last wishes and see that he passed out of this life at peace.

Grandmother's eyes flared, and she lifted her hand to her heart. "You did what?"

Maggie swallowed, wishing she hadn't said anything, but she couldn't take her words back now. "I told Nate I wouldn't accept the money. His father is only trying to soothe his guilty conscience, and I don't want any part of that."

"Margaret Ann, what a dreadful thing to say!" Grandmother stepped back from the kitchen table and dusted the flour from her hands.

A pang of guilt struck Maggie's heart, but she refused to let it sink in.

Grandmother looked at Maggie over the top of her spectacles. "From what I've heard, Mr. Harcourt is very ill and may be dying."

Maggie dipped her chin, trying to forget the painful look in Nate's eyes when he'd told her that same news.

Grandmother continued, "Mr. Harcourt wants to put his affairs in order and leave this world with his debts paid and his conscience clear."

"I'm sure he does, but doesn't it bother you that he never tried to pay us the money until now? That seems very dishonorable to me."

"I suppose he had his reasons." She searched Maggie's face, concern in her eyes. "Really, my dear, you shouldn't be so quick to judge people's motives, especially those of someone like Mr. Harcourt, who is so highly respected."

"He may be respected by some people, but I have my reasons for not trusting the Harcourts."

Grandmother clicked her tongue. "Surely you don't feel that way about Nathaniel. I thought you considered him your friend."

Maggie's throat tightened, and she had to push out her words. "I did, years ago, before the accident."

"He's a good, brave man who has done his duty for king and country, fighting the Boers. He deserves your appreciation and respect."

Maggie lifted one shoulder in a small shrug, unable to deny the truth of her grandmother's words.

"I'm sure his father has good intentions."

"How can you defend him?"

"I'm not defending him. I'm simply choosing *not* to be offended by him." Grandmother smoothed her hand down her apron. "Now, if you want my opinion, you'll write to Nathaniel and tell him you'll be glad to accept the money."

Maggie clenched her fists. "I can't do that."

"Of course you can. That money is a blessing from God, and we are not going to turn up our noses and refuse it."

"A blessing from God?" Maggie huffed and turned away.

"Yes, that's exactly what it is. I've been praying for a way to afford the repairs on the roof. And don't forget, we're also going to have a bill from the hospital for Violet's stay after the accident, and we're very low on supplies for the shop."

Maggie sighed. Why were finances always such a struggle? "I can't write to Nate and ask for the money now. I'd feel like I was begging."

"There is a big difference between humbling yourself and begging."

Maggie rolled her eyes and suppressed a groan. Her grandmother always had an answer for everything.

"Just tell him you've had time to consider it and you've changed your mind. Adding a few kind words of gratitude wouldn't hurt our cause either." Grandmother turned toward the kitchen table, plunged her hands into the bread dough, and continued kneading as though the decision had been made.

Maggie paced across the room, silently debating what to do.

"This money comes at the perfect time." Grandmother sprinkled flour over the dough and folded it into the mixture. "Even if Mr. Harcourt's motives for withholding the funds were not as honorable as we'd like, God knows what we need and He's seeing we receive it—and more besides." She chuckled and rolled the dough into a neat loaf. "Put on the tea kettle, Maggie. I think this calls for a little celebration."

Maggie turned toward Grandmother. "I didn't say I would write to Nate."

"But you will . . . Mark my words, you will."

Maggie lifted the soggy blouse from the laundry basket and clipped one shoulder to the clothesline in the courtyard behind her grandmother's shop. She looked up at the heavy clouds overhead and sighed. Perhaps this wasn't the best time to hang the clothes outside.

"Maggie, is that you?" Lilly looked over the stone wall separating their back courtyards. Her friend and neighbor wore a white cap over her blond hair, but a few short curls escaped to frame her face.

"Lilly, what are you doing home?" Maggie stepped away from the clothesline and crossed to the wall. Lilly's duties as housemaid at Morningside Manor usually kept her there all week, except for Sunday afternoons when she was free to visit her friends and family.

Lilly looked over the wall. "Mrs. Harcourt sent me to have her shoes repaired. The strap is broken, and she wants to wear them for the funeral."

Maggie's heart lurched. "Funeral?"

"Yes, didn't you hear? Mr. Harcourt passed away this morning."

A tremor shook Maggie, and she reached toward the wall to steady herself. "Oh no! That's terrible."

Lilly nodded, her face reflecting proper sadness. "Of course we knew he was nearing the end, but it's still been a bit of a shock for everyone."

Maggie's thoughts flashed to Nate. Had his visit with her that morning caused him to miss those last moments with his father? She focused on Lilly again. "Who was with him when he died?"

"Mrs. Harcourt and Miss Clara." Lilly clicked her tongue. "You never heard such moaning and crying as came from Mrs. Harcourt when it was all over. The doctor had to give her medicine to calm her down."

"What about the younger Mr. Harcourt?"

"They sent Andrew off to look for him, but by the time he made it back to the house, his father had passed."

Maggie's shoulders sagged. She hoped Nate had already said good-bye and would have no regrets, but thinking of the years of separation from his family and the short time they'd been reunited, she doubted that was true. She understood all too well the pain that followed losing a parent.

Conflicting feelings flooded her heart. Her refusal to accept the money had prevented Nate from fulfilling his father's dying request. No doubt her decision added to the grief he was feeling now.

"Maggie, are you all right?"

She blinked and looked at Lilly again. "Yes, I'm just a bit stunned by the news."

"It is dreadful to think about, but I'm glad the younger Mr. Harcourt had a little time with his father before he passed. That should ease his mind and help him accept the loss."

Maggie nodded, though she wasn't sure how Nate would deal with his father's death. "He was a loyal son. He wanted his father's passing to be peaceful."

Lilly tilted her head. "How do you know that?"

Maggie hesitated, her face warming. "He came by the shop . . . and told me as much."

"He came to see you at your grandmother's shop?"

Maggie nodded. "Yesterday he was passing by on the street when Violet was struck by a motorcar."

"Oh, my goodness. I hadn't heard about that. Is she going to be all right?"

"She has a broken leg and had to stay at the hospital overnight, but the doctor says she'll be fine in time. We're very grateful. It could've been so much worse."

"I'm glad to hear she's on the mend. Please tell her I'll say a prayer for her." Lilly looked around and then focused on Maggie again. "We've had some bad news as well. Rob's father had an accident at Clifton."

Maggie gasped. "What happened?"

"His hand was caught in some machinery, and it's doubtful he'll be able to go back to work there."

"That's dreadful."

Lilly nodded. "It means more hard times for his family, and it means putting off our wedding plans as well."

Maggie reached for Lilly's hand and gave it a squeeze, her heart aching for her friends. "I'm so sorry."

Rob and Lilly had worked hard to save for their marriage, and now it seemed they would have to wait longer. His mother, Rose, was a dear friend to Grandmother, and Rob's sisters were sweet and caring girls. Maggie hated to think of them suffering because of the accident and loss of income.

"We'll be all right. Bad times can't go on forever." Lilly straightened her shoulders. "So, what were you saying about Nathaniel Harcourt?"

"Oh, he stopped to help Violet after the accident and carried her to the hospital. Then he came by this morning to see how she was doing."

"Really? He was here today?"

"I'm sure he didn't realize this was his father's last day or he would never have left his side."

"Yes, you're probably right about that. It certainly was kind of him to help Violet and then come to the village to look in on her." Curiosity lit her friend's eyes, and she studied Maggie. "I remember you saying you and Nathaniel Harcourt were friends when you were younger."

Maggie looked away. "That was years ago."

"I've only seen him a few times." Lilly sent her a teasing smile. "He's not nearly as good looking as my Rob, but he's quite handsome, don't you think?"

Maggie's face warmed. How had their conversation turned in this direction? "It doesn't matter what I think of Mr. Harcourt. We shouldn't be discussing this, especially not when his father has just passed away."

Lilly pulled back. "I'm sorry. I didn't mean to upset you."

Now she'd done it. If she wasn't careful, her friend would realize there was more to her meeting with Nate than a little kindness between old friends. "It's all right. I'm not upset."

Lilly leaned toward the wall again. "You don't have to pretend with me. I can see something's wrong."

Maggie debated a few more seconds, then blew out a breath. "All right. I'll tell you, but you must promise not to say a word to anyone else."

Lilly gave an eager nod and stepped closer. "I promise."

"Nathaniel Harcourt did come by to check on Violet, but he also came because Mr. Harcourt owed my father a large sum of money at the time of his death."

"Really?"

"Yes." Maggie leaned toward Lilly and whispered the amount.

Lilly's blue eyes grew round. "Oh, my goodness! That's more than enough to meet your needs for a long while and put away a sizable dowry besides."

Maggie shook her head. "I don't think I should accept it."

Lilly's mouth dropped open, and she looked at Maggie as if she'd lost her senses. "Of course you should. Why wouldn't you?"

Maggie stiffened. "Mr. Harcourt didn't care about us. He just wanted to ease his guilty conscience."

"Why would you say that?"

"I told you how they treated us after my parents and sister died."

"Yes, but that was years ago. I'm sure they're all sorry for it now."

"I'm not sure of anything, except that I don't trust the Harcourts."

"Maybe they're giving you the money as a peace offering, to make up for what happened."

"I won't be bought off. Not by Nate—I mean Mr. Harcourt—or anyone else."

Lilly frowned and looked toward the shop. "What does your grandmother say?"

Maggie sighed. "She wants me to take it."

"There's your answer, then."

"She doesn't understand. It's not that simple." Maggie shifted her gaze away and crossed her arms. Why didn't she just do as her grandmother asked, write a letter, and accept the money? She sighed and shook her head. That would be like saying what the Harcourts had done didn't matter, that all was forgiven . . . and she could never say that.

Nate walked down the main staircase at Morningside and followed his stepmother, Helen, toward the drawing room. There was much to be done, but she had requested a private word with him before he contacted his father's solicitor and the board at Clifton Engineering to inform them of his father's death.

Would his stepmother tell their extended family, or would that be his responsibility as well? He rubbed the back of his neck where a headache had been building during the last hour.

Helen crossed to the sofa and took a seat. "Sit down, Nathaniel. We need to discuss the funeral arrangements." Her grim, authoritative tone set his teeth on edge, but he determined not to react in a similar manner. She had become a widow today, and he wanted to give her as much grace as he could muster.

He sat in the chair opposite her. "I can speak to the curate at Saint Peter's and take care of the funeral arrangements, if you'd like."

Her eyebrows rose. "I would like to have some say in the matter."

"Of course, I was only trying to save you the trouble."

"It is no trouble to see that my husband has a proper funeral. You may meet with Reverend Samuelson, but I expect you to convey my wishes."

"Very well." He rubbed his hands on the arms of the chair. He'd never met Reverend Samuelson. He must have arrived at the parish while Nate was away. "Did you have some specific instructions you want me to convey to the reverend?"

"First, we need to set the date."

Nate nodded. "I believe Saturday would give everyone adequate time to prepare."

Her nostrils flared. "That's not nearly enough time. Next Wednesday is the earliest date I will consider."

Nate frowned. "I don't see why we should wait a week."

"We need to notify our friends and relatives and give them time to make their travel arrangements."

"And who are these friends and relatives that need an extended amount of time to travel to the funeral?"

"Your father has several business acquaintances in London who will want to attend. And my friend Lucile Pierpont lives there as well. Perhaps you don't remember, but her husband owns an investment company, and he can't leave his business and travel to Northumberland with only a day's notice."

"And you believe the Pierponts would like to attend Father's funeral?"

"I should hope so. She is one of my oldest and dearest friends." She glared at him as though he had insulted her.

"I'm sorry. I didn't realize they would want to be included. I don't recall them being in the habit of visiting Morningside."

She lifted her chin, and her gaze turned steely. "His business keeps them in town, and they have a very busy social schedule. But I'm quite certain they will attend if we give them sufficient notice."

Nate's stomach churned. He did not look forward to playing host to a large group of people he barely knew. But it seemed he had no choice in the matter. He had promised his father he would take care of Helen, and seeing that she had her way with the funeral arrangements was part of that responsibility.

"All right. I'll ask Reverend Samuelson if the funeral can be scheduled next Wednesday."

"Set the time for eleven, then we can serve luncheon here after."

Nate shifted in his seat. "Is that necessary?"

"Of course it is. Some people will travel a great distance to attend, and we can't send them off without offering a meal and time for conversation."

"Very well." He pulled his thoughts back to the decisions at hand. "Do you have any thoughts about the service itself?"

"Whatever the reverend suggests will be fine, as long as it's proper and respectful." She thought for a moment, then narrowed her eyes. "But I don't want him to ask Mrs. Sylvia Gatling to sing. She has a dreadful voice, and it will strain my nerves past the point of breaking if I have to listen to her sing at my husband's funeral." She paused, but only long enough to take a quick breath. "And another thing, I don't want him giving any long, dour sermons. Facing a crowd for the first time after losing my husband will be trying enough. I don't want the day made more dismal by his warnings of God's judgment and hellfire." She lifted her eyes toward the ceiling with a dramatic sigh. "That's the last thing anyone wants to hear at a funeral."

Nate clenched his jaw and drummed his fingers on the arm of the chair. He'd never felt close to his stepmother, but this conversation was rapidly making the distance wider. "I'm sure Reverend Samuelson will want to encourage people to consider the brevity of life and offer the hope of heaven for those who place their faith and trust in Christ."

She looked at him as though he were speaking a foreign language. "People want to be comforted at a funeral, not condemned."

"I'm sure he would not condemn anyone."

Her mouth pinched into a tight line. "Just make my wishes clear. He may include uplifting scripture and speak about your father's accomplishments and good character, but I will not tolerate any warnings of judgment or hellfire. Do you understand?"

Nate leveled his gaze at Helen. "I don't believe it's my place to dictate the reverend's message."

"Then you can remind him that a good portion of his salary comes from our family's gifts to the parish, and if he wants those to continue, he will keep my requests in mind."

Nate shook his head. Her presumption was unbelievable.

She rose and crossed to the window. "Now, what shall we serve for the luncheon?"

"I'm sure you and Mrs. Burnell can plan the menu with the cook." He rose from his chair. "I'm going to send a telegram to Father's solicitor and arrange a meeting with him."

"Tell him to come to Morningside. I don't want to travel to Newcastle upon Tyne any time soon."

The band around Nate's chest cinched tighter, and it took every ounce of his self-control to keep his tone in check. "As you wish." He turned and strode out of the drawing room.

He'd forgotten how difficult his stepmother could be. She liked to give the impression that she deferred to her husband in important matters, but she had not been able to hide her desire for control from Nate. And now that his father was gone . . . He sighed and shook his head.

But he had promised he would look after her, and he intended to keep his word.

One of the maids hurried across the great hall, looking lost in thought. In her hands she carried a pair of women's black shoes. As she drew closer, her head popped up and her eyes widened. "I'm sorry, sir. I didn't see you."

"It's all right."

She looked at him, and her expression softened. "I'm very sorry for your loss, sir."

Her gentle tone caught him by surprise. She was the first member of the staff to acknowledge his father's death. All the others had avoided looking his way and remained silent.

His throat tightened. "Thank you." He nodded to her. "Excuse me." Then he strode up the stairs, strangely touched by the maid's kindness.

It wasn't only his stepmother who had suffered a loss today. He had lost his father. This was the end of an era at Morningside and in his life. There would be no more opportunities to strengthen his relationship with his father. He must look to the future and try to live a life that reflected the best of his father's character. To those qualities he would add the practical wisdom he was gaining from his newfound faith.

The path ahead might be foggy and uncertain, but if he put that strategy into action, surely God would bless his efforts and show him the way.

Maggie kissed her grandmother and Violet good night, then climbed the stairs to her bedroom. She placed the lantern on the bedside table and glanced around the cozy space with its mismatched desk, chair, dresser, and two narrow beds.

Violet would sleep downstairs with Grandmother tonight, giving Maggie some rare private time. She crossed to the window, pushed aside the lace curtain, and looked down at the small courtyard behind the shop. All was quiet now. A soft breeze drifted in through the open window, carrying the scent of rain.

She lifted her eyes to the sky, where the sunset's golden glow darkened to deeper shades of blue beyond the trees. Overhead, one tiny star blinked at her between the drifting clouds.

The events of the day rolled through her mind . . . bringing Violet home from the hospital, Nate's visit that morning, and Lilly's news from Morningside. She and her grandmother had spent a good part of the evening talking about all that had happened. Her grandmother's words came back to her now.

"Your father would want you to accept the money from Mr. Harcourt, especially now that he's gone and can do nothing more to make things right."

Maggie stared across the village rooftops. Was that true? Would her father want her to take the money and forgive the Harcourts?

If only he were here to counsel her and help her understand why she struggled so with this decision. Her father had always been wise and kind. He would know the perfect words to comfort her heart.

A mosaic of memories came flooding back . . . jaunts through the fields with her father, fishing trips to the Upper Coquetdale, gathering shells by the seashore, visits to Bamburgh Castle, and walking along the ancient Hadrian's Wall.

Oh, how she missed him! More than words could ever say.

She walked to the small trunk at the end of her bed and lifted the lid. Her father's last journal lay on top of the stack of neatly folded blankets, along with her mother's Bible and Olivia's soft green shawl. Those were the only family mementos she'd kept. The rest had been sold or given away after she and Violet had been whisked off to Scotland following the accident.

Bile rose in her throat, and she swallowed hard. She took the journal from the trunk and gently ran her hand over the leather cover. She'd kept it locked away until now, but perhaps it would be a comfort to read a few entries written in her father's hand.

She carefully opened the book, turned the first page, and read the inscription. Her father's handwriting flowed across the page with beautiful curves and loops, each letter distinct, his artistic talent obvious in his elegant signature:

The Journal of Daniel Lounsbury. Begun 14 March 1897.

She scanned the first few entries, and a smile tipped up the corners of her mouth. Each day he recorded his progress on the landscaping projects at Morningside, his interactions with the Harcourts and his assistants, as well as notes about the family. He mentioned a trip to Newcastle upon Tyne and seeing the first signs of spring in the garden, accompanied by an illustration of daffodils.

She loved to see his drawings, and it made her long to take up her own nature journal again. She'd set it aside since she'd come to Heatherton to live with Grandmother. It was too painful to look back at what she'd shared with her parents—their carefree life, with time in the country to explore nature and record and illustrate the plants and animals she'd discovered.

She turned the page and read the next entry.

27 March

I came across Mrs. H. today almost a mile from the house, a most surprising encounter. When I greeted her, she seemed quite upset and her eyes looked red, as though she had been crying. I asked if she was all right, and she said there was no need for me to be concerned. She was on her way home and would be fine.

I offered to escort her back to the house, thinking that would ease her distress. But a fearful expression crossed her face, and she quickly declined. Then she hurried away without another word. Very strange indeed.

I don't know Mrs. H. well, although I've been a dinner guest in their home several times. She has a rather strong personality and is not afraid to speak her mind. I'm afraid she and Mr. H. do not enjoy the same closeness I have with Abigail. I suppose few couples share that level of contentment after so many years together. But I can honestly say I am blessed beyond measure with my dear Abigail, my closest companion and the other half of my heart.

I pray Mr. and Mrs. H. will one day enjoy that same closeness.

Maggie looked up, her heart warmed by her father's comments about his feelings for her mother. Knowing they loved each other deeply and were happy together was a great comfort.

But the comforting warmth faded as the memory of the boating accident rose in her mind. Her father was a strong swimmer. If she could make it to shore, then there was no doubt in her mind that he could have as well. But he had refused to leave his wife and daughter, and his love and devotion to them had cost him his life.

She pressed her lips together and blinked back her tears. What a hard and painful choice to make. Would she have the courage to give up her life for someone she loved? Would anyone ever love her with that much devotion?

She looked back at the journal and read the first line once more.

I came across Mrs. H. today almost a mile from the house, a most surprising encounter.

A fuzzy memory stirred in her mind and came into focus. She'd been thirteen years old at the time, a year after she and her family had first come to Morningside Manor . . .

"Margaret Lounsbury, what in the world do you think you're doing?"

Maggie gasped and gripped the swaying elm branch. "Nate! You nearly made me fall!"

Nate placed his hands on his hips and glared up at her. "Come down out of that tree before you kill yourself!"

The rough bark scraped her hands and ankles as she inched forward, but she ignored the pain. "I can't come down. There's a perfect little wren's nest up here, and I must have a look."

"Oh, for heaven's sake! You're risking your life to inspect a bird's nest?"

Maggie wrinkled her nose at him. "I want to see if there are any eggs, and I can't very well do that from the ground." Just because Nate was sixteen, and heir to Morningside Manor, he thought that gave him the right to lord his age and position over her. Well, she might be three years younger, but she was just as clever and strong as he was, and she would prove it.

He shook his head, his dark-brown eyes flashing. "You know very well you're being ridiculous!"

"I am not! How can I paint the eggs if I don't know what they look like?"

"No bird's eggs are worth falling out of a tree and breaking your neck."

"I won't fall if you'll stop shouting at me." She crept forward, straining toward the nest.

He huffed and paced across the grass, then looked up at her again. "Your father may be our landscape architect, but that doesn't mean you can wander all over the estate and climb trees like a monkey."

Her face flushed. She did not climb like a monkey! How dare he say that!

"If your father saw what you're doing, you know you'd be in trouble. And if my father or stepmother found out, heaven only knows what kind of explosion would follow."

"My father has gone to the village, and your father is too preoccupied with his inventions to venture outside."

"Thank heaven for small favors, but what about my stepmother?"

"You know she rarely walks past the edge of the rose garden, so there's little chance of anyone finding out." Maggie peered down at him through the leaves, and a touch of worry pricked her conscience. "Unless you tell them. You won't, will you?"

His brow creased as he looked up at her, but his expression softened. "Not as long as you stop this foolishness and climb down."

She didn't like to upset Nate. In spite of his sometimes lofty attitude, he was a good friend. But she wouldn't turn around now, not when she was so close. "I can't. Not until I see what's in the nest."

He straightened his shoulders and looked up at her. "All right, then I am coming up after you."

She gasped. "Don't even think about it! You'd break the branch for sure."

He started toward the trunk.

"Nate, please! I'm almost there. I'll just take one look and then be on the ground before you know it. I promise."

He stopped and muttered something under his breath, then placed his hands on his hips again and watched her creep the last few inches.

She peeked into the nest, and a smile broke across her face. "I knew it!"

Four pale blue eggs with faint brown speckles lay in the center of a neatly woven circle fashioned from tiny twigs, dried grass, and seedling fluff. She studied the scene, hoping she could capture the fragile beauty when she sketched it in her nature journal and then used her watercolors to bring it to life.

Were the eggs smooth or did the speckles give them texture? She reached out and ran her finger over the closest eggs.

Suddenly, a squawking bird dived toward her, flapping its wings and circling her head.

She screamed and flung out both hands, trying to bat the bird away.

"Maggie!" Nate dashed closer, holding out his arms.

She scrambled back along the branch, her heart pounding wildly. The bird swooped in again. She ducked to the left and lost her balance. A scream caught in her throat as she plunged toward the ground.

Nate broke her fall, and they tumbled into the grass.

All the air whooshed out of her lungs, and she lay on top of him, stunned and breathless. She blinked a few times, pushed herself up on shaky arms, and brushed her dark hair out of her face. "Sorry, Nate."

She scanned his still form, and the hair on the back of her neck prickled.

His eyes were closed, and his lips barely parted. Why didn't he sit up and scold her for landing on top of him? A cold wave swept over her.

"Nate?" Her voice sounded like a hoarse whisper, but he didn't open his eyes.

She gasped and scrambled off. Had she killed him?

Kneeling beside him, she laid her head on his solid chest and listened to his heart. The strong, steady beat eased her fear, but that relief lasted only a moment. She might not have murdered her friend, but she had certainly knocked him unconscious.

She bit her lip and gently brushed his dark-brown hair off his forehead. No cuts or lumps were visible on his face, but what if his injuries were the more serious kind that you couldn't see?

"Oh, Nate, I'm so sorry. I didn't mean to flatten you—really I didn't. Please wake up. I'll listen to you next time. I promise I will! No, there won't be a next time. I give you my solemn word that I'll never climb another tree as long as I live!"

One corner of his mouth quirked up. Then his eyes popped open, and he smiled up at her. "Promise?"

She gasped, then leaned back and slapped his shoulder. "Oh, you're terrible! How could you tease me like that?"

He sat up, grinning, and brushed the grass off his shirt. "Well, you nearly did knock me out. I had no idea you were so heavy."

She sat back on her heels and scowled at him.

"Oh, come on, Maggie. Don't be angry. I was just having a little fun."

"I thought I killed you." She crossed her arms and looked away.

He laughed. "Not this time."

She continued to glare, but she couldn't stay angry, not when he looked at her with that teasing twinkle in his eyes. "You must promise never to do that again."

"All right." He sent her a cheeky grin and rose to his feet. "Come on. We'd better get back. Your parents will be looking for you."

"I haven't been gone that long." She glanced up at the sun through the tree's limbs, trying to guess the time.

"It's almost four. We'll miss tea if we don't hurry. And you know your mother wouldn't like that." He held out his hand.

She grabbed hold and rose, a smile stealing across her lips again. Nate could be bossy, and he took more of her father's time and attention than she cared to give, but she enjoyed his company.

He only came home to Morningside for Christmas and summer holidays. The rest of the year he attended school in London. When he was home, he spent more time with her family than his own. Her father had taken him under his wing as he oversaw the work of transforming the rocky and heather-covered moors around the estate into beautiful woodlands, expansive lakes, and flower-filled gardens.

She would miss Nate terribly when he went back to school again.

They started down the path leading through the woods around Tumbledon Lake. It was only a fifteen-minute walk back to her house, which was just a short distance from the manor house where Nate lived with his father, stepmother, and younger sister, Clara.

She and Nate had been walking only a few minutes when she heard voices off to the left. Apparently Nate heard them too because he held out his hand and stopped her. Maggie peered through the bushes, but she didn't see anyone. She exchanged a quick glance with Nate, and he returned a quizzical look.

Was it Mr. McDougall, the head gamekeeper, or one of his assistants? They often made their rounds through this part of the estate, checking on red deer, pheasants, and quail that were raised for hunting.

"I don't understand. You promised you'd speak to her." The female voice was hushed but insistent.

Maggie tilted her head to listen. The woman sounded like Nate's stepmother, Helen Harcourt, but she couldn't be sure.

Nate frowned toward the trees, his gaze intense.

"I tried, but she's been ill," a man replied, his tone matching Mrs. Harcourt's.

Maggie didn't recognize the man's voice. She lifted her eyebrows and sent Nate a questioning glance, but he waved her off and leaned forward to better hear the voices.

“So you’ll speak to her when she recovers?” Impatience sharpened the woman’s words.

“Yes, of course. As soon as I feel she’s able to handle the news.”

Why were these two meeting here in the woods so far from the manor house? What was the news the man was hesitant to tell?

Nate leaned toward Maggie. “Let’s go before they see us,” he whispered, then started down the path.

Maggie grabbed his arm. “Don’t you want to hear what they’re saying?”

“No.” He pulled away.

“But, Nate—”

He looked back, his brow furrowed and his mouth set in a grim line. “Your parents will be worried.” He shot a quick glance toward the voices in the woods. “We need to go.”

Maggie bit her lip. Something wasn’t right. Why was Nate so intent on leaving rather than listening to the rest of the conversation? She followed him a few steps down the path, then slowed and looked over her shoulder. A flash of purple showed between the trees and then Mrs. Harcourt’s profile came into view.

A cool, stony look covered her face like a mask.

A chill shot down Maggie’s back. Whoever Mrs. Harcourt was talking to, Maggie wouldn’t want to be in his shoes.

7

Lilly swirled her spoon through her tea, rested her chin in her hand, and stared across the servants' hall table. Thoughts of Rob and his family filled her mind. How was his father's recovery coming along, and how was his mother bearing up under these new burdens?

Rob was still reluctant to accept the money she'd offered, but she was working on a plan to help his family in practical ways. If she mentioned her idea to a few friends, she was certain they would all want to contribute. It was time for them to pull together and take care of one another.

But what if the workers at Clifton continued to press the management for changes? What if their demands were ignored and they called for a strike? Almost every family in the village would feel the pain if they did. She grimaced and pushed those thoughts away. Today had enough trouble. No need to borrow from tomorrow.

"Lilly?"

She blinked and pulled her gaze back into focus. "Yes?"

Sophie sent her a curious look across the table. "You seem to be miles away. Did you hear my question?"

"No, sorry. What did you say?"

"I asked if you had plans for your half day?"

Lilly shook her head. "Not yet." Most of the staff were released from their duties after church on Sunday. She usually spent time with her father and brother in the village and then shared a meal with Rob and his family before he walked her back to Morningside by eight o'clock. She sighed as those happy memories faded. What would the future hold for her and Rob now? How long would they have to postpone their wedding plans?

Andrew walked into the room, carrying a small stack of envelopes. "The morning post, sir." He handed them to Mr. Jackson.

The butler sorted through the pile and looked up. "Lilly."

"Yes, sir?"

"This one is for you." Mr. Jackson passed her an envelope.

Her heartbeat quickened. She rose, clutched the envelope to her chest, and hurried outside. Rob was the only one who wrote to her, and she wanted to read his letter in private.

She sat down on a crate outside in the back courtyard and tore open the letter.

My dear Lilly, how I miss you! You are never far away from my thoughts and always in my heart. How I wish we could sit by the fire this evening, talk about our day, and enjoy the comfort of life together. I hope and pray that day will come soon. But for now I will have to be content to write to you, tell you my news, and ask you to keep me in your prayers.

The doctor told us today that Father's hand is healing, but it won't be much use to him. It's good it is his left hand. Still, he won't be able to return to work at Clifton, and I'm not sure if he'll be able to find another job. Of course we are all discouraged by this news, but Mother and the girls are putting on cheerful faces, though I know their hearts are aching too.

I've decided to take on extra hours at Clifton. I spoke to Charlie Gilmore, and he said he needs someone to help with cleaning the warehouses on Sundays.

Lilly stared at the letter, her heart sinking. How could Rob work seven days a week? He'd wear himself out and end up getting sick. What would his family do then?

Knowing I won't be able to see you on Sunday afternoon is weighing very heavy on me. Spending time with you is always the best part of my week, but it's a sacrifice I have to make to take care of the family. I hope you'll understand and forgive me.

Your letters give me hope and lift my spirits, so please write to me when you can. Until then, know that I am thinking of you and praying for you.

With all my love,

Rob

Tears flooded her eyes as she lowered the letter to her lap. *Oh, Rob, what are we going to do?*

Nate slowly climbed the stairs. Only three days had passed since his father's death, but so much had happened, and the weight of his responsibilities made him feel like he carried a heavy pack on his shoulders.

The unsettling conversation with his stepmother replayed in his mind, stirring his frustration. Helen had taken control of Morningside in February when his father had grown too ill to carry out his duties. She was proud of the way she'd handled every decision concerning the house and staff, and she didn't relish giving up control now, especially to Nate.

He was too young, she insisted, too inexperienced.

Nate disagreed as tactfully as he could. He might be only twenty-four, but he had been through naval training and a war, and he was confident he could manage the estate and learn what was needed to carry out his responsibilities at Clifton Engineering as well.

But Helen was not ready to concede. When the conversation ended, they'd faced each other in heated silence for several seconds, both aware they'd reached a stalemate.

He blew out a deep breath and shook his head. If they could just get past the funeral, perhaps Helen's emotions would settle and she would be able to accept the changes his father's death had forced on them all. He was the heir. The estate had passed to him, and she needed to accept that fact. He was committed to caring for her and Clara, but he would not relinquish leadership of the estate to her.

As he walked down the hallway to his room, another unsettling thought rose in his mind. Yesterday Mr. Geoffrey Rowlett, his father's business partner at Clifton, had come to Morningside to offer his condolences and assure Nate there was no need for him to worry about matters at Clifton Engineering.

A few minutes into that visit Nate realized the conversation was nothing more than a veiled attempt to keep him away from Clifton. Why didn't he want Nate involved? Did he share Helen's opinion that Nate was too young and inexperienced to take an active role as a partner and a member of the board? Or was there some other reason?

The sound of a woman crying stopped him halfway down the hall. He cocked his head and listened, then followed the sound. Muffled sobs came from Clara's room.

He stopped in front of her door and listened for a few seconds. Poor girl. She had put on a brave front since their father's death, but it had obviously impacted her more deeply than she'd let anyone see.

He glanced down the hall and then back at her door. Should he walk away and pretend he hadn't heard or go in and try to comfort her? He didn't know Clara very well, and he wasn't sure what he could say that would help. But her crying continued, and he felt he must try.

"Clara?" He tapped on her door.

The crying stopped, but she didn't reply.

He knocked again. "It's Nate. May I come in?"

A few more seconds passed. "All right."

He slowly pushed the door open. Two small lamps glowed on either side of the bed, and flames flickered in the fireplace, illuminating the room. Clara sat in a high-backed chair by the hearth. Her shoulders sagged, and misery lined her face.

She met his gaze, then quickly looked away. Her eyes were red, and she clutched a wrinkled handkerchief in her hand.

He stood in the doorway. "I'm sorry to disturb you. But I heard you crying and I thought—"

"What? That you'd come in and rescue me?" Her bitter tone took him by surprise.

"No, I thought it might help if I looked in on you."

"Well, you needn't bother." She sniffed and wiped her nose with the handkerchief. "I'm all right. I just have a cold."

"I think there must be another reason for your tears."

Her gaze darted back to him. "I don't know why you would care."

He crossed the room and stood on the opposite side of the fireplace. "I care because I am your brother."

"Half brother, you mean."

He tipped his head slightly. "True, but we've been part of the same family since you were born."

"So you think that gives you some kind of special knowledge about me?" He opened his mouth to reply, but she cut him off. "You don't know me. You left when I was fourteen, and you never bothered to write to me or visit me. Mother and Father didn't talk about you often, but when they did, I could tell you had hurt them."

He stilled, struck by her words. He could make excuses, say his naval training or the war kept him away. But the truth was, he'd had extended leave a few times and could've made the trip home. Instead, he'd chosen to stay away and nurture his grievances.

He straightened. "You're right. I wish I could go back and make different choices, ones that wouldn't hurt the people I care about, including you. I'm sorry, Clara."

Her tense expression eased, and a small light flickered in her eyes.

"I should've come home sooner and tried to work out the problems that kept me away."

"Why didn't you come home?"

He shook his head. "I don't want to burden you with my troubles."

"I'm not a child anymore. You don't have to try and protect me from the truth. I know you were angry with Father and Mother when you left."

"That's true, but it won't do any good to raise those issues now. Father and I made our peace before he passed, and I'm glad of it."

"What about Mother?"

Nate took a moment to weigh his words. "Your mother and I still have some matters we need to resolve, but we'll work through them."

"So . . . you're not going to make us leave?"

His gaze darted to meet hers. "No, whatever gave you that idea?"

She lifted one shoulder. "I know you inherit everything, and Mother and I are not your real family. I thought you might send us away."

He sat on the stool next to her chair. "Clara, you are my sister. I promised Father I would look after you and your mother. Morningside is your home, and you will always have a place here as long as you'd like."

Her face brightened. "You mean that?"

"Yes, of course."

She lifted her hand to her heart. "Oh, that's such a relief. I couldn't stand the thought of leaving Morningside on top of everything else. That's why I was crying."

"I thought it might be because you're missing Father."

Her eyes glistened. "Of course, that too." She blinked away her tears. "He'd been ill for quite a while, and I tried to prepare myself for his passing, but I didn't know it would feel like this . . . so final, so painful."

Nate nodded. "No one knows what it's like to lose a parent until you go through it."

She looked at him with the glow of sympathy in her eyes. "And you've lost both of yours."

He swallowed. "Yes, I have."

"Yet you don't seem broken by it." She sat back in her chair. "I suppose that's because you're a man and you don't feel things the way women do."

Nate suppressed a smile. "I'm not sure about that, but I think men aren't as willing to show their feelings."

"No, I suppose not."

"But I did love Father, and I am very sorry we didn't have more time together."

"Yes, I feel the same." Clara released a weary sigh. "The future seems uncertain without Father, but at least you're not asking us to leave."

"I'm glad I can put that fear to rest." He smiled as he rose and held out his hand to her. She reached out and took hold, but she ducked her chin, looking embarrassed by the gesture.

"Now I'll say good night and wish you peaceful dreams."

"Thank you, Nathaniel," she said softly.

"I think you should call me Nate."

She lifted her head and sent him a tremulous smile. "Very well. Good night, Nate."

8

Maggie looked at her reflection in the mirror on the shop counter and adjusted the small black hat to the proper angle. With a careful touch, she slid a hatpin through the back of the crown. There was a bit of a breeze today, and she didn't want her hat to fly off across Saint Peter's churchyard during Mr. Harcourt's graveside service.

Grandmother pushed the curtain aside and stepped into the shop. "You look very nice, my dear."

"Thank you." Maggie brushed her hand down the skirt of her black dress and checked her appearance in the mirror once more. "You don't mind if I wear the hat?"

"Not at all. Someone might as well get some use out of it." Grandmother hobbled across the room and stepped behind the glass display case opposite Maggie. "I'm sorry you have to go to the funeral alone."

"It's all right. I don't mind. Thank you for staying with Violet."

Grandmother nodded, her gaze intense. "It's more important that you go."

A prickle of unease traveled through Maggie. What did her grandmother mean by that?

Grandmother reached across the counter and adjusted the netting on Maggie's hat. "Be sure to give my condolences to the Harcourts when you speak to them after."

Rather than replying, Maggie reached up and touched the cameo pinned at her neck.

Grandmother's eyebrows rose slightly. "Have you written to Nathaniel and told him you'll accept the money?"

Ah, here was the real point of this conversation. Avoiding her grandmother's eyes, Maggie stepped away and straightened a light-blue hat on a nearby wooden stand. A week had passed since she'd seen Nate. Her stormy emotions had calmed, but she still couldn't decide what to do about the money. "I'm sure he's been busy with family matters and preparing for the funeral."

"But you said he was eager to settle the matter." Grandmother stepped into Maggie's line of vision. "Why don't you speak to him today?"

Maggie walked around the end of the glass case. "I don't think his father's funeral is the right time for that discussion."

"But if he brings it up, I hope you're ready to give him your answer."

Maggie's frustration bubbled up in her voice. "Even if it comes up, I don't know what to say to him."

"God will help you. All you have to do is ask." Grandmother's tone was gentle, but her words still felt like rough sandpaper rasping across Maggie's sore heart.

"The book of James says if anyone lacks wisdom they should ask of God," Grandmother continued, "and He will give it to them."

Maggie almost rolled her eyes, but she didn't want to hurt her grandmother. Her faith seemed unshakeable. She had a scripture ready for every situation, and she was not shy about sharing them with Maggie or anyone else.

A sliver of guilt pricked Maggie's heart. Her parents had been very much like her grandmother, weaving scriptures into their conversation as naturally as they practiced those principles in their daily lives . . . but in the end, it hadn't helped them.

Maggie shook her head. "I don't mean to be disrespectful, but I don't think God hears or answers my prayers."

Grandmother leaned toward her. "Oh, Maggie, how can you say such a thing?"

A lump lodged in Maggie's throat, and she could barely push out her reply. "How can you even ask me that?"

Grandmother's expression softened, and she released a sigh. "I know you're still carrying a load of hurt from everything that happened to your parents and Olivia, but you've got to turn it over to God and let Him carry it for you."

The storm inside Maggie swirled into a tempest, and her words rushed out. "You've always said God is good and kind, that He answers prayer and watches over those who trust Him, but how can that be true? He could've saved my parents and sister, but He closed His heart to their cries and let them drown." Her voice choked off.

Grandmother's hand trembled as she laid it on Maggie's shoulder. "You're not the only one who was dealt a terrible blow that day. I lost my daughter, son-in-law, and granddaughter, and it still grieves me. I don't understand why God allowed it, but I've chosen to let Him carry that load and walk with me through my grief." A tender light filled Grandmother's eyes. "God hears and answers prayer. Those answers are not always the ones we'd hoped for. But I've asked Him to strengthen my faith, and He has met that need time and again. I put my trust in Him, and in return He comforts me and gives me strength to carry on." She gave Maggie's shoulder a gentle squeeze. "He wants to do the same for you, Maggie."

Tears burned Maggie's eyes, and she blinked them away.

How could her grandmother just let it all go? It didn't make sense. It hurt too much. If God heard everyone's prayers, then surely He'd heard her parents' calls for help and her own cries for mercy.

Why didn't He answer? If He was good and kind, He wouldn't have let them die. How could she trust a God who allowed such painful things to happen to her and those she loved?

A light breeze stirred the air, cooling Nate's face and giving him a small measure of peace as his gaze took in the somber scene at Saint Peter's churchyard.

Only a dozen or so people remained behind after his father's graveside service; they quietly waited to speak to his stepmother and Clara. He didn't know most of them, so he stepped away, needing a break from shaking hands with strangers and searching for polite responses to their comments about his father and the funeral service.

Reverend Avery Samuelson approached Nate. "I'm sorry for your loss, Mr. Harcourt. Your father was certainly a gifted man. He made quite an impact with his inventions and leadership at Clifton Engineering." His tone was sincere, unlike that of some of the others who had spoken to Nate today.

"Thank you." Nate clasped the reverend's hand with a firm grip. Samuelson had a keen mind and spoke with sincerity and kindness. He was only a few years older than Nate, and though their backgrounds were quite different, Nate sensed a connection with him that could lead to friendship.

"I hope you'll let me know if there is anything I can do for you or your family."

"I will. I appreciate you conducting the service today. Your message was very meaningful."

Samuelson's solemn expression softened, and his gray eyes glimmered with understanding.

When they'd met last week to discuss plans for the funeral, Nate had conveyed his stepmother's wishes, but he'd also added his own, giving the man freedom to craft his message however he saw fit. Nate promised there would be no repercussions if Samuelson spoke clearly about salvation and the promise of heaven for those who received Christ as Savior—and Nate had not been disappointed.

His stepmother, however, had stiffened like a poker at the mention of life after death and sent Nate a heated look. But Samuelson's message was caring as well as truthful, and that was what mattered most, at least to Nate.

The line of mourners waiting to speak to his stepmother finally dwindled. Only Clara and his mother's cousin, Elizabeth, and Elizabeth's daughter, Amelia, waited with her. Nate crossed the grass toward them. Samuelson followed, and Nate steeled himself, hoping his stepmother would not be too unkind to the young reverend.

Helen's expression hardened as they approached.

Reverend Samuelson gave a slight bow. "Mrs. Harcourt, your husband was obviously respected and loved by many people. I offer you and your daughter my most sincere condolences."

Helen lifted her white lace handkerchief to her nose. "Thank you." But it was the stiffest and least sincere reply Nate had heard her give all day.

Samuelson continued, "Please let me know if there is any way I can be of assistance to you and your family in this time of grief."

"I sincerely doubt we will be contacting you for any assistance." Her tone cut like a knife, and she narrowed her eyes. "How could you ignore my wishes and give such a troubling message?"

Cousin Elizabeth's eyes widened, and Amelia sent Nate a questioning glance. What could he say? He could have predicted Helen's response down to the letter.

Reverend Samuelson blinked and raised his eyebrows. "Troubling?"

"Yes, I specifically asked for an uplifting message that would ease our grief, not one that would add to it."

The reverend's face flushed, and he paused a few seconds before he replied. "Mrs. Harcourt, I'm sorry you found the message . . . unsettling. I hope you will allow me to call on you and answer any questions you might have about my comments."

She lifted her chin. "That won't be necessary. I don't wish to discuss it any further." She turned away from Samuelson. "We need to return to Morningside. Our guests will be waiting." She took Clara's arm and started toward the carriage. Elizabeth and Amelia followed. After taking a few steps, Helen stopped and looked back at Nate. "Are you coming?"

He dreaded the thought and wished there was some other way he could return to the house. No doubt Helen would make her displeasure known during the entire ride back to Morningside. But it was his duty to accompany them.

He was about to answer when he spotted Maggie standing at the gate to the churchyard. He'd looked for her at the funeral service, but the church had been crowded with mourners and he hadn't seen her among them.

She looked his way, but she came no farther than the gate.

He shifted his gaze to Helen. "I'll be along in a few minutes."

Helen's eyes flashed. "But what about our guests? We don't want them to arrive at the house and find no one there to greet them."

"I need to speak to someone."

"Who?" Helen squinted across the churchyard. "Is that the Lounsbury girl?" Her lips puckered as though she'd tasted something bitter.

Irritation shot through him. "Yes, that is Margaret Lounsbury, and if you'll excuse me, I want to speak to her."

Helen huffed. "We'll wait for you in the carriage. Don't be long."

He strode off without replying.

Maggie stepped through the gate and walked toward him. She wore a simple black dress, hat, and gloves. The dress's high neckline, slim waist, and flowing skirt flattered her feminine figure. Once again he was struck by how much Maggie had grown and changed. She was no longer a child, but a lovely young woman. Her position in society might be different now, but at her essence, Maggie was still the same free-spirited and determined girl he knew . . . and for that, he was grateful.

She drew near and met his gaze. "I'm truly sorry for your loss." Her blue-gray eyes searched his, reflecting empathy and some other emotion he couldn't name.

"Thank you. I appreciate you coming." It was the standard reply he had given so many times today, but this time he actually meant it.

"I wanted to come," she said softly. "I remember what it's like."

He nodded, touched by her caring words and comforted by the knowledge of their shared experiences.

She pressed her lips together and looked down. "I haven't properly thanked you for stopping to help Violet the day of the accident. I appreciate what you did."

"No thanks needed. I was glad to do it."

Her gaze shifted to his father's grave and then back to Nate. "I'm sorry it delayed you from seeing your father."

He glanced away, considering her words. When he'd stopped to assist Violet, he hadn't realized how little time his father had left; still, he was glad he'd been there that day. "It was no trouble. How is Violet? I hope her recovery is going well."

"It is." She hesitated and glanced around, her hands tightly clasped and her brow creased. Was she remembering their last conversation and the unresolved issue between them? "I hope your last visit to the shop didn't keep you from seeing your father that day."

"I spoke to him earlier that morning before I came to the village."

Sorrow clouded her eyes. "I hope you had time to say everything you wanted."

He swallowed and nodded. "I did, and I'm grateful for it."

The horses stirred, and he looked over his shoulder. Helen and Elizabeth had climbed into the carriage, but Amelia and Clara waited by the door. Helen looked out the window and sent Nate an impatient frown.

He turned back to Maggie. Her gaze was fixed on Clara and his cousin. Then she looked his way with questions in her eyes.

His face warmed. "That's my cousin Amelia with Clara. We have a luncheon planned at the house for the out-of-town guests."

Disappointment clouded her eyes, and she stepped back. "Of course." Her voice turned cool. "I don't want to keep you."

"Excuse me, Mr. Harcourt." The coachman approached with a wary expression. "I'm sorry to interrupt, sir, but Mrs. Harcourt is eager to return to Morningside. She asks that you join her as soon as possible." He stepped back but waited nearby.

"I should go." He leaned toward her and lowered his voice. "But I hate to leave with things so unsettled between us."

Her eyes widened. She pressed her lips together and looked down. Was she unwilling to discuss the issues that separated them, or did she simply feel this wasn't the right time or place? Either way, her silence left him no choice. He would have to wait to settle matters with Maggie.

He touched the brim of his hat and nodded to her. "Good-bye, Maggie." Then he turned and strode away.

His shoulders sagged as he walked toward the carriage. He not only grieved the loss of his father and all that meant; his stepmother's abrasive attitude was wearing him thin and making everything more difficult. But worst of all, one of his oldest and dearest friends was barely speaking to him, and there seemed little he could do to change her mind.

Father, please help me carry these burdens and find the right path forward. I can't do this on my own. I need You.

Maggie stepped through the back door of the shop, removed her hat, and pulled off her gloves. With a weary sigh, she crossed to the sink and filled a glass with water.

She'd spent the entire walk home from the funeral replaying her conversation with Nate, and now her head throbbed and her stomach felt queasy.

She knew how painful it was to lose a parent, and she felt sorry for Nate, truly she did. But that didn't mean she could forget the way he and his family had been so uncaring toward her and Violet after the boating accident.

They never should have sold all her family's belongings and sent her and her sister away to Scotland. It wasn't right. Nate should have stood up to his parents and at least attended the funeral for her family members.

Perhaps now Nate would realize what a great loss she'd suffered and regret the way he'd ignored her pleas for help in her time of need.

She took a sip of water. Of course she wanted him to understand the way he'd hurt her and ask her forgiveness, but this wasn't how she'd wanted him to learn that lesson. He'd looked exhausted, and it was obvious his stepmother was making matters painfully hard for him.

The image of his pretty blond cousin, waiting by the carriage with Clara, flitted across her mind, and she stilled. Did she live nearby? It was strange he'd never mentioned her before. What did she think of Nate? And a more important question—what did Nate think of her?

Maggie stifled a groan and refilled her glass. That was a ridiculous line of thinking. She didn't care who the girl was or what Nate thought of her . . . at least not very much.

The curtain separating the shop from the back room swished to the side, and Grandmother hobbled through. "I thought I heard you come in. How was the funeral?"

Maggie turned toward Grandmother. "The service was long. The church was cold, and it was so crowded I had a hard time finding a seat."

Grandmother nodded. "I thought there would be a good number attending."

Maggie slowly sipped her water, hoping to put off her grandmother's questions.

"You were gone longer than I expected. Did you speak to the family?"

So much for that hope. "I spoke to Nate after the graveside service."

Grandmother's eyebrows rose. "And . . . ?"

"I offered my condolences." Maggie finished her drink and set the glass aside. "Where is Violet?"

"I set her up in the shop with a stack of drawing paper and pencils."

"I'm sure she'll enjoy that." Maggie crossed the room toward the shop.

Grandmother reached out to stop her. "Did you tell Nate you would accept the money?"

Heat flared in Maggie's face. "No, I didn't."

"Oh, Maggie. Why didn't you speak up?"

She bristled and stepped away. Why couldn't her grandmother understand and let it go?

"Kindness and humility will take you much further in life than pride and a stubborn spirit."

Maggie faced her grandmother. "My decision about the money has nothing to do with pride or a stubborn spirit."

"Then why not accept it?"

"I have my reasons."

"And they are?"

Her gaze darted around the room as she searched for an answer. "I don't want to feel an obligation toward the Harcourts."

Grandmother slowly shook her head. "Accepting that money would be a step toward healing the breach that separates you."

"What if I don't want it healed?"

"Then I'm afraid the Lord may have to teach you that lesson another way."

Maggie snatched her hat and gloves off the table and darted up the stairs, her heart hammering and her grandmother's words echoing through her mind.

"Violet, wait for me!" Maggie grabbed hold of her hat and dashed down the street after her sister. "You're going to plant your face in a puddle if you don't slow down!"

Violet vaulted ahead on her crutches, swinging herself forward with huge steps. "We're almost there," she called, undaunted.

"Dr. Hadley will not appreciate your pace or the muddy splashes on your cast."

Violet flew around the corner and didn't stop until she reached the side door to the village hospital. She turned and sent Maggie a gleeful smile. "See, I didn't fall." That was true, but her cheeks glowed bright pink and several strands of hair had come loose from her braids.

Maggie lifted her eyes to the sky. "Heaven only knows why."

"Good day, ladies."

Maggie glanced over her shoulder and pulled in a sharp breath. Nate crossed the street toward them, wearing a charcoal-gray suit and hat and looking every bit like the handsome new master of Morningside Manor. She squelched that thought with a silent reminder not to make a fool of herself.

He tipped his hat to them. "Violet, you travel at an amazing speed."

Her little sister grinned. "I don't mind the crutches at all."

"I can see that." He smiled and pleasant lines creased the area around his eyes and mouth. He darted a glance at Maggie. "I was actually on my way to see you."

"You were?" Her cheeks warmed, and she silently scolded herself again.

"Yes, I thought I'd stop in and check on Violet."

"We're just on our way to see Dr. Hadley."

A hint of concern lit his eyes. "I hope everything is all right."

"Oh, I'm sure it is. We just want him to look at Violet's cast. She cracked it coming down the stairs this morning."

"The stairs?" He lifted his dark eyebrows.

"Yes." Maggie looked away and shifted her weight to the other foot. She probably shouldn't have given in to Violet's pleas and let her make that climb. But her sister had been begging for days and insisting she was strong enough. Going up had gone relatively smoothly, though Maggie had held her breath and followed close behind. When it was time to come down this morning, Violet had done it so quickly she'd smacked her foot into the wall.

Violet looked down at the cast. "It's just a small crack, but Maggie said we had to come."

"Yes, I did, though I expect Dr. Hadley will give us both a scolding. I should've made you stay downstairs."

Violet pushed out her lower lip. "But I missed you, Maggie. And besides that, Grandmother snores like a bear."

Nate lifted his hand to cover his mouth, but he couldn't hold back his chuckle. Maggie soon joined him, her heart suddenly feeling light. How long had it been since she'd put aside her worries and laughed with a friend? Much too long.

Violet looked back and forth between them with a puzzled expression. "What is so funny?"

Nate grinned. "We're just enjoying your observations about your grandmother."

Violet's eyes widened. "You mustn't tell her I said that. She wouldn't like it."

"Don't worry. Your secret is safe with me." He winked at Violet.

Relief flooded Violet's face. "Thank you!"

The hospital door opened, and Mr. Alvin Neatherton, owner of Neatherton's Shoes and Boots and Maggie's neighbor, stepped out. "Good morning, Maggie, Violet." He glanced at Nate with slightly narrowed eyes.

"Good morning, Mr. Neatherton." Maggie introduced the two men.

Mr. Neatherton lifted his chin. "So you're the new lord of Morningside Manor."

Nate straightened. "My father's estate has passed to me. But there's no hereditary title."

"Ah, that's right. Your father might have been a baron, but that title went with him to the grave." His tone held a slight challenge.

Maggie's eyes widened. Mr. Neatherton was a proud man, but she'd never known him to be unkind. Her gaze darted to Nate, but he didn't seem bothered by the comment. In fact, a kind, open expression filled his face.

"I understand you make the finest boots in Northumberland."

Mr. Neatherton's chest puffed out. "Well, folks do say that here in the village, though I would never be so bold as to make that claim myself."

"Your son, Joseph, says it's true, and I am in need of a new pair of boots. Might I come by your shop later this morning? I'd like to see what you would recommend."

Mr. Neatherton rubbed his chin and eyed Nate's boots with an arched eyebrow. "Of course. I'd be glad to show you what we have to offer and measure you for a fine pair of boots."

"Very good. I have a few other items of business to see to. Will you be back at the shop by eleven?"

"Yes, sir. I'm headed that way now."

"Very good. I'll see you later this morning." Nate waited for Mr. Neatherton to leave, then he turned back to Maggie. "Well, I'm glad to know Violet continues to improve."

"Yes, we're grateful." She pressed her lips together, debating her next words. Should she invite him to stop by the shop after he finished seeing Mr. Neatherton? He had no reason to visit now. He had business to attend to and an estate to run . . . but would he come if she asked him to?

He glanced around, then back at Maggie. "I suppose I should be going." But he didn't step away.

She swallowed, wishing he would say he would see her later, but he didn't.

Violet hopped forward on her crutches. "Are we going in?"

"Yes, of course." Maggie started toward the door.

"Let me get that for you." Nate stepped past her and pulled it open. He looked at Violet. "Be sure to check your speed and guard that cast."

She grinned and nodded. "I will."

He turned to Maggie and touched his hat brim. "Take care, Maggie."

"Thank you. I will." She nodded to him as she walked past.

Goodness. She sounded almost breathless. That would never do. The ties of friendship they'd shared in the past no longer held them together. Nate had inherited a fortune and with it entry into the best society had to offer. Why would he ever want to continue his friendship with her?

Nate ran his hand over the supple leather of the tall brown boots on the counter at Neatherton's shop. "These are very fine. I'd like a pair just like them."

"It will take me a few days to craft boots as fine as those, but they're a good choice." Mr. Neatherton motioned toward the back of the shop. "Come with me, and I'll measure your foot."

Nate followed him behind the counter.

"Stand right here." Neatherton pointed to a piece of paper he'd placed on the floor, then he knelt beside Nate, grunted, and looked up at him.

Nate removed his shoes and stood in place while the man drew around his right foot with a charcoal pencil. "Not many still do it this way, but I say if you want to be sure you have the proper fit, then you trace both feet each time you make a pair of boots. A man's foot can change from year to year."

"It sounds like an excellent method." Nate watched the man draw around his left foot.

Neatherton slowly rose, and Nate was sure he heard the man's bones creak. "Now let me check a few more things." He pulled a tape measure from his trousers pocket and motioned toward a wooden chair. "Have a seat, sir."

Nate obliged and watched the man measure across the top of his foot, then write the numbers on a small pad of paper.

"It must be good to have your son working with you." Nate glanced around the shop. "I thought he might be here today."

Mr. Neatherton jotted down another number. "He's gone to the station to pick up a shipment coming in from London. We only buy the finest materials for our shoes and boots."

"Ah, I see." Ever since he'd met the younger Neatherton, he'd been curious to know a bit more about him and his connection with Maggie. "He must be a great help to you."

Mr. Neatherton nodded but continued making notes.

"I met him when I was next door at Mrs. Hayes's millinery shop."

"Yes, he keeps a good eye on them and helps out whenever he can. It's not easy for them, being on their own like they are without a man to watch over them. And he and Maggie—"

Nate's breath caught. "He and Maggie . . . ?"

Neatherton cleared his throat and waved his words away. "You've not heard it from me. That's my son's business, not mine."

The bell over the shop door rang, and both men looked that way.

Reverend Avery Samuelson walked in the door. "Hello, Mr. Neatherton." He nodded to Nate. "Mr. Harcourt, it's good to see you again."

Nate smiled. "I'm just being fitted for a new pair of boots."

"Then you've come to the right place," Samuelson added. "I don't want to interrupt. Please, finish with Mr. Harcourt."

"I believe we are finished." Nate glanced at Neatherton.

"That's right. I have what I need. I'll set to work on these right away. Check with me next Friday. They should be ready by then."

"Very good. Thank you." Nate started toward the door.

"Mr. Harcourt. Would you mind waiting a moment? I'd like to speak to you."

"Of course." Nate stood by the door and waited while Samuelson paid Neatherton and picked up a pair of shoes that had been resoled.

Samuelson led the way outside, and Nate followed. "Would you have time to take a meal with me, perhaps at the Red Lion?"

Nate glanced toward Maggie's shop. He had hoped he might see her again today, but the front door was closed and no one was about. He let go of that hope and turned back to Samuelson. "Thank you for the invitation. I'd be glad to join you."

"Good. That will give us time to talk."

They set off down the street and a few minutes later entered the Red Lion.

The proprietor greeted them and took their orders. Nate scanned the room, searching for an open table.

"There's one at the back." Samuelson nodded toward the far corner, and they passed through the main room to the open table.

When they were seated, Samuelson turned to Nate. "I'm not sure how much time you have, so I'll get right to the point. I'm concerned about the situation at Clifton Engineering."

"Why is that?"

"In the last few months, since your father became ill, tensions have increased."

Nate shifted in his chair. "Go on."

"A few of the wives whose husbands work there have spoken to me. I think there may be trouble brewing."

Nate frowned. "What kind of trouble?"

"There is a long-standing conflict between the management and the workers, and from what I've heard, ill feelings are building again."

"What are the issues?"

"Wages, hours, and safety, the same kind of thing you hear workers all over the country speaking up about. The men work long hours, six days a week, and they haven't had a raise in pay for almost three years."

Nate rubbed his chin. "I've only just begun to get my feet under me at Morningside. I haven't looked into matters at Clifton yet. But I have my first meeting with the board of directors next week."

"So you are planning to step into your father's role there?"

Nate nodded. "I have inherited his half ownership in the company, and that should give me some say in how things are run. Unfortunately, I haven't set foot in Clifton for more than five years, and I know very little about day-to-day operations. But I'll look into these matters. I'm sure my father would want the workers treated fairly."

A smile broke across Samuelson's face. "Thank you. I had a feeling I could count on you to help resolve matters peacefully."

Nate straightened. "Do you think there's a threat of violence?"

"I'm not sure. Some men are quite agitated. A few have mentioned the possibility of a strike if the issues are not addressed."

"A strike would have a negative impact on the entire community."

"Yes, but some feel that may be the only way to convince the management to listen."

"Surely matters are not that serious yet."

"There was an accident not long ago. One man was severely injured when his hand was crushed in one of the machines."

Nate's stomach tensed. "I'm sorry to hear it."

"With the heavy equipment and long hours, it's a wonder there aren't more accidents. The men have been asking for more safety measures for quite a while, but those in charge have refused to make any changes."

"I see." Nate's gaze traveled around the room. Did any of these men or members of their families work at Clifton? They were a major employer in the area with almost sixteen hundred men on their payroll, that much he knew.

The company had flourished for more than thirty years, building industrial cranes, drawbridges, and taking on other large engineering projects, but Nate knew very little about the relationship between the management and the workers.

When he was younger and living at home, his father talked about the unrest among workers around the country and the rise of unions, but Nate didn't realize they were dealing with those issues here in Heatherton. Were the workers at Clifton being treated unfairly? What would the other board members say about these matters?

It was time he learned more about the inner workings at Clifton and found the answers to those questions for himself.

Lilly accepted the bag of flour from one of her neighbors in the village, Mrs. Edith Miller, and placed it in her basket. "Thank you. I know the Carters will be very grateful."

"I'm glad to help. We went through hard times when George was sick last year. We wouldn't have made it without the help of our friends. You tell Rose I'm praying for her and her husband."

"I will."

Edith reached up and took a small jar from her kitchen shelf. "Let's add these cherry preserves too. That will be a nice treat for them."

Lilly thanked her again and placed the preserves in the basket with the other food items she had collected from several friends. "I should be going. I want to drop these things off and pay them a short visit before I walk back to Morningside."

Edith's brow creased. "How's that young man of yours? I heard he's working extra shifts at Clifton."

Lilly's smile melted away. "Yes, ma'am. Rob is working hard, doing all he can for his family."

"That's all the more reason for us to lend a hand." Edith clicked her tongue. "He's a fine young man. I'm sure his parents are proud of him."

"I believe they are." Lilly bid Edith good-bye, tucked the basket over her arm, and set off down the village lane. Fewer than five minutes later, she knocked at the Carters' front door, and Rob's sister Jane answered.

"Oh, Lilly, it's so good to see you. Please come in." Fourteen-year-old Jane was a bright-eyed blonde with a sprinkle of freckles over her nose and cheeks. Since Lilly had no sisters, she especially enjoyed spending time with Jane and her younger sister, MaryAnn.

The scent of fresh-baked bread drifted past, making her empty stomach contract as she stepped inside. "Is your mother home?"

Jane nodded. Her gaze dipped to the basket, then darted back to Lilly. "She's upstairs with Father. I'll let her know you're here." She turned and hurried up the stairs.

Lilly glanced around the simple cottage. Bunches of herbs and a few onions hung from the low-beamed ceiling of the kitchen on the right. A small fire glowed in the kitchen fireplace, and six chairs stood around the plain wooden table. A pitcher filled with bluebells and tulips sat in the middle of the table on a lace doily. White linen curtains edged with lace hung at the kitchen window.

Lilly released a soft sigh. Rob's home was always neat and cozy, and so much more welcoming than the rooms behind the boot shop where she had lived with her father and brother until she went into service at Morningside. Lilly's mother had passed away when she was six, and all those special touches a woman brought to a home vanished with her. Lilly hadn't even realized what was missing until she began spending time with the Carters.

Rose Carter, Rob's mother, came down the stairs, and her eyes brightened when she spotted Lilly waiting in the kitchen. Eleven-year-old MaryAnn sent Lilly a shy smile as she followed her mother into the room. MaryAnn was a sweet, quiet girl who wore her long golden-brown hair in two braids that hung to her waist.

"Lilly, it's so nice of you to come." Mrs. Carter crossed the kitchen toward her. "With Rob working today, I didn't know if we'd see you."

Lilly smiled. "I wanted to stop by and see how Mr. Carter is doing and bring you these gifts from your neighbors and friends." Lilly held up the basket.

Mrs. Carter's face flushed, and she shook her head. "Oh, I don't know what to say." She gazed at the basket, soft longing in her eyes.

"There's no need to say anything. Everyone was happy to share what they could, and they all send their love and prayers for you and Mr. Carter." Lilly stepped closer, holding out the basket and praying she would accept their gifts. "Edith Miller sent the cherry preserves and the flour. She said she remembers how friends helped them when her husband was sick."

Rob's mother finally accepted the basket. "It's very kind. We're grateful. You must tell me who contributed so I can thank them." She set the basket on the kitchen table, and Jane and MaryAnn gathered around.

"Look, Mother, there's cheese and ham and carrots and peas." Jane grinned and took out the cherry preserves. "Sarah Miller says her mother's preserves are the best in the village."

MaryAnn looked up at her mother. "May we have some with our tea?"

Mrs. Carter smiled and nodded. "Slice some bread and toast it, then you can take a tray up to your father while I visit with Lilly."

The girls bustled around the kitchen, preparing the tea tray for their father while Rob's mother told Lilly about the doctor's visit and her husband's slow recovery. When the girls carried the tray upstairs, Mrs. Carter and Lilly sat at the table, then Mrs. Carter poured her a cup of tea.

"How is Rob?" Lilly asked. "I had a letter from him a few days ago, but I'm worried about him working so much."

Mrs. Carter's brow creased, and she brushed a bread crumb from the table. "He's tired by evening. In fact, sometimes he falls straight into bed after dinner. I hate to see him give up his only day of rest."

"I wish there was more I could do to help."

"You've done more than enough, bringing us that basket and cheering me with your company." Mrs. Carter's blue eyes softened. "Rob is a strong young man with a good heart. I couldn't ask for a finer son."

Lilly's own heart warmed, hearing Rob's mother speak so highly of him.

Mrs. Carter offered Lilly more tea and refilled her own cup. "I've been thinking of ways I might be able to bring in some extra money."

Lilly straightened. "What did you have in mind?"

Rob's mother gazed at the flowers on the table. "I'm creative and skilled with a needle. I could take in sewing or mending, but you know what I'd really like to do?"

"What?"

"Make hats." Mrs. Carter glanced away, but a smile lifted one corner of her mouth. "I'd love to try my hand at that."

"Making hats sounds like a lovely idea." Lilly had always admired Maggie's millinery skills. It was a blessing she had a grandmother who had trained her, and one day Mrs. Hayes would pass on the shop to Maggie. That would give her an income and security. What would Lilly's life be like if she'd learned to fashion hats rather than going into service?

Mrs. Carter took a sip of tea. "I doubt there'd be enough business for another millinery shop in Heatherton, and I wouldn't want to take business from Mrs. Hayes and her granddaughter."

"No, I suppose not."

"Well, enough of that dream. I need to be practical, which probably means taking in mending or ironing."

"What about dressmaking or sewing curtains?"

Mrs. Carter nodded, her smile returning. "I could do that."

"I'm sure you could."

Jane came down the stairs, and MaryAnn followed behind, carrying the tray. "Father says it's time for his medicine."

"I need to go up." Rob's mother stood. "You're welcome to stay and visit with the girls, if you'd like."

Lilly glanced at the clock on the kitchen wall. "I wish I could, but I need to start back to Morningside."

Mrs. Carter reached for her hand. "Thank you for coming, Lilly."

"Please tell Rob I stopped by." Lilly reached into her skirt pocket. "And would you give him this letter?"

"I'd be glad to." She laid it on the kitchen table. "Take care, Lilly." She turned and started up the steps.

Lilly said good-bye to Jane and MaryAnn, then slipped out the door and took the lane past the old mill on her way back to Morningside.

10

Maggie poured her grandmother a cup of tea and placed the pot on the table. Flames leaped and crackled in the fireplace, spreading welcome warmth throughout their small kitchen. She took a seat opposite her grandmother and looked across the table. Lines creased her grandmother's forehead, and the woman's shoulders sagged. Was she weary from their busy day at the shop, or were other concerns weighing her down?

A pang of guilt struck Maggie's heart. Grandmother had not mentioned Maggie's refusal to accept the money from Nate since their last painful conversation three days ago, but she had mentioned the need to pay the bill for Violet's hospital stay and her frustration with their leaky roof.

Maggie sighed. They both worked long hours, Grandmother doing what she could and Maggie styling hats until her back ached and her fingers were sore. But their income barely covered their regular expenses, and extra bills caused a great strain.

Maggie shifted her gaze away and took a sip of tea, the weight of her grandmother's concern tugging on her heart.

"I hope word about that money you've turned down doesn't make its way to the village."

"I wouldn't worry about that."

"I suppose you're right. I doubt Nathaniel would speak of it to anyone, and no one else knows about it." Grandmother sent her a cautious glance. "Unless you mentioned it to someone."

Maggie looked down and wrapped her hand around her teacup. "The only person I told is Lilly."

Grandmother clicked her tongue. "Well, now the whole staff at Morningside will hear about it before the day is out."

It had been almost two weeks since she'd spoken to Lilly about Nate's offer, but she didn't want to tell Grandmother that. "I don't think Lilly will talk about our private affairs up at the manor."

"Really?" Grandmother looked at Maggie over the top of her spectacles. "Remember how she used to delight in telling us her brother had been scolded for some misbehavior, or report her father's conversations with a difficult customer?"

"That was when she was much younger. She's not like that now." At least Maggie hoped she wasn't. She shifted in her chair, wishing she'd asked Lilly to keep their conversation private. Perhaps she should send her a note and make sure she knew the information should not be shared with anyone.

"It's too bad you're set against taking the money." Grandmother gazed toward the fire. "Think of all you could do, maybe even take a holiday."

Maggie huffed. "Why does everyone think I ought to take a holiday?"

Grandmother's eyebrows rose. "Everyone?"

Heat infused Maggie's cheeks. "It's just that . . . Nate suggested the same thing."

"He did?" A soft, dimpled smile creased Grandmother's cheeks.

"Yes, but it was only a suggestion, and a silly one at that. Imagine me taking a holiday when there's so much to do here."

"Well, whether you want to go or not, it was very sweet of Nate to suggest it."

Maggie had to squelch the desire to roll her eyes. "*Sweet* is not the word I would use to describe Nathaniel Harcourt."

Grandmother tipped her head. "How would you describe him, then?"

Dashing, clever . . . handsome. Those thoughts rode through her mind before she could rein them in. She straightened in her chair. "He's the master of Morningside Manor and the new business partner at Clifton."

"Those are his positions, not who he truly is on the inside. I'm talking about his character and convictions and how he lives those out."

"Whatever those may be, his position is what's most important to him and everyone else." But Maggie's own words sounded hollow to her as she took another sip of tea and stared at the fire, remembering Nate's visit to the shop and the way he'd helped Violet the day of the accident. Each time, he'd treated them with respect and consideration. And when she'd expressed her hurt and anger toward him and his family for their lack of concern in the past, he'd shown restraint rather than answering in the same way.

She bit her lip, recalling all she'd said and the way she'd stormed off—twice.

Nate didn't deserve that.

Their friendship had begun when she was twelve years old, and she'd always admired him—his eagerness to learn from her father, his admiration for her family, and his willingness to include her in his adventures around the estate. But he'd also been proud of his position as future heir of Morningside and didn't hesitate to remind her of that.

But she had to admit he seemed different since he'd returned, more thoughtful and caring. Was it his time in the Navy and his involvement in the war that brought about those changes? One would think going off to war might harden a man and make him less caring toward others . . . but the opposite seemed to be true of Nate.

And those changes made him even more attractive to her.

Maggie blew out a breath and gave her head a shake. What was she thinking? She had refused the money, and when he'd tried to broach the subject again, she'd remained silent. She'd done it on principle to emphasize her point, but she was beginning to wonder if it had more to do with her pride.

Perhaps someday she might be able to forgive Nate and his family, but she wasn't going to put her heart on the line or allow herself to hope for what could never be. There was too much that separated her from Nate Harcourt. Even an ongoing friendship was unlikely, let alone anything more.

That thought took hold, and a painful ache swelled in her chest.

Enough! She would not think about Nate anymore.

She pushed to her feet. "I'll check on Violet, then I'm going up to bed. Is there anything I can get for you?"

Grandmother searched Maggie's face. "Trials and suffering come into everyone's life, Maggie. Don't let the pain of the past cloud your view of the future. Keep your heart open to what God wants to do."

Maggie pressed her lips together and tried to ignore her grandmother's convicting words, but they sank in deep and hit her heart.

She bent and kissed her grandmother's cheek and caught a whiff of lavender, Grandmother's favorite scent. She pulled in a deep breath, and it soothed the ache in her chest a bit. "Good night, Grandmother."

"Good night, dear. God bless you with sweet dreams and restful sleep."

Those were the same words she said every night, but for some reason they made Maggie's eyes sting tonight. She blinked and tried to shake it off. She was just worn out from the long day.

She looked in on Violet and found her fast asleep in Grandmother's bed, her casted leg sticking out of the blankets. Her sister looked completely at peace, with her wavy brown hair spread out across the pillow and her long, dark eyelashes falling against her creamy pink cheeks.

Maggie stepped closer, pulled the blanket up to her sister's chin, and gently brushed a strand of hair from her sister's face. "Good night, Vi," she whispered, then leaned down and kissed her sister's forehead.

Grandmother's parting comments resurfaced in her mind as she climbed the stairs to her room. Why did she struggle so with letting go of hurt and disappointment? She was just trying to be sensible and realistic, but were her painful memories of the past truly clouding her view of the future?

She huffed out a breath and dismissed the thought. It was time to put those questions away for the night. She lifted the lid of her trunk and took out her father's journal. Perhaps if she spent a few minutes reading his entries, it would give her some comfort and direction.

Opening the journal, she carefully turned the pages and stopped at an entry in early May that featured a drawing of bluebells outlined in ink and painted in watercolor. The lovely, detailed drawing stirred pleasant memories, and a smile touched Maggie lips.

Closing her eyes, she recalled their walks through the woods and the carpets of bluebells that covered the shady forest floor. What a delight they were after the long, cold winter. She turned to where she'd left off reading last time.

20 August

Today I came upon Mrs. H. and a man quite unexpectedly on the path by Tumbledon Lake. As soon as the man saw me he broke off his conversation and hurried off down the path, away from us. I turned and started back in the direction I'd come, but I'd only gone a few steps when Mrs. H. called out to me. I didn't want to stop and speak to her, but I felt I must.

She was coy at first, smiling and trying to make light of the encounter, but I'd seen their startled looks and the guilt on both their faces when I came upon them. It is not the first time I've seen them together. She questioned me, trying to discover my intention. I felt I owed her an honest reply, and I urged her to speak to her husband, so I would not feel the need to.

She tried to look unruffled, but I could tell the opposite was true. "Why would you want to embarrass and upset Mr. Harcourt? There's no need to say anything to him or anyone else." Her hands fluttered like a nervous bird all the time she was speaking, and I could see her true feeling of anxiety behind her words.

I gave her my answer. "I've seen you with that man before, and if it means nothing, then you won't be hesitant to tell Mr. Harcourt about it."

Her coy expression faded and hardened. "If you take it upon yourself to interfere in my private life, you'll be risking your position and reputation."

I stared at her for a moment, stunned that she would say such a thing to me, when she was the one walking down such a troubled path.

"You will promise me your silence," she continued, "or I will go to my husband and tell him you've been making advances toward me, then you'll be the one paying the price for what you think you saw today."

A wave of shock jolted through me, then anger that she would threaten me with that lie. I made my decision then and told her what to expect. "I will give you three days to speak to your husband and settle this matter or I will go to him myself."

Her face flushed, and her eyes snapped with fire. "You will regret the way you've spoken to me today!" With that, she spun away and marched off.

I stood my ground for several seconds, shaken by her foolish, angry words, but I have no choice. Mr. H. is my employer and friend. I cannot keep what I've seen a secret. I hope and pray Mrs. H. will stop meeting that man and confess her misdeeds to her husband, but if not, my loyalty demands I speak to Mr. H. and give him the opportunity to deal with it as he sees fit.

My heart is very heavy, thinking of the pain and suffering that comes when marriage vows are not honored and trust is broken. But there is always hope if all parties are willing to be honest, forgive, and rebuild trust. I pray that will be the case for Mr. and Mrs. Harcourt.

Maggie stared at the page. How terrible that Nate's stepmother had been so desperate to hide her misdeeds that she threatened Maggie's father. She turned the page to read on, but the next page was blank.

She quickly flipped through the rest of the journal, but there were no more entries. She glanced back at the date of the last entry, and dizziness swept through her.

Two days later they'd taken the boat out on Tumbledon Lake and . . .

She closed the journal and squeezed her eyes shut. She did not want to think about that day. What good would it do now? Nothing could change what had happened or bring her family back.

She set aside the journal, climbed onto her bed, and lay back on her pillow. Questions tumbled through her mind as she stared at the ceiling.

Had Mrs. Harcourt confessed to her husband about her meetings with the man in the woods? How had Mr. Harcourt responded? What if she had accused Maggie's father instead? Did Mr. Harcourt believe her?

She tried to recall her family's conversations at home before the accident, but as far as she could remember, her father had given no hint that he was caught in the middle of a conflict between Mr. and Mrs. Harcourt. Had he told her mother about it? She had seemed lighthearted the day of the picnic. Maggie hadn't sensed any trouble brewing when they'd first set out across the lake that day.

But she had been only seventeen, and looking back now, she realized how little she'd understood about the real world and what was going on in the hearts and lives of those around her.

A sudden thought jolted her, and she sat up.

What if Mrs. Harcourt wanted to stop Maggie's father from speaking to her husband? Could she have learned of their plans to take the boat out that day? If she had, could she have arranged for the boat's hull to be damaged so it would sink?

No, that was ridiculous!

Mrs. Harcourt might have been involved with another man, and she might have threatened her father with a false accusation, but she wouldn't plot to murder him and his whole family . . . would she?

A chill traveled down Maggie's back. Could that be the reason the Harcourts had been so eager to send Maggie and Violet away? Was that part of Mrs. Harcourt's plan to make Maggie's family disappear so that no one would be able to expose her secret?

The scent of smoke drifted past Maggie. She wrinkled her nose and sniffed. It smelled different than the scent of their kitchen fire. She rose from the bed and glanced toward the window. Sometimes the wind blew smoke toward them from the neighbor's chimney. Perhaps that was all it was.

She crossed the room and pushed aside the lace curtain. A wispy cloud of smoke drifted up past the window from the direction of Neatherton's. Maggie's heart lurched. She swung around, then hurried out of her bedroom and down the stairs.

11

Nate strolled down the village street, replaying his conversation with Reverend Samuelson and the three workmen from Clifton Engineering. The stories they'd told about accidents related to long hours and poor working conditions sent a troubling wave of concern through him and stirred more questions in his mind.

How did those in charge at Clifton expect the men to produce quality products when they were overworked and waiting in fear for the next accident to happen?

Something had to be done. Every man's life was important. But as the newest member of the board, with little working knowledge of the company, he wasn't sure they would listen to him. He huffed out a breath. Somehow he must document the facts and then do what he could to help the workers.

He walked on, noting the lanterns glowing in the windows of the homes he passed. One window gave him a view of a family seated around the fireplace. Bits of conversation floated out the open doorway. The scene lasted only a second or two as he walked on, but it stirred a longing within him.

What would it be like to enjoy a quiet evening with his family seated around the fire as they talked about the events of the day? Evenings at Morningside were something he endured rather than enjoyed. They consisted of a stiff, formal dinner with Helen and Clara and then a few minutes of stilted conversation in the drawing room before he excused himself for the night.

He shook off those thoughts and walked on. He was the head of the family now. It was up to him to change the atmosphere in his home and forge stronger relationships between himself and his stepmother and sister.

When he reached the Red Lion, he debated stopping in for a meal before he started home, but he decided against it. If he was going to influence Helen and Clara, he must spend time at home and work on strengthening the bonds among the three of them. He walked around back to the stable where he'd left his horse just a few hours earlier and paid the young groom who had watched over him.

A man burst out the back door of the inn, his eyes wide. "Grab a bucket! There's a fire down the street!"

Nate swung around. "Where?"

"Neatherton's boot shop."

Alarm shot through Nate. He dashed out the door and ran around the corner toward Maggie's. A small crowd had gathered in the smoky street in front of Neatherton's. One man shouted orders while another organized a bucket brigade.

Nate ran past all of them and banged his fist on the millinery shop's front door. "Maggie! Mrs. Hayes!"

The door swung open and Maggie looked out. Her wide-eyed gaze darted to the crowd past his shoulder. "What is it?"

"There's a fire at Neatherton's!"

"I thought I smelled smoke. I was just coming down to check." She stepped outside and looked toward the neighboring shop. "Is everyone out?"

"I'm not sure. But it would be wise for you and your grandmother and sister to come a safe distance away until the fire is under control." He didn't want to frighten her by suggesting their shop might also catch fire, but it was a very real possibility. Only a narrow passage separated the millinery shop from Neatherton's, and their roofs almost touched.

"Yes, of course. I'll wake Grandmother and Violet."

"I'm awake." Mrs. Hayes hobbled across the shop and joined them at the front door. Maggie quickly explained the situation, and her grandmother sent an anxious glance toward the neighboring shop.

"I suggest you take your grandmother across the street, out of harm's way."

Maggie's eyes darted toward the curtain separating the shop from the family's private rooms. "Violet is in the back room, next to the kitchen."

"I'll get Violet. You take care of your grandmother."

Maggie nodded, then ushered her grandmother outside.

Nate hurried through the hat shop and into the kitchen. A hazy veil of smoke already curled through the air close to the ceiling. He clamped his mouth closed and pushed past the blue curtain, into the small bedroom. Violet lay in the bed, fast asleep.

He threw back her bedcovers and scooped up the girl. Violet startled and her eyes flew open. "It's all right, Violet. I'm carrying you out to join your sister and grandmother." He started toward the doorway.

"My crutches!" She pointed to the wall near the bed. He shifted her weight and grabbed the crutches with one hand, then he carried her through the lowering haze and out the front door.

When they reached the street, he darted a glance at the neighboring shop. The roof was fully ablaze, and flames were visible through the front windows as well. Even from a distance he could feel the intense heat. A few men threw buckets of water on the building, but most of the crowd had pulled back, watching the blaze from a safer distance, across the street.

"Throw water on the neighboring shops," one man called to the others, directing them toward Maggie's shop on the right and the druggist on the left.

Nate studied the scene with growing dread. The village men hadn't been able to slow the fire's raging appetite, and the boot shop was nearly engulfed.

He turned away and carried Violet through the crowd, searching for Maggie and Mrs. Hayes. He spotted them standing with two other women by the door to Mrs. Fenwick's Teashop, on the opposite side of the street.

Relief flooded Maggie's expression as he approached with Violet. She stepped forward and took the crutches from his hand. He lowered Violet to the ground beside her. She looked her sister over and smoothed her hair, then whispered reassuring words to the frightened girl.

Nate turned back toward the fire, weighing the situation. There was still time to rescue a few items from the millinery. He turned to Maggie. "Do you have any valuables you want to bring out?"

Maggie's eyes widened. "I keep some money in a box upstairs in my room."

"Oh, Maggie." Grandmother lifted a trembling hand to cover her mouth.

He had no idea how much money the box held, but if it was important to Maggie, he would do his best to retrieve it.

Maggie laid her hand on her grandmother's arm. "It's all right. There's time. I'll go back." She stepped toward the street.

Nate reached for her arm. "No. You stay here. I'll go."

"But you won't know—"

"Just tell me where it is. I'll bring it to you."

She darted a glance at the shop and then turned back to him. "It's in the trunk at the foot of my bed in a wooden button box with a green velvet lid."

He gave a quick nod and started to turn away.

"Please be careful!" Maggie called, her voice urgent, her eyes sending a message of concern.

His heart lifted. "I will," he said, then hustled across the street and into the smoky shop.

The air grew thicker as he made his way up the steps. Soon his eyes stung and his nose filled with the acrid smell of burning wood. He lifted the corner of his suit coat to cover his mouth and nose, hoping that would keep the smoke out.

He spotted the trunk at the foot of the bed, knelt, and quickly lifted the lid. A Bible lay on top of a folded shawl. He pulled them from the trunk and laid them on the floor. Pushing aside several other items, he spotted the small wooden box and lifted the lid. A few one- and five-pound notes lay folded in the box.

He waved the smoky air away from his face, then grabbed the box and picked up the Bible and shawl from the floor. If the shop truly was going up in flames, they might be a comfort to Maggie. He squinted and looked around, searching for anything else of value she might want, but his stinging eyes made it impossible for him to continue his search for long. He rose and hurried down the stairs.

Holding his breath, he ran through the shop and out the front door. Once on the street, he stopped and pulled in several deep breaths, then made his way through the crowd, searching for Maggie.

She hurried toward him. "Are you all right?"

He coughed and nodded, then handed her the box, shawl, and Bible. "I thought you might want these."

She bit her bottom lip. Her eyes glistened with unshed tears as she looked up at him. "Thank you. These belonged to my mother and sister."

Nate nodded, thankful he'd been able to bring them out as well.

A loud crash sounded behind them. Maggie gasped and clutched the shawl and Bible to her chest.

Nate swung around, and his spirits plunged. Neatherton's roof caved in with a roar. Sparks flew through the air and flames licked the peak of the millinery shop's roof.

"Oh no!" Maggie's strangled voice tore through him.

Violet burst into tears and clung to her grandmother.

"There, there." Mrs. Hayes patted Violet's back, but her own chin trembled as she watched the flames leap across the gap and spread to her roof.

Maggie stared at the shop, her solemn expression frozen on her face. The crowd continued throwing water on the front wall of the shop, but soon flames swept across the wooden roof shingles.

Nate stepped closer to Maggie, wishing he could shield her from the terrible sight and protect her from these dreadful losses.

He slipped his arm around her shoulders. "It will be all right." But his words blew away on the smoky wind.

Maggie stared at the dying flames, then rubbed her eyes as though that could wipe away the terrible scene before her. How could their shop, home, and everything they owned burn down to this heap of charred rubble in less than an hour? It was impossible to take in.

Grandmother stood between Maggie and Violet, her thin shoulders stooped as she surveyed the smoldering remains of the shop. "I've seen many a sorrowful sight in my time, but this is . . . There are just no words."

Maggie nodded, her chest aching and frightening thoughts tumbling through her mind. Where would they go now? What would they do?

She clenched her jaw and tried to calm her trembling. She must collect herself and try to say something to comfort Grandmother and Violet. She turned toward them, struggling for words. "No one was hurt. That's what's most important. We still have each other."

Grandmother's shawl fluttered in the wind, and she slowly shook her head. "Everything we've built is gone—our home, our business." Her voice was hushed, as though she hadn't even heard Maggie's efforts to comfort her.

A shiver raced down Maggie's back. Should she ask Grandmother if the shop was insured against fire? What if it wasn't? That possibility was too upsetting to consider, let alone mention to Grandmother tonight.

Even if it was insured, would the coverage be adequate to rebuild? How would they support themselves until they could open the shop again—if that were possible? Maggie's thoughts careened ahead into their unknown future, and she felt like she had walked into a long, dark cave without a light.

She closed her eyes and swallowed, trying to block it all out of her mind.

"Why don't you come inside and have a cup of tea while you sort out what's to be done?" Their neighbor Esther Fenwick slipped her arm around Grandmother's shoulders.

Grandmother's chin trembled. "That's good of you, Esther. Thank you."

"Maggie." Nate walked toward them through the thinning crowd with Reverend Samuelson at his side. Soot smudged Nate's glistening face, and his trousers and jacket were splattered with water and mud. "I'm sorry. I wish there was more we could've done." He glanced back at the smoking ruins, weary lines creasing his forehead.

Maggie's throat ached, and she had to force out her words. "It's not your fault. You did what you could."

"It was a very gallant effort," the reverend added, "and very heartening to see so many men working together to fight the fire."

"Yes, but two families lost their homes and businesses tonight." Nate placed his hands on his hips and glared down the street. "If we had proper firefighting equipment, we might have been able to keep the fire from spreading."

The reverend nodded. "Perhaps it's time the village invested in a fire wagon and recruited volunteers who could be trained in firefighting techniques."

"That's an excellent idea." Nate turned back to Samuelson. "I'll look into it and see what we need to do to start the process."

Reverend Samuelson focused on Maggie and her grandmother. "I'm very sorry for your loss. I'd like to offer my assistance. The rectory is quite small, but I could make inquiries and find someone who would allow you to stay with them until you can find permanent lodgings."

Maggie glanced at Grandmother, uncertain if they should accept the reverend's offer.

"There's no need." Nate stepped forward. "They're coming to Morningside with me."

Maggie sent him a surprised look. "Thank you, but we cannot accept." He might be the master of Morningside, but she would not be ordered around by him or anyone else.

His eyebrows rose. "But Morningside has several empty guest rooms. You'd be quite comfortable there, and I'd feel much more at ease knowing you had a safe place to rest and recover." He studied her a moment and seemed to notice her stiff posture and raised chin. He softened his tone. "At least spend the night. Tomorrow we can sort things out."

Perhaps she ought to consider it. "How would we travel there?"

"I'll rent a carriage and hire a driver."

Grandmother touched her arm. "It's a sensible plan, Maggie."

The journal entry she'd read earlier that evening rose in her mind, and her stomach tensed. What if her suspicions about Mrs. Harcourt were true? How could they stay in the same house with the woman who might be responsible for the deaths of her parents and sister?

That thought repulsed her, but if she did agree to go to Morningside, she might be able to find some evidence that would link Helen Harcourt to their deaths. It wasn't too late to see her punished for the crime if she was the one responsible. A visit to Morningside could bring her closer to the truth, and that would be worth suffering the discomfort of being around Mrs. Harcourt.

She glanced at Nate, and a wave of uneasiness traveled through her. What would he say if he knew she suspected his stepmother of wrongdoing? Would he welcome her into his home, or would he turn his back on her as he had four years ago?

Since Nate's return she'd allowed his kindness and attention to soften her resolve to keep her distance from the Harcourts. But she would not let it go any further. She must protect herself and her family at all costs.

Most of all she must remember the Harcourts could not be trusted.

12

Maggie looked out the carriage window as they rolled up the hill toward Morningside Manor. A half-moon peeked out between heavy clouds, spreading pale, silvery light over the winding drive and gardens. Nate rode his horse alongside the carriage, though he was only a shadowed figure in the moonlight.

When they reached the top of the hill, torches lit the wide, circular front drive.

The house rose before her like a huge, dark castle set against the rugged mountainside. Gravel crunched under the carriage wheels, and the springs squeaked as the driver slowed the horses.

Maggie picked up her mother's Bible, sister's shawl, and the money box from the seat beside her and glanced across the carriage. Violet sagged against Grandmother's arm, her eyes closed and her mouth slightly open. The poor girl looked exhausted; no wonder, it was well past midnight.

Nate dismounted his horse and opened the carriage door. Maggie looked out, expecting a footman or butler to meet them. But since the hour was so late, she supposed the household staff had already gone to bed.

Nate held out his hand to help her down. She took it but looked away and slipped her fingers from his as soon as her feet touched the ground. Nate helped Grandmother down next, then handed out Violet's crutches. Grandmother took them.

Nate turned to Maggie. "Shall I carry Violet in?"

"Yes, please." Maggie and her grandmother stepped back, waiting for Nate to lead the way. But as he carried Violet toward the house, Maggie sprang ahead, shifted her belongings to one hand, and pulled open the massive front door.

"Thank you," he murmured as he passed through with her sister.

Maggie and Grandmother followed him into the dimly lit entryway and then into the larger great hall.

Round glass globes that looked like large bowls turned upside down sat on top of the corner posts at the bottom of the stairs. They glowed softly and sent a pale-yellow light around the room.

"Look at that," Grandmother whispered, her gaze fixed on the globes.

"Yes." Maggie had heard about the strange inventions Nate's father had placed around the house, including the unusual lights, hot water for bathing on the upper floors, and a lift to bring food up from the kitchen to the dining room. They were powered by something called hydroelectricity, which was created by moving water. Maggie couldn't imagine how water could light the house and run all those inventions, but it appeared to be true.

Perhaps that was why people called Mr. Harcourt the Magician of the North. But she was not superstitious. She knew it was not magic but science behind the lights and other inventions at Morningside Manor and Clifton Engineering.

Nate set Violet down, and Grandmother passed her the crutches.

"Clara! Where have you been?" A woman's voice rang out from the shadowed upper gallery at the end of the great hall. "Come upstairs this instant!"

Nate frowned toward the woman's voice. "It's Nathaniel, not Clara, and I have some guests with me."

"Guests? At this hour?" Helen Harcourt appeared at the top of the stairs and started down, carrying a lantern. She wore a light-blue dressing gown, and her silver-blond hair flowed over her shoulders. As she came closer, her gaze swept past Grandmother and Violet and settled on Maggie. Her lips compressed into a firm line, and she narrowed her eyes slightly.

Nate motioned toward Grandmother. "This is Mrs. Hayes, and perhaps you remember her granddaughters, Margaret and Violet Lounsbury."

"Yes, of course." Helen's brow creased, her gaze flicking from Maggie to Nate. "You look dreadful. What happened to you?"

"There was a fire in Heatherton. Neatherton's Boots and Mrs. Hayes's millinery shop were destroyed. That was also their home, so I've invited them to stay with us at Morningside."

Helen sent Nate a sharp look that made it clear she was not pleased by the invitation. "I'll ring for Mrs. Burnell."

Nate put out his hand. "It's too late for that. Don't disturb the housekeeper. I'll show them up to their rooms."

"Very well. Good night." But Helen's chilly tone betrayed her true feelings. She turned away and swept up the stairs.

A muscle in Nate's jaw contracted as he watched his stepmother disappear into the darkness of the upper gallery. "I'm sorry. It's late. I'm sure she'll be in a better mood in the morning." He motioned toward the stairs. "Let me show you to your rooms."

Maggie, Grandmother, and Violet followed Nate toward the stairs, but Violet stopped at the bottom and looked up.

"Would you like a lift?" Nate's mouth tugged up in a smile.

"They do look awfully steep." Violet turned toward him.

He lifted her into his arms. Maggie passed her belongings to Grandmother, then took Violet's crutches, and she and Grandmother climbed the stairs after them.

When they reached the upper landing, Maggie glanced down at the shadowy great hall, and a shiver traveled down her back. Morningside Manor had always seemed to be a huge, imposing house, with its mysterious inventions and aloof master and mistress. But tonight it seemed even more peculiar and threatening.

Nate lit the lantern and set it on the bedside table in the Devonshire guest room. "You and Violet should be quite comfortable here." His gaze traveled around the room, taking in two canopy beds with blue curtains and plush bedspreads to his right. Straight ahead, heavy blue-and-gold drapes hung over two east-facing windows. To his left, a tall cherry wardrobe and dressing table with mirror and a padded bench stood on either side of a fireplace.

He'd chosen the largest of their seven guest rooms for Maggie and Violet. In the morning they'd have a view of the front gardens and the bridge that crossed the ravine and stream. He knew how much Maggie had loved exploring those gardens when she was a girl, and he hoped the view would lift her spirits.

"Thank you." Maggie cast a glance around the room, but rather than looking pleased, as he'd hoped, a little line creased the area between her eyebrows. Was she ill at ease because Morningside was such a large, stately home compared to her grandmother's modest millinery shop, or was it something else? He studied her a moment more, then dismissed his questions. It was after midnight. They were all tired. This was no time to draw conclusions about her opinion of Morningside.

He turned to her grandmother. "Mrs. Hayes, if you'll come with me, I'll show you to your room."

Her silver eyebrows rose. "Oh no, I'll be just fine here."

"But there are only two beds."

"Violet and I can share." Maggie stepped closer to her sister and laid her hand on the girl's shoulder.

He motioned to the hallway. "There is another guest room directly across the hall."

"I'd rather stay here with the girls," Mrs. Hayes added. "No need to take up two rooms when the three of us can share one."

He glanced at Maggie, waiting for her to speak, but she shifted her gaze away, looking as though she wanted to shield her thoughts from him.

"All right. If that's what you'd like."

Mrs. Hayes gave a firm nod. "It is."

"Very well. Let me show you the bathroom. It's just down the hall."

"You go ahead, Maggie." Grandmother slipped her shawl from her shoulders. "I'll help Violet get to bed."

Maggie shot her grandmother a quick glance as though she did not like that suggestion, but the older woman was already folding back the blankets for Violet.

Nate led Maggie down the hall and pushed open the bathroom door. "We have hot and cold running water. There are extra towels in that cabinet by the window. If you need anything, just ring the bell on the wall and one of the servants will come."

"Even at this hour?"

"There is a hall boy sleeping downstairs by the bell board. He'll wake a maid or the housekeeper if needed."

Maggie looked past his shoulder into the bathroom, but she stayed in the hall a few feet away from him.

Was it the lateness of the hour or the trying events of the day that made her put up that shield and keep everyone at a distance . . . or was she simply trying to keep *him* away?

Whatever the reason, he hated the way she seemed unwilling to renew their friendship. He took a deep breath, determined to try to bridge that gap if he could. "I'm truly sorry for all that's happened," he said softly.

Her gaze flashed to his, then she quickly looked away. "Thank you." But her tone carried no warmth.

"Maggie, what is it? Have I done or said something that's upset you?"

She stilled, keeping her gaze averted. "No, you haven't."

"Then why do I feel as though there is a thick wall between us?"

Seconds ticked by as she pressed her lips together and glanced down the hallway. "Coming to Morningside brings back memories, and most of them are not pleasant."

He frowned, sorry that her connection to his home made her uncomfortable. Was she thinking of the times she'd come to the house with her parents before the accident claimed their lives? Of course that would be a painful memory. But what about all the times he and Maggie had tramped through the woods, exploring the trails, fishing, watching birds, and chasing rabbits? Those had always been some of his fondest memories. Why didn't they linger in her heart?

He studied her face again. "I can understand why you might be uncomfortable here. But I hope this stay will create new memories, ones that will ease the pain of the past."

She stared at him for a moment. "I'm not sure that's possible." Her reply was soft and strained.

"Of course it is. We can't change the past, but the future is an open door. We can make the path ahead as bright and carefree as you'd like."

She lifted her gaze to meet his, and moisture glittered in her eyes. "Sometimes the hold of the past is too great."

Her heartfelt words and sorrowful expression struck him like a blow to his chest, and he had to look away. If there was one thing he could not stand, it was seeing Maggie—his strong, vibrant Maggie—so close to tears.

He swallowed hard. "I'll leave you, then. Good night." He strode away without waiting for her answer.

But just before he turned the corner to the east wing, her soft reply reached him. "Good night, Nate."

Maggie watched Nate disappear down the dim hallway, and her heart clenched. Shielding her thoughts and feelings from him had been difficult enough when she only saw him occasionally in the village. How would she keep them hidden if she was staying in his home and would surely see him at all hours of the day?

She shook her head. She must keep her reason for coming to Morningside front and center in her mind. Yes, they needed shelter, but she was also seeking answers to the questions that had risen after reading her father's journal.

She slipped into the bathroom to wash her face and prepare for bed. A few minutes later, she stepped out of the bathroom into the hallway. Soft footsteps approached.

Maggie stilled and stared into the darkness. "Hello?"

The footsteps stalled, and a shadowy female figure appeared a few feet away. "Betsy, is that you?" the woman whispered.

"No, it's Margaret Lounsbury." With the faint moonlight streaming through the hall window, Maggie could see that the woman was Clara Harcourt, Nate's sister. She wore a dark hooded cape and carried a small satchel. What was she doing dressed like that at this time of the night? Why didn't she carry a lantern or candle?

Clara stared at her. "Miss Lounsbury, I don't understand. What are you doing here at Morningside?"

"I'm sorry. I didn't mean to startle you. Let me explain. There was a fire in the village tonight. Our shop was destroyed, and your brother offered us shelter."

"Us?"

"Yes, my grandmother and my sister Violet are with me."

"Oh, I see. I didn't realize there'd been a fire." Clara's tone softened. "I'm sorry to hear about your shop." She looked over her shoulder, then back at Maggie. "Please don't say anything to my mother about seeing me. She'd be very angry if she discovered I'd gone out."

Maggie hesitated. "I'm afraid she already knows."

Clara's eyes widened. "How could she?"

"I'm not sure, but when we first arrived, the great hall was dark. She couldn't see who we were, and she called out for you from the upper gallery. She seemed quite upset when she came down. I wasn't sure if that was because of our unexpected arrival or her concern for you."

Clara sighed and slipped off her hood. "Probably both. Mother doesn't like to be surprised or defied."

A smile touched Maggie's lips. "Yes, I could see that."

"My mother likes to be in control, and that means she keeps a stranglehold on me and everyone else in this house. But I'm almost eighteen. I won't allow her to have that kind of power over my life any longer."

Conflicting thoughts coursed through Maggie's mind, making her uncertain how to reply.

"Well, I don't want to keep you. It's late." Clara stepped away. "I hope you sleep well, Miss Lounsbury."

Maggie bid Clara good night and walked back to the guest room. Where had Clara been at this hour? Should she say something to Nate? Clara wanted Maggie to keep her secret, but was that wise? If someone caught her sister sneaking in at this time of night, Maggie would want to know.

Waves of weariness washed over Maggie. Her thoughts felt foggy and her steps leaden. It was too late to make sense of it all tonight. She would deal with it and the one hundred other things weighing on her mind in the morning.

Early the next morning, Mrs. Burnell gave Lilly a dress and undergarments for Violet. She said they used to belong to Clara, and she would look for some clothing for Maggie and Mrs. Hayes later.

Lilly took the clothes and undergarments to the guest room and helped them dress, then she led them down the servants' stairs to the lower hallway and past the kitchen. "I'll show you where we have our meals."

News of the fire that had destroyed her father's shop had spread through the staff like lightning and left Lilly reeling. Where had her father and brother gone? What would they do now? Just thinking about her poor old father having to deal with this kind of disaster at his age made her heart ache. And he wasn't the only one grieving losses today. Maggie and Mrs. Hayes's shop had burned down as well.

It was almost too much to take in.

Lilly noted the weary slope of Mrs. Hayes's shoulders and the shadows beneath Maggie's eyes. No doubt they were shocked by all that had happened and had not slept well.

Lilly stepped into the servants' hall. "Just have a seat, and I'll let Mrs. McCarthy know you'll be eating—"

Mrs. Burnell walked through the doorway. "Thank you, Lilly. I've already taken care of that." She turned to Mrs. Hayes and motioned toward the table. "You may be seated. Breakfast will be ready soon."

"Thank you." Mrs. Hayes pulled out a chair and sat down while Maggie helped Violet with her crutches. Sophie, Andrew, and several other staff members took seats around the table.

Lilly sat next to Maggie and placed her napkin on her lap.

Maggie leaned toward her. "Have you heard from your father or brother?"

"Not yet. I'm sure they're both terribly upset."

Maggie nodded. "I'm sure they are. I still can't believe it. When I woke up this morning, I thought it was all a bad dream, then I smelled the smoke in my hair and I knew it really happened."

She was about to answer when Mr. Jackson walked in and all the staff quickly rose to their feet.

"You may be seated." Mr. Jackson looked toward Mrs. Hayes. "We're sorry to hear about the fire and the loss of your shop. If there's anything we can do to assist you or make your stay with us more comfortable, please let me know."

"Thank you, sir." Mrs. Hayes nodded to the butler. "We are quite comfortable. Everyone has been very kind."

"Good." Mr. Jackson's gaze shifted to the staff. "Before breakfast is served, I want to make you all aware of a few changes to our schedule today."

Lilly listened until her duties had been listed, then her thoughts drifted to Rob. How she wished she could see him and tell him about the fire, but today was only Tuesday and she wouldn't be free to return to the village until Sunday. Even then she might not be able to speak to him if he was working that extra shift at Clifton.

She could write him another letter, but it wasn't the same as speaking to him face to face. Lilly sighed and made up her mind. Exchanging letters was better than silence. As soon as she had a spare minute, she'd go up to her room and tell Rob everything that had happened and ask him to pray for her and her family, and for Maggie and her grandmother too.

Nate strode into the dining room, glanced at the empty table, and came to an abrupt halt. His stepmother always took breakfast in her bedroom, but he had expected to see his guests and sister seated and waiting for him. A quick look around the room told him the only person present was his aging butler, standing guard by the sideboard.

"Jackson, did one of the maids wake our guests this morning?"

"There was no need, sir. Mrs. Hayes and her granddaughters were up quite early."

Nate glanced at the covered dishes on the sideboard and frowned. "Have they already eaten?"

Jackson's silver eyebrows rose. "They're having breakfast in the servants' hall."

Nate frowned. "Why are they eating downstairs?"

"Mrs. Harcourt sent a message to Mrs. Burnell earlier this morning with those instructions."

Nate drew in a slow, deep breath. His stepmother had overstepped again. She obviously still thought of herself as mistress of the manor and the one who should give orders to the staff concerning their guests. It was time he set the record straight, and he would begin with Jackson.

He turned to the butler. "As you know, I am the master of Morningside now. Mrs. Harcourt no longer has the final word concerning how this house will be run or how my guests are to be treated."

Jackson straightened. "Yes, sir. I'm sorry, sir."

"There is no need to apologize. We all need time to adjust to these new roles."

"Shall I go down to the servants' hall and ask your guests to come up and join you in the dining room?"

"No. I'll see to it myself." Nate motioned toward the table. "Set three more places."

"Very well, sir." Jackson nodded to Nate and then shuffled off.

Nate strode out of the dining room and took the servants' stairs to the lower level. Voices in the kitchen caught his attention as he rounded the corner of the hallway.

Mrs. McCarthy, the cook, bustled across the room, carrying a heavy, steaming pot. She plopped it down on the large worktable in the center of the kitchen. "Mary, take that tray into the servants' hall, and be quick about it."

The young kitchen maid scooped up the tray filled with a platter of toast and two pots of jam and turned toward the door. Her mouth dropped open when she spotted Nate, and her eyes grew as round as boiled eggs. "Good morning, sir." She dipped a curtsy and jostled the tray.

Mrs. McCarthy spun around and lifted her hand to her heart. "Mr. Harcourt! Oh my. Is everything all right? What . . . can we do for you, sir?"

"Everything is fine. No need to be alarmed. I've just come down to speak to Mrs. Hayes and her granddaughters."

"They're in the servants' hall. We're just about to serve breakfast." The cook gave the kitchen maid a shove on the back. "Go on now, Mary. Don't keep them waiting." The cook's words seemed to bring Mary out of her stunned state.

"Yes, ma'am." She bobbed another curtsy to Nate, then scurried down the hall.

Nate followed her through the doorway to the servants' hall. The conversation around the table died away, and the staff quickly rose to their feet. Maggie, Mrs. Hayes, and Violet all looked up at him from their seats on the far side of the table.

"I'm sorry to interrupt your breakfast. Please be seated."

The footmen, maids, and hall boy settled on their chairs again, but Mrs. Burnell, the housekeeper, crossed to meet him. "Can I help, sir?"

"Yes, there seems to be a misunderstanding about our guests." He glanced at Maggie, but she didn't meet his gaze. "I was expecting Mrs. Hayes and her granddaughters to join me upstairs for meals while they're staying at Morningside."

A frown creased Mrs. Burnell's brow. "Mrs. Harcourt said they're to take their meals downstairs with the staff."

"I understand, but that was not my intention, nor my request."

Mrs. Burnell pursed her lips. "She won't like it."

"She is no longer in a position to make those decisions."

Mrs. Burnell's face flushed. "Yes, sir."

Nate didn't want to upset the housekeeper or appear rude, but he was done with staff members bowing to Mrs. Harcourt's whims. He softened his tone. "I am sorry for the confusion. Our guests arrived late last night, and I failed to make my wishes clear to Mrs. Harcourt. I'll inform her—"

"That's not necessary." Maggie looked his way. "We're quite comfortable eating with the staff."

"That we are," Mrs. Hayes added with a quick nod. "Please don't trouble yourself or Mrs. Harcourt. We have friends among the staff." She glanced across at one of the maids, and the maid returned a brief smile.

"It's no trouble," Nate continued. "Please, come and join me upstairs. I've asked Jackson to set places for you, and I'm sure Mrs. McCarthy can send up your meals."

Maggie and her grandmother exchanged an uncomfortable glance. He had put them in an awkward position, but it couldn't be helped. He would not allow his stepmother to dictate who would eat at his table.

Maggie rose, and she and Mrs. Hayes followed him into the hallway. Violet clumped along on her crutches.

Maggie caught up with Nate in the lower hallway. "We don't mind eating downstairs." She glanced toward the servants' hall and lowered her voice. "We don't want to create an uncomfortable situation between you and Mrs. Harcourt."

"It's all right. My stepmother needs to understand her role at Morningside changed when my father breathed his last."

Mrs. Hayes sent him a surprised look.

"I don't mean to sound harsh, but I won't tolerate her treating my guests in an unkind manner. Banishing you to the servants' hall is totally unacceptable."

A hint of a smile lifted the corners of Maggie's mouth. "Are you sure?"

"Yes, quite sure, and quite hungry. Please, let's go upstairs and enjoy our breakfast."

Grandmother sent a cautious glance toward the upper floors. "What will Mrs. Harcourt say?"

"She always takes breakfast in her room. I'll speak to her later." He motioned toward the stairs. "After you, ladies." He turned to Violet. "Unless you'd like me to carry you up."

Violet wrinkled her nose as she scanned the steps. "I don't mind. These are like our stairs at home. I can do it."

"All right. You go first, and I'll follow behind just in case you need any assistance."

Maggie sent him a smile, and this one actually lit up her eyes.

Warmth flowed through him, and his chest expanded. If watching out for

Maggie's sister and inviting them to share his breakfast table could bring that kind of warm response, maybe there was hope for bridging the gap between them after all. That thought buoyed his spirits and made his steps light as he climbed the stairs.

Horses' hooves sounded outside on the gravel drive. Maggie pushed aside the guest-room curtain and looked out the window. A carriage pulled by four horses drove around the side of the house and rolled to a stop in front of the main entrance. When Maggie heard the door open downstairs, she leaned closer to the glass. A footman sprang into sight and opened the carriage door.

Mrs. Harcourt and Clara crossed the drive and climbed inside. The footman closed the door and stepped back. The driver called to the horses, and the carriage rolled off down the drive.

Maggie's heartbeat quickened. This was her chance. With Mrs. Harcourt and Clara away from the house and her grandmother and Violet occupied in the library, she could begin her search for something that might connect Helen Harcourt with her parents' and sister's deaths.

But where should she start?

A knock sounded at the guest room door, and Maggie turned from the window. Who could that be? Nate had left after breakfast to meet with the board of directors at Clifton, and he didn't expect to return until midafternoon.

She smoothed her hand down her dress. "Yes?"

"It's Lilly. May I come in?"

Relief rushed through Maggie. She hurried across the room and pulled open the door. "Oh, Lilly, I'm glad you've come. Have you had some news from your family?"

Her friend stepped into the room and closed the door behind her. "Yes, a message arrived a few minutes ago."

"Are they all right?"

Lilly nodded. "Of course they're upset about the fire, but they're safe and already making plans to rebuild the shop."

"Did they have insurance?"

"Yes, but Father says he's not sure it will cover all their losses."

Maggie nodded. Grandmother had said the same thing before breakfast that morning. She was protected in case of fire, but she doubted their coverage would be enough to rebuild and restock. Maggie pushed those worries away and focused on Lilly again. "Where are they staying?"

"With my uncle James, on his farm a few miles west of the village."

"It's good you have family close by. I'm sure that puts your father's mind at ease."

"I don't know about that. Joseph said Father was in a terrible state last night. He feared he'd have a heart attack watching everything he'd built burn to the ground." Lilly shuddered and rubbed her arms. "It must have been a dreadful sight."

Memories of the scorching heat and roaring blaze flew through Maggie's mind and sent a dizzy wave over her. "I've never seen anything like it, and I hope I never do again."

Lilly's expression softened. "I'm sorry for all you've lost. I know how much that shop meant to you and your grandmother."

Losing everything in the fire had been a terrible blow. How long would it take for those frightening memories to fade and loosen their grip on her heart? She blew out a deep breath, determined to refocus her thoughts. "No one was hurt. That's what matters most."

"Yes. That is a blessing." Lilly sent her a sympathetic smile. "It was kind of Mr. Harcourt to invite you to stay at Morningside until you can rebuild."

"We've only agreed to stay one day."

Concern lit Lilly's eyes. "Where will you go?"

Maggie glanced away, uncertain how to reply. She ought to be making inquiries to solve that problem and contacting the insurance company rather than plotting to search the house for clues about Mrs. Harcourt's actions. But she would not waste this opportunity. She reached for her friend's hand. "I need your help, Lilly."

"Of course. I'll do whatever I can for you."

"Do you know how long Mrs. Harcourt and Clara will be away?"

Lilly's brow creased. "I'm not sure. I believe they're visiting the Willmingtons at Everly Hall. That's about an hour's drive. So I expect they won't be home for at least three hours."

Maggie nodded, her spirits lifting. That should be enough time to begin her search. "Do you know if Mrs. Harcourt keeps a diary?"

Lilly thought for a moment. "I've seen her write in a book."

"Where does she keep it?"

Lilly hesitated. "Why do you want to know?"

"I just want to take a look and see . . . what she's written."

"Why?" Doubt shadowed Lilly's expression.

Maggie looked away with a rush of guilt. She and Lilly had been close friends for many years, and Lilly had never betrayed her confidence—surely she could trust her. Maggie turned back. "I thought I'd look back and see what she wrote around the time of the accident."

Lilly stilled. "You mean when your parents and sister died?"

Maggie met Lilly's gaze. "Yes."

"But what would Mrs. Harcourt have to say about that?"

"I'm not sure, but if I read her diary, I might find a connection."

Lilly cast a nervous glance toward the window. "I don't know. We would be in a world of trouble if we got caught."

"Just show me where she keeps her diary, then you can leave me there and go back to your duties."

Lilly studied her a moment, obviously debating her reply. Finally, she glanced toward the door. "It's in her sitting room, on the desk."

Excitement pulsed through Maggie. "Will you show me?"

Lilly hesitated a moment more. "All right. I'll take you there."

Relief flowed through Maggie. "Thank you, Lilly."

"Don't thank me. You haven't found anything yet."

"No, but I have a feeling I will."

Lilly smiled and tipped her head toward the door. "Come on, then."

14

Nate walked down the central aisle of Building Number Four at Clifton Engineering Works with Mr. Michael Waller, one of the lead engineers. The clang of tools and grinding of the heavy equipment rang in Nate's ears while the smell of burning oil and molten metal assaulted his nose.

Men wearing coveralls called out to each other as they hefted sections of metal framework into place for welding.

A few men looked up as Nate and Mr. Waller passed, some with curious glances, others with dark, suspicious looks. Nate didn't see any of the men he and Reverend Samuelson had talked to in the village, but he wasn't surprised. Clifton employed more than seven hundred men at this site near Heatherton and another nine hundred at the Newcastle upon Tyne location.

"What are they building?" Nate raised his voice to be heard above the din.

Mr. Waller slowed and turned toward Nate. "They're assembling sections for hydraulic cranes."

Nate glanced at the nearest structure, and a burly man looked his way. The man's face glistened with sweat and grime. He wore thick leather gloves and held a welding torch in his hands. A young man who looked to be no more than sixteen and was as thin as a rail stood beside him, holding up a section of metal framework.

Nate studied the design, but it made no sense to him. There was so much he didn't know about his father's business, and now that he had inherited a leadership role at Clifton, he had much to learn.

Nate looked at Mr. Waller again. "How are the cranes used?"

Mr. Waller's mouth tipped up on one side. Was he amused by Nate's lack of knowledge, or was he simply a good-humored man? Nate hoped it was the latter. He didn't like to appear as though he was uninformed or, worse yet, a fool.

"They're used for loading and unloading goods off ships, but they have applications to railroads and other industries as well."

"I see." There was more Nate wanted to ask, but the noise level and the desire not to appear ignorant made him hold his tongue.

"Clifton's cranes are in demand all over the country, but we also build bridges, water systems, and just about anything else requiring engineering and hydroelectric power."

They continued on through the building and entered the offices at the far end. As soon as the door closed, the noise, smell, and hustle faded. Dark-paneled walls and plush rugs on the hardwood floor gave the office a look of comfort and prosperity.

A woman seated at the reception desk looked up as they approached. She wore a neatly pressed white blouse, a masculine tie, and wire-rimmed spectacles that gave her a no-nonsense appearance. Threads of silver in her light-brown hair made Nate guess she was in her late forties.

Waller stepped forward. "Good morning, Miss Larson. Will you please tell Mr. Rowlett that Mr. Harcourt and I are here?"

"Yes, sir." She picked up a cone-shaped device connected with a cord to a small box on her desk, then pressed a buzzer on the side and relayed Mr. Waller's message.

Nate only had a moment to stare at the machine before he heard a man reply, "Send them in."

Nate shot a glance at Mr. Waller. "I've never seen anything like that before."

The engineer smiled. "It's a relatively new invention."

"Was it my father's idea?"

"No, but I believe he had it installed just after he saw it exhibited in London two years ago."

Miss Larson rose from her chair. "Please follow me, gentlemen." She led them down the hall and opened the second door on the right.

Nate passed through the doorway and into the inner office, followed by Mr. Waller. Six men were seated around a long table in the center of the room.

Folders and papers were spread out among them along with half-full cups of coffee or tea.

The meeting appeared to be well underway, although they had arrived at the appointed time. Nate's stomach tensed. "I'm sorry, gentlemen, are we late?"

Mr. Geoffrey Rowlett rose. "No, you're on time. Please come in."

Nate sent a questioning glance around the table.

Rowlett's face turned ruddy. "We had a few matters to discuss in preparation for our meeting with you."

Nate didn't like the sound of that. Why had they started without him and Mr. Waller? What had they discussed out of his hearing?

Rowlett motioned to the two empty chairs. "Please have a seat."

Nate took one of the chairs Rowlett indicated at the end of the table and glanced around at the other men. He had seen most of them at his father's funeral, though he could only remember two of their names. He must make an effort to learn what he could about them and commit their names to memory. If he was going to step into his father's shoes at Clifton, he would need as many allies as possible.

Rowlett remained standing at the head of the table. "First, we would like to express our sincere condolences concerning your father's passing. We all admired him. He will be greatly missed."

Nate nodded. "Thank you."

"We want to assure you," Rowlett continued, "that we'll do everything in our power to carry on his fine legacy here at Clifton."

"I appreciate that. Father spoke highly of you all, and I know he would be grateful for your patience and consideration as I learn what's needed to take on my role here."

As Nate looked around the table, each man glanced away and seemed unwilling to meet his gaze.

Geoffrey Rowlett took his seat, giving Nate a moment to observe the man more carefully. His dark hair was streaked with silver, and his eyes were even darker. He had smooth, olive-toned skin and sharp features. His bearing and suit were stylish and impeccable.

Rowlett had managed the business side of things at Clifton for years, while Nate's father had been the mastermind behind most of the inventions. The two men had been associates and friends as long as Nate could remember, but Nate had never been comfortable around Geoffrey Rowlett. His odd reception today did nothing to change those feelings.

"We appreciate you coming," Rowlett continued as he settled into his chair. "You must have your hands full, learning what's needed to manage Morningside, as well as caring for Mrs. Harcourt and Miss Clara during this . . . difficult time." Was that a sincere look of sympathy in Rowlett's eyes, or was it simply put on to appease Nate?

"Thank you for your concern. Learning to manage Morningside will be a challenge, but I have a skilled estate manager and a diligent staff. With their help, I'm confident we'll do quite well." Nate glanced around the table once more. "I'm very interested to learn all I can about Clifton and take on my responsibilities here. In fact, I'm quite looking forward to it."

Rowlett shifted in his chair. "We are more than willing to continue managing Clifton's day-to-day operations and guiding the company toward even greater heights of profitability and productivity."

Nate held his gaze steady. "Thank you, Mr. Rowlett. I look forward to joining you in that effort."

Rowlett's brow creased slightly. "Of course you're more than welcome to sit in on our meetings and learn how we operate, but I hope you'll do as your father has done and leave the daily management to this capable board."

"I will certainly look to the board for direction," Nate continued, keeping his tone even, "but I plan to take an active role in decision making, especially as it relates to working conditions for the men employed by Clifton."

A ripple of unease traveled around the table, and the board members exchanged wary glances.

Mr. Judson, seated on Nate's left, leaned forward slightly. "Do you have some particular concerns?"

"Yes. I understand there was an accident recently and a man was severely injured. From what I've heard in the village, that seems to have unsettled the men and stirred up negative feelings toward management."

Mr. Judson tipped his head, acknowledging Nate's comment. "The men work with heavy equipment. Accidents are bound to happen. That one you mentioned wasn't the first, and it won't be the last."

Heat rushed into Nate's face. "We're talking about a man who lost the use of his hand. He won't be able to return to his job here, and it's doubtful he'll be able to support his family."

"That is regrettable, but the men know the risks. It's a chance they take when they sign on at Clifton."

"But isn't it our responsibility to make sure our equipment is safe and the workers are protected as much as possible?"

Judson frowned. "We have safety inspections once a year."

"If accidents are as common as you say, then perhaps we need better training and more frequent inspections."

"We have to close down operations for inspections, and that would cost us a great deal."

"But think what we would gain—the goodwill of our workers and a safe, efficient facility. That could increase our productivity in the long run."

Judson pressed his mouth into a firm line and glared at the open file on the table in front of him.

Nate would not be put off by Judson's stony silence. "Another issue related to safety is the length of the workday," he continued. "Most of the men work ten-hour shifts. I believe shortening their day to nine or even eight hours would help them be more alert and better able to avoid accidents."

Mr. Judson huffed. "I'm sure they'd all like to stay in bed another hour or two, but that won't put food on the table for their families or make a profit for us."

Rowlett lifted his hand. "It is commendable of you to speak up for the workers' concerns, but you don't understand the impact your suggestions would have on the company."

Nate narrowed his eyes at Rowlett. "Adequate safety inspections, a shorter workday, and a small pay raise don't seem like unreasonable requests to me."

Rowlett shook his head. "That's exactly what I mean. You don't understand. We operate with a very slim profit margin. If we shorten the men's hours and raise their wages, we could put the company in a very dangerous financial position."

"Really?" Nate locked gazes with Rowlett. "You have so little confidence in your management skills that you couldn't make a few concessions to give the men decent wages and safer working conditions and still make a profit?"

Rowlett's expression hardened. "Mr. Harcourt, this is your first board meeting. You're not familiar with our policies and practices. Do you really think it's appropriate to make these kinds of recommendations when you have very little knowledge of how we operate and no experience managing a large enterprise like Clifton Engineering?"

Nate stilled, stung by Rowlett's sharp words. He might not like it, but Rowlett had a point. Nate had based his requests to the board on his conversations with Reverend Samuelson and a few workers. He hadn't looked into the company's financial records or spoken to the men overseeing daily operations. Perhaps he was overstepping or at least not coming at this in the wisest way.

He pulled in a deep breath. "It's true I'm not familiar with the policies and procedures at Clifton, but I do have four years of experience in the Royal Navy. I fought in a war and rose to the rank of lieutenant. I learned to take orders and issue them. I organized and equipped men to perform with valor and do their duty to God, king, and country. Those experiences, along with my commitment to learn more about how Clifton operates, should give me a voice on this board."

Mr. Waller met his gaze, and a glint of respect showed in his eyes. Rowlett, Judson, and the other men's solemn expressions remained unchanged.

The truth was clear. Waller might appreciate what he'd said, but Nate wouldn't win the rest of them over until he did a more thorough investigation and could show them facts and figures to back up his requests. But was there time for that? If tensions continued to rise, they might all regret delaying their response.

Nate looked around the table. "I must warn you, gentlemen, unrest is stirring among the workers. Some are talking about the possibility of a strike."

Rowlett's dark eyes flashed. "That is just senseless talk from a few hot-tempered men who are trying to cause trouble."

"Are you sure about that?"

Rowlett glared across the table at Nate. "Mr. Harcourt, we have been dealing with issues like these for years. Talk of a strike comes from a few troublemakers who want to push their will on the others. I can assure you we have everything under control."

"You may consider those men troublemakers, but I believe they're strong leaders who have great influence over the others. If you want to see Clifton's production and profits increase, then you'll have to seriously consider the concessions the workers request."

Deep lines slashed Geoffrey Rowlett's ruddy face. "That is not a decision we will be making today."

Nate's intense focus remained on Rowlett. "Then we're in for trouble, and you'll have to prepare to deal with it."

Maggie slipped down the upper hallway with Lilly. All was quiet, and no one seemed to be about, but Maggie couldn't shake her uneasy feelings. Was someone watching, or was it only her guilty conscience giving her that impression?

Lilly stopped in front of the fifth door on the right. "This is Mrs. Harcourt's sitting room. It connects to her bedroom." She pushed open the door and stood back.

Maggie stopped on the threshold and looked in. It was a feminine room with peach satin wall coverings and ivory lace curtains. Two comfortable chairs and a settee were grouped around the marble fireplace. Above the mantel hung a large family portrait of Mr. and Mrs. Harcourt, Nate, and Clara. Nate looked to be about fifteen, the age he'd been when he and Maggie first met.

"I dust and tidy up in here on Tuesdays and Fridays," Lilly said softly. "She usually keeps her diary on her desk." She nodded toward the elegant desk and chair in the corner.

Maggie swallowed. Did she have the courage to enter Mrs. Harcourt's sitting room and look through her private papers? And if she did find some kind of evidence that tied Mrs. Harcourt to the boating accident, what would she do then? Maggie pushed aside those questions and straightened her shoulders. She would do this for her parents and sister, and for her own peace of mind.

"I should get back to work." Lilly glanced over her shoulder. "I don't want Mrs. Burnell to come looking for me."

Maggie nodded. "I'll just take a quick look."

"I hope you find what you're looking for." Lilly sent her a half smile, but apprehension flickered in her eyes.

"Thank you, Lilly."

"Be careful and put everything back as you found it."

"I will." Maggie squeezed her friend's hand.

Lilly returned the same, then hurried off down the hall.

Maggie slipped inside, but she didn't want to make any extra noise by pulling the door shut, so she left it slightly ajar. She crossed the room and approached the desk. A few unopened letters and a fountain pen lay on the large blotter in the center. Other papers and letters were tucked into the compartments at the back of the desktop. A leather-bound book lay to the right of the blotter. Helen Harcourt's name was embossed on the cover.

Maggie flipped it open and read the inscription on the first page:

This is the private diary of Helen Harcourt. Begun the first day of January 1901.

Maggie's heart sank. That was more than a year after the boating accident. Could there be an earlier journal that would cover the dates she was looking for? She quietly closed the book and pulled open the top-left desk drawer. Envelopes, stationery, and a few letters tied with a blue ribbon were neatly stacked in the drawer, but there were no other diaries. She pushed it closed and opened the drawer below.

Four slim leather books stood together with their bindings face-up. They looked just like the diary on the desktop but were in various colors—blue, black, green, brown.

She reached in and pulled out the first book. Opening the cover, she read,

This is the private diary of Helen Harcourt. Begun the first day of January 1899.

Maggie's breath caught in her throat, and her heart began to pound. Eighteen ninety-nine was the year her parents and sister drowned. What did Helen Harcourt write about that terrible day?

"Miss Lounsbury, can I help?"

Maggie gasped, dropped the journal in the drawer, and spun around. "Mrs. Burnell, you startled me."

The housekeeper glanced at the open drawer. "May I ask what you're doing, looking through Mrs. Harcourt's desk?"

Maggie's mind spun, and she swallowed. "I need to write some letters . . . about the fire . . . and make some inquiries." That was true, but not the whole truth. "I thought I might borrow some stationery and a pen."

Mrs. Burnell scanned Maggie's face, doubt reflecting in her cool gray eyes. "If you need something, please ring for a member of the staff and allow us to bring it to you."

Maggie forced a smile. "Oh, I didn't want to bother anyone."

"Mr. Harcourt left instructions that we're to attend to your needs and those of your grandmother and sister." She pursed her lips. "But I don't think he would approve of you looking through Mrs. Harcourt's desk."

Maggie smoothed her hand down her dress. "I'm sorry. I didn't mean to cause any trouble."

Mrs. Burnell crossed the room, the keys on her chatelaine jingling as she walked. She pulled open the top drawer and took out several sheets of stationery, a few envelopes, and a fountain pen. "You may use these and return the pen to me when you're finished. We receive morning and afternoon posts. You can leave your letters with Mr. Jackson or one of the footmen, and they'll send them out."

"Thank you." Maggie accepted the ivory paper, envelopes, and fountain pen.

Mrs. Burnell lifted her chin and met Maggie's gaze. "Will there be anything else?"

"No, thank you. That's all I need." Maggie turned and walked out of the room, clutching the stationery to her chest. As soon as she reached the hall, she quickened her step and hurried toward her bedroom.

Did Mrs. Burnell suspect she'd been snooping or trying to steal something? Would the housekeeper tell Mrs. Harcourt she'd caught Maggie looking through her desk? Perhaps she should go back and ask Mrs. Burnell not to say anything to her mistress, but that would make Maggie's guilt certain.

Closing her eyes, she blew out a breath. The nudge to pray and ask God for help rose from her heart . . . but it had been years since she'd uttered a prayer and believed it would be answered. That hope had died along with her parents and sister.

Still, she sensed this problem was bigger than she could handle alone. But what could she do? Who would believe her? Who cared enough to search for the truth and take up her cause to see that justice was done?

Nate rode around the side of the manor house and headed for the stable, all the while replaying the frustrating events of the board meeting.

Why were those men so opposed to his suggestions? The workers' concerns made sense. Their leaders were not power-hungry agitators. Reverend Samuelson stood with them, giving credence to the men's claims about the unsettling situation at Clifton.

Didn't the board members realize a strike would hurt everyone, management and workers alike? The whole village and surrounding area would be impacted if these issues weren't resolved in a timely and peaceful manner—to say nothing of his own situation. How would he maintain Morningside and pay his staff if there was a prolonged strike? Would he be forced to let some of the staff go or sell some of his property?

He'd never hear the last of it from his stepmother if that happened.

Nate shook his head. He must convince the board to listen to the workers' grievances and make the necessary changes. And the only way to persuade the board would be to present facts and figures, and to give them those, he needed a better understanding of Clifton's financial status and proof of dangerous working conditions.

Mr. Waller had called him aside after the meeting and offered his help and support. As lead engineer he understood the board's point of view as well as the workers' concerns. Nate had barely been able to contain his emotions when Waller offered to meet with him later in the week to help him gather the information needed for the next board meeting in May.

That was weeks away, but he would not be discouraged. Instead, he would use that time to learn all he could and build a case the board could not refuse. Too much depended on them coming to a peaceful and speedy resolution. He would not let them push these issues under the table or wait until another man was injured or killed.

A young groom hustled out to meet Nate as he approached the stable. "Shall I take your horse, sir?"

"Yes, give him a good rub down and something to eat." Nate dismounted and handed the reins to the groom. Ginger curls poked out from beneath the groom's cap, and freckles covered a good portion of his face. "What's your name, lad?"

"Ethan, sir. Ethan Holloway."

"Well, Ethan, take good care of him." Nate patted Samson's warm neck.

"I will, sir. He's a fine horse." His eyes shining, the boy looked Samson over.

"Yes, he is. Thank you for looking after him. I appreciate it, and I'm sure Samson does as well."

Ethan smiled. "I'm glad to, sir. I always try to do my best for you and the family."

"Good man. I'm sure you do." Nate strode down the path toward the house, his thoughts returning to the troubling situation at Clifton. But feminine laughter from the other side of the hedge caught his attention. The low chuckle that followed definitely sounded masculine.

Nate frowned. Was it a harmless conversation between two members of his staff, or was there something else transpiring on the path to the gardens? He glanced toward the house and considered alerting Jackson or Mrs. Burnell, but he was master of Morningside now, and it was his duty to make sure his staff conducted themselves properly.

He rounded the corner and halted in his tracks. Clara stood very close to a young man dressed in brown tweed and a matching cap. Was he someone from the village or a member of the outdoor staff? Whoever he was, a private meeting with his sister behind the hedge was not an appropriate way to spend his time.

"Clara?"

She spun around, her eyes wide. "Nate!"

"Who is this?" He nodded to Clara's companion.

The young man straightened. "I'm Owen Campbell, sir, Mr. McDougall's nephew and the junior gamekeeper."

Nate frowned and looked him over. His attire matched that worn by Morningside's senior gamekeeper, Mr. John McDougall. "I don't believe we've met. I am Clara's brother, Nathaniel Harcourt, the new master of Morningside."

Owen Campbell whipped off his cap. "I'm pleased to meet you, sir." But the young man looked more startled than pleased.

"I'm curious to know, Mr. Campbell, what business does a junior gamekeeper have on the path to the gardens?"

The young man's face turned ruddy. "I was just . . . looking for my uncle."

Nate sent the boy a doubtful glance. "Then I suggest you check the gun room, the gamekeeper's lodge, or the woods beyond. You won't find him here."

"Yes, sir. I will, sir." Young Campbell shot a glance at Clara, then returned his cap to his head and hustled off down the path.

Clara watched Campbell disappear past the garden wall, then turned and glared at Nate. "How could you be so rude?"

Nate pulled back. "Rude?"

"Yes. We were only talking. We've done nothing wrong. You've no cause to scowl and treat Owen with disrespect."

"I don't believe I was disrespectful. I simply encouraged him to carry on with his duties, and I suggest you do the same."

"What duties? Do you want me to go inside and practice my French? Or perhaps I should review my dance lessons or paint another landscape?" Her face flushed pink, and her voice grew more intense with each phrase.

Nate frowned. What were Clara's duties? Did she actually have any?

"Did you know, now that we're in mourning," she continued, "I won't be going to London for the season?"

"The season?" Surprise rolled through him. "Clara, you're only seventeen. Surely your mother wasn't planning to take you until next year."

She lifted one shoulder in a slight shrug. "We had discussed it, and she was almost convinced . . . until Father fell ill. Then all our plans had to be set aside."

How had she managed to swing the conversation away from her meeting with Owen Campbell? And why did she consider showing proper respect for their father's passing less important than an early debut? That thought irked him more than the meeting with young Campbell. "I'm sorry your plans for coming out have changed, but I'm more concerned that you're sneaking off to meet some young man of questionable character."

Clara lifted her chin. "There's nothing questionable about Owen Campbell's character!"

"Then he ought to call on you properly rather than meeting you behind the hedge."

Hope filled Clara's eyes. "Do you think Mother would allow it?"

Nate rubbed his hand down his face. Why had he suggested the boy call? He knew very well his stepmother would make them all miserable if he agreed to it. "I don't think that is a good idea."

"Why not? Owen is from a good family. He's a fine, respectable man."

"Man? That boy hardly looks old enough to be out of school."

"He's twenty, and he's been working at Morningside for more than six months. But he has higher goals than that. He wants to be a veterinarian. He's saving now to take his training."

Nate crossed his arms. "It sounds as though you know quite a bit about Owen Campbell."

She lifted her chin and looked away, making her long blond curls cross over her shoulder. "We have become friends."

"And is sneaking out at night to see him part of that friendship?"

Her gaze darted back to meet his. "Who told you that? Miss Lounsbury?"

Nate frowned. What did Maggie have to do with it? "No, Helen was looking for you last night when we arrived around midnight. Apparently, she believed you'd gone out without her knowledge."

Clara's countenance fell. "Please don't say anything to her about Owen."

"I don't think keeping secrets from your mother is a good idea."

"But if she finds out, I'm afraid she'll send Owen away."

Nate's frown deepened. Like everyone else, Clara seemed to think Helen had the final word concerning the hiring and firing of staff.

He faced her with a serious gaze. "Clara, Owen Campbell may be a fine young man with good plans for his future, but you know your mother would not approve a courtship with him, and as your brother, I believe I have some say in the matter as well."

Clara glared up at him. "You don't even know Owen. How can you be so set against him?"

"He is a member of our staff, and that makes him an unlikely suitor."

"He is now, but he won't always be!"

"That is beside the point."

Fire burned in her eyes. "Oh, you're just like Mother!"

Nate pulled back, stung by the insulting comparison.

"I'm not a child!" Her voice rose, and her face flushed again. "I should be allowed to make my own decisions about whom I will see and where I will go."

"Clara, you're only seventeen, and that's not nearly old enough to have the final word about such important matters."

Her face crumpled and she turned away, but not before he saw tears flood her eyes.

Blast! He forced himself to calm down and soften his tone. "You have your whole life ahead of you. I'm sure you don't want to tarnish your reputation and hurt your future prospects for marriage by seeing any young man in secret and without a chaperon."

She swung around. "You don't understand! Owen is not any young man. I love him!" With that she grabbed up her skirt and ran toward the house.

Nate closed his eyes and rubbed his forehead. As if the trouble at Clifton was not enough, now he had to deal with a heartbroken, foolish sister who didn't want to listen to reason.

Maggie sat at the desk in the Morningside library and added a few more lines to the letter to the insurance company. She glanced across at her grandmother. "Do you think we should say our display cases were used when we bought them?"

Grandmother shifted on the settee and looked Maggie's way. "They were only three years old, but yes, we should mention it. We can't expect the Lord to honor our prayers for a favorable outcome with the insurance company unless we're honest about our claims."

Maggie wasn't sure if her grandmother's prayers would make any difference, but her parents had taught her the importance of honesty in all areas of life. She added the information and scanned the letter once more, weighing each word. Their future depended on her presenting their case as clearly as possible.

To that end, they'd spent the last hour creating a list of all that had been lost in the fire, including the finished hats and supplies in the shop, as well as the furniture and other items in their private rooms.

Violet flipped a page of the large book she held on her lap and quietly studied the next colorful illustration. She looked up at Grandmother seated next to her. "Do you think we'll see birds like these at Morningside?"

Maggie glanced over at the book, and longing rose in her heart. She would so much rather be out on a walk, exploring the gardens and enjoying the flowers and birds, than laboring over this letter, but her grandmother needed her help.

She turned back to her task and read the letter one more time. Finally, she rose from the desk, crossed the room, and handed the letter to her grandmother. "What do you think of this?"

Grandmother pushed her spectacles up her nose and read what Maggie had written. When she finished, she looked up. "Very nicely done, my dear."

"Thank you." Maggie sent her grandmother a pleased smile.

Grandmother handed it back. "I'm sure someone from the company will want to visit the shop and speak to us after. Why don't you tell them they can reach us here at Morningside Manor?"

Maggie stilled, and a prickle of unease traveled across her shoulders. "We haven't settled that with Nate."

"I'm sure that was his intention when he invited us last night."

"I wouldn't exactly say he invited us—it was more like a command." She frowned toward the fireplace, remembering how he'd practically ordered them to spend the night at Morningside.

Grandmother looked at her over the top of her spectacles. "For goodness' sake, Maggie, you ought to be grateful. Remember how he ran back into the shop to rescue Violet and retrieve the money you left upstairs? Then he fought the fire side by side with the village men, trying to save our shop. I don't know too many gentlemen who would risk their own safety or get their hands wet and dirty like that."

It was true. Nate had gone out of his way to alert them to the fire and make sure they were safely away before he joined the others to do what he could. Still, Maggie didn't want to give him too much credit. Their shop had been destroyed, and all they owned was lost. It was too little too late . . . again.

She crossed her arms over her chest as though protecting herself from a chill. "I didn't appreciate him ordering us to come here. We're not junior seamen on one of his Navy ships, and he is not our commanding officer."

"I'm sure he only spoke that way because the hour was late and we were all exhausted."

"I doubt that's true." Nate had a habit of using his position to influence others and get his way, or at least he had in the past. He did seem different since he'd returned, but she didn't want to be fooled by an outward display of kindness that covered a proud and demanding heart.

"Well, I wasn't offended by what he said or the way he said it," Grandmother continued. "In fact, quite the opposite. I was glad someone was willing to welcome us into his home, and you should be as well."

A sting of guilt pricked Maggie's conscience as she walked back to the desk. Grandmother could be right, but Maggie didn't want to concede her point.

Grandmother watched Maggie with a concerned look. "You should be careful, my dear. We're in a difficult position, without a home or income for a time. If Nathaniel is willing to allow us to stay at Morningside, we should do all we can to express our gratitude and remain in his good graces."

"What about Mrs. Harcourt? I'm not sure she'll be too pleased by an extended stay, especially when we have no idea how long it will take to rebuild our shop."

"Well, she might not like it, but Nathaniel has invited us and we are his guests. Besides, I don't know anyone else who has the room and desire to take us in."

Maggie glanced toward the window. Surely there must be someone else who would open their home to them. Should she contact Reverend Samuelson and ask for his help?

How could they continue to stay in the same house with the woman who might be responsible for the deaths of her parents and sister?

What did Nate know about the accident? The more time she spent with him, the more torn she felt. Was he only offering his friendship to keep her off balance and squelch her suspicions? Or was he a true friend who wanted to make up for the painful way his family had treated them in the past?

What if Nate learned she suspected Helen Harcourt was involved in a plot to murder her father? Would he side with his stepmother to protect his family from the scandal, or would he stand with Maggie and allow the truth to be told?

Nate strode into the library. "Ah, here you are."

Maggie swallowed hard. How long had Nate been outside the library door? Had he heard her remarks to her grandmother?

He looked her way, his expression warm and open, as though he had nothing to hide. "I'm sorry to leave you on your own all morning. The meeting at Clifton took longer than I expected."

"You mustn't worry about us." Grandmother looked up at him with a smile. "We're fine. We've just been composing our letter to the insurance company." She motioned toward the desk where Maggie sat. "Perhaps you could read it and give us your opinion?"

"Of course. I'd be glad to." He crossed toward Maggie.

She hesitated a moment, then held out the letter. Would he approve of what she'd written? She looked away and silently scolded herself for caring.

He scanned the first page, then quickly read the second. "This is well written." He looked up and met Maggie's gaze, appreciation in his eyes.

Maggie straightened. "Thank you."

"But I think it's important to add that the fire started in Neatherton's shop and then spread to yours. You want to absolve yourself of as much responsibility as possible. You don't want the company to claim you were careless or at fault for the damages and deny your claim."

Maggie pulled in a sharp breath. "Could they do that?"

"I have heard of some instances where that was the case." He glanced down at the letter again. "You'll also want to list the value of the property you lost."

Of course he was right. Why hadn't she thought of that? It wasn't enough to simply list the contents of the shop. They had to assign value to each item if they wanted to receive a fair settlement for their claim.

"And you should also include the amount of income you're losing by not being able to conduct your business."

"Yes, I suppose Maggie and I could come up with a weekly average without too much trouble."

"I'm not sure if your policy covers lost income," Nate continued, "but sending that information along might speed up processing the claim."

Grandmother clicked her tongue. "Well, it's a good thing we showed you our letter. It looks like we have some more work to do before we post it."

Nate glanced at Maggie, a hint of expectation in his eyes. Was he hoping she would praise him for his suggestions? She couldn't quite bring herself to do that.

But what if they hadn't shown him the letter? Would the insurance company have been happy to give them a smaller settlement?

"Thank you, Nathaniel. We're grateful for your help with our claim and for allowing us to stay at Morningside." Grandmother rose and crossed to stand beside Maggie.

Nate sent a surprised glance at Maggie, then nodded to Grandmother. "I'm pleased you've decided to stay."

"It's very kind of you to allow it." Grandmother paused, giving Maggie a meaningful look. "Isn't it, Maggie?"

"Yes, very kind." But Maggie couldn't look Nate in the eye when she spoke.

He reached toward the desk and pulled open one of the side drawers. "It might carry some weight if you wrote the letter on Harcourt stationery. And you'll want to make a copy to keep for your own records." He took out an envelope and several sheets of ivory paper with the gold Harcourt crest at the top.

He held them out to Maggie. "You may list my name as the person to contact, if you'd like."

She stiffened. Was he hoping to somehow control the outcome of the insurance claim, or was he simply trying to be helpful? Either way, she didn't want that kind of help. "Thank you, but I'd prefer to speak with them directly." He studied her face. Her cheeks warmed, and she had the distinct impression he could read her troubled thoughts.

He stepped back. "As you wish."

"Nate," Violet called from her spot on the settee, "do you ever see birds like these at Morningside?" She pointed to the open book on her lap.

"Let me see." He joined her on the settee, and they talked for several minutes about the birds he'd spotted on his walks.

Maggie focused on revising and copying the letter on the Harcourt stationery. With some help from her grandmother, she assigned values to their lost property and came up with a figure for their lost income.

Grandmother read the final copy and showed it to Nate. He nodded his approval. "I'll ring Jackson and ask him to take care of this for you." Nate pressed the bell to summon his butler, then turned to Maggie. "It's a lovely afternoon. I was thinking about taking a ride. Would you like to join me?"

Maggie blinked, surprised by his invitation. The thought of escaping the house and enjoying a ride in the fresh country air was almost too much to resist. "I haven't ridden for years." Four to be exact, but she didn't want to make that painfully clear.

"Then perhaps it's time you climbed back in the saddle." A hint of challenge lit Nate's eyes.

Maggie's heart tugged her to accept, but she shook her head. "I don't have any riding clothes."

"That outfit is fine. There's no need to change."

Grandmother took his arm and lowered her voice. "I think what Maggie is reluctant to say is that we brought no other clothing with us, and if she soils that dress, she'll have to stay wrapped up in a blanket in our room until it's washed and dried."

Heat surged through Maggie. Oh, what a lovely picture.

"Of course." Nate's face flushed. "I didn't think of that." He rubbed his chin and turned to Maggie. "You and Clara are about the same height and . . . size." He quickly shifted his gaze away. "I'm sure she has some clothes you could borrow until you have an opportunity to see the dressmaker."

"Oh, we've no need of a dressmaker." Grandmother chuckled. "We sew all our own clothes."

Maggie did most of the sewing since Grandmother's fingers had stiffened with arthritis, but her grandmother still did some and advised her each step of the way. "Yes, we're quite capable of sewing new dresses. We just need some fabric and a few supplies."

"I can help make a new dress." Violet looked up with an eager smile. "Maggie has been teaching me to sew. I've already made an apron and a blanket for my doll."

Nate grinned. "That's excellent." He shifted his gaze to Maggie. "I'll speak to Mrs. Burnell and see what we have on hand, and if that's not satisfactory, I'll arrange for you to take a trip into the village."

"Thank you." But her feeling of gratitude was quickly overshadowed by an uncomfortable realization. Morningside was at least four miles from Heatherton. It would take her well over an hour to walk there if the need arose, but it would be difficult for Violet and impossible for Grandmother. They were completely dependent on Nate or one of his staff if they wanted to return to the village. It was almost as if he held them captive at Morningside. Maggie bristled at that thought.

Nate looked her way with that open, hopeful expression. "So . . . would you like to join me for that ride?" Some unnamed emotion flickered in his eyes. Was it vulnerability, or was he seeking to hide something from her?

Perhaps if she agreed to go she could discover what was behind that look. She glanced at her grandmother.

"Violet and I will be fine. Go and enjoy the ride."

"All right." Maggie nodded to Nate. "I'll come along."

Violet released a wistful sigh. "I love horses, but I've never ridden one." She looked up at Nate with longing in her blue eyes.

Maggie laid her hand on Violet's shoulder. "And you won't be riding until that cast comes off your leg."

Violet's face fell. Immediately, Maggie regretted squashing her sister's dream, but it couldn't be helped.

"I have an idea." Nate crossed the room and knelt in front of Violet. "Perhaps you and your grandmother would like to sit on the bench out front and enjoy the sunshine. Then Maggie and I could bring the horses around so you could see them."

Violet's face brightened. "Oh, would you?"

"I'd be glad to, but first I must go up and change. Enjoy your book, and I'll send word when it's time for you to join us."

Violet gave a quick nod. "I'll be ready."

Before he could rise, Violet threw her arms around his neck and laid her head on his chest. "Thank you."

He slowly lifted his hand and patted her on the back. "You're welcome," he said with a catch in his voice. Then he stood and sent Maggie a quick smile before he walked out of the library.

Maggie watched him go, her heart warmed by his kindness toward Violet. He seemed sincere, and she found herself wanting to believe his words and actions matched what he was truly thinking. But was that wise? Was she simply being swayed by a few kind words? Could she truly trust Nate?

Nate changed into his riding clothes without waiting for his valet. He didn't want to give Maggie time to change her mind about joining him on the ride.

He frowned as he buttoned his jacket, recalling her shuttered expression and brief replies. For some reason, she'd pulled back even further today. Was she still troubled by painful memories from the past, or was it something else?

He hustled downstairs, and as he crossed toward the library, his stepmother's voice carried out into the great hall. A jolt of concern made him quicken his steps, but then he stopped and listened by the door.

"The cottage will be much more suitable and give you the opportunity for some privacy." Helen's tone was polite but firm. "Jackson will make the arrangements, and you can move there later this afternoon."

Nate stifled a growl and strode into the library. "Helen."

Her eyes widened for a split second, but she quickly recovered a neutral expression.

"What is this about?" He walked to the middle of the room and faced her.

"I was just explaining that our former housekeeper, Mrs. Potter, recently vacated one of our cottages on the north drive, and I thought it would be more convenient for Mrs. Hayes and her granddaughters to stay there."

Maggie was seated with her grandmother and Violet on the settee. She shifted her questioning glance from Helen to Nate.

Nate pulled in a deep breath, giving himself a moment to calm his voice. "It seems there is a misunderstanding. Mrs. Hayes and her granddaughters will be staying here with us until their shop can be rebuilt."

Helen's forehead creased. "I don't see why we need to house them here when—"

"Please step into the hall." His firm tone made it clear he expected her to comply.

Helen set her mouth in a tight line, then turned away with a swish of her skirt and strode out the door.

"Excuse me, ladies." Nate followed her out, praying for patience.

Helen stopped a few feet from the library door, but Nate motioned for her to follow him across the hall.

He waited until she came closer, then lowered his voice. "I don't want to be unkind, but you must understand our roles have changed."

"What do you mean by that?" The challenge in her expression was unmistakable.

"Your responsibility as mistress of Morningside ended the day my father died. I am the heir, and I will decide who stays in my home."

Helen's eyes sparked. "I have been mistress of Morningside for almost twenty years. You're not married. You have no wife to take up those duties."

Nate steeled himself against her jabbing words. "The fact that I am not married does not mean I am incapable of running this house."

"But the fact that you invited those . . . village people to stay here certainly calls it into question."

Fire flashed through Nate. "Daniel Lounsbury spent the last five years of his life at Morningside transforming our rugged, barren property into beautiful, lush gardens. I see no reason we shouldn't help his family when they're facing difficult times. He was an honorable man, a respected landscape architect, and one of Father's most trusted friends."

She sniffed. "That shows how little you know about the situation."

"What do you mean by that?"

"Just a few days before he died, Daniel Lounsbury tried to blackmail your father."

"Bah! I don't believe that."

"I know you admired the man, but it's true. He betrayed your father's trust."

"Again, I don't believe it. Besides, what could Daniel Lounsbury have known about Father that would give him grounds for blackmail?"

"It won't do any good to dredge up those painful details now. Let it suffice to say, Lounsbury discovered matters that could have caused a great scandal, and rather than being a gentleman and proving his loyalty to our family, he threatened to ruin us."

Nate shook his head. It couldn't be true, could it? Why would Daniel Lounsbury want to destroy his father's reputation? What had he discovered?

Nate focused on Helen. "I insist you tell me the details. I have a right to know."

Helen raised her chin. "Very well. I suppose, as the heir, you ought to know the truth." Her mouth pinched into a painful line. "After your mother died, your father was romantically involved with a woman."

Nate clenched his hands. He was only two years old when his mother died, and he'd spent most of his early childhood in the care of nannies and nursery maids. He remembered very little about his father's response to her death or his actions after.

Helen watched him with an eager, almost haughty expression.

Nate shook his head. "I find that difficult to believe."

"I know it may seem out of character for your father. But they met in 1882 when he traveled to America. She was a stage actress in New York City. Unfortunately, she became pregnant and had a child. A girl."

Shock jolted Nate, and his thoughts flashed back to his father's final requests. He had urged Nate to continue sending money to Natalie Fredrick, a woman in America. Was she the actress or the daughter?

"Daniel Lounsbury discovered your father's secret and threatened to go to the newspapers unless your father paid him a huge sum."

Nate frowned. "You're saying he did it for the money?"

"Yes, of course. He wanted to secure his future. But before Lounsbury could carry out his threats, he drowned, and that put an end to it."

Nate stared at her, trying to process the information. If it was true, he had a half sister in New York, the daughter of an actress. And a man he had greatly admired had planned to betray his father.

"So you can see why I don't want them to stay. I have no idea if Daniel Lounsbury told them about all this, but I certainly don't want to give them an opportunity to take up where their father left off and cause more problems for our family."

Doubts stirred in Nate's mind. He'd always held Daniel Lounsbury in high regard, and it didn't seem likely he would blackmail his father. But why would Helen make up a story like this? He focused on his stepmother. "Even if what you say is true, I don't believe Maggie would ever try to hurt our family."

"That shows how little you know about the situation and about her!" Helen shot a heated glance toward the library. "That girl knows more than she's saying. I can feel it. And I'm sure when the time is right, she'll try to use it against us. She's just as devious and threatening as her—"

"That's enough!" He clamped his mouth closed to gain control of his temper before he continued. "I promised Father I would take care of you and Clara, and I intend to keep that promise. But I will not allow you to poison my opinion of my friends. You must release your controlling grip on matters here at Morningside and be respectful toward my guests."

Helen lifted her chin. "And if I don't choose to obey you?"

He held his gaze steady. "Then you may find yourself occupying that cottage on the north drive."

Maggie gripped the pommel and urged Juniper up the stony hillside. The wind whistled around her and blew her hair back from her face. Nate followed close behind, riding Samson. They reached the top of the hill, and she pulled back on the reins. Her heart lifted as she scanned the view spreading out below them.

Rolling hills painted in shades of green and brown flowed on for miles, with higher mountains rising in the north. Closer to them, a few ancient stone walls separated lush fields where sheep grazed. To the south she could see Heatherton, with the stone church tower rising in the center of the village and Clifton's buildings just outside the village.

Nate reined in his horse and stopped beside her. He turned toward Maggie, his face ruddy from the ride and his hair windblown. "It's quite the view, isn't it?"

"Yes, it's lovely." She brushed a strand of hair from her face. The sun broke through the clouds and sent warm rays across her shoulders. The wind died down for a moment, and the scent of damp grass and yellow gorse filled the air around her. It was a beautiful spot, and he'd brought her here to see it.

Nate looked out across the valley to the high hills beyond. "I thought you'd like it." He looked her way with a winsome smile.

She couldn't help but return the same. The ride seemed to have transported them back in time, to the days when they'd been close friends and spent countless hours exploring the estate together. Those memories, along with the way Nate had stood up to his stepmother and insisted they stay on at the main house, drew her toward him and made her want to let down her guard.

She welcomed his brighter mood for another reason. When they left the stable, he'd seemed subdued and said very little. But as they rode across the estate, she'd asked him about his plans for Morningside. That drew him into conversation and seemed to ease his tense expression, but this was the first time he'd smiled since they'd left.

She shifted her gaze away, not wanting him to see how carefully she observed him. Lifting her hand, she shaded her eyes. "You can certainly see for miles."

"Yes." He pointed to the east. "That faint blue line is the North Sea."

She squinted and scanned the horizon. "I believe you're right."

"Of course I am. I'm a Navy man. I'd know the sea anywhere."

She laughed, and he smiled again, obviously pleased by her response.

"Would you like to get down and stretch your legs for a bit?"

"That sounds like a good idea." She shifted in the saddle, hoping she could dismount without embarrassing herself.

He swung down from his horse with ease and came around on her left side. She lifted her knee over the pommel on her sidesaddle and faced him. He held out his hand, ready to assist her if needed.

She took the reins in her right hand, then placed her other hand on the pommel, turned, and started to slide down. But halfway down she jerked to a stop. With a gasp, she fell backward into Nate's arms.

"Whoa." He grabbed her around the waist.

"My skirt is caught!" She reached for the bunched-up fabric and tried to pull it away from the stirrup.

"Do you need my help?" Nate held her tight against his chest while she struggled with her skirt. His warm breath fanned out across her cheek.

A tremor passed through her, and she silently scolded herself for her reaction and her clumsy dismount. "No, I'm sure I can get it." She tugged harder, her skirt came loose, and she slid to the ground.

Nate loosened his hold, but he didn't let go all the way.

She glanced up at him. Their gazes held, and her heart pounded hard against her ribs.

One side of his mouth pulled up, and a touch of mischief lit his eyes. "I knew that outfit would be perfect for riding."

She narrowed her eyes and sent him a scolding look. "Nate!"

He laughed and released her. "Just trying to lighten the moment."

She pulled in a deep breath, giving herself a second to steady her wobbly legs. She hadn't ridden for years. That must be the reason she felt unsteady. It had nothing to do with her close contact with Nate. Nothing at all.

He placed his hand on her shoulder. "Are you all right?"

"Yes, yes . . . I'm fine." She turned toward him.

"Shall we walk?"

She glanced at Samson and Juniper. "Will the horses be all right?"

He nodded. "We won't go far."

"Then a walk sounds perfect."

His smile returned. "Come on, then."

She fell into step beside him, and they tramped across rough tufts of grass and low heather. Soon they reached a rocky outcropping with a view to the west. Nate held out his hand and helped her climb up a bit higher.

"You can see the manor house from here." He looked down on Morningside, and his expression grew solemn, his eyes troubled.

She studied his face. "What is it, Nate?"

His expression eased. "Nothing for you to worry about."

"Whatever it is, I'd be glad to listen."

His solemn gaze remained fixed on Morningside for several seconds, then he looked her way. "There is something I want to say."

She stilled. "I'm listening."

"I know it's a sore subject, and I won't ask you again if you tell me your decision is final, but would you reconsider and accept the money our family owed your father?"

Maggie bit her lower lip and glanced away, uncertain what answer to give.

"I know you're hoping the insurance settlement will come through soon and you'll be able to rebuild your shop, but until then, the money could be a great help."

It was true their needs were greater now that the fire had destroyed their business and home. They would have no income until the shop was rebuilt.

Grandmother's words came back, reminding her that pride and a lack of forgiveness should have no place in her heart.

"Your father earned that money, Maggie. It would've been passed on to you." Nate studied her face, his expression hopeful. "He was a fine man. I respected him a great deal."

Her throat tightened at the mention of her father, and she had to force out her words. "He was very fond of you as well." She hesitated but then met his gaze. "I think he would want me to accept it."

Nate nodded, looking relieved, then he turned and gazed out into the distance again. "I'm sorry I didn't come to the funeral."

The old wound tore open. She clenched her jaw and looked away.

He placed his hand on her arm. "Maggie?"

She wouldn't look at him. She couldn't.

"You must believe me. I would've come if I'd heard the news in time."

Her gaze snapped back to meet his. "What?"

"It wasn't that I chose not to come. I didn't hear about the accident until almost a week later."

She squinted at him. "How could that be?"

"I was visiting my cousins in Newcastle upon Tyne. My parents never sent word."

"You were with your cousins?" Maggie stared at him, dumbly repeating his words. "You didn't know they'd drowned or that Violet and I nearly died with them?"

"No, of course not. I would've come home immediately."

Maggie blinked, trying to weave this new information into her memories of those painful events. "I thought your parents didn't want you to come to the funeral, and you bowed to their decision."

"If they'd told me to stay away, I wouldn't have listened. But as it happened, I didn't arrive home until you'd left for Scotland."

"Why didn't you answer my letters? I wrote three times asking for your help."

His face darkened. "I never received them."

Confusion swirled through Maggie. Had someone intercepted her letters and kept them from him? Why would they do that? She searched his face, and his sincere expression bolstered her courage. "I asked you to speak to your father and try to find some way for us to stay on at Morningside. But when you didn't come to see us or attend the funeral, I gave up hope."

"Why didn't you stay in Heatherton with your grandmother?"

"She was ill at the time. No one knew if she would recover. As soon as the funeral was over, your parents insisted Violet and I go to my great-aunt's in Edinburgh."

He scowled. "They told me you'd gone to Glasgow."

Maggie cocked her head. "Was that a mistake, or do you think they purposely gave you the wrong address?"

"Oh, it was probably the right address, but the wrong city." Nate shifted his gaze to the mountains. "I was determined to find you, but everyone I met in Glasgow insisted they'd never heard of you or your great-aunt."

Maggie's breath caught. "You went to Scotland to look for us?"

"Yes, I was furious with my parents for sending you away." He turned to her. "As for it being a mistake or intentional, I don't know. But I do remember they did not approve of me spending so much time with your family."

Maggie crossed her arms, the view of the valley blurring before her eyes. Helen Harcourt had always been cool toward her. Last night's reception and Helen's plan to move them to an estate cottage seemed to confirm her opinion had not changed.

Maggie looked up at Nate. "I don't understand. Your father respected mine. We lived at Morningside for almost five years. Why would they care if you spent time with us?"

He shook his head, but she could see him turning something over in his mind. Finally, he looked her way again. "I think Helen was not in favor of my growing attachment to you."

Maggie stilled, unable to even form the question rising in her heart. "Attachment?"

He picked up a stone and tossed it off the cliff. "She warned me I might give you and your family the wrong impression."

The wind rushed up the hillside, and her skirt fluttered around her. Without warning, huge raindrops splattered on the rocks near them.

Maggie gasped and lifted her hand over her head, but it did little to shelter her from the sudden downpour.

"Come on!" Nate grabbed her hand, scrambled down the rocks, and ran back toward the horses. He helped her mount, then swung up into his saddle. "Do you want to find somewhere to wait this out or ride for home?"

She lifted her face to the rain, letting it splash across her cheeks and eyes. Laughter bubbled up from her heart. She turned toward him with a teasing smile. "I'll race you back to Morningside."

His laughter rang out, and they charged off down the hill.

Maggie wrapped the blanket tighter around herself and stepped closer to her bedroom fireplace. The ride back to Morningside in the pouring rain had been exhilarating, but she'd been drenched long before they reached the manor house.

She smiled, thinking of the startled look on the old butler's face when she and Nate walked into the entry hall, laughing and dripping puddles of water all over the tile floor.

Lilly picked up Maggie's wet dress and undergarments from the screen in front of the fireplace and draped them over her arm. "I'll take these down to the laundry and see what I can do."

"Thank you, Lilly. I'm sorry to add to your workload."

"Don't worry about that. I just hope you don't catch a dreadful cold."

"I'm sure I'll be fine." But Maggie shivered, and she could hardly keep her teeth from chattering.

Lilly's brow creased. "Would you like me to bring up some tea?"

"Thank you. That would be wonderful." She grinned at her friend. "I can't very well go down for tea like this."

Lilly's smile broke through. "No, you can't." She turned and started toward the door.

"Before you go, there's one more thing."

Lilly turned and waited.

"This morning, when I was in Mrs. Harcourt's sitting room, I found the journal from ninety-nine."

Lilly's eyes widened. "Did she write anything about the accident?"

"I don't know. Before I could read the entries, Mrs. Burnell walked in."

Lilly gasped. "Oh no! What did you say?"

"I told her I wanted to write a letter to the insurance company and needed some stationery." Maggie tried to squelch the guilty feeling that rose in her heart. She didn't like deceiving the housekeeper or anyone else, but she had to find out the truth.

"Did she believe you?" Lilly asked.

"I think so, but she wasn't happy to find me there."

"Of course not."

"She probably thinks I'm an ill-mannered snoop, but I doubt she suspects why I was looking through Mrs. Harcourt's desk."

"Mrs. Burnell has eyes and ears all over this house. I hope you're not planning to sneak back into Mrs. Harcourt's rooms."

Maggie sent her friend a pleading look. "Do you think you could slip in and bring me the journal? I'm sure no one would be the wiser."

Lilly's eyes widened, and she shook her head. "I couldn't. They'd sack me for sure if they found out I'd taken something from her desk."

"It's not really stealing. We're just borrowing it. I'll take a quick look, then return it as soon as I'm done. No one will know."

"But what if I get caught?"

"Please, Lilly. It's important." Maggie crossed toward her friend and lowered her voice. "Today Nate told me Mr. and Mrs. Harcourt kept the news of the accident from him, then they tried to stop him from finding me in Scotland."

"Why would they do that?"

She thought through her conversation with Nate earlier that afternoon. Did his parents consider her and her family unworthy of Nate, or were they motivated by guilt and hoping to keep Maggie as far from Morningside as possible?

She looked at Lilly. "I'm not sure, but they sent me away and they lied to Nate about where I'd gone."

Lilly raised her eyes to the ceiling, the struggle evident on her face. "Oh, all right. I'll look for the journal, but not until Friday, when it's my regular day to dust and tidy up in her rooms."

Maggie reached for Lilly's hand. "Thank you."

"Just pray I don't get caught." Lilly sent her a serious look. "I'm the only one in my family with an income right now."

Another guilty pang struck Maggie's heart. She was asking a lot of her friend. She wasn't sure God heard her prayers or was inclined to answer, but at least she could try. "Of course I'll pray."

Lilly gave her a quick hug, then slipped out the door.

Maggie watched her go, her stomach sinking. Then she closed her eyes. "God, I'm not sure if You're listening, but if You are, would You protect Lilly and help me find out the truth about what happened to my family?" Her whispered words seemed to bounce off the ceiling, and the silence pressed in around her.

What was she doing? God didn't want to hear from her. She'd closed her heart to Him a long time ago, and she shouldn't expect Him to hear her prayers or do her any favors.

She sighed, confusion and longing tugging her emotions in opposite directions. She might not know if God heard her prayers, but two things were clear: she had misjudged Nate, and she had more reasons not to trust Helen Harcourt.

Maggie pushed the needle through the hem of the new navy-blue dress and took a few more stitches. It was not a very pretty color, but she'd given the light-green fabric to Violet, and Grandmother said she preferred the burgundy.

Maggie leaned back on the settee, reminding herself she should be grateful for the fabric Mrs. Burnell had given them. At least now she would have another dress to alternate with the plain brown one she'd worn since the fire. But it was hard to stir up much enthusiasm for the dull color and stiff fabric.

Violet clomped across the room on her crutches and gazed out the window. "Can we go outside?"

"Not right now, dear." Grandmother cut another length of thread from the spool and struggled to thread her needle.

"But Maggie said we'd take a walk this afternoon."

Maggie looked up from her sewing. "I need to finish this hem, and you need to learn to be patient."

Violet mumbled something under her breath.

"Be careful, young lady." Maggie looked up from her sewing.

Violet swung around. "Oh, I'm just going to supplicate if I don't get some fresh air!"

Maggie stifled a laugh. "You mean suffocate?"

"Yes! It's so stuffy in here. Please let me go outside."

"I'm halfway around the hem. Find something quiet to do until I'm finished."

Violet leaned on her crutches and swung her casted leg back and forth. "Why can't I go outside by myself?"

"For goodness' sake, Violet. The last time I let you go out by yourself, you were hit by a motorcar and ended up with a broken leg."

"That was an accident!"

Maggie lifted her eyes to the ceiling. "Yes, a very serious one."

"All right, girls. Let's not argue." Grandmother set her needle and thread aside and rose from her chair. "These old eyes of mine need a break from sewing. I'll take Violet out for a walk."

"Thank you!" Violet vaulted across the room on her crutches.

"Slow down, dear," Grandmother called and followed Violet into the great hall.

Grandmother's voice faded, and Maggie heard the front door open and close. She looked out the window and watched Violet fly across the front drive and start down the path toward the stable. Grandmother followed at a slower pace. Maggie smiled and shook her head. This was their third full day at Morningside, and Violet's love for horses had grown by leaps and bounds since they'd arrived.

Nate had brought Samson around front again for a short visit that morning. And yesterday he'd taken Violet to the stable to see his other horses. She returned with a glowing face and nonstop descriptions of every horse he owned.

It was kind of Nate to take time for Violet, especially when he had so many other responsibilities. He seemed to understand how hard it was for her sister to be cooped up in the house and weighed down by her cast. He never seemed to tire of her endless questions and chatter; in fact, he seemed to enjoy them.

Maggie released a soft sigh and picked up her needle again. Like Violet, she'd always loved being outdoors. She supposed that came from the hours she'd spent with her father on jaunts around the estate and through the countryside. But after her parents and sister passed away, she'd learned to put her work first and do what needed to be done.

The library door opened, and Clara walked in with several dresses draped over her arm. "Ah, here you are. I've been looking for you."

Maggie stood and greeted Clara.

"I've brought you some dresses." She crossed the room toward Maggie.

A ripple of surprise flowed through Maggie, and her gaze traveled over the colorful assortment: aqua, mint, coral, pink, and a sky-blue dress made from a shimmering satin. "Oh, they're lovely."

"Yes, they are, and I can't wear them since we're in mourning." Clara sighed and laid the dresses over the end of the settee.

Was she giving her the dresses or lending them until Maggie could sew more of her own? Either way, Maggie was happy to accept them. "Thank you, Clara. That's very kind."

"It was Nate's idea. He thought we're about the same size, and since Mother and I will be wearing black for at least a year, someone ought to enjoy them. Feel free to alter them to fit." She gave the dresses one more wistful look and ran her hand over the top gown. "I also gave Lilly some undergarments for you. She put them in your room. And after you decide which dresses you'd like, you can come to my room and choose some hats and gloves."

Maggie wasn't sure which Clara mourned more—the loss of her father or the separation from her colorful dresses. She silently scolded herself for that unkind thought. Clara was only seventeen. She might not have been as close to her father as Maggie had been to hers.

"The pink dress is a few years old and quite a bit smaller," Clara said, fingering the sleeve. "I thought you might be able to cut it down for Violet."

"I'm sure we'll make good use of them all." Maggie ran her hand over the smooth fabrics. Each dress looked beautifully made. Each had ruffles and sashes, and the sky-blue dress had beading on the bodice. If she started on it right away, she might be able to make the needed alterations and wear one of them tomorrow.

Clara glanced around the room and then looked back at Maggie. "May I ask you something?"

"Of course."

Clara sat in the chair opposite Maggie. "If there was a young man who caught your eye and you grew very fond of him, but your parents didn't approve, what would you do?"

Maggie looked up and met Clara's gaze. "I don't have the benefit of my parents' guidance. They passed away four years ago."

Clara's cheeks flushed. "I'm sorry. I knew that. I wasn't thinking of you in particular."

"So the question is . . . hypothetical?"

"Yes, exactly." Clara clasped her hands. "I was just wondering how someone in that kind of situation might . . . overcome her family's objections and convince them she was mature enough to make her own decisions."

Maggie looked down at her sewing and pondered her reply. Clara was obviously talking about herself, and that put Maggie in an awkward position. If she encouraged Clara to follow her heart and take a stand against her family, that would no doubt upset Mrs. Harcourt and most likely Nate. But if she advised her to accept her family's decision, would she destroy Clara's chance for love?

Maggie tucked the needle into the fabric and set aside the dress. "Our emotions can easily override our good judgment when our affections are involved. That's why it's usually wise to listen to our family's advice, especially when it comes to matters of the heart."

Clara's hopeful expression dimmed, and she sank lower in the chair.

"But if the young man is a worthy suitor," Maggie added, "then there's nothing to fear."

"Nate says Mother would never accept Owen." Her eyes widened, and she lifted her hand to her heart. "Please don't say anything to Mother. I haven't told her about him, and I don't want her to know yet."

Clara looked so troubled that Maggie couldn't help but feel sorry for her. "I understand. I won't say anything to your mother."

The light returned to Clara's eyes. "Thank you, Miss Lounsbury."

"Please call me Maggie."

"All right." They exchanged smiles, and memories of conversations Maggie had shared with her sister Olivia sent a bittersweet pang through her heart.

Clara leaned forward. "It's difficult to care for someone and know he cares for you, but then find so many obstacles blocking the path of true love."

Maggie sent her a kind smile. "True love?"

"Yes, I love Owen, and he says he loves me. He hopes to train to be a veterinarian, but right now he is working as one of our gamekeepers, and Nate says that makes it impossible for us to be together."

Disappointment flooded Maggie's heart. How unkind of Nate to rule out Clara's young man simply because he was a member of the staff. Of course, Clara was young, and Maggie had no idea if she and Owen would be a good match. There might be other reasons Nate disapproved. "I'm sorry, Clara."

"Well, I'm not giving up. There must be some way to convince Nate and Mother to accept Owen." She rose and paced across the room. When she reached the window, she spun around and faced Maggie. "I know!" She hurried over and sat beside Maggie. "You could speak to Nate for me."

Maggie stared at Clara. "I don't think that would help your cause."

"Oh, I'm sure you could convince him."

"Whatever makes you say that?"

"I've seen the way he watches you when you walk into the room and how he listens to you at dinner." Clara's eyes glowed. "I think my brother is quite fond of you."

A delightful mixture of hope and embarrassment flooded Maggie's heart. "Your brother and I are old friends, nothing more."

Clara tipped her head and studied Maggie. "Perhaps, but I think there's a possibility for something more if you're agreeable."

Maggie gave a self-conscious laugh and turned away.

"And if you told Nate that Owen Campbell has fine prospects and would be a good match, I'm sure he would listen."

It was tempting to think she might be able to sway Nate to do as she asked. But did she want to test her power of influence by speaking up for Clara and Owen? She didn't know the young gamekeeper, and she wasn't sure about his intentions or character.

But another question rose in her mind, demanding an answer. How did Nate feel about her? She pushed the question away. It was foolish to listen to Clara. The girl was love-struck and imagining romance wherever she looked. Maggie should guard her thoughts and not let them travel in that direction. If she didn't, it would only lead to discomfort and heartache.

She and Nate might be old friends, but she worked in a millinery shop and made barely enough money to care for her grandmother and sister. He was a wealthy gentleman now, master of a large estate, and part owner of the largest engineering firm in the north of England. If he didn't approve of Clara's involvement with Owen Campbell, surely he would never allow himself to be committed to Maggie. Her hope sank like a stone tossed in the lake, and she released a soft sigh.

Love might not be on the horizon for her, but she could speak up for Clara and her beau, and perhaps they would find their happily-ever-after.

Nate led Juniper through the open stable doorway and started up the path toward the house at a gentle pace. He looked up at Violet, perched happily in the sidesaddle. "Are you enjoying your ride?"

"Yes, very much!" Her blue eyes sparkled, and dimples creased both her rosy cheeks.

Mrs. Hayes walked on the opposite side of the horse, keeping a careful eye on her granddaughter. "Be sure to hold on."

Violet gripped the pommel and stretched a bit taller in the saddle. "I can see over the garden wall!"

Nate exchanged a smile with Mrs. Hayes. "Yes, I'm sure you have quite a nice view from up there."

"I can see everything!" She smiled, looking like a little princess riding her noble steed.

He chuckled. Today he'd finally consented to give Violet a short ride on his gentlest horse as long as her grandmother agreed.

"I love Juniper. She's so pretty." Violet leaned forward and ran her hand over the horse's neck.

"She seems to like you as well." He studied Violet for a moment, pondering the fondness he felt for her. He'd never been very close to Clara, but for some reason Violet, with her bright-blue eyes, sweet smile, and sunny outlook, captured his heart. He was afraid he'd have a hard time saying no to anything she asked.

She looked out across the estate with a dreamy expression. "Someday I'll ride all the way to the ocean."

He grinned. "You're fond of the seashore?"

She shrugged. "I haven't really been there."

Nate's steps stalled. "You've never been to the sea?"

"No, but Maggie read me a story once and showed me the pictures."

He looked across at the girl's grandmother. "The sea is only thirty-five miles away. I'm surprised you haven't taken her."

Mrs. Hayes glanced at him over the top of her spectacles. "We're not in the habit of taking holidays at the seashore, or anywhere else for that matter."

"But surely a short visit would not be out of the question."

"Our lives are quite different from yours. We can't often take time away from the shop."

"Of course," he said, regretting his remarks. Then an idea struck, and he looked her way again. "While you're waiting for your shop to be rebuilt, perhaps we could arrange a visit to the seaside."

"Oh no, that's too much trouble. You've already done so much for us. We couldn't ask you to take us to the seashore."

"You didn't ask me. I'm offering."

Mrs. Hayes's soft smile returned. "Well, it's a lovely idea." She looked up at her granddaughter. "What do you think, Violet? Would you like to see the ocean?"

The girl gave an eager nod. "Oh yes, please!"

As they approached the house, Maggie stepped out the front door. When she saw Violet atop Juniper, her brow creased and her gaze darted to Nate.

Before he could reassure her, Violet called out, "Look, Maggie! I'm riding Juniper!"

"Yes, I see." Maggie's cool tone made it clear she was not pleased. She crossed the drive and met them in the middle.

Nate stepped forward. "We kept a slow pace, and I never left her side."

"I should hope not."

His irritation flared, but he reined it in. She was concerned for her sister's safety; still, he was disappointed she didn't trust his judgment. He reached up and carefully lifted Violet down. "There you go."

Mrs. Hayes came around Juniper and passed Violet her crutches. The little girl slipped them under her arms and looked up at Nate. "That was a nice ride, but next time I hope we can go faster."

Maggie flashed him a warning look and stepped closer to Violet.

"Let's make sure your leg is healed first." His reply was more for Maggie's sake than Violet's.

Mrs. Hayes bent and whispered something in the child's ear. Violet looked up and beamed Nate a smile. "Thank you for the ride."

Warmth spread through his chest, easing away his irritation. Even if Maggie didn't appreciate what he'd done, he'd made her little sister happy. "You're welcome, Violet."

"We're grateful for your kindness." Mrs. Hayes nodded to Maggie, as though urging her to add her thanks, but she said nothing. Mrs. Hayes placed her hand on the little girl's shoulder. "Come along, Violet. It's time for us to go inside and finish our sewing."

Violet sighed and sent Juniper one last look. "Good-bye, Juniper. I'll see you soon." She turned and started toward the house with her grandmother.

Maggie watched them go, but she made no move to follow. As soon as they passed through the doorway, she turned to Nate. "I wish you would've asked me before you took Violet for a ride."

"You weren't there, so I asked your grandmother. And it wasn't actually a ride—it was just a short walk from the stable to the front drive."

"But she has a broken leg."

"I lifted her in and out of the saddle. She was perfectly safe."

Maggie looked away, her lips pressed in a tight line.

Why was she upset with him? He'd gone out of his way to fulfill Violet's wish. There was no danger in that little walk. But Maggie didn't seem to see it that way, and if he was going to regain lost ground with her, then he'd better soften his stance. He leaned toward her. "I hope you know I'd never let anything happen to Violet."

Her taut expression eased. "I'm sorry. I don't mean to be cross. I suppose I'm overprotective at times."

He made an effort to see things from her perspective. "If you are overprotective, then I'm sure it's only because you're a caring sister."

"I try to be, though she doesn't make it easy. She takes off on those crutches like a racehorse."

He smiled at the comparison. "I understand. She has a broken leg, and you don't want to see anything like that happen again."

"Yes, but it's more than that." Her voice wavered.

He watched her closely, waiting for her to explain.

"Violet and Grandmother are all I have left of my family." Her voice choked off.

He stilled, struck by her words and the vulnerable look in her eyes. Though four years had passed, she had not fully recovered from the tragedy of losing her parents and sister. And those wounds were easily opened when circumstances reminded her of that terrible day.

A powerful urge to comfort her flooded through him. If only there was some way he could take away her pain and make up for those losses. But he couldn't bring back her family or replace what she'd lost. He'd tried to help by repaying his family's debt and opening his home after the fire. If she would let him, he would do more.

"I didn't realize giving her a ride would upset you." His voice sounded low and husky. "That was certainly not my intention."

She looked away. "I know I shouldn't let it bother me, but it's hard to let go of those memories."

He nodded, searching for something else to say, but no words came.

"I don't mean to be gloomy. I know Violet adores you and your horses." She reached out and patted Juniper's neck.

"I must confess I'm quite fond of Violet as well."

Her weary expression eased, replaced by the hint of a smile.

He motioned toward the stable. "I'm walking Juniper back. Would you like to come along?"

She hesitated a moment, then nodded. "All right."

They set off down the drive, Nate holding Juniper's reins as the horse trailed behind them.

Maggie bent and plucked a little blue flower from the side of the path. "Your sister brought me several dresses."

Nate nodded, glad for the change of subject and that Clara had finally followed through on his suggestion. "That's good to hear."

"When I thanked her, she said it was your idea."

"Well . . . I did mention you'd lost most of yours in the fire."

She sent him a sideways glance. "Thank you."

Warmth infused his chest. "It was nothing, really."

"I wouldn't say that."

Their gazes met and held. A renewed sense of connection flowed between them, making his steps lighter. They both smiled. Maggie looked away first, but the soft glow on her face didn't fade for several seconds.

They reached the stable, and Nate handed off Juniper to the young groom. Maggie glanced toward the house and then back at Nate, looking as though she wasn't sure if she should go or stay.

He definitely wished they could continue their conversation, and he had an idea that might help. "If you have a moment, there's something I'd like to show you."

"What is it?"

"Come with me."

She nodded, and he headed around the side of the stable. He hadn't shown anyone else. And for some reason it seemed right that Maggie should be the first to see what had been delivered that morning.

18

"Where are you taking me?" Maggie's trust in Nate was growing, but small vines of doubt wove around her heart at the most unexpected times, choking it out.

Nate grinned as he glanced over his shoulder, looking unaware of her unsettled feelings. "It's right around here." He motioned toward a beige canvas tarp covering something quite large. "Can you guess what it is?" He lifted his eyebrows, his face bright with expectation.

It didn't look tall enough to be a new carriage, but it was definitely something about that size. "Is it some sort of wagon?"

"You're close, but not quite right."

She lifted her hands. "I have no idea."

"Very well. I'll show you." He grabbed the tarp and pulled it off, revealing a shiny new motorcar.

Maggie gasped and lifted her hand to her mouth. "Oh, Nate!"

"It was just delivered a few hours ago. What do you think?"

It had a dark-green exterior and padded black leather seats. "Do you know how it works?"

"The man who delivered it showed me the basics. It doesn't seem too difficult. But I think I'll need a bit more practice before I take anyone else with me."

The memory of the accident in Heatherton and Violet's broken leg stirred her concern. "Motorcars can be dangerous. I hope you'll be careful."

Nate nodded and walked around the vehicle, inspecting it carefully. "I'm sure I can learn what's needed to be a safe driver."

She studied him for a moment. "I never would've guessed you'd order a motorcar."

"I didn't."

She lifted her eyebrows.

"Apparently my father ordered it a few months ago, before he got sick, and it was just now delivered."

She pulled in a quick breath. "Oh, I'm sorry. I didn't realize."

"It's all right. It was a surprise to me as well. When it first arrived, I told the deliveryman it was a mistake." He reached out and touched the steering wheel. "But then he showed me the paperwork with my father's signature."

"So you decided to keep it?"

"Yes. They're all the rage in London, and I can see how it would help us get around much more quickly."

Maggie glanced toward the stable. "But you'll keep your horses and carriages, won't you?"

"Yes, of course. I'm not sure Helen will even ride in a motorcar."

Maggie stiffened at the mention of Helen's name. Nate's stepmother avoided Maggie and her grandmother, but her disapproval of them seemed to permeate the atmosphere of the house.

Nate cocked his head. "What is it?"

She waved away his question. "Nothing."

He frowned. "Has my stepmother said something to upset you?"

"She has barely said a word since she tried to send us to that cottage."

"I'm sorry. I know she can be difficult, but if she ignores you, it's probably for the best." He gave a dry chuckle. "I wish she would ignore me."

"You don't really mean that, do you?"

"There has never been a close bond between us, and she can't seem to accept the changes that have occurred since my father passed away."

"You mean you taking on your father's role?"

"Yes, she's reluctant to release her grip on running Morningside, and she's even tried to influence my decisions about Clifton."

"It sounds like she is making things difficult for you."

He sent her a small smile. "Don't worry about me. I'm determined to ride out the storm and make a new way forward for us all."

Maggie studied Nate's expression, trying to read the meaning behind his words. If only she could tell him what she suspected and enlist his help in her search for evidence. But what if he didn't believe her? What would she do then?

Friday morning after breakfast Maggie settled in the drawing room with the sewing basket and the dresses she needed to alter. Clara was taller than Maggie and fuller in the waist and above. With a sigh, Maggie opened the sewing box. She had always been slim with modest feminine curves, taking after her mother. She told herself it didn't matter, but lately she found herself wishing she filled out her dresses the way Clara did. Perhaps then Nate might—

She clamped a lid on that thought and plucked a needle from the pincushion.

The drawing room door opened, and Lilly looked in. "May I have a word with you, Maggie?"

"Yes, of course." She set aside her sewing and rose from her chair.

"My goodness, Lilly, there's no need to be so formal." Grandmother sent her a quizzical look. "Come in and join us."

Lilly's eyes widened. "Oh no, I can't . . . I have to get back to work."

"It's all right. We understand." Maggie hurried across the drawing room and out the door, tugging Lilly with her. "Did you find Mrs. Harcourt's diary?" she whispered.

Lilly nodded. "I put it in your room, bottom drawer of the dressing table."

"Thank you!" Maggie squeezed her hand.

"Oh, Maggie, I feel like a thief!" Lilly looked over her shoulder and leaned closer. "Look through it quickly and return it as soon as you can."

"I will. I promise." Maggie's heart rate picked up speed. If Helen Harcourt had written something about the accident in her journal, Maggie might find the proof she needed.

"I have to go back upstairs. Mrs. Burnell will have my head if she finds out what I've been up to." Lilly glanced toward the door to the servants' stairs at the end of the great hall.

"She won't find out. I'll make sure of it." Maggie squeezed Lilly's hand again. "Thank you. I'll never forget what you've done."

"Just be careful," Lilly whispered, then she hurried across the great hall and up the stairs.

Maggie returned to the drawing room and took up her sewing, though she longed to run upstairs and start reading Helen's diary.

"What did Lilly want?" Grandmother snipped the thread on the side seam of the pink dress they were cutting down for Violet.

Maggie lifted one shoulder. "Oh, she just wanted to tell me about something she found."

Grandmother's brow creased. "What are you girls up to?"

Maggie sorted through the spools of thread and ignored her grandmother's question.

"Maggie?" Grandmother's voice held an edge that could not be ignored.

She slowly lifted her head and met Grandmother's gaze. "I can't say, at least not right now."

Concern shadowed Grandmother's eyes. "Be careful, my dear. Secrets can wield a double-edged sword."

Maggie plucked the spool of thread from the basket. "Yes, they can, but sometimes they're necessary."

Grandmother studied her a moment more, then resumed her sewing. Maggie released a slow, deep breath. She wished she could tell her grandmother what she suspected, but she couldn't, not until she had the evidence in hand.

The morning passed at an achingly slow pace. Maggie didn't feel she could slip away until after luncheon. Violet begged to take a walk in the garden, and Grandmother agreed to go along.

"Come with us, Maggie," Violet called as she vaulted across the great hall on her crutches and headed toward the front door.

"You two go ahead." Maggie glanced up the stairs. "I have some reading I'd like to do."

Grandmother's steps slowed, and she looked at Maggie with a quizzical frown. "Reading rather than a walk? That doesn't sound like you."

Maggie avoided meeting Grandmother's gaze and hurried up the steps. "Enjoy your time in the garden."

She slipped into her room and quietly closed the door. Though she had not seen anyone in the hallway, she crossed the room on tiptoe and pulled open the lower drawer of the dressing table. Mrs. Harcourt's brown leather diary lay on top of the pile of folded handkerchiefs. Her hand trembled as she took it out and sat on the bench.

She ran her fingers over Helen's name embossed in gold on the cover, then opened to the first page:

This is the private diary of Helen Harcourt. Begun the first day of January 1899.

Maggie stilled. This was it. If Mrs. Harcourt was behind the boating accident, Maggie would find the proof here—she was sure of it.

Nate glared at the note from Geoffrey Rowlett and tossed it on his desk. The finely worded reply could not veil the man's disdain for Nate or his suggestion that they meet privately before the next board meeting to talk through the issues with the workers and try to avoid a strike.

He'd spent several hours with Mr. Waller, discussing the projects and working conditions at Clifton. They'd even convinced Miss Larson to give them access to the financial records for the past three years. He'd gathered enough facts and figures to support the workers' cause. But how could he follow through on his promise to Reverend Samuelson and the men unless he convinced Rowlett to listen to his conclusions and soften his stance?

He would have to contact Samuelson, give him the news, and discuss their next move.

Helen strode into the library and crossed toward his desk. Though it was almost two o'clock, it was the first time he'd seen her that day. "Good afternoon, Helen."

She looked down at him with a furrowed brow. "There is a serious situation we must address."

Nate steeled himself. "What is it?"

"Your sister has been sneaking out at all hours to see a young man, and he is our junior gamekeeper!" Her lips curled in disgust. "I want you to speak to her immediately and put a stop to it."

He forced himself to remain calm and sat back in his chair. "I've already spoken to her."

"What?" Helen pulled in a sharp breath. "Why didn't you say anything to me? I had to suffer the embarrassment of hearing about it from my maid!"

Nate held his gaze steady but didn't reply.

"Well? What did you say to Clara?"

"I told her you would not approve and she should break it off." He almost regretted his words now, knowing they put him in the same camp with his stepmother.

"Was she convinced?"

Nate released a deep breath. "No, she was not."

"Then you must send the young man away, and do it today."

Nate wasn't sure which he disliked more, his stepmother's demanding nature or her meddlesome ways. He leveled his gaze at her. "I don't believe that's necessary."

"Not necessary!" Helen's face flushed, and she looked as though she might burst a blood vessel. "Do you want your sister's reputation ruined?"

"Of course not, but Clara is quite taken with him." He could hardly believe he was arguing for his sister's cause, but he couldn't let his stepmother think he would simply fold and do whatever she demanded.

"Poppycock! She is young and easily influenced."

"Clara is almost eighteen, the same age my mother was when she married my father."

Helen's eyes practically shot fire at him. She never liked to be reminded his father had been married before and she was his second wife . . . his second choice. "That has nothing to do with this situation."

"I think it reminds us some young people are mature enough to make an excellent choice at a young age."

Her nostrils flared. "I will not have my daughter involved with a game-keeper!"

"She says he has plans to study to become a veterinarian."

"That's not the life I want for Clara! You must send him away before the news circulates and our family's name is dragged through the mud!"

"Really, Helen, I think you're overreacting."

"I am not overreacting! This is a very serious matter. And this proves you know very little about the rules of society. I shouldn't be surprised. You've been away in the Navy for years, serving with rough, vulgar men."

Nate rose to his feet. "That's enough!" His voice boomed. "You may insult me, but I will not allow you to slander my men or fellow officers."

Helen froze and stared at him.

"I may have been away fighting in a war, but I know enough about families and society to realize you are overstepping your bounds."

She straightened. "You never liked the way your father confided in me or the way we shared the responsibility of running Morningside. But now that he's gone, you want to rip that all away from me."

"Things have changed, Helen. If you want to remain at Morningside, you must accept that."

"Or what, you're going to cast me out, send me to that dreadful old cottage? How can you treat me like this?"

He pulled in a calming breath, determined to maintain his temper no matter how much she goaded him. "I mean no disrespect. I'm simply trying to carry out my duties as head of our family and master of Morningside. And as such, I am the one to decide who stays and who goes."

Her eyes widened and her face paled.

He was referring to Owen Campbell, but from her shocked response it was clear she thought he meant her. He debated if he should explain his meaning but decided it might be helpful for her to remember who his father had left in control.

"Very well." She lifted her chin. "But remember this, if Clara's hopes for a happy future are ruined by your neglect, you will have no one to blame but yourself." With that, she whirled away and marched out of the library.

Nate sank back onto his chair, closed his eyes, and ran his hand down his face. What an exasperating woman! How had his father put up with her for so many years?

He might not like his stepmother's controlling nature, but for his sister's sake he must find a way to work through these issues and do what was best for the family. But what steps should he take? That was the question.

Maggie turned the page and continued scanning the entries in Helen's diary. She mentioned attending luncheons and dinner parties, trips to visit friends in Cumbria and London, and occasional meetings with the Women's Missionary Aid Society in the local parish hall, but nothing about Maggie's parents or anything out of the ordinary—until Maggie found an entry dated 13 August 1899.

R. came again this afternoon. Thank heavens Mr. Harcourt was away. I thought after his last visit, eight months ago, that would be the end of it and I would never see him again. But I should not have believed him. This time, I have one week. That's all the time he'll give me.

Maggie stared at the page. Was R. the man her father saw with Mrs. Harcourt in the woods a few days before the accident? If not, who was he? What did she mean about him giving her one week? The first part of the entry sounded like she might be describing a lover who reappeared after an eight-month absence, but what did the rest of it mean?

A knock sounded at her door.

She gasped, slammed the journal closed, and shoved it in the open drawer. "Who is it?"

"It's Nate."

Her heart thumped hard in her chest as she crossed the room and opened the door. Nate stood in the hallway, his brow creased and a look of unease in his eyes.

Panic flashed through her. Did he know what she was doing? Had he come to confront her? She straightened, ready to do battle. "Yes?"

"I'm going out for a walk, and I wondered if you might like to join me."

"A walk?" Her voice came out soft and a bit shaky.

He sent her a questioning look. "Yes, I have something I wanted to ask you." He glanced down the hall and then back at her. "But I'd rather do it in private."

"All right. Just a moment." Questions thrummed in her mind as she took her sister's shawl from the chair by the door and wrapped it around her shoulders.

They walked downstairs and out the front door without any more conversation. The day was cool, but the sun peeked through the clouds, highlighting the bright-green grass and tulips along the drive.

They started down the path toward the garden and stable, and he glanced her way. "Have you had any opportunities to talk with Clara? I mean, besides at meals?"

"We've spoken a few times." Her last conversation with Clara came to mind. Although she hadn't promised Clara she would speak to Nate about Owen Campbell, she'd meant to. Perhaps it wasn't too late to help Clara and Nate come to an understanding about her young man. But she would have to tread carefully.

Nate clasped his hands behind his back as he walked and frowned at the gravel path. "She has developed an interest in a young man, but my stepmother is not in favor of it. She insists I put an end to it immediately. But I'm not sure that's the best way to handle things."

"What do you think of the young man?"

"I don't really know him. I met him just once. We spoke only briefly when I found them together." He nodded to the left. "Behind that hedge."

Maggie's cheeks warmed. "I suppose that was awkward."

"They were only talking, but yes, it was uncomfortable for them and for me. I sent him on his way and asked Clara for an explanation. She was quite upset and ran off in tears."

Maggie sighed, unsure what to say.

"I probably should've handled things differently. And now Helen is adamant that I speak to Clara again, but I'm not sure what to say." He glanced at her. "I thought I might ask your advice."

He wanted her opinion, and he was humble enough to ask for her help? Her heart warmed. "I'd be glad to help you if I can."

"Thank you." His tense expression eased a bit. "Here's the question. How can I convince her to be reasonable and see the situation more clearly?"

"And what exactly do you want her to see?"

"First, that she should listen to her family. And second, that she should not give her heart away to someone she barely knows."

Maggie nodded, encouraging him to continue.

"She says she loves him, but she's young and impressionable, and I doubt she understands the true meaning of the word. And even if she does have strong feelings for him, she shouldn't choose a husband based on feelings alone. There are much more important things to consider."

"Such as?"

"What kind of man is he? Will he be able to provide for her? Would he be a loving husband and father? Does he have a good reputation, a strong faith, and proven character? What about his family and background?"

"Those seem like reasonable questions to ask."

"She says he hopes to study to be a veterinarian, but how do I know if he will follow through on that plan?"

Maggie wasn't sure how to answer that question.

"Since my father is gone, I'm responsible for her." He grimaced. "Along with her mother, of course."

"And you agree with your stepmother? Owen Campbell is not a worthy suitor for Clara?"

He stopped and looked at her, a hint of accusation in his eyes. "You knew about this?"

She gave a reluctant nod. "Clara told me about him the day she brought me the dresses."

"I see." He frowned. "And you didn't think you ought to tell me?"

She considered that for a moment. "Clara wanted me to speak to you and try to convince you to let Owen call on her. But I wasn't sure if that was wise." He was obviously disappointed, and she regretted her decision to remain silent. "I'm sorry. I should've spoken up sooner."

Nate shook his head. "It's all right. I don't blame you for not wanting to get involved."

"If I thought there was any real danger, of course I would've come to you right away."

He nodded, seeming to accept her explanation.

"Also, I wasn't sure if I should be involved in a private family matter."

"Well, Clara and I have both confided in you, so you are involved whether you want to be or not." He walked on a few more steps, then said, "I'd welcome any words of wisdom you have to share."

She pondered the situation as they entered the enclosed garden.

"I could dismiss Campbell and send him away, as Helen suggests." Nate continued, "But if I do, Clara will be hurt and angry. I could face that, but what if she runs off and tries to follow him?"

"Do you think she might?"

"She's always been headstrong, so I have to consider the possibility."

Maggie hoped Clara would not make that choice. The consequences would be painful for everyone. "If you send him away or insist Clara never see him again, you might push her to defend her position and draw them even closer. But if you listen to what she has to say with an open mind and show a bit of sympathy for her feelings, I think she might be more open to your concerns."

"I can't pretend I'm in favor of her involvement with Campbell."

"No, I don't suppose you can be . . . especially when you don't know him."

"Are you suggesting I get to know him?"

She smiled. "I think a conversation with Owen Campbell might help you discern his character and intentions, and you could help him see the seriousness of his actions. But I don't think you should do it in an overbearing or threatening way."

"Hmm, I'll have to think about that."

Maggie considered the situation for a few more seconds. "I think the best chance you have to influence Clara is to come alongside and treat her with sympathy and respect. When she knows how much you care about her and her future, then she'll be more likely to listen to what you have to say."

Andrew crossed the garden toward them. "Excuse me, sir. Mr. Hendricks of the Portsmouth Insurance Company has arrived. Mrs. Hayes would like Miss Lounsbury to return to the house to meet with him."

Nate nodded. "Very good."

The footman turned to go.

"Thank you, Andrew," Maggie added.

He looked back. "You're welcome, miss."

"We should go in. I'm sure you're anxious for this meeting." Nate motioned toward the house.

Maggie hesitated. Nate had been humble enough to ask her opinion about his sister's predicament. Perhaps it was time she asked for his help as well. "Will you join us when we speak to Mr. Hendricks? I'd appreciate your input about the insurance settlement."

He gave a quick nod, looking pleased. "Of course. I'd be glad to. Hopefully, we can make sure the matter is settled in your best interest."

"Thank you." She could barely hold back her smile as they walked to the house. Not only had he confided in her, he'd also welcomed her advice on an important family matter. Now she would show him the same measure of respect and listen to his advice concerning their conversation with Mr. Hendricks.

Maggie shifted in her chair and studied Mr. Hendricks, the insurance adjustor, while he wrote one of her answers in his notebook. He was a stout man of about forty-five, with a drooping brown mustache, and he wore a wrinkled gray suit.

They were seated in the library with Grandmother and Nate. Mr. Hendricks had asked them a series of questions about the fire, their business, and the contents of the shop and their private rooms, all without giving his opinion or offering any conclusion.

Maggie glanced at the clock, then shifted her gaze to Mr. Hendricks. The interview seemed to be coming to a close, and he had yet to tell them how much money they could expect to receive in the settlement. She didn't want to appear presumptuous, but they needed an answer. She looked at Nate, hoping he might read her thoughts and ask the question for them, but he remained silent while he watched Mr. Hendricks.

Mr. Hendricks wrote a few more lines in his notebook, then looked up. "If you could give me the names of a few witnesses who were there at the time of the fire, I can contact them to verify these details."

Nate leaned forward slightly. "I was in the village when the fire broke out."

Mr. Hendricks's eyebrows rose, and he sent Nate a skeptical look. "Were you?"

"Yes, I had just finished a meeting with Reverend Samuelson at Saint Peter's and walked to the Red Lion to pick up my horse when a man charged in, yelling there was a fire at Neatherton's. I immediately thought of Mrs. Hayes and her granddaughters and went to warn them. Neatherton's was already ablaze when I ran past, and men were gathering to fight the fire. I knocked on Mrs. Hayes's door and encouraged them to leave the shop for their own safety."

Mr. Hendricks wrote as Nate spoke, then looked up. "So you can verify the fire started at the neighboring shop?"

"Yes." Nate thought for a moment and added, "Once the ladies were safely away, I returned to their shop and collected a few personal items for them."

Mr. Hendricks's brow creased. "What kind of personal items?"

Nate shot a quick glance at Maggie before he answered. "Miss Lounsbury's mother's Bible, her sister's shawl, and a box holding money from their shop."

Mr. Hendricks glanced at Maggie. "I didn't see any of those items mentioned in your letter."

Irritation coursed through Maggie. Was he trying to trap her? "No, they were saved from the fire, so there was no need to list them."

"Ah yes." Mr. Hendricks looked up. "Is there anyone else who could verify the story you've told me?"

She didn't like him calling it a story, but perhaps giving him the names of other witnesses would settle the matter. "Mrs. Fenwick owns the teashop directly across the street from our shop. She was with us while the men fought the fire. And of course you can speak to Mr. Alvin Neatherton and his son, Joseph."

Mr. Hendricks jotted the names in the notebook. "All right. I believe that's all the information I need." He rose from his chair and slipped his notebook into a small leather case.

Grandmother adjusted her glasses, looking weary. "Thank you for coming, Mr. Hendricks."

Maggie's breath caught. That was all her grandmother was going to say? They couldn't let the man go without pressing him for some answers.

She stood and faced him. "Mr. Hendricks, I'm sure you can understand how eager we are to make plans to rebuild the shop and open for business again. When do you think we can expect to receive the payment of our claim?"

"Well now, I'm not sure about that. It will take some time to collect all the facts and interview the witnesses." He studied her through narrowed eyes. "You'd be surprised how many people fabricate their stories, hoping for a larger settlement."

Nate rose to his feet and towered over Mr. Hendricks. "I hope you're not suggesting Miss Lounsbury and Mrs. Hayes are being dishonest in their statements."

Mr. Hendricks tugged his vest back in place. "No, sir. I'm simply stating the facts and letting the ladies know I have to verify the details they've given me before we can move ahead."

"I'm sure when you do you'll find everything exactly as we've told you."

Mr. Hendricks tucked his leather case under his arm. "Even eyewitnesses who see the same event may report it in a very different light."

"Perhaps, but the facts remain unchanged." Nate held his gaze steady. "I'm confident the witnesses will confirm the events as we've relayed them, and when they do, I'm sure you'll see these ladies receive a quick and generous settlement to their claim."

Mr. Hendricks's face flushed, and he eyed Nate a moment longer. Then he placed his bowler hat on his head and turned to the ladies. "Mrs. Hayes, Miss Lounsbury, I'll be in touch."

Maggie could barely contain herself until he disappeared out the door. "Oh, what a pompous man! He practically accused us of lying. I can't believe someone like that holds our future in his hands."

Grandmother rose from the settee. "If that were true, we would be in a sorry situation. But we've no need to worry."

Maggie stared at her grandmother. "How can you say that?"

"Our future is in the Lord's hands, Maggie. And He's proven Himself faithful time and again. I'm sure He'll look out for us in this matter as well."

Maggie lifted her hand. "If that's true, why did He allow the fire in the first place?"

Grandmother and Nate exchanged a glance. It looked as though they shared a private understanding Maggie did not grasp, and it frustrated her to no end.

"Honestly, I don't know how you can accept what Mr. Hendricks said or the way he said it. I think we ought to write a letter to the company and report him to his superiors."

Nate's mouth tugged up at one corner. "I don't believe that would help your case." Was he amused by her comments or simply not as anxious as she was about the situation?

Maggie crossed her arms and tried to let go of her frustration, but her stomach continued to churn. "I suppose we can't very well report him, not if we want our case to be settled any time soon. We'll just have to wait to see what happens."

Nate crossed to stand beside her. "Perhaps there is something else we can do."

Maggie looked up at him. "And what would that be?"

"We could go ahead and make plans to rebuild your shop, with the hope and expectation your claim will be upheld and the funds will be forthcoming."

Grandmother chuckled. "Now that sounds like a fine idea."

Maggie rubbed her forehead and suppressed a groan. No matter what they said, the outcome of their claim was still undecided and very much in Mr. Hendricks's hands. How could they dismiss the man's rude behavior and be confident everything would be resolved in their favor?

She supposed her grandmother's optimism sprang from her faith. Was the same true for Nate? He had mentioned prayer and God's guidance a few times in their conversations, but she had assigned it to custom or his upbringing.

But as she thought of how Nate conducted himself, the way he spoke and treated her and others, she saw a definite similarity to her father's character and actions—and he had been a man of strong faith.

From the time she was a little girl, her father had spoken to her about the wonder and beauty of God's creation and His love and care for all His creatures.

When she was young she had taken her father's faith and actions for granted, but when she was fourteen, there had been an incident that made her think about it more deeply . . . She and her father had been on one of their jaunts across the estate and were climbing to a particularly high, rocky point. Maggie was out of breath but pushed on to stay close to her father as he climbed higher.

Father turned and looked over his shoulder. "Come on, Maggie girl, we're almost there."

"I'm coming." Her leg muscles burned, but she wasn't about to complain or give up, not when they were so close to the top.

Father set off again, using his walking stick to help him up the steep trail. She puffed along with the help of her own walking stick, slowly making her way among the rocks and crags. Suddenly, off to the left, she heard a soft bleating. Turning her head, she strained to listen. After a few seconds it came again.

"Father, did you hear that?"

He stopped and glanced back at her. "What?"

"Some animal is crying. I think it's down there." She pointed to the left over the cliff.

They stopped to listen, and Maggie turned toward the cliff. Had she truly heard an animal, or was it just the sound of the wind rushing up the mountainside?

The cry came again, soft and faint.

Father's eyes lit up. "I hear it!" He scrambled across the rocks and looked over the side of the cliff. Maggie followed more slowly, making her way between the boulders and over the scratchy heather.

Father knelt and leaned out over the edge, searching the rocks below.

"Father!" Maggie grabbed his jacket and held on tight, fearing he would slip over the side.

He sat back. "It's all right, Maggie. I'm not going to fall. Trust me."

She searched his face, then loosened her grip. He turned back toward the cliff and continued his search. A tired bleat reached them once more. Maggie crept forward, looked over, and spotted the small lamb caught between a scraggly bush and the rocky hillside about fifteen feet below. "There he is!"

"Yes, I see him." Father slipped his knapsack off his shoulders and took out a rope.

Maggie's stomach tensed. "What are you going to do?"

He met her gaze. "I'm going down after him."

Maggie's heart lurched. "You can't! It's too steep."

"I'll be all right." He placed his hand on her shoulder. "You hold tight to this end of the rope. I'll wrap it around the lamb, and we'll bring him up together."

Maggie glanced over the side once more, and a dizzy wave washed over her, making her head swim. "Are you sure?"

"Yes. He needs our help."

"But you could fall."

"If we don't rescue him, he'll die." Father sent her a tender smile. "Say a prayer and trust the Lord. We're on His mission of mercy. I'm sure He'll help us."

Maggie nodded and tried to swallow past the dreadful lump in her throat.

"Have faith, Maggie girl." He patted her cheek, then he turned and slowly lowered himself down the side of the cliff. Maggie scooted closer, lay on her stomach, and peered over the edge. Small bits of rock fell away as Father took another step down, searching for the next foothold.

She pressed her lips together and held her breath. What would she do if her father fell? How would she rescue him? Her father's reminder to pray rose in her mind, but she didn't know what to say.

She recited formal prayers at church and joined the family for mealtime prayers, but she rarely spoke to God on her own. There were those few times when she'd disobeyed her mother and been sent to her room to wait for her punishment. Those pleas for mercy had rarely been answered, and she'd been punished anyway.

She pushed those confusing thoughts away. They were certainly in trouble now and needed God's help. She squeezed her eyes tight. *Please, God, take care of my father. Help him rescue this lamb, and please bring them both back up safely. Amen.*

She opened her eyes and scanned the scene below.

Her father searched for the next handhold as he descended closer to the lamb. The frightened animal continued to issue pitiful cries that twisted Maggie's heart. Finally, her father reached the stranded lamb and quickly secured the rope around him. He looked up and called to her, "I'm going to climb up, but I need both hands. You'll have to pull up the lamb. But be careful. Don't get too close to the edge, and be sure of your footing."

Maggie hopped up. "I'm ready!" She tightened her grip on the rope and pulled it up a few feet. The lamb was surprisingly heavy. She took a step back, securing her feet behind a large rock, and pulled up the rope another foot.

"Take it slow," her father called.

From where she stood, Maggie couldn't see her father, but she trusted his voice, adjusted her grip on the rope, and pulled slower.

"That's the way." A few seconds later Father called, "Hold it right there."

Maggie locked her arms, straining against the pull of the rope, and waited.

Finally, Father's head appeared above the edge of the cliff, his face red and his cap askew, but he sent her a broad smile. Then he climbed up over the edge and grabbed hold of the rope. "I've got it now. Come help me, and we'll bring him up over the top."

Maggie scrambled back to her father's side, and together they lifted the lamb up over the rocks beside them.

The lamb squirmed and bleated. Maggie knelt next to him and ran a hand over his soft wooly coat. "Is he hurt?"

"It doesn't seem so, but let me take a look." Father did a quick assessment while Maggie held the rope tight. "He looks all right. Let's see if we can lead him down to the rest of the herd."

Father held out his hand, and Maggie handed him the rope. The frisky lamb tugged ahead. After they'd gone a few steps, Father had to adjust the rope around the lamb's neck and midsection. "He seems like a strong little fellow."

About ten minutes later, they reached the bottom of the trail and started across the sheep pasture. The lamb bleated and tugged hard on the rope again.

"It seems our little friend is eager to return to his family."

Maggie grinned and nodded. "Shall I untie him?"

"Yes, I think he's safe now."

She quickly loosened the rope, and the lamb leaped away and ran across the pasture toward a group of ewes. They welcomed him back with bleats that echoed up the hillside.

Maggie couldn't help but smile as she watched the happy reunion. "I'm glad he's safely home with his family."

Father nodded, his eyes shining. "So you think it was worth the risk to rescue him?"

"Oh yes. I'm glad we did."

"You weren't so sure at first, up on the trail."

"I was afraid you'd fall and I wouldn't know how to save you."

"Faith is the antidote to fear, Maggie. I'm not talking about wishful-thinking kind of faith, but genuine trust and belief in God's goodness and love."

Maggie tried to understand what he meant, but she wasn't certain.

"You must never let fear stop you from doing what the Lord calls you to do." Father's eyes glowed with sincerity. "Especially when it's in the service of those who cannot help themselves."

She swallowed and nodded, taking his words to heart.

"Maggie?" Grandmother's voice brought her back to the moment. "My goodness. You seem to be miles away."

"I was just . . . remembering something that happened a long time ago."

Grandmother sent her a curious glance.

Nate stepped into her line of vision. "I hope it was a pleasant memory."

"Yes, it was." Looking at Nate, she couldn't help but sense his likeness to her father.

"What do you think of Nate's idea?" Grandmother asked.

"I'm sorry. I didn't hear what he said."

"I'm going to Heatherton tomorrow afternoon, and I thought you might like to come along. I hope to meet with Reverend Samuelson, then we could make some inquiries and see about rebuilding your shop."

Maggie's heart lifted. "That sounds wonderful. Thank you, Nate."

He nodded. "That way, when the insurance money arrives, you'll have a plan in place and be ready to move ahead."

Grandmother stepped closer and linked her arm through Maggie's. "That's a fine idea, isn't it, Maggie?" Before she could answer, Grandmother continued, "I can already see us in our new shop, greeting our customers and friends and making the loveliest hats."

Maggie patted Grandmother's hand. She hoped Nate and Grandmother were right and the insurance company would soon provide enough money to put them back in business . . . but what if their claim was denied? And what if the money from Nate wasn't enough to rebuild? How would she provide for her grandmother and sister?

She pushed those thoughts away for now. Perhaps it was time she put some of that faith her father spoke about into practice.

Maggie didn't have a moment alone to read more of Helen Harcourt's diary until the next morning after breakfast. Grandmother took Violet up to the bedroom to do a fitting of her new pink dress. Maggie followed them up, then slipped the diary into the folds of her dress and took it outside to a quiet spot in the corner of the garden. She settled on a wooden bench in the shade of a cedar tree and opened to the page she'd marked with the ribbon attached to the spine.

A chill ran through her as she read the entry for August 13 again. Who was the mysterious R. Helen had mentioned? And what could the reference to "one week" mean? She had no idea how to find the answers to her questions without asking someone else. But whom could she trust?

She turned the page to the next entry and glanced at the date.

Shock jolted through her, and she looked away. Clenching her jaw, she turned back and focused on the diary again.

22 August 1899

We received the most disturbing news today. Daniel Lounsbury, his wife, and eldest daughter drowned in Tumbledon Lake this afternoon. We are stunned and can hardly believe it's true. The staff were visibly shaken when they were told, and one of the maids broke down in tears. Mr. Harcourt is shocked and grieved for the loss of the man he believed was his friend.

The timing of it is certainly surprising. It is a tragedy to be sure, but it means Daniel Lounsbury will no longer be able to carry out his threat against us, and for that I am glad.

The two younger daughters survived, and now we must decide what to do with them. Margaret, the older girl, is seventeen, but she is too young to take care of her much younger sister on her own. They have a grandmother in the village, but she is ill and elderly and cannot take them. There is an aunt in Scotland. Sending them to her seems the most likely course of action. We've sent one of the maids to stay with them tonight.

Mr. Harcourt considered sending a message to Nathaniel and calling him home from Huntsford Hall, but I convinced him to wait. I do not want to interrupt his visit. My hope is that he will become better acquainted with his second cousin, Amelia. She is an accomplished young woman of marriageable age and would be a good match for Nathaniel. It's time he made his choice and settled down. I've had more than enough of his free-spirited gallivanting around the estate with no purpose or direction.

The Lounsburys have no other family nearby, so it is left up to Mr. Harcourt to see that funeral arrangements are made. I can't even think about it and doubt I will attend. The sooner we get past this dreadful incident and put it out of our minds, the better.

Clara says she is growing too big for her pony and is begging for a new horse for her fourteenth birthday. I told Mr. Harcourt to ask Mr. Kennedy to start the search. Her birthday is less than a month away, and I don't want her to be disappointed.

Tears stung Maggie's eyes, but she blinked them away. How could Helen Harcourt write about the deaths of her parents and sister one moment and the next about ordering a horse for Clara? How could she be so coldhearted?

Maggie shook her head. As much as Helen's careless words hurt, Maggie must set aside her emotions and look at the facts.

Scanning the entry once more, she frowned. Helen seemed surprised about the boating accident. That cast doubt on her being the one behind it. But she could have written the entry that way to avoid suspicion. She seemed to write freely about her feelings and actions, but perhaps it was all done to cover up her shocking crime.

Her mention of Maggie's father carrying out a threat against them matched what Maggie had read in her father's journal. Maggie considered her father's determination to report what he'd seen to Mr. Harcourt a warning rather than a threat, but Helen was motivated by the fear of being found out and her desire to continue deceiving her husband. While her father was motivated by honor and loyalty to his friend and employer.

But that day on Tumbledon Lake had changed everything. Daniel Lounsbury, his wife, and eldest daughter had perished before the deadline he'd given Mrs. Harcourt, and Helen's secret had drowned with them.

Except for the entry he'd written in his journal. But that had burned in the fire, and now Maggie was the only one who knew the truth about Mrs. Harcourt and her disloyal and deceptive ways.

Maggie reread Helen's statement about being glad she didn't have to worry about Maggie's father's threat and released a shuddering breath. How selfish and disgusting! But there was nothing there to prove she had plotted to drown Maggie's family.

She scanned the paragraph about Nate, and the ache in her heart eased a bit. His stepmother's words confirmed everything Nate had told her. He was not at Morningside the day of the accident, and his parents had not called him home after. The reason for that was clear as well. Helen hoped he would choose Amelia as his future wife.

Had Nate considered proposing to her? As far as Maggie could remember, Nate had never mentioned her, except when she had attended his father's funeral. The image of the pretty blonde standing with Clara by the carriage after the graveside service rose in Maggie's mind, and a tremor passed through her.

Did Helen still hope that Nate would marry Amelia now that he'd returned to Morningside?

An unexpected ache swelled in Maggie's chest, and she lifted her hand to her heart. Why was she even considering those questions? Nate was a friend who had stepped forward to help her and her family in their time of need. She could not expect anything more from him, no matter how much she wished the situation were different.

That thought surprised her, but she couldn't deny the truth any longer. Though she'd tried to guard her heart, her attraction to Nate was growing stronger every day. The more time she spent with him, the more she admired him, and the more she wished—

Enough! She rose from the garden bench and strode back toward the house, tucking Helen Harcourt's diary into the folds of her skirt again. It was past time she reined in her emotions and put romantic thoughts of Nate out of her mind. If she didn't, she was bound for heartache.

20

Nate adjusted his cap, lowered his goggles, and glanced across at Maggie. "Are you ready?"

She looked over her shoulder to the motorcar's backseat, checking on her grandmother and Violet. The older woman slipped her arm around Violet's shoulders and nodded.

Maggie turned back with a smile. "We're ready if you are."

She looked quite fetching as she settled back on the padded bench seat next to him. Her blue dress was almost the same color as her eyes, and she'd tied a filmy white veil over her broad-brimmed hat and knotted it under her chin. A few strands of her dark-brown hair peeked out from under her hat and curled around her face. Her cheeks were flushed pink, and she gripped the armrest on her side.

"You've nothing to fear. I've been practicing every day. You're quite safe."

She eased her hand into her lap. "I'm sure you wouldn't suggest we ride along with you unless that was true. Still, it's my first time in a motorcar, and I'm not quite sure what to expect."

"I'd say you're in for a great surprise." He took hold of the steering wheel and signaled the young man standing out front to turn the crank. The engine roared to life. Nate adjusted the choke and slowly pressed the gas pedal. The car rolled forward, he shifted gears, and they set off down the drive, headed for the iron bridge over the ravine.

It was a perfect day for a drive. The roads were dry, and only a few clouds were scattered across the sky. Once they passed the main gate and set off on a relatively straight road, he would take the motorcar up to twenty miles per hour. At that speed they would reach Heatherton in a matter of minutes.

The wind rushed past as they picked up speed, and Maggie lifted her hand to her hat. Her smile spread wider, and she looked across at him with shining eyes.

"You like it?" he called over the roar of the motor.

"Yes! It's wonderful!"

He grinned and then glanced at the backseat. Violet waved and sent him a gleeful smile, and Mrs. Hayes looked almost as delighted as her granddaughters. He chuckled as he focused on the road again.

Bringing Maggie, her grandmother, and Violet to Morningside had been an excellent idea. Their presence lifted the gloomy atmosphere that seemed to shroud the house. He looked forward to his conversations with Maggie, their rides across the estate, and their strolls through the gardens. Those times reminded him of how they used to take walks through the countryside with her father, collecting plant specimens and observing the birds and animals. Those were happy memories he was glad to call to mind.

But the most pleasing turn of events was Maggie's growing openness toward him. He rarely saw the cool formality she'd shown the first few days of her stay. She seemed to have overcome her ill feelings toward his father, and that eased his mind.

There was still a strained distance between Maggie and his stepmother, but he wouldn't blame her for that. Helen had been cool and unpleasant since the day they'd arrived. She continued to make her feelings obvious most evenings at dinner by excluding Maggie from the conversation. And when she did speak to her, her remarks were brief and condescending.

He tried to ease the situation by bringing Maggie into the conversation when he could. She answered his questions politely and seemed to appreciate his efforts, but he could see his stepmother was not pleased.

His thoughts shifted to Helen's private comments to him about Maggie's father and his attempts to blackmail Nate's father.

Had Daniel Lounsbury actually planned to extort money from his father? It seemed very unlikely. Mr. Lounsbury had always spoken highly of Nate's father and shown him the utmost respect. But if it wasn't true, why would Helen relay the story? What could she gain by blackening the name of a man who'd been dead for almost four years?

He shook off those disturbing thoughts. Until he knew more about the situation or had it confirmed by someone besides his stepmother, he would not credit the story or hold it against his memory of Daniel Lounsbury. More important, he certainly would not allow it to color his opinion of Maggie. Even if by some strange circumstance it happened to be true, it was in the past and had nothing to do with her. She was innocent of any plot against his family and deserved much better treatment than she had been receiving from Helen.

He hoped to make up for his stepmother's behavior and unkind remarks by helping Maggie and Mrs. Hayes find a respected builder who could be trusted to repair their millinery shop. It would take time to clear away the rubble, raise the walls and roof, and finish the interior. Then they would have to restock their shelves before they could open for business again.

The money Maggie had finally agreed to accept from him would get them started, and when the insurance claim was settled, they'd have more than enough to finish the job.

A frown creased his forehead. As soon as the shop was repaired, their stay at Morningside would end. Maggie would move back to the village and take up her life where it had left off . . . and he didn't like the sound of that at all.

Maggie felt almost breathless as the motorcar flew down the road, whizzing past hedgerows and fields dotted with sheep. What a thrill to see it all and be seated next to Nate on her very first motorcar ride.

She stole a glance at him, and her lips tipped up in a smile. He looked quite handsome wearing his motoring cap and goggles, his face red from the wind. Though he was a relatively new driver, he handled the motorcar with ease and confidence. He'd proven his skills by guiding them safely around several rough spots in the road and avoiding a collision with a stray sheep.

As they approached the village, he downshifted and slowed the motorcar to a respectable speed. She relaxed back in the seat, glad he would not race through the village like that careless man who had struck and injured her sister.

Nate adjusted his gloved hands on the steering wheel and glanced her way. "Where would you like to go first?"

"Could you take us to Mrs. Fenwick's Teashop? I'm going to ask her to watch Violet while we meet with the builders." She hoped their friend wouldn't mind caring for her sister while Maggie, her grandmother, and Nate took care of their business in the village.

Nate nodded and rounded the next corner. Three women ran past, followed by an older man quickly limping along with a young boy of nine or ten. Maggie scanned their anxious faces. Why were they in such a hurry?

The sound of shouts rose in the distance, and Maggie shot a glance at Nate.

"Something's not right." He lifted his goggles and scanned the street as two more women hurried past. He pulled the car to the side of the road but left the engine idling.

Martha Hemsworth, the druggist's wife, scurried toward them, carrying a large wicker basket over her arm. "Oh, Maggie, there's trouble coming!"

Maggie sat forward. "What is it, Martha? Why is everyone running?"

The plump woman fanned her red face. "There's a crowd of men gathered on the village green." She wagged her head toward the center of town. "One of them is shouting and stirring up the others."

Nate's brow furrowed. "What's the issue?"

"I don't know the particulars, but I'd stay away if I were you." Martha looked past them, down the street. "I have to get back to the shop before Mr. Hemsworth comes looking for me. I don't want him to get caught in the middle of that mob."

No sooner had she finished speaking than a group of men strode around the corner and marched toward them. Some hooted and shouted, while others waved their fists in the air. Maggie counted at least a dozen men, but they kept coming and she lost count.

Martha gave a wide-eyed yelp and ran off down the street.

"Hold on!" Nate wrestled with the gears, looked over his shoulder, and started backing down the street. The angry crowd surged forward and surrounded their motorcar. Nate had no choice but to stop or run over some of them.

He jerked up the hand brake and rose to his feet. His eyebrows drew down in a V as he scanned the crowd. "What is the meaning of this?" His commanding tone startled some of the men, and a few stepped back, but the rest of them continued shouting and waving their arms, blocking any way of escape.

A young man in a shabby brown coat and plaid cap stepped forward, turned to the crowd, and lifted both arms. "He wants to know our meaning! Let's tell him, boys!"

"We're the men from Clifton!" another man shouted. "And we're on our way to make the owners listen to our demands!" A rowdy cheer rose from the swarming crowd.

Maggie gripped the armrest and shot an anxious glance at Nate. Did the men realize Nate was one of those owners?

Nate shook his head. "They won't listen if you come like this, shouting your demands and frightening the good people of this village."

A stout man in a green coat moved forward and jabbed a finger toward Nate. "That's Harcourt! He's on the board!"

Catcalls, boos, and hisses emanated from the group.

"Ha! Look at the mighty lord, riding around in his fancy motorcar!"

"What gives you the right to live like a king while we can barely afford to feed our children?"

"How do you expect us to provide for our families on the measly wages you pay?"

"We're tired of working ourselves into an early grave for men who care nothing for us!"

Maggie's gaze darted from one man to the next as she tried to see who shouted each phrase, but the shifting of the crowd and overlapping voices made it nearly impossible.

Nate lifted his hand, trying to calm the men. "I am Nathaniel Harcourt, yes, and I'm a member of the board at Clifton, but this is not the time or place to air your grievances."

"Why not?" "Are you afraid to hear what we have to say?" "This is as good a time as any!" "You just don't want to listen!"

Nate lifted his hand again. "I've only recently returned from serving in the Navy and taken over my father's position at Clifton, following his death. I understand there are serious issues that need to be addressed. I've met with some of your leaders to hear your grievances, and it's my hope—"

"That was weeks ago! Nothing has changed!" The man in the green coat stepped forward again. "You and Reverend Samuelson promised you'd speak to the board for us, but you've not kept your word."

"That's not true. I did speak to them, but we haven't come to an agreement on what's to be done."

Loud boos, hissing, and shouting drowned him out.

"We're tired of waiting for changes!" The man in the green coat lifted his fist. "Three men were badly burned today when their welding equipment exploded."

Nate gripped the upper edge of the windshield and stared at the man.

"Ha! You don't even know what happened, and you're a member of the board!"

Nate glared at him. "I'll look into it."

The man huffed and shook his head. "That accident wouldn't have happened if your equipment was safe and the men weren't worn out from working night and day." He stepped forward and gripped the motorcar's door frame. "We're done waiting, Harcourt! You tell the board to meet with us face to face, listen to our demands, and make those changes, or we're going to strike!"

The crowd exploded with more shouts and wild cheering. Some slapped the shoulders of the men next to them, while others pounded on the front and sides of the motorcar.

Maggie leaned toward Nate, her heart thudding in her throat.

"Take that message back to those money-hungry tyrants!" "We're done letting you lord it over us!" "Listen to us, or we'll close down Clifton!"

"Gentlemen, gentlemen! This is no way to conduct yourselves!" Reverend Samuelson strode forward through the crowd, and the men stepped aside. When he reached Nate's side of the motorcar, he turned and faced the men.

"Nathaniel Harcourt has heard your complaints in meetings with your leaders, and he stands with you in your cause. He is your friend, not your enemy. But if you persist in this kind of reckless behavior, he may change his mind, and with good cause."

The crowd died down, and several of the men looked away with guilty glances.

"Now, I urge you to remain calm, pray for your friends who were injured today, and encourage your leaders to pursue a peaceful resolution." Reverend Samuelson looked around the group with a stern expression. "I'm willing to meet with your representatives Monday evening, seven o'clock, in the church hall." He looked at Nate. "Will you join us?"

Nate considered it for a moment, then nodded. "I'll be there, ready to listen and respond to your questions and concerns."

"Very good." Reverend Samuelson turned to the crowd. "You've all heard Mr. Harcourt's reply. I trust you'll accept that and return to your homes."

Maggie held her breath and searched the men's faces. Would they listen to Reverend Samuelson and leave peaceably?

A few at the back of the crowd turned and trudged off. Others glanced around, waiting to see what their friends would do.

"Come on, boys." An older man with a long gray beard slapped another man on the back. "I'm paying a visit to the Red Lion before I go home. Who wants to join me?"

Most of the crowd shuffled off, but the man in the green coat and two others lingered, hard expressions lining their faces.

Reverend Samuelson nodded to the man in the green coat. "John Palmer, you have something to say?"

"I do." Palmer turned his steely gaze on Nate. "One of the men who was burned today is my brother, Todd. He's a fine, God-fearing man with a wife and six children. He's worked for Clifton for eighteen years."

Nate studied Palmer's face. "I'm sorry to hear that."

"Sorry isn't going to heal his burns or feed his family. What are you going to do about that?"

A muscle in Nate's jaw rippled. He glanced at Reverend Samuelson and then looked back at Palmer. "I'll see that he gets the best medical care possible and make sure his family has financial help."

Palmer huffed. "The management at Clifton isn't known for taking care of the injured or their families."

"You have my word. I'll see to it, even if the funds have to come out of my own account."

Palmer's eyes burned with doubt and resentment. "I'll believe that when I see it." He spun on his heel and strode off down the street. The last two men fell into step beside him.

Nate slowly lowered himself to the seat and turned to Reverend Samuelson. "Thank you. Your timing and choice of words couldn't have been better."

"I'm glad I heard the shouting."

"So am I." Nate gave a solemn nod, then turned to Maggie. "I'm sorry about all this. Are you all right?"

"Yes, I'm fine." Maggie glanced at Grandmother and Violet in the backseat.

Grandmother sat forward. "I was praying the whole time. I didn't know how God would answer, then He sent Reverend Samuelson at just the right moment."

Maggie wasn't sure if her grandmother's prayers or the reverend's good hearing were responsible for him coming; either way, she was grateful.

Nate and Reverend Samuelson spoke for a few more minutes, discussing how they would help the injured men and their families. When they'd agreed on a plan, Reverend Samuelson bid them good day and walked toward the church.

Nate released the hand brake. "I'll take you to Mrs. Fenwick's, but I think it's best if we go the back way."

"Yes, it sounds wise to avoid the center of the village."

Nate backed up a short distance, then turned into the narrow alley that ran behind the shops on that side of the street. They met no one in the alley, and Maggie was glad of it.

"There it is." She pointed to the back entrance of the teashop.

Nate left the motor idling. He walked around to open the rear passenger door for Grandmother and Violet and helped them down. "Why don't you wait inside the shop? I'll park the motorcar and come back for you."

Grandmother handed Violet her crutches and guided the girl toward the rear entrance of the teashop. Nate opened Maggie's door.

She glanced down the alley. Was it safe for him to go on alone? "Why don't you leave the motorcar here?" She took his hand as she stepped down.

"I don't want to block the way. Someone else might want to get past."

Maggie nodded but held tight to his hand. "Please be careful."

A hint of surprise flickered in his eyes, followed by a warm smile. "Don't worry. There's a shady spot in the lot behind the church. I'll park there and be back in a few minutes."

Maggie swallowed and nodded, but she still felt uneasy. "Perhaps I should come with you."

He shook his head. "I'll be fine, and I'd rather you wait inside the shop where I know you're safe."

"All right." She tightened her grasp for just a moment, then slipped her hand from his and walked toward the teashop. As she opened the door, she looked back. He stood in the alley, watching her and waiting to see that she was safely inside. She lifted her hand and he did the same, then he climbed into the motorcar and drove away.

Maggie sighed and closed the door, concern for Nate clouding her thoughts. She admired the way he'd stood up to the men from Clifton, but what if they were watching and waiting for a chance to vent their anger on him in a more dangerous way? Her heart clenched at that thought.

"Maggie?" Violet swung toward her. "Mrs. Fenwick says I can have a scone. Is it all right?"

She forced her worries away and focused on her sister. "Yes, it's fine. Be sure to thank her."

"I will." Violet hopped away.

The scent of fresh-baked apple cinnamon scones floated toward Maggie as she followed Violet into the front room of the shop.

Her grandmother sat at a table with Mrs. Fenwick while two younger women scurried around preparing tea for them. Did she have enough time to sit down and enjoy a cup before Nate returned? Either way, she would buy something for him as a way to say thank you.

She studied the baked goods in the glass case, trying to imagine what he would like, and decided on the apple cinnamon scones.

It wasn't much, but she wanted him to know she appreciated his willingness to drive them to the village and help them today. He didn't have to do that. Yet he'd taken time out of his busy schedule and ended up facing an angry mob.

She glanced out the window, and a shiver traveled down her back. All was quiet now, but how long would that last? Would Nate and Reverend Samuelson be able to calm the men and convince the board to listen to their grievances, or would a strike break out and spread anger and turmoil through the whole village?

An hour later, Maggie stood with Nate and Mr. Horace Ledbetter in front of what remained of her grandmother's millinery shop. She and Nate had finished interviewing the first builder, Mr. Robert Daniels, thirty minutes earlier. He came highly recommended, but he was a grim, hard-faced man who made Maggie decidedly uncomfortable. She hoped this second builder would be a better fit.

Mr. Ledbetter rubbed his chin as he scanned the front wall's charred stones, then he took a small pad of paper and pencil from his jacket pocket and made a few notes. "Now, don't you worry, Miss Lounsbury. We can set things right for you in no time at all. And when we're done, your shop will look as good as new, even better, or my name is not Horace Ledbetter."

Maggie liked the man's friendly, confident manner. He would certainly be easier to work with than Mr. Daniels.

Nate motioned toward the scorched stones and charred timbers. "Can you give an estimate of how much it will cost to complete the reconstruction?"

Maggie nodded, eager to hear what he'd say.

Mr. Ledbetter tipped up the brim of his hat and scanned the burned storefront once more. "Well now, I'll need to look inside and take some measurements. That should give me a better idea of what's needed." He started toward the front entrance. Nate and Maggie followed.

When they reached the doorway, Mr. Ledbetter noticed Maggie behind him. "There's no need for you to soil your dress, walking through all the ash and soot. I can look things over."

"All right." Maggie stepped back, relieved she didn't need to climb through the burned debris.

Nate pushed open the scorched door. "I'll go with you."

"If you'd like." Mr. Ledbetter nodded to Nate.

Gratefulness warmed Maggie's heart again, and she sent Nate a smile as he followed Mr. Ledbetter through the doorway.

"Watch your step," the builder called. "There's broken glass and nails."

Maggie crossed her arms and watched them disappear into the shop. The lower story was faced with stone, which still stood, though blackened by the fire. But the wooden upper story had burned and fallen in on top of the rest. She sighed and shook her head. What a waste.

The sound of horses' hooves down the street drew her attention, and she turned. A wagon pulled by two strong bays and filled with building supplies stopped in front of what remained of the neighboring shop.

Joseph Neatherton hopped down from the driver's seat, and his father slowly climbed down after him. Joseph lifted his hand to Maggie and walked toward her.

She met him halfway. "Hello, Joseph. How are you?"

"I'm well." He nodded to her, his eyes shining. "It's good to see you, Maggie. I was worried about you after the fire. I didn't know where you'd gone. Then Lilly wrote and told me you were staying at Morningside."

"Yes, the Harcourts have been kind." At least that was true of Nate, though Helen remained cool and unpleasant. Maggie put aside that thought and focused on Joseph again. "I was concerned about you and your father as well."

"We're all right. We're staying with my uncle on his farm near Millcrest until we can move back to the shop." Joseph looked toward the scorched shell of the building. "We've got our work cut out for us. There's no doubt about that. But we're ready to take it on." He looked her way again. "And what about you and your grandmother? Will you rebuild?"

"Yes. That's why I'm here today. Mr. Ledbetter is looking around inside now. He's going to give us an estimate."

Joseph crossed his arms. "He's a good man. I'm sure he'll do a fine job for you."

"That's good to hear. Several others have recommended him as well."

"So the money from your insurance claim came through?"

"Not yet, but we have some savings. That will help us get started."

"It's lucky you had some money put away." Joseph glanced at his father.

Was it luck or divine provision? She dismissed that thought. "When the insurance money arrives, we'll be able to finish up and restock the shop." She tried to infuse her voice with confidence, but an unsettled, anxious feeling stirred in her heart again. Would they receive the money that was due them? Were her grandmother's prayers and optimistic feelings enough to justify hiring a builder and starting the work? Nate seemed to think so.

She glanced at the wagon stacked with wood. "It looks like your claim was settled in record time."

"No, it was denied."

"Why? What did they say?"

"It seems Father missed making some payments recently, and they don't look too kindly on that."

"Oh, Joseph, I'm so sorry!" Maggie shook her head, her heart aching for her friends.

"Father was beside himself when the letter arrived. He has spent his whole life working in that shop, and my grandfather before him."

She reached out and touched Joseph's arm. "If there's anything we can do to help you . . ." She wasn't sure what practical help she could give, but he certainly deserved her sympathy.

He laid his large, rough fingers over hers and looked into her eyes. "Thank you, Maggie. That means a lot to me."

Heat flooded her cheeks, and she slipped her hand away. She must be careful not to give Joseph a reason to hope for more than friendship.

"We'll be all right," Joseph said. "My uncle James owns a lumber mill. He gave us that load of wood and some tools and supplies and refused to take more than a few pounds for them. And last week several friends came and helped us clear away the rubble."

"I'm glad to hear it."

"Rebuilding may take longer than we'd like, but we'll open our shop again, even without the insurance company's help."

"With a determined spirit like that, I'm sure you'll finish in no time." Maggie's gaze shifted to Mr. Neatherton. "Your father must be very grateful for all you're doing."

Joseph watched his father give orders to two young men who were unloading the wood from the back of the wagon. "He's not one to offer thanks often, but I think he's glad for my help."

"I'm sure he is."

Joseph glanced at Maggie again, his smile returning. "We'll be working here most days, but I could come to Morningside to see you on Sunday afternoon."

Maggie's breath caught, and she tried to think of a reply that wouldn't hurt her friend's feelings. "Oh, Joseph, that's a long way for you to come."

"I don't mind. The trip wouldn't take more than two hours if I borrowed one of my uncle's horses."

"But Sunday is your only day to rest. I'd hate to see you spend it riding back and forth to see me when we'd only have time for a short visit."

He reached for her hand. "Please, Maggie. I miss you more than I can say."

Her tongue suddenly felt thick and stuck to the roof of her mouth. She'd known Joseph cared for her, but she didn't think he would declare his feelings today, not right here in the street where she had no easy way to avoid giving him an answer.

Nate bent and picked up a small piece of melted blue-and-white pottery. Had it been a piece of a china plate or part of a teacup transformed by the fire into this colorful round nugget? He tucked it into his pocket to show Maggie. Perhaps it would be meaningful to her.

"Can you tell me how large the front room of the shop should be?" Mr. Ledbetter lifted his bushy dark eyebrows and poised his pencil over his notepad.

"I'm not sure of the dimensions. Shall I ask Miss Lounsbury?"

Mr. Ledbetter held up his hand. "Not yet. I'll jot down a list of questions to ask her after we're finished in here."

Nate nodded, then he clasped his hands behind his back and looked into the remains of the glass display case. It was nothing more than a pile of melted metal and glass now. He was glad Maggie had not come in. It was difficult enough to look at the ruined shop from the outside. If she had to walk through this charred and melted mess, it would be even more painful.

Mr. Ledbetter climbed over several blackened beams and examined the south wall. He sighed and shook his head, then made a note on his pad.

"Now that you see the condition of the interior, how long do you think it will take to finish the job?"

"It's hard to say." Mr. Ledbetter used his foot to push aside one of the charred beams. "We'll have to clear away all this wreckage before we can start rebuilding." He pointed to the front wall. "Some of that stone can stay, but other sections will have to be knocked down and replaced before we can do much on the inside or add the upper story."

"Do you think two months or maybe three?"

Mr. Ledbetter frowned. "That might be enough time, if everything goes smoothly, but that's rarely the case. More likely it will take four months, possibly five, if we run into any problems or delays. And you can almost count on that."

Nate glanced around once again. "I understand."

Maggie might not be happy to hear her shop wouldn't reopen until late summer or early fall, but he wouldn't be sorry to have her stay at Morningside longer than he'd expected. Surely that would be enough time to strengthen their friendship and affection for each other.

Thank You, Lord. It's like You to take the painful loss from the fire and turn it around for good. Please give me wisdom and show me how to help Maggie through this challenging time. Soften her heart toward me, strengthen our friendship, and if it's Your will, open the door for more.

A ripple of surprise traveled through him. Was that what he was truly considering, a deeper, long-lasting commitment to Maggie? Of course he'd always been fond of her and admired her spirit and determination, her caring heart, her creativity.

That summer before he'd left Morningside to take up his naval commission, his feelings for Maggie had begun to change from friendship to affection. But then her parents and sister died, and the years of simmering conflict between him and his father and stepmother came to a head. He'd left home determined to make his own way in the world and put the past behind him.

All those years he'd kept his memories of Maggie locked away, and he thought that was all they were: fond memories to be taken out and enjoyed when he was feeling low or alone . . . until he returned to Morningside and their paths crossed again. Now he was beginning to believe there might be a future for them.

"I think I've seen everything I need for now." Mr. Ledbetter's words pulled Nate out of his reverie. The builder tapped his pencil on his notepad and motioned toward the entrance. "After you, sir."

Nate made his way toward the front door, eager to rejoin Maggie and discuss the builder's projections. When he stepped outside, he spotted Maggie a few yards away, engaged in conversation with a tall blond man.

Recognition flashed through Nate, and his shoulders tensed. The look on Joseph Neatherton's face reflected longing . . . and much more.

Nate set off toward them. When he was only a few feet away, Joseph reached for Maggie's hand and leaned toward her with a beseeching look.

Alarm shot through Nate. "Maggie!" His voice rang out louder than he'd intended.

She turned, her eyes wide.

Nate's gaze darted from Maggie's face to their clasped hands.

Her cheeks flushed, and she slipped her hand from Joseph's. Was she embarrassed to be caught holding Joseph's hand, or was she upset with Nate for interrupting them? She straightened and met his gaze. "Are you and Mr. Ledbetter finished inside?"

"Yes, and he has a few questions for you." Nate glanced over his shoulder. Mr. Ledbetter stood in front of the shop making notes on his pad.

"I'll go speak to him now." She turned back to Joseph. "Excuse me."

Joseph nodded to Maggie. As she turned and walked away, he shot a perturbed glance at Nate.

Nate met Joseph's challenge with one of his own. He walked a few steps toward Joseph and lowered his voice. "I'd suggest you keep a proper distance from Miss Lounsbury to protect her reputation and your own."

Joseph squinted at Nate. "Just because your family owns a big estate and a fancy manor house, that doesn't make you lord over everyone else."

"I'm not suggesting it does. I'm simply looking out for Miss Lounsbury."

"And what gives you the right to do that?"

"I've taken Miss Lounsbury and her grandmother and sister into my home and offered them my protection."

"Protection . . . is that what you call it?"

"Yes, that's exactly what it is. And I take my role very seriously."

Joseph stepped toward Nate, determination glinting in his eyes. "You'd better watch yourself, Harcourt."

"What do you mean by that?"

"I mean Maggie has had enough hurt in her life, losing her parents and sister and struggling to provide for her grandmother and Violet. And now she's lost her home and business. She doesn't need you breaking her heart."

Nate clamped his jaw. He would not let Joseph's words shake him, but they stung all the same. "You should keep your own warning in mind."

Joseph glared at him. "I've looked out for Maggie ever since she came to Heatherton, and I don't intend to stop now." He narrowed his eyes. "If you do anything to hurt her, I'll—"

"I would never hurt Maggie."

"You'd better not or you'll find me on your doorstep more than ready to settle the score." Joseph shot him one more heated glare, then turned and marched over to join his father and the other men unloading the wagon.

Nate's pulse pounded in his temples as he replayed Joseph's words. He might not like the way Joseph issued the warning, but the fact remained, Maggie had been hurt in the past and she was in a vulnerable position now.

He glanced her way, and the reality of his responsibility toward her became clear. If he wasn't ready to declare his feelings and propose, then he must guard his words and actions. He should think of her like a sister and treat her as he would Clara.

But could he ever be satisfied with that?

He shifted his gaze from Maggie to Joseph. Did she love him? Had she set her heart on marrying Joseph Neatherton? Was the young boot maker just waiting to propose until his shop was rebuilt and he had a steady income again?

A powerful ache filled Nate's chest, and he shook his head. He must not let that happen. He set his jaw, determination coursing through him. No matter the obstacles or how long it took, he would win Maggie's heart and show her that he was worthy of her trust and love.

Lilly sat in the servants' hall and stared at the mesmerizing flames dancing in the fireplace. Another Sunday had come and was almost gone, and she had not seen Rob. That morning, she'd attended church with her father and brother, then shared a meal with them at the Red Lion. After she bid them good-bye and they set off for her uncle's farm, she stopped in to visit Rob's family. She spent almost two hours with Mrs. Carter, Jane, and MaryAnn and had a pleasant visit, but all the while she'd been missing Rob. Finally, she took the lonesome walk back to Morningside.

She fingered the ruffle on the bottom edge of her white apron. Rob must be home by now. If only she could have stayed in the village long enough to see him, but if she had, she would not have returned in time to stay in the good graces of Mrs. Burnell and Mr. Jackson.

Andrew strode into the servants' hall. He spotted her, and a teasing smile lifted the corners of his mouth. He crossed the room and handed her a folded piece of paper.

"What's this?"

He lifted his brows. "A note for you."

"Who is it from?"

He leaned down and lowered his voice. "If you don't want to cause a stir, I'd suggest you read it outside in the courtyard."

She pulled in a sharp breath and rose from her chair. "Thank you," she whispered, then walked out of the servants' hall. One glance at her name written on the folded note and her heart leaped. It was Rob's writing. She was sure of it.

The sun had dipped behind the house when she stepped outside, but a rosy glow spread across the courtyard as she opened the note and read his message.

I'm waiting for you just past the main gate. Come and see me if you can. But if it would cause you too much trouble, don't come. I'll understand.

Love,

Rob

She slipped the note into her apron pocket, and with a quick glance over her shoulder at the empty courtyard, she started down the path toward the main gate. She walked at an easy pace, as though she was just out for an evening stroll. No one would question her for that, would they?

Her heartbeat quickened as she neared the tall stone gate. Would he still be waiting? Would she finally be able to hear his voice, see his dear face, and know he was all right?

Insects hummed a quiet evening song as she passed through the open gateway. Her steps slowed, and she scanned the trees on the right and the left.

"Psst, Lilly. Over here."

She turned, following Rob's voice, and spotted him just beyond the tree line, wearing his dark blue jacket and his cap pulled low over his eyes. A large brown horse stood beside him, and he held the reins in his hand. She hurried toward Rob, and they ducked into the trees, letting the cool, shady woods conceal them from view.

Rob reached for her hand. "I missed you, Lilly. I hope you're not upset with me for coming."

Warmth spread across her cheeks, and she smiled. "Of course I'm not upset. I'm always glad to see you."

Relief flashed in his eyes. He pulled her close for a quick hug, then stepped back. "I heard about the fire at your father's shop. I rode over there before I came up." He shook his head. "Have you seen it?"

"Yes, we walked by after church." She swallowed and tried to banish the awful memory of the burned wreckage. "Such a terrible waste."

"I'm awful sorry."

His sympathetic words eased away some of the pain. "I keep telling myself to be thankful. Father and Joseph could've been killed. Still, Father is terribly upset about losing the shop."

"Of course he is. That's his life's work gone up in smoke."

Lilly nodded. She'd been shocked when she'd seen her father that morning. He looked like he'd aged several years since the fire, and Joseph looked discouraged as well.

"Will they rebuild?"

"Yes, they've already started. My uncle and some friends are lending a hand."

"That's good to hear." He wove his fingers through hers. "And how are you holding up? I hope the news of the fire hasn't been too much for you."

His tender touch and gentle words made her eyes sting. "I'm all right, but I've been worried about you, working such long days and having no time off on Sunday."

He rubbed his thumb over the top of her hand and smiled at her. "You've no need to worry about me. I'm young and strong, and I'm keeping my head above water just fine."

She returned his smile, the burden she'd been carrying feeling a bit lighter. "How is your father?"

His smile faded away, and he gave his head a slight shake. "He's out of bed for a short time each day, but his mood is dark, and it's hard on my mother."

Lilly had noticed the tired lines around Mrs. Carter's eyes during her visit. When Lilly asked her how she was doing, Mrs. Carter waved away her concern and said all was well, but Lilly could tell she carried a burden. Maybe it was more than just concern for her husband's healing. Perhaps she'd heard the talk about mounting tensions at Clifton as well.

Lilly looked up at Rob. "Maggie told me some of the men from Clifton were marching through the village, shouting and making trouble."

Rob's brow creased, and he looked away.

A ripple of fear zinged down her back. "You weren't with them, were you?"

"I went along, but I stayed in the back of the crowd."

She pulled her hand from his. "Oh, Rob! How could you join a mob like that? Maggie said they forced Mr. Harcourt to stop his car, and they were making threats. It scared her and her grandmother and sister. And Mr. Harcourt wasn't too happy either."

"It wasn't as bad as that. We were just marching through the village, and Mr. Harcourt came driving toward us. Some of the men surrounded the car, and there was a discussion, but Reverend Samuelson came out and made everyone settle down and listen."

Her panic mounted. "Did Maggie see you? Did she know you were there?"

He shook his head. "I was far from the motorcar. She didn't see me."

"Are you sure?"

His mouth pinched into a tight line. "There were at least fifty men, and as I said, I was in the back."

Lilly huffed out a breath and pointed at his chest. "Robert Carter, if you get yourself sacked for stirring up trouble, you'll have no one to blame but yourself."

"I had to go, Lilly. They would have called me a coward if I didn't."

She crossed her arms and turned away. Didn't he realize if he lost his job, not only would their dreams be destroyed, but his family would suffer as well? "There are worse things than being called a coward."

He laid his hand on her shoulder. "Please, Lilly, don't be mad. I did it for us."

She spun around. "How can you say that?"

"Our cause is just. Those changes are long overdue."

"How is that *for us*?"

"We're asking for a wage hike, shorter workdays, and more safety inspections. All those things will help me support my family and, some day, I hope and pray, you as well."

"But if you keep pressing for change and anger the owners, it could all blow up in your face. They could sack everyone who protests. Then where would we be?"

Rob blew out a breath and looked toward the sky, obviously not convinced.

Heat flooded through her. "I won't stand by silently while you put your job at risk by going along with a strike."

"No one is striking yet."

"But that's what's coming, and I can't support your family as well as mine on a housemaid's wages!"

His eyes narrowed and turned steely. "I never asked you to support my family."

She pulled back, hurt by his tone and words. "Fine. If that's the way you want to be." She swung away from him and stomped through the trees toward the road.

"Lilly, wait." She heard his footsteps behind her, but she didn't stop. "I'm sorry."

Her eyes stung, and her throat felt so tight she couldn't speak.

He reached for her arm and gently pulled her to a stop. "Please, listen to me."

She slowly turned and met his serious gaze.

"I love you. I want us to be together. That's always the first thought in my mind. Trust me on that."

She pulled in a shaky breath. Could she trust him? Would she?

"I'll be careful and think things through the next time they ask me to join them." He ran his hand down her arm. "But I have to do what I think is right."

She swallowed hard. "So you'll go along with a strike if they call for one?"

"Only if there's no other choice." His gaze softened. "Now, can we please set this aside?"

She released a slow, deep breath. She didn't want to be at odds with Rob, but she couldn't totally banish her fears. "Just promise you'll be careful."

"I will." He slipped his arms around her and looked into her eyes. "You have my word."

She could tell Rob meant what he said, but his choices were only a small part of the puzzle. What would happen if the other men continued to push their demands forward? Would the owners make changes, or would they refuse to listen? If they ignored the workers' demands, would anger boil over into violence?

Was there still hope to prevent the strike, or would it come no matter what they did and crush all their hopes for the future?

Maggie spent an hour Sunday evening scanning Helen's diary. She read several more entries after the one about the accident, then released a heavy sigh. There were no more mentions of the mysterious R. or any references to the boating accident. But there were several entries detailing Nate's return from Huntsford Hall after the funeral, the stormy confrontation with his parents that followed, and his trip to Scotland to search for Maggie and Violet.

Nathaniel's misplaced loyalty to Daniel Lounsbury and his family is straining our ties to the breaking point! How can he choose them over his own flesh and blood? I cannot tolerate his selfish, willful behavior any longer. Mr. Harcourt must put a stop to it before Nathaniel does something even more foolish and ruins our family name.

Maggie's throat burned. How could Helen write those things about Nate? His only crime was trying to make up for his father and stepmother's heartless treatment and offer Maggie and Violet some consolation.

She turned the page. There was a lapse of several weeks, and the final entry was dated 25 December 1899.

We have little to celebrate this Christmas. Mr. Harcourt was downcast and silent, and when I questioned him, he admitted he was disappointed he had not heard from Nathaniel. I told him his naval training might have prevented him from writing, but he was not convinced and stalked off to sulk.

Clara was disappointed with her gifts and spent a good part of the afternoon carrying on and in tears. Selfish child! Pleasing her is next to impossible.

I gave the servants a bowl of punch and wished them all a happy Christmas, but even they seemed reluctant to enjoy the day when their master was so gloomy.

As for me, I did not receive even a card or letter from my cousins. Why do they neglect me and treat me with such scorn?

Maggie closed the diary and shook her head. Helen's selfish remarks were depressing, but nothing she'd written that Christmas night tied her to the boating accident.

Was Maggie's search futile? Should she give up and put her suspicions to rest?

No! Her father's journal clearly stated that trouble had been brewing in the Harcourt family for a long time. His confrontation with Helen and her threats toward him occurred only days before the accident.

Helen Harcourt had to be involved!

She closed her eyes, her churning thoughts becoming a silent prayer. *You talk about truth and justice in Your Word, about light shining into the darkness and good overcoming evil. I long for that in my life, to know what truly happened that day on Tumbledon Lake and to see justice done, but it seems impossible now. What am I supposed to do?*

She waited, listening, hoping for some divine impression or sense of direction, but no answer came. With a huff, she turned away.

Why would God answer her prayer? She'd turned her back on Him a long time ago, and she had refused to listen each time He spoke to her in the quiet beauty of a glowing sunset or through her grandmother's kind words and actions. She had ignored His voice and hardened her heart to His gentle yet relentless call to release her hurt and come back to Him.

Bone-aching weariness washed over her. She was so tired of carrying her burden alone, tired of trying to balance the scale of justice in an unjust world.

The load was too heavy for her, but giving it to God and allowing Him to carry it for her seemed impossible. That would mean yielding her heart and accepting God's will. And she didn't know if she had the courage to do that.

She pushed those thoughts away and rose to her feet. It was time to return the journal and be done with this fruitless search.

She stepped out of her bedroom and stopped in the hallway. Downstairs, she heard Clara playing the piano in the music room. Helen's voice rose from the great hall. It sounded as though she was speaking to one of the servants. That might give Maggie just enough time to take care of her task. Still, she'd have to be quick about it and hope she didn't run into Mrs. Burnell or another member of the staff.

She slipped down the hall and pushed open the door to Mrs. Harcourt's sitting room. On tiptoe, she crossed the room, opened the desk drawer, and placed the diary with the others.

Footsteps and hushed voices sounded in the upper hallway.

Maggie stifled a gasp. Her gaze darted around the room, searching for a place to hide. The door to Helen's bedroom stood open, and behind it was a secluded corner next to the tall wardrobe. She darted toward the corner, slid behind the door, then pulled the door open a few more inches to shield herself from view.

The footsteps entered the sitting room. Maggie held perfectly still, but her heart thundered in her chest.

"Quickly, shut the hall door. I don't want the servants to see you."

That was Helen Harcourt's voice.

A low laugh from a man followed. "Don't worry. No one will see us. I'll make sure of that. Haven't I always?"

"Stop this nonsense!" Helen's voice was hushed and insistent. "What do you want?"

"I've had some extra expenses in the last few weeks. I need a little more money to tide me over until next month."

"That's impossible. I can't give you any more money."

"But you must have access to everything now that Old Moneybags is gone. I'm sure he left you a tidy sum."

Maggie's eyes widened. Who would dare call Mr. Harcourt *Old Moneybags*? She leaned down and peeked through the keyhole into Helen's sitting room. A pudgy, middle-aged man with straggly blond hair and a shaggy mustache faced Helen.

"Nathaniel inherited everything." Disdain filled Helen's voice.

"He may be the heir, but your husband wouldn't leave you without an income. And besides that, I know you must have some funds secreted away."

"I only receive a small allowance, but it's not nearly enough to pay for my expenses. Clara and I must go to Nathaniel and beg for every shilling. It's humiliating."

"Well now, that's quite a change, isn't it?" The man laughed again.

"Yes, it's a change, for me and for you." Helen paused and glared at the man. "Your days of counting on me for an income are over. You'll have to find some other way to cover your expenses."

"Now, Helen, that won't do. You've always found a way to keep our agreement, and I'm sure you can find a way now."

"I can't! Everything has changed! I must do as Nathaniel says—he has threatened to banish me to a small cottage at the far end of the estate."

"That young upstart! Why do you let him treat you like that?"

"I have no choice. He controls everything now. What do you expect me to do?"

"I expect you to keep your word and pay me what you promised."

"Roland, you're not listening! I have no way to—"

"Shh! Someone's coming!"

Their voices hushed and footsteps passed in the hallway. Silence followed for a few seconds.

"Thirty pounds should see me through until June." Roland's voice was a harsh whisper.

"Don't you understand? I can't give you thirty pounds or three hundred, and there won't be a payment next month!"

"You listen to me, Helen." Roland's voice was low and threatening. "You'll send me the payment we agreed on or I'll make sure your dirty little secret is printed on the front page of every newspaper in the country. And when that happens you will be forced to leave Morningside, but you won't be living in a modest little cottage—you'll be going to jail!"

Quick steps trod across the room. The door to the hallway opened and then closed.

Maggie held her breath, counting the seconds.

Helen's fierce growl vibrated through the room, then glass shattered against the far wall. Footsteps marched toward the corner where Maggie was hidden.

Maggie froze and squeezed her eyes tight, not daring to breathe.

The door swept away from Maggie and slammed with a loud bang.

Stunned, Maggie opened her eyes and scanned the empty sitting room. A broken vase lay shattered on the fireplace hearth, but Helen had retreated into her bedroom.

Maggie's knees went weak. She gripped the side of the wardrobe and pulled in a steadying breath. Then she ran across the room, stepped around the broken glass, and slipped into the hallway. A quick glance to the left and right told her no one was watching.

She bolted down the hall, entered her bedroom, and quietly closed the door. Pulling in a ragged breath, she leaned her forehead against the door.

"Maggie, what in the world are you doing?"

She gasped and whirled around. Grandmother sat in the overstuffed chair by the window, a book in one hand. She looked at Maggie over the top of her spectacles. "Well, are you going to tell me what you've been up to?"

Maggie swallowed, her thoughts spinning. "What do you mean?"

"You know very well what I mean. You've been sneaking around the house and hiding something from me. I'm disappointed, Maggie. That's not like you."

Maggie's heart sank. She had kept her search a secret, but she'd never intended to hurt her grandmother. "I'm sorry. You're right. I have kept something from you, but that's only because I didn't want to say anything until I knew if my suspicions were true."

Grandmother frowned. "What suspicions?"

Maggie crossed the room and sat in the chair opposite her grandmother. She glanced toward the bed to make sure Violet was asleep, then she turned back to Grandmother. "You may find this hard to believe, but I think Mrs. Harcourt may have been behind the boating accident that killed my parents and sister."

Grandmother's eyes widened. "My goodness, Maggie. That's a serious accusation."

"Yes, very serious."

Grandmother set aside her book. "Mrs. Harcourt is certainly a cold, unfeeling woman, but I can't believe she would plot a murder. What makes you say such a thing?"

"I never suspected it either until I read Father's journal."

Grandmother's silver eyebrows rose. "I didn't know your father kept a journal."

"He did. But after the funeral, the Harcourts sent people to clear out our house. All the furniture, clothing, and personal items, including my father's journals, were given away or destroyed, except for his last journal. I took that with me when they sent me to Scotland."

Grandmother clasped her hands in her lap. "Go on."

"I kept it locked away in my trunk with Mother's Bible. I knew it would be painful to read it, so I never opened it until a few weeks ago. Then, on the night of the fire, I read Father's final entry . . . That's when I knew his death was not an accident."

"What did it say?"

Maggie recounted her father's description of Helen's rendezvous with a man in the woods and the confrontation that followed.

Grandmother listened intently, clearly caught up in the story. "Mrs. Harcourt actually said she would accuse your father of . . . making advances toward her if he told Mr. Harcourt what he'd seen?"

"Yes! At first she tried to pretend it all meant nothing, but Father had seen them together before, and he felt he couldn't ignore it any longer. He urged her to go to her husband and tell him the truth. That's when she threatened Father."

Grandmother huffed out a breath. "How dare she!"

"Helen was angry with Father and wanted to silence him. I think she must have learned about our plans to take the boat out and then paid someone to damage it."

Grandmother's face had gone pale. "And all this is written in his journal?"

"Well, most of it, but the journal was lost in the fire."

"So there's no proof." Grandmother sighed. "Isn't there a possibility it was just a dreadful coincidence?"

"No, I'll never believe that, especially not after what I just overheard."

Grandmother lifted her silver eyebrows. "What do you mean?"

Maggie leaned forward. "A man named Roland came to see Mrs. Harcourt, and she whisked him off to her sitting room so no one would hear them talking."

"And how do you know this?"

"Well, I was putting back . . . something I borrowed when I heard them coming, so I hid in the corner of her sitting room behind the door."

"Maggie, you ought not be in Mrs. Harcourt's sitting room or eavesdropping on her conversations." Grandmother smoothed her hand across her skirt. "Still, this sounds like an important matter. What did they say?"

"He asked her for money, and from what I heard, it sounds like she pays him every month to keep him quiet about something he called her 'dirty little secret.'"

Grandmother lifted her hand to cover her heart. "Oh dear, that does sound like terrible business." She pondered for a moment. "You think the secret she wants to keep hidden is her involvement in the boating accident?"

"Yes, what else could it be?"

"She might be paying him to keep her affair with that man a secret."

"That's what I thought at first, but the last thing Roland said was that if her secret got out she would be forced to leave Morningside and would go to jail. So it must be something illegal, not just something improper."

Grandmother gave a slow nod.

"Society might raise their eyebrows if they learned Mrs. Harcourt had a long-standing affair, but her husband is dead," Maggie continued. "There's no one to send her to jail for that now."

"No, I suppose not."

Maggie stood and paced across the room, her thoughts shifting from one conclusion to the next. "Perhaps I should go to the police."

Concern flooded Grandmother's eyes. "I'm not sure that's the best course of action, at least not yet."

"But we know Mrs. Harcourt threatened Father, and now it's clear she was paying someone to keep her secret."

"She does sound guilty, but without your father's journal, it would be your word against Mrs. Harcourt's. And I'm afraid the police would be much more likely to believe her."

Maggie moaned and sank into a chair. Her grandmother had a point. Maggie's suspicions and theories were not enough to convince the police Mrs. Harcourt was at fault. They needed solid evidence, and Maggie had nothing to give them.

Even if she could convince the police to question Nate's stepmother, that might prompt Helen to destroy evidence or find a way to pay Roland or someone else to keep silent. And what if Helen learned Maggie was the one making the accusation? She might turn her anger on Maggie and her family. Maggie couldn't put her grandmother and sister in danger. They must be safely away from Morningside before she made any of this public.

Grandmother leaned forward in her chair. "I think we should pray and wait on the Lord to make our next steps clear."

Resistance tugged at Maggie's heart. She did want to make sure her family was safe before she went to the police, but she would not wait indefinitely for her grandmother to sense the timing was right. "I can't just stand by and do nothing, not when I believe that woman is responsible for the deaths of my parents and sister."

"I know this is difficult, Maggie, but listen to me. There's more to waiting than just biding our time. Our job is to pray and trust the Lord to reveal what's hidden and bring the full truth to light."

A lump lodged in Maggie's throat. What if her suspicions were unfounded? What if she was wrong about all of it? Then again, what if she was right?

Grandmother reached for Maggie's hand. "It's time to put your hurt and suspicions into the hands of the One who knows the truth and has the power to do something about it." Warmth and confidence flowed from her grandmother's work-worn hand into Maggie's. The soothing flow wrapped around her heart like a comforting blanket.

Could she cross that bridge and renew her trust in God? If she did, would He take up their cause and see that justice was done? With everything in her she wanted to believe Someone had the power and wisdom to help her learn the truth, even if it was a truth she didn't want to accept. But even more than that, she wanted to believe that Someone loved her and would meet her on that bridge when she stepped out in faith.

Did God still love her even after she'd turned her back on Him for so long? She pulled in a shuddering breath and stepped out.

Help me, God, I want to believe.

23

Nate shifted on the hard wooden chair and glanced around the circle of men gathered in the church hall. Reverend Samuelson sat on his right, and eight workers from Clifton filled the other seats. The tense conversation had gone on for almost two hours, with the men listing their grievances and Nate responding as best he could with his limited knowledge of Clifton. He glanced at Samuelson, hoping his friend could find a way to end the meeting on a positive note.

Samuelson met his gaze, then looked around at the men in the group. "The hour is late, and we need to draw this meeting to a close. I think we've all learned a great deal tonight. You've made your points clear and given Mr. Harcourt the information he needs to take back to the board."

"But will they listen? That's the question." John Palmer shifted his hard gaze to Nate.

"I'm sure Mr. Harcourt will do his best to—"

"Can he promise us a meeting with the full board to negotiate our grievances? That's what we want."

Nate's chest tightened, and he tried to rein in his frustration. He couldn't make that promise. But if he was going to keep these men on the job and avert a strike, he had to convince them he would do his best.

Nate looked across at Palmer. "I promise to speak to the board and explain these issues in the most persuasive way possible."

A few men nodded, looking satisfied, but Palmer and the two men on either side of him sent Nate doubtful frowns.

Nate's conscience bore down on him. It was wrong to lead them to believe he could control the board or that the outcome was certain. He had to tell them the truth, even if they didn't like it or him. "I will do everything in my power to help you, but I cannot guarantee the board's response."

Murmurs and sharp glances traveled around the circle.

Samuelson lifted one hand. "Gentlemen, I hope you'll make an effort to understand Mr. Harcourt's position. He has made a commitment to speak to the board, but he is only one member. He does not have the final say in all matters at Clifton."

A man seated next to Palmer pointed at Nate. "Your father founded the company, and you own a good portion of it now. That ought to give you a say in how the company is run."

Nate nodded. "I do have some influence, and I will use it to make sure the issues we've discussed have a fair hearing."

"No!" John Palmer's shout echoed around the room. "That's not good enough! We've been put off time and again." He turned and glared at Nate. "We'll give you one week, that's all. If we don't have a promise from the full board to meet with us, then we will bring it back to our men and they'll vote to strike."

Palmer's friends nodded and clapped their hearty agreement.

Samuelson leaned forward, his expression intent. "Gentlemen, I urge you to keep working toward a peaceful solution. Talk of a deadline to strike will stir up animosity and put everyone on the defensive, and that will only end up hurting your cause."

"If they won't listen, we have no other choice."

"Fortunately, it hasn't reached that point yet. There's still time to bring both sides together and work things out in a peaceful and reasonable way."

Palmer shook his head. "If they want a peaceful solution, then the board will have to meet with us. If not, then we're ready to take a stand against them."

Samuelson's gaze traveled from one man to the next. "A strike would mean great hardship for you and your families."

"True, but if that's what it takes, we won't be the only ones who suffer." Palmer rose from his chair. "Come on, men. We're done talking tonight."

As the men walked out of the room, Nate sat back and blew out a deep breath. His course was set. If anyone was going to stop the strike, it was up to him—he must convince the board to negotiate with the workers. Still, he felt defeated as he remembered the board's determination to stand strong against negotiating with the men.

"Don't look so worried." Samuelson rose and clamped a firm hand on his shoulder. "There's still time to prevent a strike."

"A short time, yes, but a strategy to see this through . . . that's what I need. I'm not sure I can convince the board to do anything."

"Then it's good to remember it's not all up to you." Samuelson looked Nate in the eye. "I suggest we pray about it and keep praying until we see men's hearts change—on both sides."

"Good idea, Samuelson."

"Shall we start now?" Samuelson bowed his head.

Nate closed his eyes and listened while his friend offered a humble yet confident prayer for a resolution to the threatened strike. The words flowed over and around him, easing away his tension and bringing him renewed hope.

He would keep his word to the men and do what he could, but the outcome was in God's hands . . . and that was where it needed to stay.

Nate quietly opened the front door and stepped into the entrance hall at Morningside Manor. With a weary sigh, he pushed the door closed, then walked toward the dimly lit great hall. The only lights on were the two globes glowing at the bottom of the stairs.

The weight of the day's events and the lateness of the hour drained away the last of his energy and made his steps heavy. All he wanted now was to fall into bed and let sleep drown out his problems.

He started toward the stairs, but a soft snore sounded off to his left. He turned and spotted Jackson seated on a chair, his head lowered and shoulders sagging. The poor old butler was evidently waiting for Nate to return before he locked the front door and went upstairs to bed.

Nate reached out and touched the man's shoulder. "Jackson."

The butler startled, lifted his head, and blinked. "I'm sorry, sir. I'm afraid I dozed off." He slowly rose to his feet.

"I'm the one who should apologize. The meeting went longer than I expected."

"It's all right, sir."

"Thank you for keeping an eye on everything. You can lock up now and be done for the night."

Jackson glanced toward the door. "I don't believe Miss Clara has returned yet, sir."

"Clara is out at this hour?" Frowning, Nate checked the tall clock in the corner. Ten minutes after eleven was certainly too late for his sister to be out.

"Yes, sir. She left just after nine." Jackson leaned closer. "Said she was going for a walk." But the lift of his silver brows made it clear Jackson believed there was more to the story.

Nate glanced at the stairs, letting go of his desire to head straight to bed. He'd promised his father he would look after Clara, and that meant more than just providing food and shelter for her. He needed to make sure she was all right.

"You may go on upstairs, Jackson. I'll go see if I can find her."

"Very good, sir." Jackson dipped his head, then shuffled off toward the staircase.

Nate watched him, fondness for the old man easing away some of his frustration. They ought to encourage Jackson to retire, give him a pension, and set him up in a cottage on the estate—or perhaps he had family who would welcome him into their home for his final years. Nate sighed. He would think about that tomorrow. Right now he needed to find his sister.

He walked outside and scanned the front drive and lawn, but there was no sign of Clara. Remembering where he'd found her with Owen Campbell, he started down the gravel path toward the walled garden.

A full moon lit the walkway and spread a silvery glow on the garden wall. He stepped through the open gateway and scanned the garden paths.

A faint voice off to the right caught his attention. At the end of the path near the far wall, Clara and Owen stood facing each other. They spoke so softly he could not make out their words, but his sister's stance and expression made him pause and step into the shadows.

Owen reached for Clara's hand and held it with gentleness and reverence. Clara glanced away with a shy smile, then slowly turned back and looked into Owen's eyes. Even from a distance Nate could read the sweet longing in her expression.

The young man lifted her hand to his lips and kissed her fingers.

Nate stilled, taking in the tender scene, surprised by the way it moved him. The two obviously cared for each other, and they seemed to be engaged in nothing more than a moonlight walk.

He remembered the way he'd spoken to them the first time he found them together, and he had a nagging sense he might have been too quick to judge the situation. Why hadn't he taken Maggie's advice and sought out Owen since then? If his sister cared that much for the man, Nate ought to at least let Owen explain his intentions.

Clara stepped back, then she kissed her fingers and waved to him. He lifted his hand, returning the farewell gesture. Owen turned and walked out the garden gate on the far wall.

Nate stayed hidden in the shadows as Clara hurried past. This was not the right time to speak to her or Owen. But when he did speak to them, he would listen first and weigh his words carefully before responding, as Maggie had encouraged him to do.

He pulled in a deep breath of damp, lavender-scented air and listened to the crickets chirping in the bushes. He waited a few more seconds, soaking in the tranquility of the moonlit garden, then he started back toward the house, his burden lighter and his mind more at peace.

Maggie followed the steep, winding path down the hillside through the rock-strewn gardens. The sound of the rushing stream rose from the bottom of the ravine, drawing her closer. Birds called to one another and darted through the evergreen trees overhead while the fragrant branches swayed in a gentle breeze.

She'd always loved following this path and seeing what lay around the next bend. Today, pink and purple azaleas bloomed on the hillsides between large boulders and low creeping heather. Beneath the tall evergreens, lush ferns, primrose, and bluebells carpeted the ground.

Her father had designed this garden his first year at Morningside, choosing every bush and tree and overseeing their planting. It was wonderful to see how much it had filled in and become even lovelier in the passing years.

All morning she'd longed to leave the house and have some time alone to think through everything that had happened in the last few days. But it wasn't until after lunch, when Grandmother and Violet were settled with sewing and books, that she'd felt she could finally slip away. What a relief to walk outside and not have to worry about seeing Helen Harcourt and having to pretend she didn't know what she had done.

She continued down the path, and her thoughts shifted to last evening. After Violet was asleep and Grandmother was absorbed in reading a novel, Maggie had written a detailed list of all she remembered about the accident and the Harcourts' actions afterward. Next she added what she'd read in her father's journal, then listed highlights from Helen's diary. Finally, she recorded the conversation between Helen and Roland, making sure she had it almost word for word. When she finished, she'd folded the sheets of paper and slipped them into her mother's Bible on her bedside table.

After breakfast she showed her notes to her grandmother, then they prayed together about the next steps to take. Maggie's prayers were halting, but she stepped out with what little faith she had and asked God for His leading and protection. She wasn't sure if it was a direct answer, but she sensed it would be best if they left Morningside and returned to the village as soon as arrangements could be made.

She reached the lower path by the stream. The sound of water rushing over and around moss-covered rocks blocked out most other sounds. It tumbled downhill, running on to join the river Coquet and then flow into the North Sea.

She left the path, stepped out on a large rock at the edge of the stream, and looked down at the colorful stones below the surface of the water. Leaning closer, she watched the little gray minnows dart between the rocks while the water gurgled and splashed over them in a hypnotic dance.

"Maggie."

Startled, she jerked, then teetered on the slippery rock.

"Whoa!" Nate reached for her, his arms encircling her waist and drawing her back toward him.

She laughed, but his nearness made her heart beat hard and fast.

"I've got you." His warm breath caressed her cheek as he held her close. "Are you all right?"

"Yes, I'm fine." But her unsteady voice sounded anything but fine. She looked over her shoulder and found his face only inches from hers.

Light glimmered in his eyes, and a slow smile lifted the corners of his mouth.

How handsome he was, with his dark, wind-tossed hair, strong chin, and deep-brown eyes. But it was more than Nate's dashing appearance that drew her to him. His kindness toward her and her family had proven his character time and again.

She looked into his eyes and felt her last bit of resistance fading. If she lifted her face toward him and let her eyes drift closed, would he kiss her? A tremor passed through her at that thought.

He tightened his hold in response, searching her eyes. "Maggie?" His voice was low and husky, and the light in his gaze flickered into a flame.

Time seemed suspended as she teetered on the edge of her decision. If she followed her heart and gave in to the feelings coursing through her, where would it take her? She cared for Nate more than she'd ever cared for any other man, but should she give away her very first kiss before she was certain of his love for her?

He must have read the uncertainty in her eyes, because his expression dimmed and he loosened his hold. "We'd better step back from the edge," he said softly, then lowered his arms and helped her down from the rock.

A thought struck Maggie, and a painful ache filled her chest. Very soon, Nate would have a good reason to distance himself from her. Once she accused his stepmother of murder, it could be the deathblow to their friendship.

He glanced down the path. "Would you like to walk with me?"

Maggie slowly lifted her gaze to meet his. "Nate, there's something I have to tell you."

"What is it?" The openness and trust in his expression only made her heart ache more.

"I sent Reverend Samuelson a letter, asking him to help us find somewhere to stay in the village."

He stilled and studied her. "Why?"

She swallowed and had to force out her next words. "I think it would be better if we were nearby when they start working on the shop."

His eyebrows dipped. "I can take you to the village whenever you'd like. You can see to your business or spend time with your . . . friends . . . if that's what you want."

She stiffened. What did he mean by that? "Mr. Ledbetter said rebuilding will take at least three months, maybe more. That's much too long for us to impose on you and your family. I think it would be best for everyone if we found somewhere else to stay."

His face had grown ruddy while she spoke. "It's because of Joseph Neatherton, isn't it?"

She pulled in a sharp breath. "Why would you say that?"

"It's obvious how he feels about you. He made that perfectly clear the last time we saw him."

"Joseph has been our neighbor and friend for years."

"And I've known you since you were twelve. Doesn't that give me just as much right to be considered your friend?"

"Of course we're friends. And I'm grateful for everything you've done for us, but I don't think we should take advantage of your generosity for months at a time."

Nate frowned. "There's more to it than that. I can see it in your eyes, Maggie. There's something you're not telling me."

She looked away. Why was he making this so hard?

"Joseph Neatherton practically knocked me down just for taking you to meet with that builder. I can assure you he has something much more permanent than friendship in mind."

Maggie lifted her chin and matched his strong tone. "What he wants and what's going to happen are two very different things."

"So you're not in love with Joseph Neatherton?"

Her mouth dropped open. "Nate!"

"What?"

"It's not fair to ask me a question like that."

He stalked a few steps away, picked up a rock, and flung it into the stream, then glared into the woods across the water. She waited, feeling torn between wanting to push him into the stream and calling him back and promising him she did not love Joseph.

He sent another rock flying, and it dropped into the deep water on the far side. Finally, he turned and walked back toward her. "I shouldn't have asked you that. I'm sorry." The lines on his face softened, and regret surfaced in his eyes. "I hope you won't stay angry with me."

"I'm not angry, just . . . confused about what I ought to do."

"Well, you can be sure of this . . . I want you to stay." His gentle tone and imploring look hit the mark.

Her heart clenched. "You might think that now, but very soon things are going to change and you won't want me at Morningside anymore." Tears burned her eyes, and her throat clogged.

He stepped closer. "Maggie, what is it?"

Tell him the truth. The Voice she had ignored for so long spoke straight to her heart.

Did she have the courage? Could she trust Nate? She blew out a deep breath, then looked into his eyes. "It's a long story."

He took her hand and drew her toward the edge of the stream to sit on a large rock. "However long it is, I'm ready to listen."

"All right." She sorted through the details, trying to decide where to start. "Do you remember the day, a long time ago, when I climbed the tree to look into that bird's nest? I think I was thirteen."

He grinned. "This must be a very long story if you are starting that far back."

She pushed his arm. "The bird attacked me, and I fell off and landed on you."

His mouth tugged up on one side. "Yes, I remember."

"On the walk home we heard your stepmother talking to a man in the woods. I wanted to stay and hear what they were saying, but you knew it was wrong, and you said we should leave."

He nodded, his smile fading.

"My father saw them too, more than once. He confronted your stepmother and urged her to break it off and tell your father everything. He said if she didn't, he would go to Mr. Harcourt himself."

Nate waited, unreadable emotions in his eyes.

"But Helen wouldn't listen. She threatened my father, saying unless he kept quiet, she would ruin his reputation by saying he had made advances toward her."

Nate's expression grew grave.

"But my father stood firm and gave her three days to tell your father the truth . . . but he didn't live long enough to follow through."

Shock flashed in Nate's eyes. "He told you this?"

"No, he never said a word to me or anyone else. He died, carrying Helen's secret with him to the bottom of Tumbledon Lake."

"Then how do you know about it?"

"I read it in his journal."

His gaze darted toward the house and then back to her. "Do you have it with you?"

She shook her head. "It was destroyed in the fire."

"So you have no proof of your father's conversation with Helen?"

"No, but I know it's true."

Nate's brow furrowed.

"There's more. A man named Roland came to the house Sunday to see Helen." Maggie told him everything she'd heard in that exchange.

"So you think this man Roland is the one she was meeting in the woods?"

"No, I think Helen wanted to silence my father, and she arranged for someone to damage the boat so it would go down. Roland knows about it, and he's blackmailing her to keep it a secret."

Nate stared at her for a few seconds. "Have you told anyone else?"

A prickle of unease traveled through her. "Only my grandmother."

"Good. I think it's best if you keep it to yourself for now."

Maggie's stomach tensed. Was Nate trying to protect his family's reputation and prevent Helen's arrest? Was that why he wanted her to keep quiet?

She had to know where he stood, even if it meant she must stand against him. "I think I should go to the police."

Nate shifted on the rock and faced her. "Your suspicions are logical, but you have no proof someone tampered with the boat." He frowned toward the water for a moment, then looked back at her. "That's the missing piece. If we can find out who she hired to damage the boat, then I think the police will listen."

"We?" Maggie's heart lifted. "You believe me?"

"Maggie, this is a serious matter. I want to find out the truth as much as you do."

"Even if it means your stepmother may go to jail?"

"If Helen is responsible for the deaths of your parents and sister, then she needs to be held accountable to the full extent of the law."

Maggie's chest swelled. "Thank you."

"I haven't done anything yet." He reached for her hand. "But I promise I won't rest until we know what happened and who is responsible."

She squeezed his hand, hoping that would convey what she couldn't say.

"Stay at Morningside, Maggie. Let's work on this together."

She looked into his eyes and wanted to say yes, but the memory of her prayer with Grandmother rose in her mind. She had sensed they should return to the village, but that was before she knew Nate believed her suspicions were justified. Surely now that he was willing to help her find out what truly happened, it made sense for them to stay. Nate would watch out for them, and with his help they'd find the proof they needed.

Ignoring the gentle tug on her heart, she smiled up at him. "All right. We'll stay."

Maggie pushed her peas around on her plate, then adjusted her linen napkin on her lap—anything to avoid looking at Helen. But with only four people seated around the dining room table, it was a challenge.

Violet could not wait until eight o'clock for dinner, so she and Grandmother usually ate earlier, then settled in for a quiet evening in their room while Maggie joined Nate, Clara, and Helen in the dining room.

It was one of the loveliest rooms in the house, with two sparkling chandeliers, a beautifully carved marble fireplace, and several remarkable paintings. But Maggie found it difficult to enjoy the room or her meal when Helen watched her with a critical eye and excluded her from most of the conversations.

Dinner was quickly becoming Maggie's least favorite meal of the day.

Helen took a sip of her water and glanced down the table. "Clara, I received a reply from the dressmaker today."

Clara looked up, her expression vague. "What?"

"I said, Mrs. Dowling wrote. Apparently she is busy sewing for a family in Newcastle upon Tyne and won't be able to come for two weeks." Helen lifted her eyes to the ceiling, and her lips puckered. "I don't know why I continue to do business with that woman."

"You've always said she is the best dressmaker in Northumberland," Clara replied.

"She is, but I told her about your father's passing and that we needed her to come immediately. I don't understand why she's putting us off like this."

"It sounds like she has a commitment to the people in Newcastle upon Tyne."

"That is no excuse! We are in mourning. What does she expect me to do while we wait for her to arrive? How can I continue to receive callers when I only have three mourning dresses?" Helen's strident tone made Maggie cringe.

Clara shot an embarrassed glance at Maggie, then looked at her mother again. "Why don't we go to Heatherton and visit one of the dressmakers there?"

Helen pulled back with wide eyes. "We can't do that. Their skills are not nearly on the same level as Mrs. Dowling's. Everyone would know, and once word spread that we had our dresses made by a village seamstress, we'd be outcasts of society."

"Really, Mother, I don't think anyone—"

"That's enough, Clara!" Helen's glare grew icy. "You are not old enough to understand, but it is important to dress in a manner equal to our position."

Clara's cheeks flushed, and she turned her face away, obviously embarrassed by her mother's scolding.

Nate sent Maggie an apologetic glance. She returned the same and wished she could do more to express her understanding and sympathy. It seemed he disliked dining with his stepmother as much as she did.

Helen pushed her plate to the side. "Jackson, take this away. We're finished with this course."

The butler stepped forward and quickly removed her plate while the footman removed Clara's.

Lilly appeared at the dining room door with a piece of paper in her hand. She motioned to Jackson, and the butler's eyes widened. He set the plate on the sideboard and crossed to the door. "What is it?" he hissed.

"This message arrived for Mr. Harcourt. The man said it was urgent and he should read it right away." Lilly kept her voice low, but Maggie could still hear her clearly. Lilly handed the note to Jackson and stepped out of view.

The butler returned to the table and silently handed the note to Nate.

"Excuse me." Nate unfolded it and scanned the message. A smile broke out across his face. "Yes!"

"Well? What is so urgent?" Helen demanded, obviously not pleased by the interruption.

"Mr. Judson has agreed to meet with the workers from Clifton." Nate looked up and met Maggie's gaze. "He's the fifth member of the board to approve the plan. That gives us the number we need to hold the meeting."

Maggie's smile spread wider. "That's wonderful."

"Yes, and we have four more days to convince the others to join us."

"Do you think they will?"

"Mr. Rowlett will be the most difficult to persuade, but now that Mr. Judson is convinced, I'd say we have a much better chance." He laid the note on the table and focused on Maggie. "But holding the meeting with the men is only the first step. The board members must truly listen to the workers' grievances and be willing to negotiate. That's the only way we'll be able to avoid a strike."

Helen's nose wrinkled as though she'd smelled something offensive. "Nathaniel, you know how much I dislike hearing business talk at the dinner table. It's not appropriate conversation."

Nate scooted back from the table. "Very well, then you'll have to excuse me." He turned to Maggie. "Shall we continue our conversation in the library?"

Helen's face turned blotchy red. "But you haven't had your pudding!"

Maggie pressed her lips together, barely able to hold back her laughter.

"That's true," Nate continued, "but I'm not really in the mood for pudding this evening."

Maggie stood. "Neither am I, but thank you for dinner. I hope you enjoy your pudding."

"Excuse us." Nate touched Maggie's back, guiding her away from the table.

"Nathaniel, how can you be so rude!" Helen's voice followed them as they walked toward the door. "I don't know why I even bother coming down. I should have my dinner sent up to my room on a tray."

"Oh, Mother, there's no need to be so dramatic," Clara added in a tired voice.

"He shows no respect for me, none at all. I am the hostess. I should be the one to decide when we're finished and when we pass through to the drawing room . . ."

Maggie and Nate continued into the great hall, and he pulled the door closed, blocking out Helen's voice.

He turned to Maggie. "I'm glad we finally had a reason to leave."

Her heart warmed, and she returned his smile. "So am I."

"Let's go into the library. There should be a nice fire, and we can have Jackson bring in some coffee when he's done in the dining room."

"That sounds perfect."

He reached for her hand as though it was the most natural thing. Surprise and pleasure traveled through her. She dipped her head but curled her fingers around his as they walked into the library.

The connection between them was growing stronger, and the walls around her heart were coming down. She had trusted him with her secret suspicions, and he had believed her and committed himself to joining her in her search for the truth. That meant the world to her.

How could she not fall in love with a man like that?

Lilly carried the basket of clean laundry up the back stairs, her mind miles away with Rob and his family and their troubles—and she couldn't forget about the fire and how her father and brother were battling to rebuild their shop on a meager budget. Overshadowing it all was the threat of a strike and what that would mean for everyone she loved.

Her steps felt leaden as she walked down the hall. She tried to push away her worries, but the unknown future seemed to loom before her like a dark path leading into a forest with no end in sight.

She knocked on Maggie's door and listened for a reply, then she stepped inside and balanced the basket against her hip as she turned to close the door.

Maggie sprang up from her chair. "Let me help you."

"I've got it." Lilly bumped the door with her other hip, and it swung closed. "I have some clean laundry for you."

Maggie reached for the basket. "Thank you, Lilly. I'll put it away. You've done enough."

Lilly released the basket to her friend.

Maggie set it on the bed, took out her undergarments and stockings, and tucked them into a dresser drawer. "I still don't feel right about you doing our laundry."

"Oh, I just brought it up. Agnes does all the laundry."

"Well, I appreciate it. Would you pass our thanks on to Agnes?"

Lilly nodded and glanced toward the window, her worries rushing back to fill her mind again.

"Lilly? Are you all right?"

Lilly pressed her lips together and nodded, but her eyes smarted and burned.

Maggie crossed toward her. "What is it?"

She pulled in a shaky breath. "I shouldn't bother you with my troubles. You have enough of your own."

"It's no bother. You always listen to me. Now it's my turn." Maggie took Lilly's hand and led her to the window seat. Then she patted the spot next to her. "Sit down and tell me what's happened."

Lilly settled on the window seat next to Maggie and pulled in a shaky breath. "I'm worried about Rob. His father's hand is healing, but he won't be able to go back to work, and that means Rob is the only one bringing any money home. And I'm afraid he's listening to the men who want to strike."

Maggie's eyebrows dipped, and she searched Lilly's face.

Lilly looked down. "He was in the crowd that day the men marched through the village and surrounded Mr. Harcourt's motorcar."

Maggie's eyes widened. "Really? I never saw him."

"He was there. He said he had to go along or the other men would call him a coward."

Maggie patted her hand. "It's hard to take a stand against others who are older and have more influence."

"What if they vote to strike? What will Mr. Harcourt and the other owners do to the men? And what if the strike goes on for a long time? How will they buy food and pay their rent? I could help a little, but it won't be nearly enough."

"Nate and Reverend Samuelson are working hard to bring the two sides together. Remember that note you brought to the dining room last night?"

Lilly nodded, remembering the family's reaction.

"That was word that another member of the board has agreed to join Nate's efforts to resolve matters. They're going to hold a meeting soon to discuss the men's grievances."

Lilly sat up straighter, her hopes rising. "Do you think they can work out their differences in time to stop the strike?"

"Nate is hopeful. He's been looking into the company's finances and procedures, and he believes there is room for negotiation if both sides are willing."

Lilly clasped her hands together. "Oh, I wish there was something I could do besides wait and worry."

"Well, you don't have a choice about waiting, but you can choose if you'll worry or not." Maggie's words were gentle, but they nudged Lilly's conscience.

Lilly ducked her head. "I know I shouldn't worry. I've struggled with that all my life."

Maggie slipped her arm around Lilly's shoulders. "You're not alone. I've had a hard time with worry myself, but that doesn't mean we have to give in to it. We can choose to focus on what's true and trustworthy and refuse those anxious thoughts when they come." She sent Lilly an encouraging smile.

Lilly pondered that for a moment. "I suppose you're right. We need to pray and trust God instead of worrying."

Maggie nodded. "That's the spirit."

"Thank you for listening." Lilly rose. "I should get back to work. Mrs. Burnell has a whole list of duties waiting for me."

Maggie reached for Lilly's arm. "Before you go, I wanted you to know I told Nate everything."

Lilly's eyes widened, and she gulped in a breath. "You told him I took Mrs. Harcourt's diary?"

"No! I said I'd read it, but I never mentioned your part in it."

Lilly blew out a relieved breath. "What did he say?"

"He agreed to help me search for the truth. We're going to speak to Mr. Hornshaw today."

"The estate manager?"

Maggie nodded. "Nate says he knew my father well. He oversees the outdoor staff and works with the tenants. Perhaps he can tell us more about my father's relationship with Mr. and Mrs. Harcourt."

Lilly fingered the edge of her apron. "That might help."

Maggie walked with Lilly to the door. "Thank you, Lilly."

"For bringing up the laundry?"

Maggie laughed softly. "Yes, and for telling me what's on your heart. I treasure your friendship." She gave Lilly a hug.

Lilly soaked in Maggie's warm embrace. "Thank you." She walked down the hall and descended the back stairs, her burden lighter.

Nate knocked two times and then pushed open the door to Mr. Hornshaw's office. He stepped to the side and let Maggie pass through first, then followed her in. The estate manager's office smelled of leather and pipe smoke. Cabinets and open shelves covered most of two walls. A stuffed fox stood atop the cabinet to the left, and a gazelle's head was mounted on the far wall above a large map of the estate.

Nate closed the door and turned to Mr. Hornshaw. "Good afternoon. I hope we're not interrupting you."

"Not at all. It's always good to see you, sir." Mr. Hornshaw rose from his chair behind his old wooden desk. He was a tall, thin man, about sixty years old, with a silver mustache and thinning hair. He wore spectacles and a neat brown tweed suit.

Nate shook hands with the estate manager and then motioned toward Maggie. "Do you remember Miss Margaret Lounsbury, Daniel Lounsbury's daughter?"

"Yes, sir, I do." Hornshaw smiled and nodded to Maggie. "Welcome back to Morningside, miss."

"Thank you, Mr. Hornshaw. It's good to see you again."

"We all admired your father. He was a fine landscape architect, and his work added great value to the estate. I know the late Mr. Harcourt thought very highly of him as well."

"That's kind of you to say." Maggie offered him a brief smile, but Nate could see the trace of sadness in her eyes.

"No one knew more about trees and flowers or had a better eye for where they ought to be planted." He shook his head. "It's hard to believe it's been four years since he passed."

Maggie pressed her lips together and nodded, her eyes growing misty.

Mr. Hornshaw sent her a sympathetic look, then turned to Nate. "Now, sir, what can I do for you?"

Nate motioned toward the two chairs facing the desk. "May we sit down?"

"Oh, yes, of course." Mr. Hornshaw waited until Maggie and Nate took a seat, then he lowered himself onto his chair.

"We're hoping you might be able to answer a few questions for us." Nate kept his tone light, wanting to put the estate manager at ease.

Mr. Hornshaw's silver eyebrows rose slightly. "Questions?"

"Yes." Nate would have to be cautious to avoid revealing too much. "Shortly before my father died, I came to see you and asked about the money he owed Daniel Lounsbury. Do you remember our conversation?"

"Yes, sir." Hornshaw's gaze shifted to Maggie and then back to Nate. "I gave you my best accounting of those funds. Is there some question about the money?"

"No, but you mentioned at the time that you were surprised about the boating accident."

He frowned thoughtfully. "Yes, sir. I believe I did say that."

"Can you tell us why?"

Hornshaw stroked his mustache and thought for a moment. "Well, your father ordered that boat from Tuttleman's that spring. They've been in business for over one hundred years and have a reputation for building the best boats in Northumberland. It was delivered in May, so the boat was only three months old when it went down. That seemed odd to me."

Maggie shot a quick glance at Nate.

"But I suppose," Hornshaw continued, "accidents happen."

"Who was responsible for the care and maintenance of the boats?"

Mr. Hornshaw sat back in his chair. "I suppose that would be Clyde Billington, one of the groundskeepers. He kept the key to the boathouse and looked after the boats."

"So Daniel Lounsbury would've needed to ask his permission to take the boat out?"

Hornshaw nodded. "I believe so."

Now they were getting somewhere. "Who else used that boat besides Daniel Lounsbury?"

"Your father made it clear the family and staff were all welcome to use the boat. I took it out a time or two myself. We just had to make arrangements with Clyde."

"So if I wanted to take a boat out tomorrow, I'd check with Clyde to see if the boat was available, then he'd meet me at the set time and unlock the boathouse?"

Hornshaw grinned. "Well, now, you'd have priority over anyone else, sir. I'm sure you wouldn't have to give notice to use a boat." He chuckled, but when he saw Nate did not join in, he sobered. "What I mean to say is, I keep the boathouse key now. Any time you want to take it out, just let me know and I'll see to it."

"What happened to Clyde?" Nate asked.

"He retired last year and went to live with his daughter in Lynemouth on the coast."

"Do you know how we might contact him?"

"Let me see." Mr. Hornshaw pulled open his top desk drawer and shuffled through some papers. "Ah, here we are. This is the address." He held up the card, then hesitated. "May I ask you something, sir?"

Nate nodded. "Of course."

"Why all these questions?" Hornshaw glanced at Maggie, then focused on Nate again.

Maggie shifted in her chair. Was she worried Nate would reveal her suspicions?

He straightened, considering his words. "As you said, there are some things about the boating accident that don't quite make sense, and we're trying to understand why the boat went down."

Mr. Hornshaw leaned forward. "Do you suspect some sort of foul play?"

Maggie's eyes widened for a split second, then she lowered her gaze to her lap.

Nate had known Mr. Hornshaw for many years, but he wasn't certain where his loyalties lay. "We're just beginning to look into it, so it's too soon for us to draw any conclusions."

Hornshaw's silver eyebrows rose, and he nodded slowly. "I see."

"This is a sensitive matter. I trust you'll keep our conversation confidential?"

"Oh, yes, sir. I won't say a word to anyone." He handed the card to Nate.

"Thank you. I'd appreciate that." Nate glanced at the address on the card. "I'd like to speak to Clyde Billington and see if he can help us. May I take this?"

"I'd be happy to copy the address for you." Hornshaw took a pen from his desk. Nate passed him the card, and the estate manager wrote down the address. When he finished, he passed the card to Nate. "I hope Clyde can help you."

"So do I." Nate rose from his chair.

Maggie stood beside him. "Thank you, Mr. Hornshaw. You've been very helpful."

"You're welcome, miss. I hope you find the answers you're looking for."

Nate led the way to the door and opened it for Maggie. They stepped outside, and he closed the door. He grinned and held up the card. "It looks like it's time for us to take that trip to the seaside."

The next morning after breakfast, Nate walked with Maggie, Mrs. Hayes, and Violet into the great hall. Sunlight poured through the tall windows above the staircase, brightening the usually shadowed room. The sky appeared to be clear, and it looked like the perfect day for their outing.

Nate turned to Maggie. "I need to dash off a note to Reverend Samuelson, then I'll fetch the car and bring it around front."

Maggie nodded. "We'll go up and collect our things from our room."

Violet swung toward Nate on her crutches. "How long will it take to drive to the ocean?"

"It's about thirty-five miles, so I'd guess about an hour and a half, maybe less." He had taken the motorcar up to thirty miles per hour on a straightaway, but he doubted that would be wise on the narrow, winding roads to Lynemouth.

Violet's eyes lit up. "That's not too long."

Nate grinned. "No, it's not."

"I can't wait!" She vaulted toward the stairs.

"Violet, slow down." Mrs. Hayes put out her hand. "You don't have to go upstairs."

"I want to go up." Violet was already clomping up the steps, looking as though she enjoyed the challenge.

Maggie shook her head, but affection for her sister glowed in her eyes. "If we could only harness Violet's energy, I'm sure we could light up the rest of the estate and the village besides."

Nate chuckled. "Violet's enthusiasm for life is contagious. I enjoy her very much."

Maggie tipped her head, her eyes shining. "I'm very glad to hear it. Thank you for that, Nate, and for everything." She sent him another heartwarming smile, then took her grandmother's arm and they started up the stairs.

His spirits lifted, his hope renewed. Ever since their conversation by the stream, Maggie's attitude toward him had changed. His commitment to help her search for the truth about the boating accident seemed to have tipped the scale in his favor.

She was opening her heart to him.

A thrill raced through him, but then a question rose in his mind. Winning Maggie's affections would be amazing, but what if their search led to a dead end? What if he failed to find the answers she wanted? What would happen then?

He shook his head and dismissed those thoughts. He would do whatever he could to help Maggie, and that would be enough. Right now he needed to focus on his plans for the day, and the first thing on his list was writing to Samuelson. He turned and started toward the library.

"Nathaniel, I need to speak to you." Helen's demanding tone scraped across his nerves.

He clenched his jaw and looked over his shoulder. His stepmother descended the stairs, passing Maggie and Mrs. Hayes on the landing without acknowledging them.

He held his peace until she reached the bottom of the stairs. "Can it wait until this evening? I'm preparing to leave for the day."

She crossed toward him, her face set in a stern expression. "Where are you going?"

Irritation coursed through him. Since when did she take a personal interest in how he spent his day? He pulled in a slow, deep breath and reminded himself to be civil. "I'm taking Mrs. Hayes and her granddaughters to the seashore."

"What about your responsibilities here and at Clifton?"

"I'm well aware of my responsibilities, and I know how to take care of them. You needn't worry."

She gave an indignant huff. "How can you justify wasting a day on an outing like that? I thought you were working with the board at Clifton, trying to save the company from the possibility of a strike."

"I thought you disliked discussing business or hearing anything about my dealings at Clifton."

"It's not appropriate dinner conversation, but that doesn't mean I'm totally ignorant of our family's business interests."

A footman entered the great hall with a tray of glasses and walked toward the dining room.

Helen frowned at the footman, then focused on Nate. "I'd prefer we continue this conversation in private." She started toward the library door without waiting for his reply.

He swallowed his frustration and followed her.

She swept into the library, then turned to him. "Close the door."

He clenched his jaw but did as she'd asked. He would listen to what she had to say, but he would not let Helen spoil the day with an argument.

Helen took a seat on an overstuffed chair near the fireplace. "Sit down, Nathaniel."

"I prefer to stand." He crossed to the fireplace hearth and faced her.

"Very well." She smoothed out her dress. "Now, tell me where you're going."

"I have business in Lynemouth, and I invited Mrs. Hayes and her granddaughters to come along."

Her brow creased. "Lynemouth is at least forty miles away."

He stifled a groan. "It's only thirty-five, but that's the beauty of motorcars. You can travel great distances in a very short time."

"At a very fast speed." She pursed her lips and sent him a disapproving look. "Racing around the countryside in a motorcar is dangerous and undignified. What will people say if they see you with that . . . Lounsbury girl?"

Ah, so that was the real issue. "Her name is Margaret."

Helen lifted her hand. "It doesn't matter what you call her. The point is, people will talk."

"Yes, they'll probably say, 'Look, there goes Nathaniel Harcourt in his splendid motorcar with his friends. Aren't they a lucky set?' "

She glared at him. "You may think you're humorous, but this is no laughing matter."

"You're right. It's becoming less humorous by the minute." He took his watch from his pocket and checked the time. "Is there some particular reason for this conversation?"

She lifted her chin, but he read a hint of apprehension in her eyes. "Yes . . . this has been an unusual month, and my allowance is simply not adequate to cover my expenses."

The conversation Maggie had reported overhearing between Helen and Roland flashed through his mind. Was Helen going to ask him for money to pay her blackmailer?

"I've had extra expenses," Helen continued, "and I'd like an advance on my allowance and an increase next month."

"What kinds of expenses?"

Helen blinked a few times. "Well, I'm sure you'll remember we hosted a very large luncheon after your father's funeral. And now that we have three houseguests, whom you invited to stay with us, we have to pay for their food as well."

"Mrs. Burnell gave me the bills from the grocer and the butcher. I paid those myself. Those expenses didn't come out of your allowance."

Her face flushed, and she glanced away. "Yes, but I had to order the flowers for the funeral, and I have to make the down payment on the headstone for your father's grave."

"Give me the bills, and I'll see that those expenses are paid."

Helen shifted in her chair. "I don't receive a bill for every expense."

"I don't understand."

"When I go to the village and buy something at one of the shops, I must pay for my purchase."

He nodded. "That's when you would use the money from your allowance."

She leaned forward. "But there are times I need something extra."

"Such as?"

She pressed her lips together for several seconds, then looked back at him. "Last week at the Women's Missionary Aid Society meeting, they were taking a special offering for the work in China. The offering plate was passed, and I wanted to give a gift, but I had nothing." She closed her eyes and shuddered. "Everyone saw. I was so embarrassed!"

A sense of regret pricked Nate's conscience. Everything in Helen's world had changed since his father's death. She was difficult and could strain every nerve, but she was part of his family and he didn't want her to be miserable. "How much did you want to give?"

"At least twenty pounds. That's how much the others were giving."

"Very well. Helping our missionaries in China is a worthy cause. I'll speak to Reverend Samuelson the next time I see him and tell him we want to give a contribution."

She sprang up from her chair, her eyes bulging. "No! That's not the point! I want to give the money myself in the meeting."

He stared at her a moment before he could reply. "Helen, I'm sure you remember what Jesus said. When you give an offering, do it in secret—don't even let your right hand know what your left hand is doing. Surely you don't want to lose your heavenly reward by making a public display of giving that money."

Her throat convulsed and her lips trembled. "You think you're clever, quoting Scripture and forcing me to beg for money, but it's not right! Your father never treated me like this. He gave me a generous allowance and never asked for an account of every penny I spent!"

At the mention of his father, fire burned through Nate, and he stepped toward her. "If my father knew what I know about you, he would've taken much more serious measures than I've done by limiting your spending."

Her mouth dropped open.

Nate tugged down the lapels of his jacket. "Now, if you'll excuse me, I have a letter to write before I leave." He motioned toward the door, indicating she should remove herself from the room.

Helen's nostrils flared, but she spun away and marched out of the library.

Nate's pulse pounded in his temples. He'd said more than he'd intended to. That might not have been wise. If Maggie's suspicions were true, Helen would not be afraid to go to great lengths to keep her secrets from becoming known. That could be dangerous for them all.

He crossed to his desk and took out paper and a pen. What he'd said might make Helen uncomfortable, but it wasn't enough to pose any real danger. They would keep looking for answers, and when they had the proof they needed, they would take it to the police and let them deal with Helen. Until then, he would keep his eyes open and tread more carefully.

Maggie took Nate's hand and stepped down out of the motorcar. Nate had parked in the shade of a large cedar tree; still, she felt a bit uneasy about leaving Grandmother and Violet there while they went inside to speak to Mr. Clyde Billington. But she didn't want Violet to hear the conversation.

"We shouldn't be long." Nate closed the car door.

"We'll be fine." Grandmother waved him off with a smile. "This is a lovely spot."

Nate pushed open the gate and let Maggie pass through first. They walked up the path toward the old stone cottage. Maggie smiled as she took in the neat front garden and charming thatched roof. The cottage looked as if it came out of an earlier century, and that was probably the case.

"I hope Mr. Billington is home." She sent Nate a sideways glance.

He offered her a brief smile, then knocked on the front door. "That would be convenient."

A few seconds later, the door opened. A middle-aged woman wearing a white apron over her simple blue dress looked out at them. "May I help you?"

"Good morning. I'm Nathaniel Harcourt, and this is Miss Lounsbury. We're hoping to speak to Mr. Billington."

The woman hesitated, a hint of concern in her eyes. "And how do you know my father?"

"He used to work for my family at Morningside Manor."

Her eyes widened. "Oh, well, I'm sure he'll be glad to see you, then. He's in the back garden. I'll go get him."

"There's no need. We'll walk around back."

"All right. Just take the path around the side of the house, and you'll find him there."

Nate thanked her, and they followed her directions. As Maggie rounded the corner, she passed under a wooden archway covered with climbing roses. It was early in the season, but a few yellow blooms had opened. Maggie sniffed the air, enjoying the flowers' sweet fragrance mixed with the scent of freshly tilled earth.

Off to her right, an elderly man knelt beside a flower bed, digging in the soil with a small trowel.

"Mr. Billington?" Nate crossed the grass toward him, and Maggie followed.

The old man looked up and squinted at them. "Yes?"

"I'm Nathaniel Harcourt from Morningside Manor, and this is Miss Lounsbury."

"Oh, my goodness." Mr. Billington reached for his cane. Nate stepped forward to give him a hand.

"Thank you." The old man looked up at Nate with a smile. "I should've recognized you right away. You look like your father when he was younger. How is he?"

Nate's smile faded. "He passed away in April."

Mr. Billington gripped his cane more tightly. "I'm sorry to hear that. He was a fine master, always fair and generous to me."

Nate nodded. "I'm glad to hear it."

Mr. Billington straightened. "So what brings you to Lynemouth? Surely you didn't come all this way just to see me."

"Mr. Hornshaw suggested we speak to you. He thought you might be able to help us."

Curiosity glowed in the old man's brown eyes. "I will if I can."

"Do you remember Miss Lounsbury's father, Daniel Lounsbury?"

He nodded. "Of course. He was a fine man, very skilled at designing gardens. Even an old gardener like me learned a few tricks from Mr. Lounsbury."

Maggie smiled, pleased to hear him speak about her father in such a kind way.

But Nate's expression remained serious. "We're looking into the events surrounding the boating accident."

Mr. Billington's brow creased. "That was a sad day, a very sad day." The old man pointed to the wooden bench nearby. "Would you like to sit down?"

"Why don't you and Miss Lounsbury take a seat?"

The old man motioned Maggie toward the bench. She sat down, then he shuffled over and sat next to her.

When they were settled, Nate focused on Mr. Billington. "I understand you kept the key to the boathouse."

"That's right, sir. I did. Also those to the gatehouse and a few other outbuildings."

"When someone wanted to take the boat out, they had to speak to you first, is that correct?"

"Yes, sir." Mr. Billington gave a firm nod. "Your father trusted me to keep a good eye on things."

"So Daniel Lounsbury made arrangements with you to use the boat?"

Mr. Billington nodded. "He came to see me a day or two before. He said he wanted to take the family across the lake for a picnic. I believe it was someone's birthday."

Maggie's throat tightened. "Yes, my sister Olivia turned nineteen that day."

"That's right." The old man pointed a knobby finger her way. "And I wrote it on the board to make sure I'd remember to come and unlock the boathouse for them."

Nate's brows lifted. "You met them there that day?"

"No, sir. I'm sorry to say I didn't see them."

Nate cocked his head. "I don't understand."

"I went down early that morning to meet your father. He took the boat out first that day."

Nate stilled and stared at him. "My father?"

"Yes, he said he wanted to do a little fishing."

"He asked you that morning?"

Mr. Billington rubbed his chin and thought for a moment. "No, I believe he came the evening before. I told him the Lounsburys wanted to use the boat for their picnic at ten. He said not to worry, he'd take the boat out about seven, but he'd bring it back in plenty of time for them to be on their way."

Nate nodded. "So you met my father that morning at seven and unlocked the boathouse for him. He took the boat out and then brought it back in time for the Lounsburys to use it for their outing?"

"Yes, sir. I believe that's right."

Nate turned to Maggie, his gaze intense. "Do you remember seeing my father that morning? Did he hand off the boat to your family?"

She glanced away with a slight frown. She didn't like to think about those events; in fact, she usually tried to block those memories, but it was important to recall them now. She thought a moment more, then looked at Nate. "We didn't see Mr. Harcourt. The boat was up on the shore. Father and I pushed it back in the water. Then we all got in and started across the lake."

Mr. Billington turned toward Maggie. "You had to push the boat into the water?"

"Yes, sir." Maggie studied the old man's troubled expression.

"I wonder why Mr. Harcourt pulled it on shore instead of tying it up at the dock." Mr. Billington stared toward the ground and shook his head.

Nate's frown deepened, and he paced a few steps away. "I suppose he thought that would be safer."

Maggie glanced at Nate. That didn't make sense. Tying up the boat would have been much easier and perfectly safe, especially since Mr. Harcourt knew her family would be using it shortly after he returned to shore.

"I think that's all we need." Nate glanced at Maggie, then looked toward the road with a slight jerk of his head.

Surprise rippled through Maggie. Why was he so eager to leave? She rose and thanked Mr. Billington.

The old man stood and turned to her. "I wish I had more answers for you." He shook his head sadly. "I don't know why that boat sank. It doesn't make sense to me, but then sometimes things happen that we don't understand."

"What you've said has been helpful." Maggie reached for his hand. "We appreciate your time."

Nate nodded to Mr. Billington, then turned and strode out of the garden. Maggie walked behind him, confused by his abrupt end to their visit. They followed the path around the house and out to the car. He opened her door without a word, then cranked the car and started the motor.

Maggie wanted to question him, but she couldn't do that in front of Violet. She'd have to wait until they reached the beach. Hopefully then she could learn more about what Nate was thinking.

Maggie shook out the lightweight blanket and let the breeze off the ocean help her spread it out on the sand. Nate carried the picnic basket and walked with Grandmother and Violet down the path toward the beach where Maggie waited for them.

She studied Nate's face as he came closer, and her stomach tensed. He'd barely said a word since they'd left Mr. Billington's. Was he simply distracted by what they'd learned, or was it something else?

She turned toward the sea, lifting her face to the sun and letting its warm rays soothe her tense shoulders. The water glistened as the waves rolled toward the shore. Gulls dipped and floated on the salty breeze. In the distance she could see the remains of an old castle on the hill overlooking the beach. Surely, in such a lovely spot on a beautiful day like this, she and Nate would be able to reconnect.

Violet swung over on her crutches and moved into Maggie's line of vision. "Can I go down to the water?"

"The doctor said you can't get your cast wet."

"I promise I'll be careful." Violet's pleading tone tugged at Maggie's heart.

Maggie laid her hand on Violet's shoulder. "Today you can enjoy the view of the ocean and the sunshine."

"Oh, please, I just want to feel the waves on my feet."

"I'm sorry, Violet, but you'll have to wait until your next visit to get your feet wet."

Violet sighed and flopped down on the blanket. "At least I can dig in the sand."

Grandmother lowered herself onto the blanket next to Violet. "Dig all you like, but you must keep the sand out of your cast or you'll be miserable." She gave Violet's knee a tap. "Swing your leg around so it's in the center of the blanket."

Violet did as Grandmother asked, then found a stick and started poking it into the sand just off the edge of the blanket.

Grandmother looked up at Nate and Maggie. "Why don't you two take a walk and test the water? We'll be fine here."

Maggie glanced at Nate. He agreed, though he didn't look especially pleased about the idea. He sat on the far side of the blanket and untied his shoes. Maggie sat down as well, turned away from Nate, removed her shoes, and slipped off her stockings. When she finished, she stood and found Nate waiting for her.

"Ready?" He motioned toward the water.

She nodded and fell into step beside him. When they reached the damp, hard-packed sand, she glanced over her shoulder to be sure they were a safe distance from Grandmother and Violet. It was time to sort through what they'd learned today. "I'm glad we were able to speak to Mr. Billington."

Nate looked toward the waves but said nothing.

She searched his face, wishing she could understand what he was thinking. "That was quite a surprise to learn your father took the boat out first that morning."

The tense lines around Nate's mouth deepened. "Yes, it was."

"It's odd that he pulled it up on shore when he could've just left it tied to the dock."

"I don't see what difference that makes."

"If someone wanted to tamper with the boat, bringing it on shore would make it easier."

He lowered his brows and looked her way. "What are you implying?"

Questions spun through her mind. Could Mr. Harcourt be responsible? Was she actually going to accuse Nate's father of murder? She blew out a breath. "I don't know. I'm just saying your father was the last one to use the boat before we took it out, and he pulled it up on shore."

Nate stopped and faced her. "That doesn't make him guilty."

She stared at him, stung by his sharp tone. "So you don't believe he could have tampered with the boat?"

"No, I don't. He respected your father and considered him a good friend. He would never purposely plot to harm him or your family."

"But you heard what Mr. Hornshaw and Mr. Billington said. The boat was practically new. There was nothing wrong with it until after your father used it that morning."

"That doesn't mean he damaged it."

Maggie lifted her chin. "That doesn't clear him of suspicion either."

Nate stuffed his hands in his jacket pockets, and his frown deepened.

Maggie's head throbbed, and sick dread built in her stomach. Of course it would be hard for Nate to believe his father could be guilty of tampering with the boat, but the possibility was growing stronger in her mind by the minute.

Nate shook his head. "It doesn't make sense. Why would he put your whole family at risk?"

"I can think of one explanation." Her voice grew more insistent. "If your stepmother followed through on her threat and accused my father of making advances toward her, your father could've been angry enough to wish my father harm."

"No! My father would never do that. Even if Helen lied to him, he would've confronted your father and given him a chance to explain."

"That's what you would do, but we're not talking about you. We're talking about William Harcourt."

Nate glared toward the water, his eyes as turbulent as the waves washing toward them.

Maggie pulled in a deep breath, trying to calm her emotions. "I know you respected your father and you want to believe the best about him, but he was the last one to use the boat, and he had a motive and the opportunity to damage it."

A muscle rippled in his jaw, and he shifted his gaze back to Maggie. "There is another possibility."

Maggie frowned. "What?"

"You said you and your father pushed the boat into the lake. Perhaps you damaged the hull and that's why it sank."

Maggie pulled in a sharp breath. "You're blaming me?"

"No, I'm just saying there could be another explanation."

Dizziness washed over Maggie. That couldn't be true! It was impossible. She lifted her chin and met his steely gaze. "Of course you'd like to shift the blame to me and absolve your father."

"Maggie, that's not true. I want to know what actually happened as much as you do, but I won't blame my father until we're one hundred percent certain he was the one responsible."

"Fine." She crossed her arms and turned away, her eyes stinging.

He placed his hand on her shoulder. "Maggie, please talk to me."

She blinked away her tears, then slowly turned to face him.

"I'm sorry for what happened to you and your family—more sorry than you'll ever know. And if I were in your position, I would fight just as hard as you are to find out who was at fault, but I think it's time you accept that what happened that day might have been an accident. A terrible, tragic accident."

She stared at him, her breath frozen in her lungs. How could he say that? She had opened her heart to him, trusted him, and believed he would help her. "After everything I've told you and all we've learned, you're going to dismiss it because you're more loyal to your family than you are to the truth?"

Nate leaned toward her, his posture rigid and his tone sharp. "I know my father. He never would've purposely planned to drown your family. It's just not possible." He turned away and strode down the beach, leaving Maggie behind.

Maggie's heart pounded in her chest, and she swallowed hard. She could go after him, but she doubted he would listen to her. And she couldn't stand hearing him defend his father one more time.

How could he betray her like this?

All the pain from the past rose like a huge wave, crashing over her and drowning out her hope. He'd turned his back on her again, just as he had after her parents and sister had died. She'd longed for his help and support, but he'd gone off and joined the Navy and left her to face her heartbreak alone. And he was abandoning her again, but this time the pain cut so much deeper. This time she'd given him her heart and he'd chosen to defend his family instead.

The sun had just dipped behind the trees on the hillside above the house when Nate dropped off Mrs. Hayes, Violet, and Maggie at Morningside's front door. He drove the motorcar around to the far side of the stable and retrieved the picnic basket from the backseat.

With a weary sigh, he started back toward the house, the distressing events of the last few hours replaying through his mind. How could a day that started out with great expectations turn into such a disaster?

What a fool he'd been to believe he could win Maggie's heart by helping her search for answers about the boating accident. He should've known the painful issues from the past would rise again and fortify the wall between them.

No matter what Mr. Billington said or how firmly Maggie argued the point, he could not believe his father would plan to harm Daniel Lounsbury or purposely damage the boat, especially not when he knew Daniel's family would be with him that day.

His father was not a perfect man, not by any means. But he was calm and even-tempered, not given to passion or revenge. It would've been totally out of character for his father to plot to murder Daniel Lounsbury, no matter what he believed the man had done.

Nate had tried to make Maggie see she was heading down the wrong path toward a faulty conclusion that would end up hurting them all. But she wouldn't listen. She had to blame someone for her heartbreak and losses, and she had decided it would be his father.

He stifled a groan and pushed open the front door. Maybe he could appeal to her one more time, but how would he convince her she was grasping for answers that were not going to be found?

He walked through the entrance hall, crossing the black-and-white tiled floor, then stepped into the great hall. The glow of the sunset through the tall windows cast a rosy light around the room. Maggie stood at the bottom of the stairs, holding an open letter in her hands. She glanced at him, then pressed her lips together and looked away.

Nate crossed toward her but stopped a few feet from where she stood.

Her hand trembled slightly as she lifted the letter. "Reverend Samuelson has found a place for us to stay in the village."

Nate's chest constricted. "You're leaving?"

"Yes, I think it's best. Mrs. Birdwell is willing to take us in until the shop is rebuilt." Her hand fell to her side, and she looked at him with a plea in her eyes.

He steeled himself. If she was determined, then he wouldn't stop her. "When will you go?"

She looked down at the letter again. "He says she'll be ready for us tomorrow."

He tried to draw in a deep breath, but his chest felt so tight it was almost impossible. He knew Maggie was strong-willed and even stubborn at times, but he didn't think she'd actually leave, not when things were so unsettled between them.

Then another thought struck, and he riveted his gaze on her face. "Are you planning to go to the police?"

Her eyes flickered and she straightened. "I think it's time I tell them what I know."

Heat rushed up his neck and flooded his face. How could she do it? Didn't their friendship mean anything to her? What about all he'd done to help her and her family? Didn't she owe him some gratitude, some loyalty?

A rustling sound in the gallery drew his attention. He looked up and scanned the upper floor, but he didn't see anyone there. The curtain by the open window shifted in the breeze, and he dismissed the sound.

It was time to face the inevitable. Maggie would accuse his father of murder and taint his family's name forever . . . and there was nothing he could do to stop her.

Again he fixed his gaze on Maggie. "If you must, I have one request, and I hope you'll honor it."

"That depends on what it is." The suspicion in her eyes hit him like a blow to the jaw. After all he'd done, she still didn't trust him.

"Wait until this business with the strike is settled. If the police come to question Helen, it will stir up a hornet's nest of trouble and I want to be here to deal with it." He gentled his voice and looked her in the eyes. "It would be best for Clara's sake."

Maggie's brow creased, and she scanned his face as though she was trying to measure the truth behind his words. Finally, she said, "All right. I'll wait until the strike is settled."

Jackson walked into the great hall. "May I take that basket down to the kitchen for you, sir?"

Nate passed him the picnic basket. "Thank you, Jackson."

Maggie turned and started up the stairs without another word.

He watched her climb the steps, pass through the gallery, and enter the west hall. The energy seemed to drain out of him, and he grasped the railing at the bottom of the stairs.

He'd lost her, and it seemed there was nothing he could say or do to make her change her mind. She would walk out of his life tomorrow, determined to falsely accuse his father of murder, and she wouldn't even look back.

27

Maggie's stomach churned as she walked into the dining room the next morning with Grandmother and Violet, but a quick glance around the room told her Nate was not there.

Jackson stepped forward. "Good morning, madam, Miss Margaret, Miss Violet. Breakfast is ready." He motioned toward the sideboard.

Grandmother nodded. "Thank you, Jackson."

Maggie glanced over her shoulder toward the great hall. "Shouldn't we wait for Mr. Harcourt?"

"He has already eaten, miss."

Violet frowned. "Nate ate breakfast without us?"

Jackson's mouth lifted at one corner, and he shifted his gaze to Maggie. "Mr. Harcourt had a meeting in the village with Reverend Samuelson. But he left instructions that a carriage was to be ready for your use this morning."

Maggie crossed to the sideboard to prepare a plate for herself and Violet, but she couldn't shake her confusing thoughts. Violet plopped down in her chair while Grandmother followed Maggie to the sideboard and served herself.

Breakfast was a quiet affair. Even Violet had little to say.

Maggie took a sip of tea and tried to wash down a bite of dry toast, but it tasted like sawdust in her mouth. She lifted her hand and rubbed the back of her neck, trying to ease her tired, aching muscles. It was no wonder she felt exhausted this morning. She'd spent half the night debating her decision and trying to calm her racing thoughts.

There seemed to be only two choices. She could go to the police, give them the information she had collected, and expose Mr. and Mrs. Harcourt's misdeeds. Or she could accept Nate's conclusion that her parents and sister had died as a result of a terrible accident, one she might have caused.

A shudder passed through her, and she pushed that second possibility away. She did not believe that was the case, not after what she'd read in her father's diary and heard Helen and Roland say to each other.

But what if she was wrong? What if she was grasping for an explanation when there was none?

She glanced at Nate's empty chair, and her spirits sank lower. She had hoped when she saw him this morning he would say he had changed his mind and would keep his promise to stand with her and see that justice was done. But he hadn't even waited long enough to say good-bye.

The events of yesterday rolled through her mind for the hundredth time, ending with that terrible look of betrayal on Nate's face when she'd told him she was leaving Morningside and going to the police. Why did she even question his decision to leave this morning without speaking to her? She was going to accuse his father of murder and expose his stepmother to public humiliation. What did she expect?

With a tired sigh, she laid her fork and knife on her plate and looked across the table at Grandmother. "What time shall we ask for the carriage?"

"It won't take long to pack. I'm sure we'll be ready by ten o'clock."

Violet slumped in her chair. "I don't want to go."

Maggie closed her eyes and rubbed her forehead. She did not have the energy to deal with Violet's dramatics this morning.

"We know, dear," Grandmother said. "But we must keep an eye on the builders while they're working on the shop, and we can't do that from Morningside."

Violet scrunched her lips together. "But I like it here."

Grandmother sighed. "Morningside is lovely, but it's time to go back to the village." She leaned forward, smiling at Violet. "And here's a thought to cheer you. Your cast comes off soon. Then you'll be able to play outdoors and see all your friends."

"But Nate is my friend, and he promised I could ride Juniper when my leg is better."

Maggie clenched her napkin in her lap, pain coursing through her. It was bad enough Nate had turned his back on Maggie. He'd also crushed her sister's dreams. She would have a hard time forgiving him for that. He should never have made promises he didn't intend to keep—to her or to Violet.

Maggie laid her napkin on the table. "I know you're sad about leaving Morningside, but we can't stay here any longer." She glanced around the lovely room. "This is not our home or our life."

Tears filled Violet's eyes. "I wish it were."

The truth hit Maggie's heart and stole her breath away. Violet wasn't the only one who'd been drawn to life at Morningside. Maggie had grown accustomed to seeing Nate every day and sharing his life with him. And in the secret corner of her heart, she'd wished he might fall in love with her and ask her to marry him. But now that could never be, and she'd been a fool to even consider the possibility.

Compassion softened Grandmother's faded-blue eyes as she looked from Maggie to Violet. "Why don't we walk down to the stable and say good-bye to the horses?"

Violet's face lit up. "I'd like that." She rose and reached for her crutches.

"You two go ahead." Maggie laid her napkin on the table. "I'll see if I can find some suitcases we can borrow and get started packing."

Violet balanced on one foot, then she adjusted her crutches and vaulted toward the doorway.

"Violet, slow down!" Grandmother rose and hustled after the girl at a surprisingly quick pace.

Jackson stepped forward and removed Grandmother's plate. "I will see to those cases for you, miss. How many would you like?"

"Two, if they're fairly large." Clara had told her to keep the dresses she'd given her, and they'd sewn a few more with the fabric Mrs. Burnell had found for them.

"Very good, miss." He shuffled over and removed her plate.

"Thank you, Jackson. You've been very kind."

He stopped and sent her a tight-lipped smile. "You're welcome, miss. It's been a pleasure having you here at Morningside."

Maggie's throat tightened. She looked away and blinked back her tears. She didn't want to embarrass Jackson or herself, so she rose and walked out of the dining room.

She'd grown quite fond of Jackson. All the staff members had served them with respect and quiet efficiency. But it was more than bidding farewell to the servants that caused her tears this morning—much more.

She climbed the stairs, her decision and departure weighing her down and making each step a struggle. When she reached her room, she crossed to the wardrobe, took out several dresses, and laid them on the bed. She ran her hand over the soft blue fabric of the top dress. She'd only worn it once, and she doubted she would have occasion to wear such a lovely dress when she returned to Heatherton. Perhaps she should return it to Clara so she could wear it when she was out of mourning.

A knock sounded at the door. Maggie looked up and called, "Come in."

Lilly entered carrying two large suitcases. "Mr. Jackson said you'll be needing these." She set them on the floor by the bed. "Are you leaving us?"

Maggie nodded and had to force out her reply. "Yes. We're going to stay with Mrs. Birdwell."

Lilly's eyebrows rose. "The old widow who lives near the mill?"

"Yes." Maggie lifted one suitcase onto the bed. "Reverend Samuelson made the arrangements. We don't know her well, but it's kind of her to offer us a place to stay." Maggie bit her lower lip. "I'm just not sure . . ." Tears flooded Maggie's eyes again, and she sank down on the bed. "Oh, Lilly. I don't know what to do."

"I hear she is a bit of a hermit, but I don't think it will be too bad."

Maggie released a half laugh, half sob. "That's not what worries me."

"What is it, then?" Lilly sat beside her, her eyes filled with concern.

Maggie tried to steady her voice. "Yesterday, Nate took us to Lynemouth, and we visited a man who used to be a groundskeeper here. He's the one who kept the keys to the boathouse at the time of the accident."

Lilly's eyes widened. "What did he say?"

"He told us Nate's father took the boat out before us that day." Maggie poured out the rest of the story, including her decision to take what she'd learned to the police and Nate's refusal to believe his father could be responsible for damaging the boat.

"Oh, Maggie, that's dreadful. I'm so sorry."

Maggie nodded, then sniffed and brushed a tear from her cheek. "You must promise not to tell anyone. I don't want word to get back to Mrs. Harcourt."

"Of course. It's our secret." Lilly glanced at the dresses on the bed. "Shall I help you pack?"

"Thank you, Lilly." Maggie walked to her bedside table in search of a handkerchief. She'd used one last night to dry her tears while she wrote down what she learned yesterday. After she finished recording those events, she tucked the papers in her mother's Bible and found comfort reading a few psalms.

Lilly folded a dress and laid it in the suitcase. "I heard the men from Clifton are meeting with the owners today. I'm praying they can settle things quickly and avoid the strike."

"Yes, that would be best for everyone." Maggie scanned her little bedside table and stopped. Hadn't she left the Bible face up? A prickle of unease traveled across her shoulders. She reached for the Bible and slid her finger to the page marked by the papers, but rather than opening to Psalm 36, where she'd left off, it opened to the fourth chapter of Ezekiel.

A tremor shook her hand, and she glanced at Lilly. "Has anyone been in to clean our room?"

Lilly shook her head. "I came in this morning, but you keep it so neat there's hardly anything to do."

"Does anyone else come in besides you?"

"Only Nancy to tend the fires." Lilly looked around the room. "Why? Is something wrong?"

"Last night I marked my place in Psalms with the papers that have all the information I've collected about the accident, but now they're in a different book."

Lilly sent her a doubtful glance. "You were upset. Maybe you forgot where you were reading."

"No, I'm sure it was the Psalms, and look, now they're in Ezekiel." She held out the Bible.

Lilly crossed toward her and glanced at the open page. "Maybe your grandmother or Violet moved them."

Maggie thought for a moment, then shook her head. "They were asleep last night when I was reading, and we were all together this morning before we went downstairs. The only time we were out of the room was during breakfast." She clutched the Bible to her chest, questions spinning through her mind.

Lilly sent a nervous glance toward the door. "I suppose someone else could've come in, but who? And why would they want to?"

"I don't know." An uneasy feeling quivered through her stomach. She was probably being silly. No one besides Nate, Lilly, and Grandmother knew about her search. She closed the Bible and placed it in the suitcase, then folded in a dress. Her thoughts turned back to leaving Morningside, and she sighed. It didn't seem right now, especially with the disagreement between her and Nate, but the decision had been made.

With Lilly's help, she finished packing in just a few minutes.

Lilly snapped the latches on the smaller suitcase. "Shall I ring for Andrew to bring these down?"

"No, I can do it." Maggie reached for the larger case and hoisted it off the bed.

Lilly lifted the other case. "I'll get this one, then."

Maggie took one last look around the lovely room, then followed Lilly out and shut the door.

As they descended the stairs, Jackson hurried forward. "May I take those cases for you, miss?"

"No, it's all right, Jackson. Lilly and I can handle them."

"Very well." Jackson crossed the entryway and opened the front door for them. "I'll send word to McGrath that you're ready to leave. He'll bring the carriage around directly."

Maggie thanked him, then set her case on the gravel drive and looked across the gardens and bridge toward Heatherton. Rather than lifting her spirits, it made her heart ache even more. This was not the way she wanted to leave Morningside.

"I'd better get back to work." Lilly sent her a worried glance. "Will you be all right?"

Maggie nodded and embraced Lilly. "Take care. Come and see us on Sunday afternoon if you have time."

Lilly nodded. "I will, or I'll send a note." She squeezed Maggie's hand, then hurried back into the house.

The sound of horse's hooves on the iron bridge over the ravine reached Maggie. She lifted her hand and shaded her eyes. A small open carriage pulled by one horse started up the winding road toward the house. An older man wearing a brown suit and cap drove the carriage, and a middle-aged woman sat next to him.

As they came closer Maggie recognized the driver and blinked in surprise. "Good morning, Mr. Billington."

"Good day to you, Miss Lounsbury." He halted the carriage beside her and tipped his hat. "I hope you're well."

"Yes, sir. I am. What brings you to Morningside?"

"We're on our way to visit my nephew, but I was hoping I might speak to Mr. Harcourt. Is he at home?"

"I'm afraid he's gone in to Heatherton. I'm not sure when he plans to return."

Mr. Billington's brow creased. "Well, perhaps you can pass on some information to him."

Maggie nodded, though she wasn't sure when she would see Nate.

"I was thinking about our conversation yesterday, and I remembered something else. It might not be important, but I thought it best to come and tell Mr. Harcourt and let him decide." He leaned down, and Maggie stepped closer. "There was another man with Mr. Harcourt the day of the boating accident."

Maggie straightened. "There was?"

"Yes. I don't recall his name. He worked in the stable, but only for a short time."

"Why would Mr. Harcourt take someone from the stable when he went fishing?"

"I suppose he brought him along so he didn't have to row and could focus on fishing."

That made sense, but it still might be important to find out more about the man. "Can you give me a description of him?" Perhaps she could ask the groomsmen if they remembered him.

Mr. Billington nodded, then squinted toward the gardens. "He was about forty, short and heavyset." He huffed out a breath. "They say he slept more than he worked. I caught him myself one day, dozing in the hay. Then Mr. Hornshaw told me he up and quit without giving notice."

"Is there anything else you remember about his appearance?"

Mr. Billington rubbed his chin. "He had light hair, pale eyes, and a drooping mustache."

The description struck a chord, and the hair on the back of Maggie's neck rose. "Are you sure you don't remember his name?"

Mr. Billington rubbed his chin. "It was something like Arnold or Ronald or . . ."

"Roland?"

The old man's eyes lit up. "Yes! That's it—Roland! Roland Dixon."

Maggie's pulse surged. The man who was blackmailing Helen had been with Mr. Harcourt the day the boat went down. That gave them another suspect, one who was definitely tied to Helen and had a reason to want to silence Maggie's father.

Mr. Billington's silver eyebrows rose. "You know the man?"

"No, but I've seen him, and I think he had a reason to damage the boat and hope it would go down."

Mr. Billington's daughter's eyes widened. "Goodness, Father. What have you gotten yourself into?"

"Not to worry, my dear." Mr. Billington patted her hand. "I'm sure Mr. Harcourt and Miss Lounsbury will know what to do about it."

His daughter glanced at Maggie with a look of apprehension in her eyes.

"Thank you, Mr. Billington. I appreciate you coming all this way."

"It was no trouble, no trouble at all. If I remember anything else, I'll be sure to let you know." He tipped his hat. "Good day to you, Miss Lounsbury." He lifted the reins and urged the horses forward.

Grandmother and Violet passed Mr. Billington's carriage as they walked back toward the house.

Grandmother stepped up beside Maggie. "Who was that?"

"Mr. Billington. He was a groundskeeper here a few years ago." She wanted to say more, but Violet swung to a stop beside them.

Grandmother's brows dipped, and she sent Maggie a questioning glance.

"I'll tell you more later," Maggie whispered.

The Harcourts' carriage rolled around the side of the house and came to a stop by the front door. The driver hopped down. "Shall I load these bags for you, miss?"

"Yes, thank you." Maggie glanced at the house, rising like a huge, dark castle against the rocky hillside. A symphony of memories played through her mind, with high notes and low, making her throat tighten and her heart ache.

A curtain shifted in an upper-story window, and Helen Harcourt looked out. Even from this distance, her piercing gaze and the stern set of her mouth relayed a silent warning.

Maggie turned away and reached for the carriage door. She would not wait for the driver to help them into the carriage. The sooner she could take her grandmother and sister away from Morningside, the safer they would be.

Helen Harcourt could not be trusted. Maggie was sure of that now.

With the information Mr. Billington had given her, she could tie Roland Dixon to the boating accident, and it was time to move forward and see that justice was done.

28

Nate knocked on Reverend Avery Samuelson's front door, then stood back and debated how he would explain arriving more than an hour early for their appointment. The truth was, he'd left Morningside before breakfast to avoid seeing Maggie, but he wasn't sure he wanted to admit that to his friend.

He frowned toward the deserted churchyard, replaying the events of the past twenty-four hours and trying to decide which bothered him more, Maggie's decision to leave Morningside and go to the police or his own poor response.

He had been so hopeful about their growing closeness. But now it seemed she couldn't wait to put as much distance between them as possible. And the speed at which everything had changed left him feeling a bit stunned.

He needed wisdom, and that was why he'd come to talk to his friend before they were scheduled to attend the negotiation meeting between Clifton's board of directors and the leaders of the workers. It was just after nine now. That should give him and Samuelson plenty of time to sort out the issues before the meeting at eleven.

The door opened and Samuelson looked out at him. His eyebrows rose. "Nate, I wasn't expecting you until ten-thirty. Did I get the time wrong?"

"No, I'm early."

"Please come in." Samuelson stepped back and opened the door wider.

Nate shifted his weight to the other foot and looked past Samuelson's shoulder into the parlor. There was no sign of Mrs. Grady, Samuelson's cook and housekeeper, but he didn't want her to overhear their conversation. "Would you care to go for a walk?"

Samuelson studied his face, a question flickering in his eyes, but then he nodded. "Let me get my jacket and hat."

Nate stepped into the front garden and glanced up at the cloudy sky. The wind ruffled the leaves of the tall elm tree by the garden gate, bringing with it the scent of rain. He hoped the shower would hold off until they returned. It wouldn't bolster his image with the board to arrive dripping wet for the negotiations.

Samuelson stepped outside and closed the door behind him. "Do you have a destination in mind?"

"I'd prefer the countryside to the village."

"Very well." Samuelson motioned to the left, and they set off at a comfortable pace.

After a few minutes they passed through the edge of the village and started down a country lane bordered by hedgerows and pastures on either side.

Samuelson glanced at Nate. "You seem lost in thought this morning. Is there something you want to discuss?"

Nate nodded and clasped his hands behind his back. He had sought Samuelson's advice a few days ago, and his friend had patiently listened to the whole story. "Remember I told you I promised Maggie I would help her look into the events surrounding the boating accident?"

"Yes, how is that going?"

Nate brought Samuelson up to date with what they'd learned from Mr. Hornshaw and their visit to Lynemouth to see Mr. Billington. Finally, Nate mentioned his father had taken out the boat the morning of the accident.

Samuelson's steps slowed, and he sent Nate a questioning glance.

Nate shifted his gaze away. "Unfortunately, Maggie and I look at those same facts and come to very different conclusions."

"What is her opinion?"

"She believes Helen lied to my father, and he was so angry he purposely damaged the boat to do away with Daniel Lounsbury."

"But you disagree?"

"Yes, of course. I don't believe my father was capable of doing such a thing. He might have been self-absorbed and more concerned about his work than his family, but he wasn't a murderer."

"So, in light of all you've learned, what do you think happened?"

"I believe the police were right from the beginning. It was a tragic accident."

He was quiet for a few seconds, considering the weight of his words. "Or perhaps Maggie and her father damaged the hull of the boat when they pushed it over rough ground and into the lake."

"That's a possibility . . . but Maggie's conclusion that your father or someone else purposely damaged the boat makes sense as well, especially after what you've told me about your stepmother and father."

Nate tipped his head to acknowledge Samuelson's comment, though he was not convinced his father was involved. "Now Maggie plans to go to the police and tell them what she thinks happened."

Samuelson rubbed his jaw. "That puts you in a difficult position."

Nate blew out a breath. "Yes, it does."

"But it might be best to let someone who is not personally involved take over the investigation."

"That may be true, but the consequences could be disastrous."

"In what way?"

"If Maggie goes to the police, they'll want to question Helen, and she won't be able to hide her affair or the fact that she's being blackmailed. And you know what kind of scandal that will cause. My reputation will be damaged at Clifton and in the community, and Clara's options for marriage will be limited at best."

Reverend Samuelson nodded, then he clasped his hands behind his back as they continued down the lane.

The muscles in Nate's neck tensed as he tried to quiet his conscience, but it was impossible. "I promised Maggie I would help her discover the truth. But how can I do that when her false assumptions will most likely destroy my family's reputation beyond repair?"

"I can see you're torn about your response."

"That's putting it lightly."

Samuelson walked on for a few seconds, then glanced at Nate. "Perhaps there's some way you could keep your promise to Maggie and still protect your family."

"I don't see how. Maggie is determined to go to the police as soon as matters with the strike are settled."

Samuelson gazed off toward the fields for a few seconds, then looked back at Nate. "If the police question your stepmother and her actions are exposed, that might be just the motivation she needs to confess her misdeeds and turn her life around."

Nate scowled. "You don't know my stepmother."

"Perhaps not, but God has a way of using challenging circumstances for good when we allow Him time and room to work."

Nate pondered that for a moment. "I know that's true. I've seen it happen in my own life, but I'm not sure Helen is listening to God or willing to change."

"You won't know unless you allow the circumstances to play out and see how she responds."

"I suppose you're right." But how would Helen react when her sinful actions came to light?

"And didn't you tell me your sister has developed a strong attachment to a young gamekeeper?"

"Yes, a fellow named Owen Campbell."

"I've come to know him and his family at the church. His father told me young Campbell hopes to study veterinary science."

"Yes, that's what Clara says."

Samuelson thought a moment more. "If Owen's feelings for Clara are sincere, I doubt he would be put off by the investigation. And if he is, then it will prove his feelings for Clara are not strong enough for marriage."

"So you're saying a police investigation might be a good way to test his character and commitment to Clara?"

"Exactly. Does he love her enough to stand with her through troubling times? Is he willing to make a lasting commitment to her in spite of all that may happen to your family?"

Nate grimaced. It was a shame his sister would have to suffer the consequences of her mother's sins. But perhaps all was not lost for Clara. If she responded well to these trials, they might make her a stronger and wiser young woman.

Samuelson looked his way, his gaze sincere and direct. "And you, my friend, are facing a similar test of your character and commitment."

Samuelson's words echoed through his mind and struck truth to his heart. Nate's steps slowed, and he gazed across the fields. Just like Owen Campbell, he faced an important decision. He might not agree with Maggie's conclusions, but he had promised to help her search for the truth, and that commitment should outweigh everything else.

He set his jaw, struggling against the sacrifices that would come with that choice.

Samuelson placed his hand on Nate's shoulder. "The question is, are you willing to keep your word to Maggie and see this through, in spite of the challenges it will present to you and your family, or will you let pride and a desire to preserve your family's reputation destroy what God wants to do in and through you?"

The weight of Samuelson's challenge pressed down on him. Once he opened the door to a police investigation, there was no guarantee what would happen. Did he have the courage and humility he needed to face this test? Could he put aside his pride and trust God to bring good from exposing his family's painful secrets to the light?

Would he take his stand with Maggie?

Maggie took the last dress from the suitcase and hung it on a peg on the wall of their bedroom at Mrs. Birdwell's. She turned, glanced around the sparse chamber, and released a soft sigh. The whitewashed walls were bare except for the faded-green curtains hanging over the window. The only furniture in the room consisted of a simple nightstand and two narrow beds covered with plain gray blankets. The three of them would barely have enough room to turn around, let alone any privacy.

What a stark contrast to their lovely, spacious room at Morningside! Maggie pushed that thought away, but it still made her heart ache. Not so much for the beautiful house, but for Nate and all she'd lost when she'd left.

Mrs. Birdwell stood in the doorway and ran her hand over her wiry gray hair, then tucked a loose strand into her bun. "I told Reverend Samuelson there wasn't room for that other bed, but he insisted on bringing it in."

Maggie blinked. Had Mrs. Birdwell expected the three of them to sleep in one narrow bed? It was a good thing Reverend Samuelson was looking out for them . . . or they might never get a good night's sleep.

Grandmother smiled, but Maggie could read the weariness in her faded-blue eyes. "I'm sure we'll be comfortable. Thank you, Mrs. Birdwell."

Violet scrunched her forehead. "Where will I sleep?"

"You'll sleep with me." Maggie sent her sister a meaningful look, then lifted the two empty cases off the nearest bed and turned to Mrs. Birdwell. "Where shall I put these?"

"Can you slip them underneath?" She motioned toward the nearest bed.

Maggie doubted they would fit, but she knelt and gave it a try. "I'm sorry—they're too large."

Mrs. Birdwell glanced over her shoulder. "I suppose you can put them out back. They shouldn't get too wet if you stack them close to the house."

Maggie's stomach tensed. That would never do. "We borrowed these cases from the Harcourts. I don't think I should leave them outside in the weather."

"Well, I suppose you can stack them in the corner of the kitchen, then. There's not much room, but I'm sure you'll be returning them shortly."

Maggie adjusted her grip on the handles. She had hoped to use the cases again when they moved into their renovated shop, but Mrs. Birdwell was right. They didn't belong to her, and the sooner she returned them to Morningside, the less obligation she would feel toward the Harcourts.

Nate's image rose in her mind, and her heartbeat quickened. He was taking part in the negotiation meeting at the town hall today, trying to head off the strike. She didn't know how long the meeting would last, but she planned to walk into the village and then speak to him when it was over. Surely when she told him what she'd learned about Roland Dixon, he would agree Dixon was a more likely suspect than his father. Perhaps he would even go with her to talk to the police.

"Come with me." Mrs. Birdwell's summons brought Maggie back to the moment, and they followed the older woman down the hall and into the low-ceilinged kitchen. A large stone fireplace took up most of the wall on the left. Logs were piled in the grate, and flames flickered under a large cast-iron pot.

Maggie sniffed, and the scent of ham and vegetables made her mouth water. "You're cooking over the fire?"

"Of course, that's the only way to make a decent meal." Mrs. Birdwell dipped a wooden spoon into the pot and stirred the thick, bubbling mixture.

At their millinery shop, Grandmother and Maggie had used a simple coal stove and oven to prepare their meals.

Grandmother stepped up beside Mrs. Birdwell and looked into the pot. "We cooked over a fire when I was a girl growing up on the farm. I'd enjoy trying my hand at it again."

Mrs. Birdwell pulled out the spoon and sent Grandmother a surprised glance. "I don't expect you to do the cooking."

"We'd be glad to help. Wouldn't we, girls?" Grandmother looked at Maggie and Violet.

Maggie gave a reluctant nod, though she had never prepared food over an open fire. She supposed her grandmother and Mrs. Birdwell could teach her what she needed to know.

Mrs. Birdwell pointed to the corner of the kitchen. "You can stack those cases over there. Just push the crates aside and move the broom." She turned back to the fireplace and sniffed the steam rising from the pot. "I made split pea soup for us."

Violet grimaced, and Maggie sent her a warning look before she deposited the cases in the corner.

Soon the table was set and they settled in to eat the midday meal. The soup was bland but filling. Maggie sipped another spoonful and reminded herself to be grateful. They had food to eat and a roof over their heads, and they would be close to their shop, church, and friends in the village . . . but they were far from Morningside.

Maggie ate the rest of her meal in silence, her thoughts focused on sifting through the information she had collected and planning what she would say to

Nate. Grandmother kept the conversation going by asking Mrs. Birdwell about her family and garden.

Violet barely touched her soup, but she ate two slices of bread, each spread with a thick layer of butter. She would've taken a third slice if Maggie hadn't reached out and stopped her.

"It's all right." Mrs. Birdwell offered Violet the first smile Maggie had seen since they'd arrived. "She's a growing girl."

"Eat your soup, Violet," Grandmother added. "Then we'll see if you have room for another slice of bread."

Violet sighed, dipped her spoon in the bowl, and swirled it through the thick green soup.

Maggie glanced at the small clock on the shelf by the fireplace and saw it was almost one. If she didn't leave soon, she might miss her chance to speak to Nate before he returned to Morningside.

"Thank you for lunch." She pushed back from the table. "I'm going to walk into the village, check on the progress at the shop, and take care of a few other errands."

Grandmother laid her napkin on the table. "I'd go with you, but I'm afraid my knees are aching today."

"May I go?" Violet looked from Grandmother to Maggie.

"I'm sorry, Violet, not today." Maggie reached for her bowl and plate and carried them to the sink.

"Why can't I go with you?" Violet stuck out her lower lip.

"It's too far to go on your crutches."

"I could do it. I'm strong."

"Yes, you are, but I think it's best if you stay here with Grandmother and Mrs. Birdwell today."

Violet crossed her arms. "Why do I have to miss out on all the fun?"

"I'm sure you can find something useful to do here this afternoon."

Grandmother scooted her chair back. "Yes, you can start by helping me with these dishes."

Violet's eyes widened, and her gaze darted from Grandmother to Maggie. "Me?"

"Yes, you." Grandmother patted Violet's cheek, and Maggie nodded.

Before their stay at Morningside Manor, Violet had helped them every day. Even after she broke her leg, she dried the dishes or folded clothes they brought in from the line. It was time she returned to those good habits.

Maggie gathered her hat and gloves from the bedroom and set off. She crossed the millstream bridge and ten minutes later reached the outskirts of the village. The street seemed practically deserted as she passed the Red Lion Inn and the village hospital. She continued on toward the shop, where she planned to make a quick stop to keep her word about checking on the progress before she walked on to the town hall in search of Nate.

As she rounded the corner and neared the shop, she heard Mr. Ledbetter call out, "Bring that wood over here." He motioned to two men unloading a stack of lumber from a wagon.

"Good afternoon, Mr. Ledbetter," Maggie called.

He touched his cap and nodded to her. "Good day, miss."

"How is the work on the shop coming along?" Maggie glanced up at the front wall, pleased to see the stone had been repaired and the wall restored to its original height.

"Very well. The weather's been fine, and that's helped us move ahead at a good pace." He motioned toward the open doorway. "Come in and let me show you what we've done."

Maggie followed him through the doorway and into the shop. All the burned debris had been hauled away, and now lumber and building supplies were stacked on the floor. Two men stood on ladders, repairing the stonework on the side wall, while another man sawed through a piece of wood set across two sawhorses.

"We finished the exterior stonework on the front wall yesterday, and we're framing the windows today." He pointed to a man who knelt on the ground, hammering a window frame together. Then he pointed to the left. "The side wall will be done in another day or two, then we can start on the interior walls and rebuild the stairway so we can work on the second floor."

Maggie smiled and nodded. "It looks like you're making good progress."

He tipped his head, and his eyes crinkled at the corners as he returned her smile. "I said we'd do our best for you, miss."

"Thank you. I'm pleased." She glanced toward the street, eager to be on her way, then looked back at Mr. Ledbetter. "I plan to stop by every few days, but I wanted you to know we're staying with Mrs. Birdwell, by the old mill, in case you needed to get in touch with us."

"Very good, miss. I'll send word if we have any questions." He bid her good day, then turned back to his work.

Maggie stepped around the stacks of lumber and made her way toward the door. As soon as she stepped outside, someone called her name, and she turned to see who it was.

Joseph Neatherton lifted his hand and jogged toward her from the neighboring shop. "Hello, Maggie." He brushed his blond hair from his eyes and sent her a broad smile.

"Hello, Joseph." She looked down the street, hoping the delay would not make her miss Nate.

"It's good to see you." His overeager expression pricked her conscience. She needed to have a talk with him and be clear about her feelings, but now was not the time.

He looked past her shoulder. "How's the work going on your shop?"

"Very well."

"Come and see what we've done." He motioned toward his shop.

"I'm sorry, Joseph. I need to be on my way." She turned and took a step.

He reached for her arm. "Maggie, wait. Why are you in such a rush? It's been so long since I've seen you." His face colored. "I've missed you."

"I'm sorry. I don't have time to talk right now. I have to go to the town hall." She slipped her arm away.

"Whoa, that's not a good idea." He stepped into her path.

She frowned at him. "Why not? What's the matter?"

He lifted his thumb and motioned toward the village green. "We drove by a few minutes ago, and there's a huge crowd of men from Clifton waiting for the strike meeting to let out. It's not safe to go there today."

"But I have to catch Nate before he leaves."

Joseph's eyebrows dipped, and a shadow crossed his face. "Why not just speak to him when you go back to Morningside?"

"We're not staying at Morningside any longer."

Surprise rippled across his face. "You're not?"

"No, we're staying with Mrs. Birdwell."

"The old widow by the mill?"

Maggie nodded. "Now I really must go. It's important that I speak to Nate as soon as he leaves that meeting." She stepped around Joseph and started down the street

"Then I'll go with you." He fell into step beside her.

Maggie blew out a frustrated breath. "If you must."

With his long legs, he had no trouble keeping up with her quick pace. "I'm glad you're staying with Mrs. Birdwell. We pass there every day on our way to my uncle's farm. Maybe I could stop on Sunday and give you and your grandmother and sister a ride to church."

Maggie was so intent on her goal she hardly heard what he was saying.

They rounded the corner and stopped at the edge of the village green. She scanned the large crowd of roughly dressed men, and her stomach clenched. It was hard to estimate the number of men filling the open area in front of the town hall, but she guessed there were at least three hundred. Some stood alone, but most were gathered in small groups, smoking and talking in low voices.

A few women and children stood at the back of the crowd, lined up by the shops facing the square. Anxious expressions lined the women's faces, and they clutched the hands of their children, keeping them close. Mistrust and hostility hardened the men's expressions, and restless energy emanated from the shuffling crowd.

Joseph stepped closer. "You see what I mean? This is no place for you to wait for Nate Harcourt."

"I'm sure I'll be fine." But a ripple of unease slid down her back. She looked around, searching for Nate's motorcar, but she didn't see it. He had probably parked it in that secluded spot behind the church to avoid the crowd after the meeting. Would he leave by the back door rather than the front for the same reason? That thought shook her from her daze, and she stepped away from Joseph and started around the edge of the square.

Joseph hustled after her. "Maggie, wait! Where are you going?" His loud voice caused several people to turn and look their way.

She shot him a heated glance. "If you're coming with me, keep your voice down."

He scrunched his shoulders and looked around, then hustled up beside her. "Why do we have to keep quiet?"

"Shh! I don't want to attract attention."

He shot her a side glance. "Maggie, you're acting crazy. What's going on?"

"I can't say!" she hissed. But the hurt in his eyes made her regret her tone. "I'm sorry, but this is urgent. I have to find Nate."

She turned and bumped into a man. "I'm sorry."

He shifted and looked her way.

She pulled in a sharp breath. "Rob?"

Ruddy color shot through Lilly's beau's face. He touched his cap and dipped his chin. "Maggie." Then he straightened his shoulders and looked toward the town hall. "Important matters are being decided today. I wanted to hear the results myself."

"Yes, of course."

He shot another glance her way. "Tell Lilly I'll see her tomorrow."

Maggie was about to explain that she was no longer staying at Morningside and wouldn't see Lilly, but the front door of the town hall opened and six men strode out. They were dressed similarly to the men waiting in the square, and Maggie assumed they were the leaders of the workers. Maggie spotted John Palmer, the man who'd challenged Nate the day the men from Clifton surrounded his motorcar.

The murmuring crowd turned toward them and settled.

"What did they say?" a man near the front shouted. "Did they agree to our demands?" His question stirred the crowd, and others called out for answers.

Palmer lifted his hands. "Quiet down and listen." His brooding gaze traveled across the village green. "We told you this would not be an easy fight."

A groan rose from some of the men.

"Tell us what happened!" another man shouted.

Palmer clenched his hands. "The board agreed to do more safety inspections, but they refused all our other demands."

Shouts and curses filled the air.

Maggie gasped. How could the board refuse to negotiate the other demands? Didn't they realize that would anger the men and force them to walk out?

"Maggie!" Joseph's voice was low and urgent. "We should leave now."

She shook her head. "Not yet!"

"So what do you say, men?" Palmer continued. "Shall we slink back to our jobs like whipped pups and keep slaving away for wages that leave us and our wives and children hungry?"

"No!" several men shouted back.

"Should we just keep our heads down and accept their decision, or will we stand up for ourselves and show them we mean what we say?"

Shouts and cheers rose from the crowd. From the far side of the village green someone shouted, "Strike! Strike! Strike!"

The cry rose and swelled as men all around Maggie raised their fists and took up the wild chant. Soon the whole crowd was stomping their feet and shouting, "Strike! Strike! Strike!"

"We have to get out of here, Maggie!" Joseph grabbed her arm and tried to pull her away from the surging mob.

29

"Strike! Strike! Strike!"

Shouts rose from the men outside in the village green and vibrated the floor of the old town hall.

Nate turned away from Geoffrey Rowlett and strode across the meeting room toward the window. His chest tightened as he took in the scene below. Men filled the square, yelling, stomping, and waving their fists in the air.

Defeat pounded through him with every shout.

He had failed, and now they would all have to pay the price.

Samuelson joined him at the window and looked out at the swarming crowd. His brow creased. "I'm sorry, Nate. I thought I could convince them to continue the negotiations."

"It's not your fault. Both sides have to be willing, and most of the board is not ready to concede the fight." Nate glanced at the men gathered on the far side of the room and shook his head. Why couldn't the board see times were changing? Workers could no longer be treated like second-class citizens who were expected to work long hours in dangerous conditions for low pay. Making changes would decrease profits, but they were necessary changes. What did they think they would gain by their refusal to negotiate the other demands?

Samuelson turned to Nate. "I should go. I have to finish preparing my sermon for tomorrow."

"I wouldn't advise leaving yet."

Samuelson glanced toward the window again. "I don't think the men would harm me."

Nate wasn't so sure. "There's no telling what might happen when they're agitated like this."

Samuelson gazed out the window, his face lined with concern. "I suppose you're right. I'll wait until things settle down."

Nate scanned the teeming crowd again while the shouting continued. He could almost see the anger and frustration rising from the village green like a foul cloud of smoke.

A flash of coral near the back of the crowd caught his eye. He shifted to the right for a better view. His heart plunged, and he gripped the windowsill. Maggie wove through the edge of the shouting throng. A tall blond man reached for her arm and pulled her to a stop.

Alarm shot through Nate. He spun away from the window and dashed across the room.

"Nate! What is it?" Samuelson's call echoed after him.

But Nate didn't slow down. There was no time to explain. He ran down the stairs and burst out the front door. Pushing past the men on the top step, he jumped to the ground. "Step aside!" He plunged into the crowd and tried to force his way through, but it felt like swimming against a raging current. He pressed on past sneering faces, with shouts and curses ringing in his ears. Finally, he spotted her coral dress. "Maggie!"

She turned, her face pale and her eyes wide. "Nate!"

"That's Harcourt!" A man grabbed his jacket and yanked him back.

Nate jerked away, but someone else grabbed him from the other side.

"We'll teach you a lesson!" A fiery-eyed man jerked Nate around, lifted his fist, and swung at him.

Nate tried to dodge the blow, but it landed in his stomach. He gasped and doubled over, blinding white pain radiating through him.

"No!" Maggie screamed and lunged toward Nate.

Nate lifted his head. Something flew through the air toward him. He ducked to the left as a glass bottle whizzed past, then hit the side of Maggie's head and shattered.

Nate's heart lurched. Maggie crumpled. Nate lunged toward her, but several men pulled him back. A tall blond man caught Maggie and scooped her up before she hit the ground.

"Stand back!" Nate pulled free. Panting, he strode forward. In a flash he realized the man holding Maggie was Joseph Neatherton. "I'll take her."

Joseph shot him a flaming glare. "No! You've done enough!" He pulled Maggie closer to his chest and strode away through the crowd.

Nate stared at them for a split second, then charged after Joseph. "Where are you taking her?"

"To the hospital." Joseph hustled down the street, and Nate matched him stride for stride.

Nate glanced at Maggie, nestled against Joseph's chest, her eyes closed and her face pale. A red rivulet snaked through her hair and dripped down the side of her face. Nate's gut twisted. "Hurry, she's bleeding!"

Joseph's eyes flashed, and he quickened his pace. "None of this would've happened if you and those greedy managers at Clifton had given the men a fair deal."

Nate steeled himself against the accusation, but it was true. Maggie had been hurt today because the board refused to compromise, and though he was a dissenting member of the board, he was still responsible. A powerful ache radiated through his stomach from the blow and the weight of his failure.

They reached the hospital in less than two minutes. Nate pushed open the door, and Joseph carried Maggie inside. A startled nurse met them in the entrance hall. She ushered them into an examination room, then ran out to fetch the doctor.

Joseph gently lowered Maggie to the examination table, then looked up at Nate. "If she is seriously hurt, I promise you I'll—"

Dr. Hadley strode into the room, and Nate pulled in a deep breath to steady himself. Surely the doctor would be able to help Maggie. But as Nate stared at Maggie's still form and the blood oozing from the side of her head, a cold wave of dread washed over him.

Maggie heard voices above her, but the words were not clear. Her head throbbed and a sharp pain pricked the side of her head. She slowly opened her eyes, then blinked at the bright lights. "Nate?"

Joseph's face came into focus, hovering over her.

Her throat was so dry she had to swallow before she could speak. "Where's Nate? Is he all right?"

Someone gripped her hand. "I'm right here, Maggie." Nate moved into view beside her, holding tight to her hand. His soothing voice sent a wave of relief through her. If Nate was here, everything would be all right.

She started to turn her head toward him, but someone stopped her. "Hold still, Maggie, I'm almost done stitching." That was Dr. Hadley's voice.

She felt another prick on the side of her head, and she bit her lip. Nate tightened his hold on her hand, compassion flowing from his brown eyes.

"Just two more stitches." The doctor leaned closer, and Maggie closed her eyes. She focused on the warmth and strength of Nate's hand holding hers and swallowed against the next prick of the doctor's needle.

"What happened?" She forced out the words.

"You received a blow to the head, and I'm stitching up the cut."

"Someone threw a glass bottle at Harcourt, but it missed him and hit you." Joseph's tone was curt and accusing.

Maggie opened her eyes. "It's not Nate's fault."

Joseph crossed his arms and looked away, obviously disagreeing with her.

"That's the last stitch." Dr. Hadley snipped the thread, then smiled at Maggie. "You're a fortunate young lady. You only needed six stitches, and the scar will be hidden in your hair." He set his needle aside. "Now let's take it nice and slow, and I'll help you sit up."

Maggie's head throbbed a bit more as she sat up. She lifted her hand and touched the skin by the cut. It was sore, but the pain wasn't too bad.

"You'll need to rest for a day or two," the doctor continued. "You may have a headache, but let me know if you have any dizziness or nausea. Keep the cut clean and dry, and come back and see me in a week. We'll check the stitches then and see if they're ready to come out."

"Thank you, Doctor."

"You're welcome." He turned to Nate and Joseph. "You'll see that she gets home?"

Both men said "Yes!" at the same time.

The doctor grinned. "I'll let you sort that out." He looked from Maggie to Joseph and Nate. "Good day." The doctor walked out of the room.

Nate turned to Maggie. "I have my motorcar parked behind the church. I'll bring it around and give you a ride."

Joseph sent Maggie a questioning glance. "Is that what you want?" She could read his deeper question, and she knew she owed him an explanation.

"Yes, it is." She shifted her gaze to Nate and smiled. "Thank you. I'd appreciate that."

He nodded, looking pleased, then walked out of the room.

"I'll head back to the shop, then." Defeat lined Joseph's face as he turned away.

Maggie's heart clenched. "Joseph, wait."

He slowly turned and met her gaze.

"You've been my good friend for a long time."

"A good friend?"

"Yes, the best. Thank you."

He nodded, but her words didn't erase the disappointment in his eyes.

"I'm sorry, Joseph. I didn't mean to hurt you."

He lifted his hand. "It's all right. I can tell by the way you look at him that he's your choice."

"I do care for Nate. I won't deny it, but I don't know if anything will come of it."

"He's a fool if he doesn't snatch you up and marry you before the week is out."

A smile tugged at Maggie's lips. "I'm not sure he's quite ready for that."

"Well, he should be. You're a beauty, Maggie, inside and out. Any man would be lucky to win your heart." He shook his head. "I'm just sorry it's not me."

She pressed her lips together, touched by his words.

He leaned down and softly kissed her cheek. "Take care, Maggie, and don't forget about your old friend."

"I won't." A lump lodged in her throat as Joseph walked out of the room, but she was glad she'd been honest with him. Joseph was a good man, and he would make some woman a fine husband. He just wasn't the right man for her.

Nate ushered Maggie toward the motorcar and opened the passenger door. She climbed in, settled on the seat, and sent him a grateful smile.

His chest swelled with hopeful expectation. She'd chosen to go with him today rather than Joseph. She was giving him another chance, and this time he would work through the issues with her.

He cranked the motorcar, then hustled around and climbed into the driver's seat.

Maggie turned toward him. "Before we go I have something to tell you."

Nate shifted in the seat to face her. "If it's all right, I'd like to speak first."

She nodded. "Of course."

He looked into her eyes. "I'm sorry for the way I responded yesterday when you suggested my father could be responsible for the deaths of your parents and sister. I didn't want to believe it could be true. But I've had time to think about it, and I realize now what's most important is that I keep my promise to you. I'll go to the police with you as soon as the strike is settled. We can tell them what we know and let them continue the investigation."

A smile bloomed on Maggie's lips. "Thank you, Nate. That's good of you."

"I want you to always feel you can count on me to keep my word."

Her eyes glowed. "I know that's true now."

The trusting look in her eyes and the sweetness of her smile stole his breath away. He reached for her hand and wrapped his fingers around hers, so grateful the wall between them was finally coming down.

"And now I'll tell you my news." Her face lit up with an eager expression. "Mr. Billington came by to see you this morning."

"Mr. Billington from Lynemouth?"

"Yes. He remembered something else about the day of the accident, and he thought it was important enough to make a trip to Morningside."

"What did he say?"

"There was another man who went out in the boat with your father that day."

He stared at her for a moment. "Who was it?"

"Roland Dixon, the same man who's blackmailing your stepmother."

Nate's thoughts spun as he absorbed this new information. "So he might be the one responsible rather than my father?"

Maggie nodded. "Helen could've told Dixon my father had discovered their secret and planned to go to Mr. Harcourt. Then Dixon decided to stop my father by damaging the boat so it would go down when he was out on the lake."

"So you think Helen and Dixon planned the accident to keep my father from learning the truth?"

Maggie nodded. "Yes. They had a motive, and now we know Dixon had the opportunity."

Nate rubbed his chin. There were still pieces of the story that didn't quite make sense, but at least they had another suspect the police could question and his father's reputation might be preserved. But if their assumptions were correct, Helen could be considered an accomplice and might face serious consequences. And that would be almost as damaging to the family's name.

"I think we're closer to the truth now than we've ever been."

Maggie's words brought him back to the moment, and he focused on her again. "Are you still willing to wait until the strike is settled before we go to the police?"

She paused for a moment, and her gaze met his. "If you think that's best."

"I do. I want to be sure I'm home when the police come to Morningside. That's the best way I can protect Clara—and Helen, if she'll allow it."

"All right. The facts aren't going to change, and I don't think Helen or Dixon are going anywhere."

Nate nodded, pleased that she trusted his judgment and was willing to wait. He glanced down the street, considering his next question. "I know the doctor said you should rest, and I can take you to Mrs. Birdwell's if you'd like, but I'd feel more at ease if you'd spend the afternoon with me."

A smile stole across her lips again. "I suppose that would be all right."

"I have a meeting with Mr. Hornshaw at three. You could rest at the house, and we could have tea after the meeting. Then I could drive you back to the village later."

She nodded, her eyes glowing with a happy light. "I'd be very happy to spend the afternoon with you."

He grinned, then revved the engine and drove off down the street.

30

They made a quick stop at Mrs. Birdwell's to let Maggie's grandmother know she was with Nate and would return before dinner, then they drove on toward Morningside.

Though the strike loomed in the days ahead and Nate was unsure what would happen after they went to the police, he couldn't help but feel optimistic. With Maggie by his side and her confidence in him restored, he believed he could overcome any obstacle that rose in his path.

He drove across the bridge over the ravine, passed through Morningside's main gate, and followed the winding drive up the hill toward the house. A young groom met them as Nate parked on the far side of the stable. He stepped forward and opened Maggie's door. Nate hustled around to meet her. She climbed out slowly, still looking a bit pale.

He pulled in a deep breath and offered her his arm. "I should've let you out by the front door rather than asking you to walk from the stable."

"I'll be all right." But she took his arm and leaned on him as they strolled toward the house.

He slowed his pace to match hers and tried to shake off his worry. The doctor said she would be fine as long as she got some rest. He would encourage her to lie down while he met with Mr. Hornshaw, then he'd see that they had an early tea.

As they approached the house, Clara and Owen Campbell walked out the front door. Clara's face brightened when she saw them. "Oh, Nate, there you are. We were looking for you." She smiled at Owen, urging him forward.

Owen nodded to Nate. "I'd like to speak to you, sir." He glanced at Maggie, questions reflecting in his eyes. "If you have time, that is."

Nate straightened and assessed the young man. Owen's flushed face and Clara's hold on his arm made Nate suspect what Owen wanted to discuss, and it couldn't have come at a more inopportune time. But it would be unkind to put them off.

"Very well." He turned to his sister. "Clara, would you take Maggie into the drawing room and wait for us there?"

His sister gave an eager nod, then hooked arms with Maggie and escorted her inside.

Nate motioned toward the front door. "Let's go into the library."

"Yes, sir." Owen walked with Nate into the house.

Nate offered Owen a chair by the library fireplace and took the seat opposite him. "Now, what did you want to discuss?"

Owen's Adam's apple bobbed in his throat. "I'm very fond of Clara, sir." His face turned a deeper shade of red, and he pressed his lips together nervously. "No, what I mean to say is, I love Clara, and I want to ask your permission to propose to her."

Nate lifted one eyebrow. "You're both quite young to consider marriage."

"I'll be twenty-one in August, and Clara is almost eighteen." Owen clutched the arms of the chair. "But of course you know your sister's age."

Nate couldn't help but feel sympathy for the young man, and he softened his tone. "I know you have your position at Morningside, but I understand you want to study to be a veterinarian. How does that fit into your plans to marry Clara?"

"I hope to have enough saved to start my training in January. That would take me away to Edinburgh for a time, but Dr. Higgs in Heatherton is willing to take me on to finish my training after that. Clara and I would like to become engaged before I go and then marry when I come back to Heatherton."

"And Clara understands you'd have to wait until you finish your training in Edinburgh to marry?"

"Yes, sir, she does."

Her life as the wife of a village veterinarian would certainly be different from her life at Morningside. Nate couldn't quite imagine his sister settled in the village, doing the cooking and most of the household chores herself. But she must be aware of Owen's circumstances and know what the future would be like if she married him. Still, Clara wasn't the only one he needed to consider.

Nate sat back and steepled his hands in front of his mouth. "Before I give you an answer, there is something you should know."

"What's that, sir?"

"In the near future, events will come to light that will cast a shadow over our family. I can't explain the particulars right now, but you might want to wait and see how those events play out before you make a decision about your future with Clara."

Owen's brow creased. "Is this about Clara? Surely she hasn't done anything wrong!"

"No, Clara is not at fault. I'm just saying these events may affect our family's reputation, and if you're connected with Clara, they will affect you as well." Nate debated telling him more, but he couldn't risk word leaking out.

"Whatever it is, I won't change my mind." Owen sat up straighter. "I'm committed to Clara, and if I have your permission, I'd like to propose."

"You're certain, even if these events become a public scandal?"

"Yes, sir. I don't listen to gossip or care about other people's opinions. I love Clara, and she loves me. We want to be married. That's what's most important to us."

Nate thought through the situation a moment more. Helen would not be pleased, especially if he made the decision without her input. But he had to do what was best for Clara and the family. And knowing the storm that was coming, Clara's engagement to Owen might be the way to protect her future.

He lifted his gaze to meet Owen's. "Very well, you have my permission to propose. I'll speak to Clara's mother and inform her of my decision."

"Thank you, sir." A smile broke out across Owen's face.

"If Clara accepts"—and Nate had no doubt she would—"I'd like you to keep the engagement private until I give you permission to announce it."

"We'll wait until you say the time is right."

"Very good." They both stood, and Nate reached out and shook the young man's hand. "You may speak to Clara, but not a word to anyone else."

"Yes, sir." Owen looked Nate in the eye. "And I promise I'll do everything in my power to make her happy."

A sense of calm assurance filled Nate. "I'm sure you will." He tipped his head toward the door leading to the adjoining drawing room. "Go on, then. I'm sure Clara is eager to hear the results of our conversation."

Owen nodded, strode across the library, and entered the drawing room, looking like a man who had won a great victory. A moment later, Nate heard Clara's happy laughter. Maggie appeared in the doorway. She slipped into the library and pulled the door closed behind her.

"So, it sounds like that went well." She crossed to meet Nate.

"Clara told you what he wanted?"

"Yes, but I guessed before she said anything." She sent him a happy smile. "So you gave them your permission?"

Nate nodded. "But I asked him to not make it public until things are settled."

She tipped her head, a question in her eyes.

"I didn't explain the whole situation. I just let him know there was trouble ahead for the family and he might want to wait, but he's determined to marry my sister."

"Do you think Helen will agree?"

"I don't think she will like it, but—"

A loud clatter sounded in the great hall, and Maggie turned toward the door. "What was that?"

"I don't know." Nate strode out of the library and into the great hall. Maggie followed close behind.

Helen was descending the stairs dressed in a gray traveling suit and broad feathered hat. She clutched a large black suitcase in one hand and reached to lift a second case that had fallen on the landing.

Nate tensed. "Helen, what are you doing?"

She gasped and dropped the suitcase. "Goodness, Nate, you startled me." She left both cases on the landing and walked down to the main floor. "I thought you were in Heatherton for the meeting with the men from Clifton."

"I was, but we finished more than an hour ago." He crossed and met her at the bottom of the stairs.

Helen cast a cool glance at Maggie. "What is she doing here? I thought she had returned to the village."

Maggie stepped up next to Nate. "We are staying with Mrs. Birdwell, but Nate invited me here for the afternoon."

Helen sniffed and looked away.

Irritation coursed through Nate as he glanced at the suitcases. "Where are you going?"

"Going? Oh . . . yes, I'm going to visit the Wilsons in Lincolnshire."

Nate frowned. "Who are the Wilsons?"

"They're old friends. You don't know them." She shifted her gaze away and fluttered her hand down her skirt. "I really should be leaving. I have to catch the four-o'clock train." She turned toward the stairs.

Nate stepped into her path. "Helen, this isn't a good time for you to visit friends."

Her eyes widened, and a hint of panic skittered across her face. "But I accepted their invitation. They're expecting me this evening. I can't disappoint them. It wouldn't be right."

He hadn't planned to confront Helen today, but there seemed no way around it. He couldn't let her take her suitcases and walk out the front door, not with the issues surrounding the accident still unresolved. He glanced at Maggie. Her firm gaze encouraged him to press on, and he focused on Helen again. "There are some important things that need to be settled first."

"What do you mean?" Her voice rose and sounded strained.

He straightened his shoulders. "We know you're being blackmailed, and we know why."

She pulled back as if she'd been struck. "Why would you say such a thing?"

"Because it's the truth."

Helen lifted a shaky finger and pointed at Maggie. "This is her fault. I told you not to trust her. She's just like her father, raising herself up and prying into our family's private affairs. You never should have brought her to Morningside."

"It won't help your cause to blame Maggie or anyone else."

"But she snuck into my room to read my diaries, then she listened to my private conversation."

Maggie gasped.

"Maggie was looking for answers about the boating accident, and I believe she found them."

"No! She wants to trap you and get rid of me!"

Heat surged into his face. "That's enough! If you expect me to show mercy toward you, then you must stop blaming others and start telling the truth."

Helen lifted her chin and looked away.

"If you won't cooperate, then I'll have no choice but to turn you over to the police and let them do the questioning."

Helen's face paled. She pressed her lips into a firm line, but her chin began to tremble.

"Were you unfaithful to my father?"

"No! Never!"

Nate scowled at her. "How can you deny it? Maggie and I saw you meeting a man in the woods by Tumbledon Lake. We heard what you said. And Maggie's father saw you with him several times as well."

"I was not meeting a lover." Her voice wavered.

"Then who was he?" Nate demanded.

"His name is Roland Dixon. He . . . he's my brother."

Nate scoffed. "Your brother? If that's true, why did you meet him in secret? Why not invite him to the house as you would any other relative?"

Helen clasped her trembling hands. "He said he would tell your father about my past, and I . . . I couldn't let that happen."

Nate stared at her, trying to recall what he knew about Helen's life before she'd married his father. They'd met in Cumbria on holiday when Nate was just a young boy, but he knew little about her beyond that.

Nate narrowed his gaze at Helen. "What was it about your past that you wanted to keep hidden from my father?"

Her face flushed as she looked from Maggie to Nate. "I'd rather not say."

"You will tell us now, or I will be forced to send for the police."

Helen clenched her hands for several seconds as she considered his threat. "All right." She released a slow, shaky breath. "Before I met your father, I was an actress in a musical review."

Surprise rippled through Nate. "An actress?" He frowned, weighing her words. "Society might look down on actresses, but you could've overcome that by having an honest conversation with my father. Why would you allow your brother to blackmail you all these years?"

She crossed her arms protectively over her midsection, and her gaze darted away.

"There must be more to the story," Nate insisted, "and you will tell us now."

Her stony expression melted, and defeat darkened her eyes. She dropped her arms. "When I was twenty-one, I married a man named Robert Maxwell. He was several years older and quite charming, but he drank more than he should and gambled away most of our money. After three years he left me. I had no idea where he'd gone or if he was ever coming back. So when I met your father I thought it was my chance to leave that life behind."

Nate stared at her. "You lied to him and accepted his proposal even though you were already married?"

She blinked and sent a desperate glance around the room. "Yes." Her voice was hushed and shaky. "A few months later, I learned my first husband died in a robbery attempt, but I was too ashamed to tell your father."

Nate frowned, trying to make sense of her story. "And that's what you've been hiding all these years?"

Helen lowered her head. "I didn't want your father or anyone else to know."

Maggie glared at Helen. "So you planned to kill my father to keep your secret from coming to light?" Her voice shook with intensity. "How could you?"

Helen lifted her head. "No! That was Roland's idea. I didn't know he was behind the accident until after it happened."

"But you told Roland about your conversation with my father, and that's what motivated him to damage the boat."

Helen nodded. "Roland only wanted to frighten your father. He didn't know the whole family was going out with him that day. He thought your father would go alone and would be able to swim to shore. Then he planned to tell him worse things would happen if he followed through on his threat to speak to Mr. Harcourt."

"Now you've done it, Helen!" A man's harsh voice boomed behind them.

Helen gripped the railing, and Nate swung around and faced the man.

Maggie gasped. "That's Roland Dixon!"

Dixon lifted a stubby finger and pointed at Helen. "I told you I was coming for you. How could you betray me after I've kept your secret all these years?"

Bright spots burned on Helen's cheeks. "You haven't kept my secret. You've used it like a weapon and held me captive with your threats and blackmail."

"You promised if I kept quiet you'd take care of me."

"I never promised you anything! You forced me into it!"

"We had an agreement!"

"Stop it, both of you!" Nate glared from one to the other. "Blaming each other won't absolve your guilt. You're both at fault, and it's time you went to the police and told the truth."

Dixon's eyes turned steely. "We aren't going to the police."

"Yes, you are." Nate took a step toward Dixon.

Dixon yanked a gun from inside his jacket and pointed it at Nate. "Stay where you are! Don't come any closer!"

Adrenaline surged through Nate, and every instinct told him to rush the man and knock the gun from his hands. But he couldn't risk Dixon shooting Maggie or Helen. He must protect them at all costs. He slowly lifted his hand. "Just calm down. We don't want anyone to get hurt."

Dixon shifted his burning gaze from Maggie to Nate. "You should've thought about that before you and that girl started snooping around."

31

A cold tremor quivered down Maggie's back as she stared at the gun in Dixon's hand. Questions darted through her mind, quickly followed by answers as the series of events clicked into place like pieces of a puzzle.

Helen must have overheard Maggie's conversation with Nate the night before. She had gone into Maggie's room that morning while they were down at breakfast and found the notes she'd tucked into her mother's Bible for safekeeping. When Helen learned what Maggie and Nate had discovered, she contacted Dixon and packed her bags, hoping to leave Morningside with Dixon before Nate and Maggie went to the police.

Dixon hadn't been afraid to harm her father four years ago, and he was in much more serious trouble now. What would he do to them? Maggie swallowed and breathed a silent prayer.

Nate focused on Dixon, his expression intense but calm. "Put the gun down, and we'll talk this through."

"It's too late for that!" Dixon's face turned scarlet, and beads of sweat glistened on his brow.

"I promise I'll do everything I can to explain your side of things to the police."

Dixon narrowed his eyes. "Why would you help me?"

"I'm a man of my word, and I don't want to see you or Helen face any more serious consequences than are necessary."

"Ha! You're a fool if you think I'd believe that." Suddenly Dixon grabbed Maggie and pulled her in front of him. She gasped, and he jabbed the gun in her side.

Dixon's rough grip sent pain shooting through Maggie's arm. His foul breath flooded the air around them. She clamped her mouth closed and turned her face away from him.

Nate's eyes flamed, but he held his ground. "Don't make your situation worse. Let Miss Lounsbury go, and put the gun away."

"Not on your life." Dixon jerked her one step to the side. "Now, all of you listen to me and do as I say. Helen, go have a carriage brought around front, then dismiss the groomsmen."

Helen's wide-eyed gaze darted from Nate to Dixon. "What are you going to do?"

He released a humorless chuckle. "I arranged one accident; I suppose I can manage another."

"Roland, no!" Helen moved toward him, her gaze pleading. "You didn't intend to kill the Lounsburys. We can hire a solicitor to defend you."

"Even if we could prove I never planned to do away with that family, I put a hole in that boat. That makes me guilty, and I'd end up rotting in prison or hanging." He cursed under his breath. "I won't die like our father!"

Helen lifted her hand to her mouth. "No, Roland, please! Don't do this!"

"Go on! Do as I say! We can't turn back now."

Helen's chin trembled as she looked from Maggie to Nate, then she strode past them and hurried out the front door.

Dixon tightened his grip on Maggie's arm again. She gulped in a breath and tried to still her shaking legs. Dixon was a desperate man, and without some kind of intervention, she and Nate were about to become the next *accident* victims.

She closed her eyes. *Please, God, help us.*

"Dixon, listen to me." Nate's voice was low and urgent. "It's not too late. You can change your mind and save yourself and your sister."

"What? You want me to turn myself in?" Dixon huffed. "I'd face the gallows for sure." He pointed the gun at Nate. "Go wait by the front door."

Nate stared at him, unmoving.

"Now!" Dixon's shout rang out, and he waved the gun at Nate.

Nate's gaze smoldered, but he walked past Maggie and Dixon toward the entrance hall and front door. Dixon shoved the gun against her side again and tugged her after Nate.

Nate glanced out the window and scanned the front drive and gardens. Maggie followed his gaze, but there was not a gardener or anyone else in sight.

Please, God! Send someone to help us.

Nate turned back to Dixon. "You won't get away with this. We have a written record of everything we discovered. If anything happens to us, they'll know who is at fault."

"We'll be long gone by then." Dixon yanked Maggie closer to the door and looked out the window. Seconds stretched into minutes as they waited. Maggie's head throbbed, and she silently sent off another prayer while Nate's gaze remained fixed on the front drive.

Finally, the carriage rolled around the side of the house and pulled to a stop by the entrance.

Dixon leaned closer to the glass, watching as the driver stepped down and walked away in the direction of the stable.

Nate shifted his gaze to meet Maggie's. His dark-brown eyes reflected determination, but they also seemed to send an appeal to trust him. Her stomach churned. What did he mean? What did he plan to do?

"Open the front door." Dixon lifted his chin toward Nate.

Nate stepped forward and pulled open the heavy wooden door.

"Now go outside," Dixon ordered, and Nate stepped out onto the gravel drive. Dixon shoved Maggie out the door and into the driveway. "Open the carriage door!"

Nate did as Dixon said, then turned and faced them.

"Get inside." Dixon shoved Maggie toward the carriage. Her foot caught on her dress, and she tripped.

Nate reached out and caught her. As they straightened, their gazes connected and held. "Whatever happens, I love you."

"And I love you," she whispered back, searching his face.

His expression grew firm, and the determination returned to his eyes. "Climb in." Nate took her hand and guided her toward the carriage.

Confusion and panic pulsed through her. How could he send her away with Dixon only two seconds after he'd said he loved her?

He nodded to her, urging her with his eyes to have faith in him. She summoned her courage and stepped up into the carriage. Once inside, she glanced around, expecting to see Helen, but she wasn't there.

Nate closed the carriage door and stepped in front of it, putting himself between Maggie and Dixon. She took a seat next to the window and looked out, her heart pounding hard while she sent off another silent plea. *Please, God, protect Nate, stop Dixon, and put an end to all of this.*

"You won't save yourself by trying to escape." Nate's voice was firm, his tone commanding. "The police will follow you, and if you take Miss Lounsbury, it will only add to your crimes."

"Oh, we'll get away, because there won't be anyone left to tell the police anything about it." Dixon raised his gun toward Nate and cocked the hammer.

Maggie gasped and lunged for the carriage door. "No!"

"Stop or I'll shoot!" Owen Campbell marched around the side of the house, flanked by Helen and Clara. He held a long hunting rifle up to his shoulder and aimed it at Dixon.

Dixon pivoted toward them, and his eyes bulged. "Helen! What are you doing?"

"The first sensible thing I've done in years."

"You'll regret this!" Dixon's hand shook as he raised his gun.

Maggie's gaze darted across the scene, her heart pounding.

Nate lunged for Dixon. The gun exploded. Clara screamed. Helen fell back and grabbed her arm as she crumpled to the ground. Owen charged forward, while Nate wrestled Dixon to the ground. Two young groomsmen came running around the side of the house and dashed into the fray between Nate and Dixon.

Maggie threw open the door, bolted from the carriage, and ran toward Helen.

Clara knelt on the ground beside Helen. "Mother, oh, Mother."

She gripped Clara's hand, her eyes squeezed tightly closed.

Maggie dropped down on the opposite side of Helen and scanned her bloody arm. She whipped off her sister's shawl, folded it, and pressed it against

Helen's wound. She looked across at Clara. "Come around and hold this against her arm."

Clara moved into place and pressed her hand against the shawl. Maggie rose and turned toward the men.

"We've got him, sir." Owen's voice rang out.

Nate rose, leaving Dixon facedown on the drive, with Owen and the two groomsmen holding him in place.

Jackson stepped out the front door, followed by two footmen. The old butler's eyes widened as he took in the scene. "Sir, are you all right? What happened?"

"I'll explain later. Andrew, use my horse to ride into the village for the doctor. Then alert the police and ask them to come as well."

"Yes, sir!" Andrew ran off toward the stable.

"Phillip, bring a length of rope and tie up that man." Nate glared at Dixon, then turned and strode toward Maggie. Lines creased his brow as he knelt on the gravel drive next to his stepmother. "I'm sorry, Helen."

"It's not your fault. None of it is." Helen pressed her trembling lips together. "I was wrong. I should've put a stop to all of this a long time ago."

Nate laid his hand on her uninjured shoulder. "Don't worry about that now."

"If I'd only been honest with your father, none of this would've happened."

"But you made the right choice today. That's what's most important. I'm grateful. We all are."

Maggie nodded, her throat too tight to speak. All these months she had blamed Helen for what had happened to her family, but now she knew the rest of the story. It was true Helen had been foolish and dishonest about her past, but Maggie's pride and anger had pushed her to make assumptions about Nate's father and stepmother that were never true. A wave of sorrow and regret washed over her. She had been wrong, very wrong, about many things. She owed Nate an apology, and perhaps she owed Helen one as well.

The footman returned with the rope and handed it to Owen. Nate called Phillip over, and they lifted Helen off the ground.

Clara rose and stifled a sob as they carried her mother into the house.

Maggie embraced her with a gentle hug and patted her back. "It's going to be all right, Clara." And for the first time in a long time, Maggie actually believed those words were true.

Nate stared into the library fireplace, watching the flames leap and dance as he recalled the events of the last few hours. The police had arrived and taken Dixon away, but they'd promised to return Monday morning at nine o'clock to question Helen and the rest of the family. The doctor came a short time later and was still upstairs with Helen.

Nate tensed, recalling his wrestling match with Dixon and the fateful shot that had struck Helen down. He'd tried to protect Maggie and his family, but he hadn't been able to prevent Helen's injury. And though she carried some blame for today's events, in the end she'd stood against her brother and tried to do what was right. He was glad for her change of heart, and he hoped it would go in her favor when the police questioned her about everything that had happened.

He turned and glanced across the room. Clara and Owen sat together, talking to each other in low voices. Owen held her hand, and her eyes glowed with tenderness as she looked at him. That young man had saved all their lives today, and he'd earned Nate's gratitude and respect.

Nate's gaze shifted to Maggie. She sat on the chair near the fireplace, watching him with a wistful hint of a smile on her lips. Her smile spread wider when she realized his focus was on her. A pretty pink flush filled her cheeks, but she did not look away. Affection and admiration stirred in his heart, and he longed for a moment alone to speak to her.

Dr. Hadley walked through the doorway, carrying his black medical bag.

Clara rose from her chair. "How is she, Doctor?"

"I believe she'll be all right. The bullet passed through her arm without hitting a bone or major artery. With rest and good care, she should recover and hopefully regain full use of her arm."

Clara clasped Owen's hand. "Oh, thank you, Doctor. May I go up and see her?"

"Yes, but I gave her some medication to help her sleep. That should take effect soon."

Clara sent Owen a questioning glance.

He nodded to her. "Go on, then. I'm sure she'll want to see you."

Clara beamed a grateful smile, then hurried out the door. Nate thanked Dr. Hadley. He promised to return the next day to check on Helen, then he bid them good night and left the room.

Nate turned to Owen. "I want to thank you for what you did today." He held out his hand, and Owen shook it. "I admire your courage, facing Dixon as you did. You not only saved my life, you saved Miss Lounsbury's as well."

Owen straightened his shoulders. "I was glad to do it, sir. We're family now, and that means we take care of each other."

Nate smiled. "You're a good man, Campbell."

"Thank you, sir. I'll say good night." He nodded to Nate and then to Maggie. "Miss Lounsbury."

"Good night," Maggie called, her eyes shining with gratitude.

Owen strode out of the library, leaving Maggie and Nate alone for the first time since the confrontation with Dixon.

Nate crossed to the settee and took a seat beside Maggie. He reached for her hand. "How are you feeling?"

She lifted her other hand to her forehead. "I have a bit of a headache, but it's not bad." She leaned back with a sigh. "I'm just thankful Dixon has been arrested and Helen is going to recover."

He sat back and ran his thumb over the top of her hand. "And I'm thankful you're all right." His throat tightened as he considered all that had happened. He could've lost her today if Owen hadn't intervened when he did.

Her gaze traveled over his face, reading the emotion behind his words. "We're both very blessed with the way things ended today."

"Yes, we are." His chest expanded. God had guided and protected them, and for that he would always be deeply grateful.

Jackson shuffled through the doorway. "Excuse me, sir, but Mrs. McCarthy is asking when you'd like dinner served and how many will be eating."

Maggie shifted on the settee and slipped her hand from his. "It's getting late. I should go."

"No, please stay."

Questions flickered in her eyes.

"You've been through two ordeals today, and I'm sure you must be tired. Why not rest here tonight?"

"But Grandmother will be worried."

"We can send a message." He rose, and she stood beside him. "And tomorrow morning I'll drive you to Mrs. Birdwell's in time to pick up your grandmother and Violet for church."

Maggie's smile returned, and she nodded. "All right."

"Then on Monday you'll want to be here when the police arrive to question everyone."

"Of course." She was eager to tell them what she'd learned.

Nate turned to Jackson. "Miss Lounsbury and I will have dinner in the dining room as soon as it's convenient. Please check with Miss Clara and see if she'd like to join us or take her dinner on a tray in Mrs. Harcourt's room. And please send a message to Mrs. Hayes that Miss Lounsbury will be staying at Morningside as our guest tonight. Also that we'll pick up Mrs. Hayes and Violet before church tomorrow."

"Very good, sir." Jackson gave a small bow and walked out.

Nate turned back to Maggie. There was so much more he wanted to say, but he could see the faint lines around her eyes and the tired slope of her shoulders. This was not the right time to talk about his hopes for the future. It would be better to wait for a special moment to declare his love and give her a memory she could treasure.

He took her hand, raised it to his lips, and kissed her soft skin.

Surprise and delight glowed in her eyes.

"We'll have dinner and get a good night's rest. Then we'll be ready to face whatever comes tomorrow."

"Before we eat, there's something I want to say."

He nodded to her. "Go on."

"I'm sorry I was so stubborn about my assumptions. Now that we know the truth, I can see I pushed too hard and was wrong about so many things." She sighed and looked up at him. "I should've taken matters more slowly and listened to you and not been so headstrong about my opinions. I was unfair and even unkind, especially accusing your father as I did. Will you forgive me?"

He clasped her hand. "Of course I forgive you. I held to my position with just as much tenacity."

"We are quite the pair, aren't we?"

He nodded. "We're both strong and determined, and those are good qualities. But if we're not careful, they can be carried to the extreme—and that's what gets us into trouble."

"Thank you, Nate." Then she leaned toward him and brushed a light and tender kiss across his cheek.

Pleasant warmth radiated through him, and for one delightful moment he forgot about everything they would face in the coming days.

32

On Sunday morning, Maggie, Nate, and Clara enjoyed a peaceful breakfast at Morningside. Maggie found her gaze continually drifting toward Nate. He had a purple bruise on his left cheek and a small cut under his right eye from his fight with Dixon, but he still looked wonderfully handsome.

He glanced her way. "What are you smiling about?"

"I was just admiring your battle scars." She sent him a teasing grin.

He chuckled. "At least I won the fight."

"Yes, you did." Her heart lifted, and she thanked God for answering her prayers and protecting them both.

Lilly walked into the dining room and sent Maggie a brief smile as she passed. "Excuse me, Miss Clara. Your mother is awake and asking for you."

Last night Lilly had spent almost an hour with Maggie, helping her prepare for bed and listening to all that had happened in the village and then with Roland Dixon and Mrs. Harcourt. No doubt the whole staff knew all about those events by now. But Maggie thought it was better for Lilly to pass on the full story rather than leaving it to their imaginations to fill in the details. Nate had also spoken to Jackson and given him information for the staff as well.

"Thank you, Lilly." Clara laid her napkin on the table, then glanced at Nate. "I'd like to stay home from church this morning so I can be with Mother."

He looked across at Clara. "We could have one of the maids stay with her, if you'd like."

"She's asking for me, and I'd like to hear what the doctor says when he comes to check on her."

"That's kind of you, Clara." Maggie sent her a gentle smile. "I'm sure that will be a comfort to her."

Clara rose and looked at Nate once more. "So it's all right?"

"Yes, it's very thoughtful. I'm glad you're willing to stay with her."

"Of course." Clara released a soft sigh. "She can be difficult, but she is the only mother I have, and I am her only daughter. We'd better learn how to appreciate and care for one another."

Nate's gaze followed Clara as she left the table. When she disappeared out the door, he turned to Maggie. "She's coming through this better than I expected."

"Yes, she is. Perhaps knowing she has a future with Owen has helped her gain perspective."

"She does have a certain glow about her, which is surprising under the circumstances. But I think you're right—we can credit Owen for that, in more ways than one."

"When will you tell Helen about their engagement?"

Nate pushed his chair back. "Not yet. I want to wait until she's feeling stronger before I give her that news."

"Good idea." Maggie laid her silverware across her plate and rose.

Nate looked her way. "It's a bit early yet, but shall we go into the village?"

"Yes, I'd like to speak to Grandmother and explain everything before we go to church. You know how news like this travels, and I wouldn't want her to hear it from someone else."

Maggie tipped her head to the side and let the breeze blow full on her face as they drove toward Heatherton. Everything seemed fresh and new on this beautiful spring morning. She glanced across at Nate, and his whispered words of love during the incident with Dixon replayed through her mind. Would he repeat those words soon? She pulled in a steadying breath, and with everything in her she hoped he would.

As soon as they arrived at Mrs. Birdwell's cottage, Violet vaulted out the door on her crutches. "Oh, Maggie, I've missed you!" She smiled at Nate. "How is Juniper?"

Nate opened Maggie's door. "She's fine, but eager for your return to Morningside. Each time I go to the stable she noses my pockets as though she is looking for a treat." A smile tugged up one side of his mouth. "I wonder where she learned that habit?"

Violet laughed. "I suppose I taught her."

Grandmother came to the doorway and lifted her hand. "Hello, come inside."

They gathered in Mrs. Birdwell's small kitchen, and she served tea while Maggie and Nate relayed all that had happened in town and at Morningside the previous day. Maggie didn't want to frighten Violet, so she was careful not to give too many harsh details. But the news of the strike and Dixon's arrest were probably already circulating throughout the village, and she decided Violet ought to know the basic facts.

When Maggie described climbing into the carriage and watching Nate face Dixon, Violet's eyes grew round and she turned to Nate. "Do you think that man would've taken Maggie away if you hadn't tackled him?"

Nate's expression grew serious. "I wouldn't have let that happen. I was just waiting until Maggie was out of his grasp before I took him down."

Maggie pressed her fingers to her lips, touched again by Nate's willingness to put himself between her and Dixon and protect her at the risk of his own life. She didn't even want to think what could've happened if Owen hadn't charged around the house when he did.

"Is that how you got that cut?" Violet pointed to the red line beneath Nate's eye.

"Yes, Dixon was quite a fighter, but we overpowered him without too much trouble. He might have been bold when he had a gun in his hand, but he howled like a wounded animal when he was facedown on the drive."

Grandmother placed her hand on her chest. "My goodness, I'm glad you subdued him but even more glad I wasn't there to see it happen. My poor heart couldn't take in such a wild show."

"I agree with you, Mrs. Hayes." Mrs. Birdwell gave a firm nod. "It's hard enough to hear them speak of it. I can't imagine living through it."

Maggie grinned. Mrs. Birdwell had been so absorbed in their story she hadn't taken a sip of tea since Nate and Maggie started talking.

Grandmother patted Mrs. Birdwell's hand. "But we can rest easy now. Maggie and Nathaniel are all right, and the man, Dixon, is behind bars."

"Yes, and it's a good thing he is. What a scheming, hard-hearted man."

Grandmother glanced at the small clock on the shelf. "Oh my, look at the time. We'll be late for church if we don't hurry."

Maggie was about to tell them what had happened to Mrs. Harcourt, but she decided it would be better to tell Grandmother later in private. There was no need to upset Violet with that part of the story.

They quickly gathered what they needed and headed out the door. Mrs. Birdwell was hesitant to ride in Nate's motorcar, but Grandmother finally convinced her it was safe, and she squeezed in the backseat with Violet and Grandmother. Maggie climbed in up front next to Nate, and they set off.

When they arrived at the church, the congregation was already singing the first hymn. They entered quietly and slipped into one of the back pews. A few people turned to stare at them. Some even whispered to the person next to them, causing a stir.

Maggie's face flushed, but she straightened her shoulders. She was proud of what Nate had done and grateful for his devotion and courage. She would stand with him in church—or anywhere else, for that matter. No one had better say a negative word about Nate Harcourt in her presence or she would give them a piece of her mind.

Nate opened the hymnal and stepped closer to share it with Maggie. She smiled up at him, hoping to convey what was in her heart, then she joined him in singing "Amazing Grace."

Nate returned the hymnal to the holder on the pew in front of them and sat down next to Maggie. His arm touched hers, and comfort flowed through the connection, stirring his affection and gratitude. She was not ashamed to be seen with him despite all that had happened, and he was confident he could count on her support in the days ahead. Maggie was a true friend, and he hoped and prayed she would soon agree to be much more.

Two pews in front of them a woman wearing a black-veiled hat turned slightly and looked his way. Her eyebrows arched. He held his gaze steady, and she quickly averted her eyes. But a moment later she leaned toward an older woman seated next to her and whispered something in her ear. The older woman looked over her shoulder and spotted Nate. She pursed her lips and sent him a disdainful glare.

Irritation burned Nate's throat. It was clear the news of Dixon's arrest at Morningside and Helen's involvement were already the focus of village gossip. Perhaps when the full story was known, people might not judge him too harshly, but it would take time for the truth to come out. There would most likely be many more uncomfortable moments ahead for him and his family.

Mr. Iverson gave the announcements for the morning, and a few more whispers traveled around the sanctuary, followed by heads turning their way.

Maggie glanced at Nate, concern in her eyes. He wanted to reach for her hand to reassure her, but that wouldn't be appropriate in church, and the last thing he wanted was to cause more gossip.

Reverend Samuelson moved into the pulpit and led them in the opening prayer, then he asked them to turn to Romans 12 and read the Scripture passage aloud. "If it be possible, as much as lieth in you, live peaceably with all men. Dearly beloved, avenge not yourselves, but rather give place unto wrath: for it is written, Vengeance is mine; I will repay, saith the Lord. Therefore if thine enemy hunger, feed him; if he thirst, give him drink: for in so doing thou shalt heap coals of fire on his head. Be not overcome of evil, but overcome evil with good."

Nate listened carefully as his friend expounded on the points in the passage and encouraged them to take those challenging instructions to heart. Considering the strike and the conflict with Helen and Dixon, the call to live peacefully with everyone was quite timely. Overcoming evil with good was a high calling and one he would need to make a matter of prayer. It would certainly take God's grace and strength to apply it in his present situation.

He glanced at Maggie a few times during the sermon, and she seemed just as caught up in Samuelson's message, her expression intent and absorbed.

When the service concluded, Nate waited until most of the congregation left the sanctuary before he rose to exit the pew with Maggie and the others. Mrs. Birdwell, Mrs. Hayes, and Violet reached the door first and thanked Reverend Samuelson for his message, then they walked outside.

As Nate and Maggie approached Samuelson, Nate extended his hand. "That was a powerful message. Thank you."

"I'm glad to hear it was meaningful for you, and I'm very glad to see you. I heard about Dixon's arrest. How is Mrs. Harcourt?"

Nate blinked. "How did you hear?"

"Mrs. Wilton came to me before the service. Her husband was one of the police officers called to Morningside yesterday. She was quite concerned about your stepmother's injury."

Nate glanced toward the door. Was Mrs. Wilton out in the churchyard now? How many others had she told about his stepmother's shameful actions and the distressing results? He shook off that thought and focused on Samuelson again. "The doctor expects Mrs. Harcourt to make a full recovery." He wished he could explain the rest of the story, but this was not the time or place, especially when Mrs. Hayes, Mrs. Birdwell, and Violet were waiting for them.

Samuelson smiled. "That's good to hear." He turned to Maggie. "And I suppose this means you found the answers you were looking for?"

Maggie sent Nate a surprised glance.

He shifted his weight to the other foot, knowing he owed her an explanation. Actually, there were still several things he wanted to tell her, but he needed a private moment to do it, and there hadn't been one yet today.

Maggie focused on Samuelson. "Roland Dixon admitted damaging the boat, though he says he only intended to give my father a warning and didn't know the whole family was going out that day."

Samuelson nodded. "I'm sure there's much more to the story, and it will all come to light now that the police can look into those events. I'll be praying the resolution brings you peace of mind as well as justice for your cause."

Maggie's eyes glimmered. "Thank you. I appreciate that."

Nate glanced out the door again. "We don't want to keep you. I'm sure you have plans for the afternoon."

"I have an invitation to dinner at the Wentworths', but before you go, I thought we might arrange a time to meet. I've been praying about the situation at Clifton, and I think we must keep looking for a way to bring the two sides together as soon as possible."

"I'm open to any ideas you have."

"Can you come and see me tomorrow?"

"The police are coming to Morningside at nine, but I could meet with you after that."

"Good. Let's say eleven o'clock, then, at my house?"

"I'll see you then." Nate placed his hat on his head, and he and Maggie walked toward the door.

As soon as they stepped outside, several people turned and looked their way. Nate lifted his gaze above the crowd and started down the path toward his motorcar with Maggie at his side. Someone called his name. He steeled himself and turned.

Geoffrey Rowlett strode toward them, his face set in a dark scowl. "Is it true? Was Mrs. Harcourt shot down by an intruder . . . while you stood by and watched?"

Maggie pulled in a sharp breath.

Nate straightened to his full height and riveted his gaze on Rowlett. "No, that is not what happened."

Rowlett narrowed his eyes. "So you're saying Mrs. Harcourt wasn't shot yesterday at Morningside?"

Nate hesitated, searching for an explanation. "It's true she was injured, but it happened when I wrestled with the man and his gun went off."

"So you're saying it was an accident?" Rowlett's tone made it clear he questioned Nate's word.

"The police will investigate the matter, and the Crown will decide how to proceed."

Rowlett huffed. "Well, this is just fine." He took a step away, then turned back and pointed at Nate. "Your father has only been gone for a little more than a month, and in that time you've managed to put all our futures at stake by pushing the workers at Clifton into a strike. Now you've failed to protect Mrs. Harcourt from serious injury, to say nothing of sullying your family's reputation and Clifton's in the bargain."

Nate stared at Rowlett, stung by his accusations.

Rowlett leaned toward him. "That's quite a list of accomplishments for such a short period of time, but I don't think your father would be pleased."

An angry tremor shook Nate. He wanted to lash back at Rowlett, but the words of the sermon rose in his mind. He pulled in a deep breath and wrestled to regain control. "Sarcasm and false accusations are not going to resolve these issues. I suggest we discuss this another day, after we've both had time to consider our words and prepare ourselves to be reasonable." Nate placed his hand on Maggie's back and guided her away from Rowlett.

Maggie shook her head. "Oh, what a dreadful man! He has no idea what he's talking about. How could he be so malicious?"

Nate tried to calm his breathing and dismiss Rowlett's accusations, but they cut deep. Not everything the man said was true, but these facts remained: Nate had failed to bring the two sides at Clifton together, and beginning tomorrow morning, the impact of the strike would be felt by everyone. He'd also failed to protect Helen, and she lay in bed at Morningside with a serious injury because he hadn't subdued Dixon in time.

What would his father think about his choices and actions? Would he understand the struggle Nate had been through, trying to do what was right but often failing to reach his desired goal? How could he resolve these issues in a way that would honor his father's memory and preserve his family's name yet still remain true to the principles of his faith and conscience?

An unexpected sense of awareness flooded through him, and with it came the first faint breeze of peace. This was not something he could accomplish on his own. It would take God's intervention to change men's hearts and the power of the Spirit, working in and through him, to see good come out of these painful times. He would hold on to that insight and let it help him form his prayers. He pulled in a deep breath, and the tension began to drain from his shoulders.

With God's help he would press on to see this through and do all he could, trusting the Lord to guide and direct him as he faced the challenges ahead.

Rob took Lilly's hand, and they started down the winding path through the hillside garden toward the stream. A light breeze carried the refreshing scent of cedar, damp earth, and moss. The sound of the water rushing over the rocks below and birds calling to each other in the tall evergreens soothed Lilly's mind.

Rob glanced at her, and his mouth tugged up on one side. "I hope the strike won't last too long, but I'm not sorry to have time off so I can spend the afternoon with you."

Lilly smiled and ducked her head. "It's a comfort to be together, especially after everything that happened yesterday."

His expression sobered, and he gazed up the hill toward Morningside Manor. "It's hard to believe Mrs. Harcourt's brother was the one behind that boat going down."

A shiver traveled down Lilly's back. "All these years, everyone thought it was an accident, but Maggie and Mr. Harcourt were set on finding the truth."

"Yes, and it almost got them killed."

Lilly had told Rob the full story as soon as they'd walked out of church that morning. She would've told him sooner, but he'd already been sitting with his mother and sisters when she arrived. She joined them in the second-to-last pew and tried to focus on the service, but she'd been bursting to relay what had happened at Morningside and hear their reactions.

The churchyard was buzzing with the story by the time they stepped outside. It seemed word had spread through the village that morning, and everyone was talking about Mrs. Harcourt's injury and the way her brother had held Maggie and Nate at gunpoint. Owen Campbell was considered a hero for confronting Roland Dixon and taking him down.

Lilly swallowed and pushed away those thoughts. "I'm just glad that man is behind bars and he'll have to face a judge and jury for what he's done."

"Do you think Mrs. Harcourt will be all right?"

"I hope so. The doctor came again this morning. Miss Clara has hardly left her side."

They reached the stream, and Rob helped Lilly step up on a large rock next to him. "How are Maggie and Mr. Harcourt? They've been through quite a bit of trouble."

Lilly smiled. "They seem closer than ever, and I wouldn't be surprised to hear some happy news from them soon."

Rob's eyebrows rose. "So you're saying there's a romance going on between them?"

Lilly shifted her shoulders back and forth, still grinning. "Maybe so, maybe not."

"You are a tease." He reached over and tickled her side.

She laughed and squirmed away, almost losing her balance.

"Careful!" He caught her and wrapped his arm around her waist, pulling her closer.

Her breath caught, and she looked up into his face. His eyes looked directly back at her, and smile lines creased the area around his mouth. He was the kindest, dearest man she'd ever known, and she loved him so much.

His gaze softened and traveled over her face. "You're a treasure, Lilly Neatherton. My life wouldn't be the same without you."

Her heartbeat sped up. "I feel the same way about you."

"Do you now?"

She smiled and whispered, "You know I do."

"Then I suppose we'll just have to find a way to move up the wedding date."

Lilly pulled in a quick breath. "What?"

"I'm tired of saying good-bye and never seeing you. I don't want to wait to save more money to have a place of our own. If we married soon, you could leave service and we could live with my family."

Hope and possibilities filled Lilly's mind. She loved Rob's mother and sisters, and she could help ease their load if she moved in with them, but she'd still need some kind of income. "Maybe I could find a job at one of the shops in the village."

"That's a fine idea. Any shop owner would be glad to have a smart, hard-working woman like you."

Lilly's cheeks warmed at his praise. "Do you really think so?"

"Of course. But what's most important is that we'd be together to face whatever comes." He studied her face a moment more. "What do you say?"

Her answer rose from her heart. "Yes!"

Rob's happy grin spread wider, and he took both her hands in his. "Let's speak to your father and then to my parents. If they're agreeable, we can go to Reverend Samuelson, have the banns read in church, and be married in a month."

Dizzy happiness spiraled through Lilly. "Oh, Rob, that sounds wonderful."

He slipped his arms around her waist and drew her near. She nestled against his chest, feeling safe and loved. She looked up, drinking in the look of love in his eyes.

He leaned down and placed a tender kiss on her lips. Her eyes drifted closed, and she kissed him back, thanksgiving filling her heart and soul.

33

Monday morning after breakfast, Maggie stood by Mrs. Birdwell's front window, watching the road. Nate had said he would send a carriage for her at eight-thirty, and she was eager to be on her way back to Morningside. Today she would finally be able to tell the police what she'd learned and turn the investigation over to them. But as eager as she was to hand it off and see that justice was carried out, she was even more eager to see Nate. His difficult encounter with Mr. Rowlett after church came to mind again. Just thinking about that man's harsh words stirred Maggie's anger. But Nate's clear and strong reply had put Mr. Rowlett in his place, and it made her admire Nate even more.

The sound of the motorcar reached her before it came into view, and her heart leaped. She leaned toward the window and smiled as the car rolled to a stop by the front gate and Nate hopped out.

"I'm leaving," Maggie called, then she pulled on her gloves and opened the door before Nate had a chance to knock.

"Good morning, Maggie." He smiled, his gaze traveling over her with a look of approval.

Pleasant warmth flooded her cheeks. "Hello, Nate. How are you this morning?" My goodness, she sounded almost breathless.

His smile widened. "Very well. And you?"

"I'm fine, thank you." The formality seemed so out of place, she laughed softly. "And I'm ever so glad to see you."

He chuckled and offered her his arm. She slipped her hand through at his elbow, and they set off down the path toward his car.

Twenty minutes later they arrived at Morningside. As soon as they settled in the library with Clara and Owen, Jackson announced Detectives Blanchard and Rider and showed them in.

Maggie stood with Nate, her stomach tense, as the detectives introduced themselves. They asked to speak to Helen first. Nate gave his permission and instructed Jackson to show the detectives to Helen's room. Clara followed them up to offer her mother support during the questioning.

Forty minutes later the detectives returned to the library and met with Maggie, Nate, Clara, and Owen. Their questions were direct, but their manner was polite, and Maggie soon relaxed. The detectives took turns questioning each of them, jotting the answers in their small notebooks until they had the full story.

Maggie gave Detective Blanchard the list of events and information she had recorded during her search.

He took a few minutes to read through the pages, then he looked up and met Maggie's gaze. "This is a good bit of detective work, Miss Lounsbury." His mustache rose on one side, giving a hint of a smile. "I'd better be careful or you'll be taking my job away from me."

"Oh, you don't have to worry about that. I only wanted to find out who was responsible for what happened to my family. I have no desire to solve any other mysteries."

Detective Blanchard flipped through the pages once more, then glanced at Maggie again. "May I take these?"

"Yes, please." Her heart lifted as she watched him slip her notes into his inside jacket pocket. It made her proud to know he appreciated her work and thought it would be useful in the investigation.

Detective Blanchard rose and turned to Nate. "I think we have all the information we need now. We'll be in touch if we have any more questions."

Maggie blinked. Were they leaving so soon? What would happen to Helen and Roland Dixon? Ever since Maggie had read her father's journal, she'd been driven to make sure those who were responsible for the boat going down were held to account, but her attitude toward Helen had softened since their confrontation with Dixon and Helen's change of heart.

Maggie stood and faced the detectives, determination coursing through her. "I hope you'll do all you can for Mrs. Harcourt. She may have been wrong to hide her past all these years, but I don't believe she intended to harm my parents or sister."

Nate looked her way, his eyes shining with approval.

Detective Blanchard tucked his notebook and pencil into his pocket. "My job is to investigate the case, interview the witnesses, and collect the evidence. The prosecutor for the Crown will decide who will be charged."

Maggie bit her lip and glanced at Nate. They both hoped Helen would not face criminal charges, but it was not up to them any longer.

The detective seemed to notice her concern. "I will say this, Miss Lounsbury. Shortly after Dixon's arrest, he confessed to drilling a hole in the boat's hull. He also told us Mrs. Harcourt knew nothing about his plans."

Maggie released a breath. "I'm so glad."

"You can expect she'll be called as a witness at the trial."

Nate's brow creased. "I don't suppose there is any way to keep my stepmother's past and the blackmail private?"

Detective Blanchard stroked his mustache. "I doubt that, sir. It will probably be in the newspaper sooner rather than later, but I wouldn't worry. Dixon's confession overshadows it all. Knowing she was being blackmailed by him, along with her injury, should put Mrs. Harcourt in a sympathetic light."

"Yes, I suppose so." Nate thanked the detectives and shook their hands, then the two men walked out of the library. Clara and Owen followed them into the great hall.

Maggie turned to Nate. "I think that went well."

"Yes, better than I expected." He stepped toward her, a teasing glint lighting his eyes. "They seemed very impressed with all the information you collected. Perhaps you should reconsider your future plans."

She lifted her chin and matched his tone. "I suppose I could do some private investigation work when we're not too busy at the millinery shop."

Nate's lips twitched. "That wasn't exactly what I was thinking."

Her heartbeat quickened. "What did you have in mind?"

He looked past her shoulder, and his grin faded.

"What is it, Nate?"

"I'm sorry. There's more I want to say, but if I don't leave soon, I'll be late for that meeting with Samuelson." He frowned at the clock, then looked back at her, a plea for understanding in his eyes.

"Of course," she said, pushing away her disappointment. Then an idea struck, and she looked his way again. "I could stay here while you go to Heatherton. That would give me time to look in on Clara and Helen, and when you come back, we could continue our conversation." She had something more in mind, but she would rather let that be a surprise.

Relief flashed across his face. "Yes, please stay."

Her smile returned. "All right. I will."

"Thank you." He leaned down and kissed her cheek, then turned and strode out of the library.

She lifted her hand and touched her cheek, and a prayer rose in her heart. *Please, Father, go with him, guide his steps, and give him Your wisdom.*

Maggie climbed the stairs and walked down the upper hallway toward Helen's bedroom. She stopped by the door, gathered her courage, and knocked twice. She wasn't quite sure what she would say, but she had the strongest impression she should speak to Helen.

"Come in."

Maggie pushed the door open, expecting to see Clara with her mother, but Helen was the only one in the room. She lay in her bed, wearing a light-blue dressing gown, her arm bandaged and propped up on a pillow beside her. Helen's eyebrows lifted when she saw Maggie in the doorway.

"I don't want to disturb you if you're resting."

"No, I'm wide awake since the visit from the police. Come in."

Maggie closed the door and crossed to Helen's bedside. "How are you feeling?"

"My arm is sore, but the medication Dr. Hadley gave me helps relieve some of the pain. At least it's better than it was yesterday." Helen glanced toward the hallway. "Have the police gone?"

"Yes, they left a few minutes ago, and Nate drove into Heatherton to meet with Reverend Samuelson."

"I see." She chewed her lower lip, then ran her hand over the bedcovers, smoothing them out. "I told the police the truth." She looked up and met Maggie's gaze. "All of it."

"I'm glad to hear it."

"I thought it would be dreadful, admitting everything I've kept hidden for so long, but it was actually a relief. I'm just sorry I waited so long to do it." She sighed. "Think how different my life could've been if I'd confessed it all to Mr. Harcourt years ago."

Maggie tensed. "You were not the only one hurt by those secrets."

A guilty shadow crossed Helen's face. "Yes, that's true. My choices had a ripple effect, and they ended up wounding many people."

"Especially my family," Maggie added, her voice thick with emotion.

"Yes, you and your family." Helen closed her eyes for a moment. When she spoke again, her voice was softer. "I'm sorry for what happened to them. I wish I'd never said anything to Roland."

"But you did, and now my sister and I will carry those painful memories for the rest of our lives."

Helen's eyes filled and a tear slipped down her cheek. She lifted her hand and brushed it away. "I didn't realize what would happen. I only thought of myself and what I wanted."

"That sounds like a very lonely and painful way to live."

Helen's lips trembled, but she managed a brief nod. "It is," she whispered.

The images of Maggie's mother, father, and sister flashed in her mind, and she gripped the side of her skirt. Helen's selfishness and Roland's greed had taken so much away from her that day on Tumbledon Lake. They'd put an end to her parents' and sister's earthly lives, but that was not the end of the story. Her parents and sister lived on in heaven, and she would see them again one day. She would hold on to that promise and allow it to help her along on her healing journey.

She swallowed and focused on Helen again. "For years I let hurt and anger rule my life because of what happened to my family. I hardened my heart and refused to listen to anyone who told me God could comfort me and heal those hurts. But that was a foolish choice that caused me even greater pain. In the last few weeks, I've seen how wrong I was to turn my back on God. He is the only One who can heal our hurts and give us new life when we turn to Him."

Tears flooded Helen's eyes again. "I know that's true, but I don't deserve God's forgiveness, not after everything I've done."

"None of us deserve it, but that's why Christ came—to pay that price for us."

Helen pressed her trembling lips together and seemed to be soaking in Maggie's words.

"I have a long way to go on my faith journey, but I'm learning to trust God and allow Him to rule in my heart again. I don't understand it all, but I have more peace now than I've had in a very long time. I suppose I owe my grandmother a great debt. She never stopped praying for me or reminding me of the truth. And Nate has helped me too by his example of living out his faith."

"He's a good boy, though he does aggravate me at times."

Maggie smiled, unsure which amused her more, Helen calling him a boy or her admitting he aggravated her. "He's the kindest and wisest man I know."

Helen sniffed and blinked away her tears. "You're in love with him, aren't you?"

Tingling swept up Maggie's neck and into her face, but she was done hiding the truth. "Yes, I am."

"Does he feel the same?"

"I believe so."

"Has he proposed?"

Her heart deflated just a bit. "No, he hasn't."

Helen huffed. "You see, I told you he could be aggravating."

Maggie's smile returned. "So you wouldn't mind if he does?"

"No, not anymore." Helen brushed the moisture from her cheeks. "The events of the last few days have helped me see everything much more clearly."

The door opened, and Clara walked in. "Oh, Maggie, I didn't realize you were still here." Her gaze darted from her mother's tear-stained cheeks to Maggie's glowing smile. "Is everything all right?"

Helen sniffed. "Yes, it is, but hand me that handkerchief and then open the drapes. I'd like to see the sunshine."

Clara sent Maggie a quizzical smile as she passed, then took a handkerchief from the bedside table and handed it to her mother.

"I'll leave you now that Clara is here." Maggie waited until Helen looked her way again. "I'm going down to the kitchen. Is there anything I can get for you?"

"No, but thank you for asking. I appreciate you coming to see me . . . and I want to thank you for what you said."

Maggie smiled. "You're welcome. I hope you'll be feeling stronger every day." With that, she turned and left Helen's room, her steps lighter and her burden lifted.

34

Nate walked through the front door at Morningside, eager to see Maggie and tell her the good news about his meeting with Samuelson.

Jackson shuffled forward to meet him. "May I take your hat, sir?"

"Yes, thank you, Jackson." Nate removed his hat and handed it to the butler. "Is Miss Lounsbury in the library?"

"No, sir. She said to tell you she's waiting for you in the servants' hall."

Nate's eyebrows rose. That seemed an odd place for her to wait, but he remembered her saying she was good friends with one of his maids. "Very well." He dismissed Jackson and strode through the great hall and down the servants' stairs.

Laughter drifted through the passageway. Nate stopped at the doorway to the servants' hall and looked in. Maggie sat at the long wooden table with three maids, a footman, and the cook, Mrs. McCarthy. He stepped into the room, and the servants all rose to their feet.

"I'm sorry to interrupt. I've just come looking for Miss Lounsbury."

The servants exchanged smiles, and he suddenly felt as though they were all in on some secret that was still a mystery to him.

Mrs. McCarthy grinned at Maggie. "She's right here, sir."

Maggie rose from the table and picked up a large basket. A blue linen cloth lay over the top, concealing whatever was inside. She smiled and held it up.

"What's that?"

"It's a picnic basket," she announced, her eyes sparkling.

"Ah, I see." He studied the basket, his delight with the surprise growing by the moment. "That must mean we're going on a picnic."

Maggie nodded. "Good thinking."

"Very well, lead the way."

She came around the table and started for the door, toting the basket. When she reached the hallway, she looked over her shoulder with another fetching grin.

"I'm right behind you."

She laughed, then pushed open the door to the courtyard.

"Let me take that basket for you."

She passed it to him, her smile revealing a dimple in her left cheek.

"Do you have a spot in mind for this picnic, or would you like a suggestion?"

"I was thinking of the viewpoint on the north drive."

"An excellent choice."

Her smile dimmed a bit, and her steps slowed. "But I wondered if we might stop by Tumbledon Lake on the way."

His breath hitched in his chest. "Are you sure?"

She glanced away for a moment, then looked back at him. "I haven't been back since the accident, but I think I'm ready."

At the mention of a picnic, he'd imagined a romantic afternoon on a sunny hillside and finally having time to tell her everything in his heart, but if some time at the lake was what she needed, then he would wait. He nodded to her. "As you wish."

They walked to the stable, loaded the basket into the motorcar, and set off up the north drive.

Feathery green ferns and dainty bluebells lined the path Maggie and Nate followed through the shady woods toward Tumbledon Lake. They'd left the motorcar parked in a safe spot and walked the rest of the way. Golden shafts of sunlight filtered through the leaves and dappled the forest floor. They rounded the bend, and Maggie caught a glimpse of the deep-blue water through the trees.

She knelt and carefully picked a small handful of bluebells. Lifting them to her nose, she closed her eyes and inhaled their sweet, spicy scent. It mingled with the cool air and the rich aroma of the moist earth, all scents her father loved and had taught her to love as well.

Nate laid his hand on her shoulder. "Are you all right?"

She rose and looked up at him. "Yes, just enjoying the moment and remembering how much my family loved it here."

He nodded, his warm gaze reflecting his empathy.

She took his arm, and they strolled down the path toward the lake. When they reached the water's edge, she slipped her arm from his. "I need just a moment."

"Take your time." He stepped back.

She walked a few steps away and gazed out over the shimmering water. Memories came rushing back, and tears filled her eyes. She lifted her face to the sunshine and let its warmth penetrate her heart and ease her pain.

This was the last place she'd seen her father, mother, and Olivia. But they were not here. Only the memories echoed back across time. Her family members were healed and whole, enjoying all the glories of heaven with the Savior they'd loved and served.

She pulled in a slow, deep breath, letting that truth comfort her heart and restore her peace. Grieving was a long journey, but at least she was finally headed in the right direction and taking the steps she needed to move forward in life.

She swallowed another round of tears, knelt by the water's edge, and tossed her bluebells into the lake. They floated off, bobbing on the ripples and taking with them some of her heartache.

She rose, and Nate stepped up beside her. He slipped his arm around her shoulders, and she let her tears fall as she rested her head against his arm. Then he turned toward her and embraced her in a gentle hug.

The wool fabric of his jacket brushed against her cheek. Beneath it she could hear the solid thump of his heartbeat, and it sent a comforting wave through her. She slipped her arms around his waist and rested against his chest.

He held her close and kissed the top of her head, waiting until she loosened her hold and stepped back.

"Thank you," she said softly. "I needed to say good-bye one last time."

He nodded and waited a moment more, tender understanding reflected on his face.

How thankful she was for his kindness and patience. She wouldn't have wanted to share this moment with anyone else. How glad she was that their friendship had been healed and restored. "I'm ready to go."

"All right." He took her hand, and they walked back up the path toward the motorcar. Nate collected the basket and a light blanket from the backseat, and they set off up the hill toward the viewpoint.

Maggie lifted her skirt a few inches so she could step around the rocks in the path. The exertion of climbing the hill washed away the sadness of her visit to the lake. It was time to push ahead and make the most of this lovely day.

"How was your meeting with Reverend Samuelson?" she asked.

Nate chuckled and looked over his shoulder. "You'll never guess what happened."

"Tell me."

"When I arrived at his house, five members of the board from Clifton were there, and three leaders of the workers."

"How did he manage that?"

"I have no idea. But he convinced them all to come and urged us to work toward finding an agreement."

"And were you successful?"

"Yes, but you'll never believe how he did it."

Maggie laughed. "Stop teasing me and tell me the rest of the story."

He grinned, obviously delighted by her comment and brighter mood. "First he reviewed some of the points from his sermon, emphasizing that we must all make every effort to live at peace with one another. Then he said the main sticking point in resolving most conflicts is that pride gets in the way." Nate turned back and offered her his hand to help her around a large rock.

She took hold and stepped up. "Go on."

"Then he said everyone must be curious to know what happened at Morningside, so he asked me to give them a report."

Maggie stopped. "Really?"

"Yes, I wasn't quite sure why he thought that was important at the moment, but I told them the facts. Partway through, Samuelson interrupted and asked me to explain why I'd pulled back from our search after we learned my father could be at fault."

"What did you say?"

"I told them I didn't believe my father could've done such a thing, but then I admitted it was my pride that kept me from wanting it to be true."

Maggie's heart lifted, and her admiration for Nate grew to new heights. "That was brave."

"I'm not sure how brave it was, but it seemed to have an impact."

"What happened after that?"

"I told them the rest of the story, all the way through the detectives' visit this morning. Then Samuelson used it as an illustration, saying how releasing my pride and working with you allowed us to find out who was truly at fault. And in the same way, the management and workers needed to put aside pride and work together to resolve our differences."

Maggie grinned. "That was clever of Reverend Samuelson to draw that parallel."

"Yes, very clever."

They reached the top of the hill, and Nate set the blanket and picnic basket on the grass. "The men were so caught up in my story that they could easily see his point. When it was time to begin the negotiations, Samuelson appealed to us again, asking that we each think about what was best for the whole community and be willing to give some ground."

"And the board went along with that?"

He smiled, looking a bit amazed. "Yes, after Mr. Waller and I presented the financial information we'd gathered, it relieved some of their fears and made it possible to move ahead with the negotiations. The board agreed to a small wage increase now and another in six months if production continues at the current rate or increases. They also agreed to shorten the workday by thirty minutes, and we'll adjust it again in three months if our output remains consistent."

"I suppose the men were pleased."

"Yes, pleased and relieved. They have to take the offer back to the workers for a vote, but I think they consider it a victory."

"I'm so glad." What a relief that so many families in Heatherton would not have to go through hardship because of an extended strike. The men would return to work with the promise of a pay increase and a shorter day.

"Yes, it's good news for everyone."

Maggie turned and gazed out across the rolling hills and green fields below. She'd come here several times with Nate and her father, but it had been at least five years since she'd climbed all the way to the top.

Ancient stone walls cut across the land, dividing it for farming and grazing. Pale green leaves brightened the trees and hedgerows lining the fields. Sturdy mountains rose in the west, hemming in the valley and reaching up to meet the clear-blue sky. "I'd forgotten how much I love this view."

"Yes, it's lovely." His tender tone made her turn toward him, and she found his gaze on her rather than the countryside below. Her stomach fluttered and warmth spiraled through her.

He reached for her hand and wove his fingers through hers, drawing her toward him. His beautiful dark-brown eyes searched hers, piercing yet intimate. "We've been through a lot these past few weeks. I'm not sure what challenges we'll face in the future, but I am sure about one thing."

She pulled in a trembling breath. "What's that?"

"You're an amazing woman, Maggie Lounsbury."

She ducked her head, savoring his words. They soothed her heart and filled in some of the broken, empty places.

"It's true." He waited until she looked up at him again. "You have a fierce love for your family, you're courageous and determined, and you wouldn't let anything stop you from discovering the truth."

Her throat tightened as she remembered everything that had happened. "I couldn't have done it without you."

"True." A teasing twinkle lit his eyes. "We make a great team."

She nodded, her heart expanding in her chest. "Yes, we do."

The twinkle faded, and his expression softened again. "I admire you for those qualities and many others, but my feelings for you go much deeper than admiration." He looked into her eyes and tightened his grip on her hand. "I love you, Maggie. I have for a very long time."

She stilled. "Truly?" Her voice came out as a breathy whisper.

"Yes, I've loved you ever since you were thirteen and you fell out of that tree and nearly killed me when you landed on top of me." His lips twitched at the corners. "I think it was your inquisitive nature that won me over."

The sweet memory washed over Maggie. "My inquisitive nature? Is that just a nice way of saying I'm a snoop?"

He chuckled and pulled her closer. "Stop making me laugh; I'm trying to be serious."

She squelched her smile. "I'm sorry. Please, go on."

"That day I caught a glimpse of your heart and a vision for who you would become."

His sweet words stirred a deep longing inside. She wanted to believe him, but doubts crept in. "That was a long time ago. We've both changed a great deal since then."

"Yes, we have. I hope I'm wiser now and better prepared to be the trustworthy man you deserve."

She had no doubt her heart was safe with Nate. He had proven himself time and again. But could she tame her own stubborn spirit and be a worthy partner for him? That was the question.

She looked up at him. "I'm afraid I might disappoint you. I'm very set in my ways, and I can be quite obstinate at times. Grandmother is always telling me I should listen more and talk less, and I definitely need to curb my curiosity."

His grin returned, and he shook his head. "Maggie, my love, you are making this proposal take much longer than I'd imagined."

He was going to propose? She lifted her hand to cover her mouth, delight filling her heart.

He looked into her eyes again, his message of love unmistakable. "I'm sure there will be times we disappoint each other, but with the Lord's help, I'm confident we can work through those issues and learn from them. Now, may I get on with what I want to say?"

She pressed her lips together and nodded.

"When I look ahead and think about the future, there's only one person I can imagine by my side, only one I want to be with every day for the rest of my life."

Her heart soared, and her mind spun with delight.

He knelt in front of her and took both her hands in his. "Margaret Ann Lounsbury, I love you with all my heart. Will you marry me?"

Happy tears blurred her vision, and she had to swallow hard before she could answer. "Yes! Oh yes!" She pulled him to his feet, and they laughed and hugged each other as a fresh round of tears coursed down her cheeks.

Nate stepped back, still holding her hands. "Oh, my darling, are you sure? My life is complicated, and it's about to become much more so with the trial and whatever comes after."

"Yes, I'm so very sure. I love you, Nate. No matter what the future holds, I want to share it with you."

He ran his hand gently down her cheek. Then he leaned closer and kissed her, tenderly, lingering as though her kiss infused him with hope and strength. Maggie's arms slipped around his waist, and she relaxed in his embrace, enjoying his sweet kiss. This was where she belonged, safe in his arms, close to his heart.

He finally stepped back, his face glowing with life and joy. "Are you happy, my darling?"

"Yes, so very happy." She reached up and tenderly touched his face, tracing his handsome jaw, drinking in the look of love in his eyes.

What wonderful gifts the Lord had given her. He had shown His faithfulness by healing her sorrow and comforting her with His love. His light had overcome the darkness and exposed the lies and secrets that had held them all captive for so long. And He had given her justice for her cause, yet He'd also taught her the value of mercy.

Nate drew her down beside him. They sat on the blanket, enjoying their picnic and talking about their hopes for the future until the sinking sun turned the sky brilliant gold and orange. When the fiery rays faded to pink and purple, they rose and collected the basket and blanket.

Maggie glanced over her shoulder at the fading colors of the sunset, and a gentle breeze fluttered up the mountainside and surrounded her. It was almost as if she could hear her father whisper his blessing over them. Happy tears filled her eyes as she received that gift and tucked it away in her heart.

Then she took Nate's hand, and they walked down the path together, her mind filled with happy expectation and her heart overflowing with joy.

Epilogue

A bright-red ribbon fluttered across the open doorway of the newly rebuilt millinery shop in the center of Heatherton. The pristine building almost seemed to glow that crisp October morning, its windowpanes sparkling and new wooden window boxes overflowing with bright fall flowers.

The sun shone down from a clear blue sky and warmed Maggie's shoulders. The faint scent of burning leaves and a whiff of cinnamon from Mrs. Fenwick's Teashop drifted past, tickling her nose. Maggie smiled as she let her gaze travel around the crowd of friends and neighbors who had gathered to celebrate the reopening of their shop.

How thankful she was that the insurance settlement had finally come through in July. Those funds had allowed them to complete the rebuilding work, furnish the shop, and restock the supplies they needed.

"Good day, Maggie." Mr. Alvin Neatherton lifted his cap to her.

"Good day to you, sir." She crossed toward him, glancing up at the scaffolding stretching across the front wall of his business. "It looks like it won't be too long before you can reopen too."

He nodded, looking pleased. "We have a few more weeks of work, but Neatherton's Shoes and Boots should be back in business before the weather turns too cold."

"I'm very happy to hear it." Maggie motioned toward his shop. "If you need anything, I hope you'll come and see us."

"I will. You and Mrs. Hayes have always been good neighbors."

She touched his arm and sent him a smile. "As you've been to us." Friends like the Neathertons were a gift and a blessing. She would never forget them even after she married Nate and moved to Morningside.

Joseph strode through the crowd toward them, his blond hair falling over his forehead and into his eyes. He wore a wrinkled pair of brown trousers and a blue shirt with the top button missing. "Hello, Maggie. How are you?"

"Very well. And you?"

"As right as rain." His carefree smile confirmed what she'd sensed the last few times they'd seen each other—he was ready to resume a comfortable friendship, and she was glad to oblige. She wondered if his happy mood was due to the fact that she'd seen him walking Ruth Horton home from church the last three Sundays. Ruth was a fine young woman, the daughter of one of the village grocers. She was known for her expert baking and delicious meals. Maggie hoped their friendship would grow into something lasting. Joseph deserved a happy future with a loving wife and family.

Clara and Owen wove through the crowd and found a spot near the front, not too far away from Maggie. Clara lifted her hand and waved. Maggie returned the greeting to her soon-to-be sister-in-law. Clara and Owen held hands and exchanged a loving look. They had a long engagement ahead of them, but they were looking forward to marrying after Owen returned from his veterinary training in Edinburgh.

Someone called Maggie's name and she turned.

Lilly and Rob made their way through the crowd toward her. Lilly embraced Maggie. "It looks like half the village has come out to celebrate with you."

"Yes, it does, and I'm so glad. I know it means so much to Grandmother." Maggie scanned the crowd and spotted her grandmother across the way with her good friend Esther Fenwick from the teashop. Grandmother's pink cheeks glowed as she continued greeting friends and catching up on the village news.

"We certainly couldn't be happier to see the shop open again." Lilly looked up at Rob with a radiant smile and tucked her arm through his.

Rob returned a proud grin and patted his bride's hand. "You're right about that."

Maggie was so happy for them. Just a few days after the strike was settled, Lilly had told Maggie she and Rob wanted to be married in June. She would be leaving service and hoped to find work in the village. She was determined to help the Carters and not be a burden to them.

As Maggie listened to Lilly talk about her hopes for the future, an idea rose in her mind. What if she and Grandmother trained Lilly and Rose Carter to make hats and eventually take over the shop? When Maggie asked Grandmother about it later, she was thrilled with the idea and said she would enjoy working with them until she was ready to retire and take on a more restful routine.

Maggie, Grandmother, and Violet would stay at the new shop until Maggie and Nate's wedding in December. After they all moved to Morningside, Lilly and Rob would take over the rooms above the millinery shop and have a place of their own. Grandmother would go into the village some afternoons by carriage to help prepare Rose and Lilly to take over the shop. It seemed like a wonderful plan that would be good for everyone.

Maggie turned to Rob. "How is your father?"

"Much better. Reverend Samuelson offered him a part-time job caring for the grounds at Saint Peter's. He doesn't have full use of his hand, but he's able to do most of the gardening tasks, and he's proud to be working again."

"That's wonderful." How kind of Reverend Samuelson to give Mr. Carter the opportunity to help support his family. Maggie admired the reverend, and she was very thankful Nate's friendship with him continued to grow.

"Look at me, Maggie!" Violet's voice rang out above the crowd.

Maggie turned, and her heart lifted as her sister passed by, riding atop Juniper. Nate walked at Violet's side, keeping an eye on her and guiding them toward the hitching post just past the millinery shop. He looked as handsome as ever in his dashing charcoal suit with the burgundy vest.

Maggie walked over to meet her sister and Nate. She patted Violet's healed leg. "You're becoming quite the horsewoman."

"Nate says I'm doing very well." Violet sent him a happy grin.

"You are indeed." Nate winked at Maggie, then took the reins, tied up the horse, and helped Violet dismount. As soon as Violet was safely on the ground, he leaned toward Maggie and kissed her cheek. "You're looking lovely this morning, my dear."

She gazed into his eyes and savored the tender message there. "Thank you."

How blessed she was to have the love of a fine man like Nate Harcourt. In spite of his commitment to manage Morningside and oversee matters at Clifton, he had made her happiness a priority these last few months, even while he guided his family through the ordeal of Roland Dixon's trial.

Helen had been called as a witness, and she'd been mortified that she had to testify in court and repeat her painful past. But the facts of the case had already circulated through the county before the trial, and the gossip died down soon after. Roland was found guilty and would spend at least fifteen years in prison.

Helen tried to visit him during the trial, but he had refused to see her. She accepted his decision surprisingly well, and she seemed to be making an effort to live a more honest life, but she could still be difficult at times. Maggie and Nate would probably face new challenges in their relationship with Helen after they married, but Maggie was hopeful they could find common ground and forge a new path through those challenges.

Maggie glanced around once more. "It looks like everyone is here except Reverend Samuelson. Have you seen him?"

Nate looked through the crowd. "Not yet, but I'm sure he'll be along." They had asked him to come and say a prayer to bless the new shop before they cut the ribbon and welcomed everyone inside.

Nate took Maggie's hand and she clasped Violet's as they walked back toward the shop entrance. She peeked through the front window, and pleasant memories filled her mind . . . happy days styling hats with Grandmother while Violet played nearby . . . and cozy evenings in the kitchen behind the shop where they gathered around the fireplace and talked about the events of the day.

She'd be leaving that life behind in two months when she married Nate and became his wife, but Grandmother and Violet would come with her.

A warm wave of happiness wrapped around Maggie's heart as she thought of all that lay ahead. She had already started teaching Lilly and Rose the basics of hat making three afternoons a week, and in exchange they were sewing her wedding dress. They'd also promised to help her carry out plans for that special day. She was thankful and blessed—so very blessed.

Nate leaned down. "Tell me the secret behind that lovely smile." His voice was soft and husky, and it melted her heart a little more.

"I was just thinking about our wedding plans."

He grinned and a mischievous twinkle lit his eyes. "Ah, no wonder you're smiling."

Maggie's cheeks warmed, but she didn't really mind his teasing. "I'm looking forward to our wedding. It will be a new beginning for us."

His teasing expression faded to tenderness, and he slipped his arm around her waist, drawing her closer. "You're right, and I'm looking forward to it as well."

Hurried footsteps sounded behind them, and Maggie and Nate turned.

Reverend Samuelson wove his way through the crowd toward them. "I'm so sorry to be late." He clutched his Bible beneath his arm and swiped his hand across his flushed face. His tie had come loose, and he looked as though he'd run all the way from the church.

Nate stepped toward him. "Is everything all right?"

"Yes, everything is fine. I just got so absorbed in writing my sermon notes, I didn't realize the time."

Nate grinned and clapped his friend on the shoulder. "No harm done. I think we're ready to begin whenever you are."

"Very well." He straightened his tie, still looking a bit flustered, and moved toward the front door of the shop.

Maggie, Nate, and Violet followed, and Grandmother joined them there.

Reverend Samuelson lifted his hand and motioned everyone toward him. "Let's all come closer." He waited while their friends and fellow merchants crowded around, then he smiled at the group. "Dearly beloved, we are gathered here today to join this man and this—"

A chuckle passed through the crowd.

Reverend Samuelson stifled a gasp and cleared his throat. "I'm sorry. Let me begin again. We've come together today to celebrate the happy occasion of reopening the village millinery shop. As you all know, Mrs. Hayes and her granddaughters suffered a terrible loss when a fire destroyed their business as well as that of their neighbors. But that is not the end of the story. A wonderful new chapter is opening for them today."

Grandmother's eyes grew glossy. She took a handkerchief from her sleeve and dabbed her eyes.

Reverend Samuelson continued, "They've asked me to offer a prayer of thanks and blessing as they begin this new phase of their lives. Won't you join me?"

Maggie held tight to Nate's hand and bowed her head.

"Dear heavenly Father, we come to You today to express our thanks for Your provision for Mrs. Hayes and her granddaughters, which has allowed them to once again open their shop. Thank You for the men who labored with great skill to make this structure strong and able to be enjoyed for years to come. We ask that Your hand of blessing would be on Mrs. Hayes, Miss Lounsbury, and Miss Violet. We also thank You for the new opportunities You are giving Mrs. Rose Carter and Mrs. Lilly Carter as they learn new skills here. We pray You will protect them all and prosper their business. May all who enter this shop sense Your presence and be blessed. We pray all these things in the name of our Lord Jesus Christ. Amen."

"Amen" echoed around the crowd. Then Violet clapped, and soon everyone joined in.

Nate grinned at Maggie. "Are you ready to cut the ribbon?"

Maggie smiled, reached into the window box, and pulled out a pair of scissors she'd put there earlier that morning. "Come on, Violet." Maggie took her sister's hand, and they stepped toward the ribbon hanging across the doorway.

Grandmother stood with them, and Maggie passed Violet the scissors. "Careful now."

Violet caught her tongue between her teeth, clasped the scissors in both hands, and clipped the red ribbon in half. A cheer rose from the crowd, and hearty applause filled the air. Violet handed the scissors to Maggie and gave a little bow.

Grandmother chuckled, then hugged Violet and Maggie. With a proud smile she pushed the shop door open wider. "Come inside, friends, and take some refreshment."

Maggie started to follow Grandmother, but Nate reached for her hand and gently pulled her aside. That twinkle was back in his eyes. "Let's not go in yet."

"Why not?"

"Because I'd like a moment alone with my bride-to-be."

She smiled up at him, love and thankfulness filling her heart. They walked a few steps away while most of the crowd flowed past them into the shop.

"You look very happy," Nate mused.

"I am, and it's not just because we've reopened the shop."

He lifted an eyebrow. "What, then?"

"I'm glad for Grandmother and Rose and Lilly, but most of all I'm glad we found our way back to each other." She wanted to say more, but her throat tightened and her eyes grew misty.

"Yes, I'm grateful too, and the best is yet to come."

She nodded, blinking away happy tears. They had come through a long time of darkness and separation when mistrust and unresolved hurt had ruled their lives, but God had not left them there. He had made a way for them to be reunited and to overcome the hold of painful memories and family secrets. And for that she would always be thankful.

Nate smiled down at her and placed a feather-light kiss on her forehead, then he tipped his head toward the shop. "I think it's time to celebrate."

"Yes, it is." She slipped her arm through his, and they walked toward the beautiful new shop and into a future bright with hope and promise.

Readers Guide

1. Grief can have a profound impact on people. How did Maggie deal with her grief following the death of her parents and sister? How was that different than the way her grandmother dealt with their deaths? What have you found to be helpful for yourself or those you know when they are going through a time of grief?
2. Maggie's suspicions led her toward several assumptions. Some were true, but some were false and hurtful to those she loved. What can we learn from that part of Maggie's journey?
3. After his father's death, Nate inherited Morningside Manor and his father's part ownership in Clifton Engineering. How did this change his life? What did you think of the way he handled those changes? If you were his friend at the time, what advice would you have given him?
4. Helen went to great lengths to hide her past from everyone. Why was this so important to her? What impact did her desire to keep her past secret have on others? How did it change the course of her life?
5. Grandmother Hayes loved Maggie and Violet and often shared advice and wisdom with them. What's one of your favorite bits of advice or wisdom from Grandmother Hayes?
6. Maggie felt a great responsibility for Violet and had a deep love for her. What did you think of Violet? What did she add to the story?
7. The fire that destroyed the millinery shop was an important turning point in the story. How did it impact Maggie? Have you ever been through a difficult time that motivated you to change the course of your life? If you could talk to Maggie after the fire, what would you tell her?

8. Maggie had an especially close relationship with her father. Even though he'd been gone for four years, she often remembered the lessons she'd learned from him. How did those memories help her?
9. The threat of the strike played a significant role in the story. What did you think of the actions Nate took to try and prevent the strike? What other people were impacted by the threat of the strike? What did you think of their choices and actions?
10. Maggie's friends Lilly and Rob faced several challenges in the story, including postponing their wedding plans to help Rob's family. How did they respond to those challenges? What advice would you give them?
11. Maggie and Helen had a challenging relationship. How did Helen treat Maggie at the beginning of the story? Near the end, Maggie and Helen seem to understand each other better. How were they able to overcome their differences?
12. Reverend Samuelson used the story of Nate's experiences and the events at Morningside to motivate the managers and workers from Clifton to negotiate their differences and settle the strike. He was a determined peacemaker. Have you ever helped settle an argument or dispute between people or groups of people? What tactics do you think are the most effective in resolving differences?

Acknowledgments

I am very grateful for all those who gave their support and encouragement and provided information in the process of writing this book. Without your help, it would never have been possible!

I'd like to say thank you to the following people:

My husband, Scott, who always provides great feedback and constant encouragement when I talk endlessly about my characters, plot, and what's happening next. Your love and support has allowed me to follow my dreams and write the books of my heart. I will be forever grateful for you!

Cathy Gohlke and Terri Gillespie, fellow authors and dear friends, who helped me brainstorm the story and make it much better than it would've been if I'd plotted it on my own. You are treasured friends! I am so grateful for all we've been through together and all the ways you've blessed my life. Let's keep encouraging one another!

Steve Laube, my literary agent, for his patience, guidance, and wise counsel. You have been a great advocate who has represented me well. I feel blessed to be your client, and I appreciate you!

Shannon Marchese, Charlene Patterson, Andrea Cox, Laura Wright, and Rose Decaen, my gifted editors, who helped me shape the story and then polish it so readers will be able to truly enjoy it.

Henrietta Heald, author of *William Armstrong: Magician of the North,* for insight into the time period, issues, and an in-depth look at the Armstrong family and Cragside Estate, the inspiration for the Harcourt family and Morningside Manor.

Kristopher Orr, the multitalented designer at Multnomah, and Mike Heath of Magnus Creative, for the lovely cover design. Thank you for inviting me into the process! I'm very pleased with the cover and feel it captures the heroine and mood of the story so well.

Jamie Lapeyrolerie, Jessica Lamb, Lori Addicott, and the entire Multnomah team for their great work with marketing, publicity, production, and sales. This book would stay hidden if not for your creative ideas and hard work. You all are the best!

Darna Michie, owner of East Angel Harbor Hats, who created the lovely hat for our cover model to wear for the photo shoot and who did it in record-breaking time. I love your hats!

My children, Josh, Melinda, Melissa, Peter, Ben, Galan, Megan, and Lizzy, and my mother-in-law, Shirley, for the way you cheer me on. It's a blessing to have a family that is so supportive!

Most of all, I thank my Lord and Savior, Jesus Christ, for His love, wonderful grace, and faithful provision. I am grateful for the gifts and talents You have given me, and I hope to always use them in ways that bless You and bring You glory.

About the Author

Carrie Turansky has loved reading since she first visited the library as a young child and checked out a tall stack of picture books. Her love for writing began when she penned her first novel at age twelve. She is now the award-winning author of seventeen inspirational romance novels and novellas.

Carrie and her husband, Scott, who is a pastor, author, and speaker, have been married for more than thirty-eight years and make their home in New Jersey. They often travel together on ministry trips and to visit their five adult children and four grandchildren. Carrie also leads the women's ministry at her church, and when she's not writing, she enjoys spending time working in her flower gardens and cooking healthy meals for friends and family.

She loves to connect with reading friends through her website, www.carrieturansky.com, and through Facebook, Pinterest, and Twitter.

Fans of Downton Abbey and historical fiction, don't miss out on the Edwardian Brides series!

WaterBrookMultnomah.com

Do you love WaterBrook & Multnomah Fiction?

Be the first to know about upcoming releases, insider news and all kinds of fiction fun!

Sign up for our Fiction Reads newsletter at
wmbooks.com/WaterBrookMultnomahFiction

Join our Fiction Only Facebook Page!
www.facebook.com/waterbrookmultnomahfiction

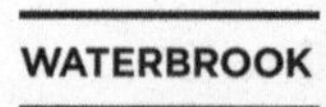

MULTNOMAH

waterbrookmultnomah.com